WHAT *the* LIGHT TOUCHES

WHAT *the* LIGHT TOUCHES

a novel

XAVIER BOSCH

TRANSLATED BY SAMANTHA MATEO

This is a work of fiction. Names, characters, organizations, places, events, and incidents are either products of the author's imagination or are used fictitiously. Any resemblance to actual persons, living or dead, or actual events is purely coincidental.

Previously published as *32 de març* by Univers Llibres in Spain in 2023. Translated from Catalan by Samantha Mateo. First published in English by Amazon Crossing in 2024.

Published by Amazon Crossing, Seattle

www.apub.com

ISBN-13: 9781662520815 (paperback)
ISBN-13: 9781662520822 (digital)

Cover design by Eileen Carey
Cover image: © Lenart Gabor, © Sergey Novikov, © MagicPics / Shutterstock; © Atlantide Phototravel / Getty; © Ildiko Neer / ArcAngel

Printed in the United States of America

For Anna and Aran and all the grandmothers and granddaughters who've created their own little world.

Paris 2008

—“What’s your name?”

—“Margaux. You know that already.”

—“What do you want to be when you grow up?”

Barbara

1

If He Were Even Alive

Surprises were better in books. She'd had enough of them in real life.

But fate, stubborn as only it can be, walks its own path. Sometimes rearing its head on a Saturday.

After climbing up five flights, loaded up like a donkey, the last thing she expected was to find someone at home. As soon as Barbara opened the door and placed the two bags with the week's worth of shopping on the floor, careful not to squash the tomatoes, she discovered a man sleeping on her couch. She didn't even have a chance to take off her jacket and gloves. The stranger—too old to be a boy, no longer a young man but not quite middle-aged—had untied his boots and, without slipping them off, placed his feet on a pillow, the very same throw pillow where, not long ago, Barbara's grandmother rested her head for her usual postlunch naps. The intruder's belly button was on full display, the waistband of his underpants peeking out over his belt buckle and his left arm splayed above his head in a sign of surrender. The other hand, with the sleeve of his black shirt rolled up, hung so that his knuckles grazed the floor. His jacket, thrown to the side, had slid down onto the tiles of the floor. Barbara didn't understand. She'd left the house at midmorning and, two hours later, here was this person, perfectly at home and without a single care in the world, as if he'd lived here his whole damn life.

Not too long ago, *Libération* had published a report she'd happened upon and read, on an epidemic of squatters in the old buildings of the Latin Quarter who, in very little time, took over entire homes—and, next thing you knew, it took an army to help kick them out. And that was in the best of cases. Often the police said that nothing could be done, that justice had gone blind, and that the latest fashion in Paris was to say you were lucky if the person who'd broken into your home was in the mafia. Because, in exchange for money, another mafia would force out the mafia staying in your apartment. The cycle of business. Half victories. You pay the price of extortion, but at least the squatters leave. What more could you want?

In the time it took her to react, Barbara dismissed the idea that her tenant was part of some perverse setup—he hadn't even grown a beard, despite appearing not to have shaved in days. He was a little too at ease in the apartment. Too calm. No amount of ruckus would have disturbed him. And it didn't look like he'd forced the lock.

She slammed the door forcefully, hoping to scare him. And wake him up.

That is, if he were even alive.

2

Not One Book or Picture

"You're Barbara, right? I just stretched out for a minute because I'm wiped from all the travel. It's impossible to sleep on that night train from Barcelona. I got here, and I just . . . plop, like someone knocked me out. I left my things in the room. I took the one that looked like it belonged to Marcel. Anyway, I didn't bring much. I don't think I'll stay for too long. Nothing but a suitcase that's heavy as a corpse, some camera equipment. That's it. Marcel didn't mention that there weren't any elevators. I'd already dragged it all from the station! I mean these little hills in Montmartre are a death trap, and when I walked through the doorway and saw I had to climb it all on foot . . . There must be, what? A hundred steps, maybe? Now, the apartment's a little shabby, but it's warm and has a charm . . . with those large windows. When I first opened the bedroom door, I thought, 'It can't be this one.' It was too neat to be my brother's room. Then I went into the bigger room—the one with more light, the one that faces out front. Honestly, clever as he is, I thought Marcel would've picked the nice room. But then I noticed that the room was full of women's stuff. Don't worry, I didn't move anything; but I saw perfumes and ducks everywhere, and I figured you must have ended up with the room . . . You're his roommate, right? Barbara? Is your name Barbara?"

She couldn't believe it. Marcel never said anything. She didn't even know he had a brother. And if he'd ever mentioned him in some conversation in the kitchen, she certainly hadn't heard, because in the months that they'd lived together on rue Chappe, they mostly kept to themselves. Barbara worked from home, glued to the computer, obsessed with her books, and Marcel woke up early, went to the firm, and, when he got home after dark, went out for a run, showered, ate something prepackaged, and shut himself in his room.

"Yes, I'm Barbara Hébrard. But I'm not his roommate. Marcel didn't tell me he was subletting his room."

"Oh no, I'm not subletting it. He's letting me borrow the room. I'm his brother. His little brother. He told me I could move in."

"In any case . . . I think he could've warned me. Same way he said, 'I've got an important case in Toulouse. I'm not sure how long the trial is going to last.' He could have just said, 'I'm giving my brother the room. He's coming from Barcelona on this exact date. He's got my keys and will let himself in when he pleases.'"

"I've had warmer welcomes."

"And then on top of it all . . . it's bothering *you*? I come home, find some guy sprawled out on my sofa, and when I go to call the police, you wake up, and *you're* offended . . . ?"

"Look, he's paying a thousand euros a month. The least he can do is let me borrow his bed . . . Don't you do whatever you feel like doing?"

"I don't know what your brother told you, but we are not roommates by any means. The apartment is mine."

"Yours?" Roger was incredulous.

"What a surprise, huh? As if!"

"Impossible." The intruder laughed. "You're kidding me. Marcel would've told me. And you . . ." He looked around the apartment with distaste. "You wouldn't have it looking like this."

"What do you mean 'like this'?"

"Not one book or picture in the whole house. If you don't mind me saying, it's decorated like an old person's house."

"If you don't like it, get that dead-body luggage of yours and go stay at a hotel." She blurted it without thinking. "If there's one thing we have in Paris, it's rats and hotels."

"Jesus, we can't be honest anymore?"

"The apartment belonged to my grandmother. She lived here her whole life. Now I live here, and because it's more than I can afford, I rented out a room to your brother for exactly 1,150 euros a month because he seemed like a clean and polite-enough gentleman with good French, always wearing that lawyer tie perfectly straight, and he hasn't broken a single rule since we've lived together."

"Oh man, us two are night and day, aren't we? If I were you, I'd marry him. He's around thirty-eight and, so far as I know, single." The intruder took his phone out of his jeans pocket. "Should I call him and ask?"

Barbara shot him a glare. Before going for the final kill, she decided to try to ignore him. She picked her two bags off the floor and placed them atop the kitchen table. Mad as she was, she opened the fridge and, without even realizing what she was doing, started shelving the half-dozen carton of eggs, the zucchini, the tomatoes, and the package of sole she planned on making that afternoon. She still hadn't even learned Marcel's brother's name. He'd gone back to sitting on the red sofa and taken off his boots and socks. Barefoot, he slowly approached the edge of the kitchen. He tried to start over, with a new tone.

"Did she die a while ago?"

"Who?"

"Your grandmother."

"My grandmother? Mine?" She turned to face him again. She found him a little too close for her liking. "Who said she died?"

"You. You said that you'd ended up with the apartment. I thought that meant . . ." He extended his hand. "Roger Narbona."

"I'm sticky from the fish. I'll shake your hand some other day."

He returned his hand to the pocket where his phone had been. Barbara turned on the faucet and washed her hands with dish soap. For the first time since entering the house, she let out a self-satisfied victory smile.

"She's a personality, she is, my grandmother. She's good and well. Mamie Margaux is my hero."

3

There's No Turning Back

Roger's room, which had been Marcel's room and must have been Barbara's room when she lived with Mamie Margaux before that, overlooked a rather old interior courtyard. The window leaned out over laundry rooms, clotheslines, and a rank odor that sometimes wafted up from the apartments below. The views, necessarily domestic, were charmless enough to justify those frosted-glass windows that hardly let in enough light for a prison cell, and were instead useful only to tell whether it was night or day outside. The built-in wardrobe next to the door was full of Marcel's suit jackets. Roger slid them over a little, careful not to wrinkle them, to make room for his two pairs of pants. They were the only two he'd brought with him. Two pairs of warm pants: one corduroy and the jeans he was currently wearing. Whatever didn't fit into Marcel's wardrobe he'd keep under the bed for the time being. He would open the suitcase, lay it flat, store it between the two legs of the bed, then drag it out whenever he needed something. The bed was big enough but a strange size nonetheless, as though it were made for one-and-a-half people. It wasn't a twin, but it wasn't quite a full-size bed, either. In his thirty-three years of life—some of it spent circling the globe more than enough times—he'd never slept on a mattress with those dimensions. He collapsed on top of it, testing it out. It was a little soft for his taste, but at least it didn't squeak or have an impression left by past inhabitants. He planned on making the most of that little corner of the world while his older brother was out of the city. He found a full-length mirror behind the door. He looked at himself, tucked his plaid shirt into his jeans, and walked out of the room, now with an idea.

"Should we get lunch? You pick the place and I'll pay."

"It's not a good time for me, honestly."

"Come on, to make up for my entrance. I didn't mean to create so much chaos. You got scared, and . . ."

"Some other day." Barbara had hardly looked up from the screen of the twenty-four-inch Mac desktop she kept on the desk in the living room.

"Something quick."

"I've got a lot of work today." She was blunt.

"On a Saturday?"

Barbara didn't feel like explaining. She realized that Marcel had at least been discreet enough not to tell his brother what she did for work. And, from what she could tell, he must also not have told Roger that, at forty-one years old, Barbara had sought refuge at her grandmother's house in Paris to escape her husband and her miserable experiences with him.

"When love is a mistake, it's better to run."

Her grandmother had given her that advice over the phone, and once she finally faced the reality of her situation, Barbara packed her bags and left Arles so that she could be done for good with Maurice. After all, she could do her job selling international rights for Giresse & Trésor from Montmartre just as well as she could from Provence. All she needed was a computer, good contacts at publishing houses, and the fine-tuned ability to sell her authors' stories. She'd gone in person to negotiate the move at Giresse & Trésor's headquarters on a lower floor of some skyscraper in the la Défense district. They said they were happy with her and that, at their company, the peace and happiness of their employees came before all else, and that Barbara should do whatever she thought was best for her. They even agreed that being in Paris would make it easier for Barbara to establish ties within the sector. Things rushed by in the capital. Sometimes there were cocktail dinners and parties that hosted editors from around the world who Barbara would've never dared to dream of meeting in Arles. And when she had to travel abroad, she'd be able to fly direct from Paris to anywhere in the world. They were all pros. And Mamie Margaux, like any grandmother, would be ecstatic to have her back. She knew that granddaughters were the joy of life. She couldn't ask for better company.

Roger didn't have much interest in eating with the landlady either. He was only trying to be nice. But if Barbara would rather stay and work and not go out for a bite, he wouldn't lose much sleep. He noticed that there was a cactus in the living room taller than he was and returned to his room. It still smelled like Marcel's things; he closed the door and began to load his backpack. He packed his Canon and, just in case, picked two lenses to help resize the world. He grabbed the wide-angle and the macro lens, because there was always a drop of water dripping from a handrail somewhere with just the right lack of urgency. He'd never forgive himself if he didn't have the right lens to capture that moment of urban poetry. Then he checked to make sure he had the keys to the apartment in one of the twenty pockets of his parka. He didn't understand why his brother carried them on that key ring. A miniature oboe did nothing for him, and music didn't mean much to Marcel either. In fact, no one in the Narbona-Bazin family cared about instruments or songs. They were all tone-deaf. And none of them knew how to dance. "Everyone here has two left feet," his mother would say, in a rather French expression. They once heard their father humming a couple of the traditional Easter caramelles he'd learned as a child as he filled boxes with apples. Their mother, Fabienne, always said that she'd studied piano until she was twelve, but when the Bazin family moved from Besançon to Fontclara, they took only the most essential items: clothes, the great-grandparents' trunk, the photo albums, and the good cutlery. Once they shuffled everything around carefully, there was just enough room left in the truck to fit that little period of mourning you need before a rebirth. And those crucial memories we hold on to when moving to new places. The rest, including the piano and the metronome, they left at home in France, in case they ever returned.

The rules. Roger wanted to know them before he left for his first walk around the neighborhood. Barbara recited all five of them like a chant she knew from memory—as though she'd grown tired of repeating them to her tenants.

Whoever cooks, cleans.

Whoever spreads out, picks up.

Don't touch the heater.

The half bathroom is for men.

And at night, make as little sound as possible.

"That's the life of a monk."

"That's how things are."

"I'm not arguing. I'm just saying."

Barbara ran her finger over her bushy eyebrows.

"Oh, and no smoking. Like I told you, if you don't like it . . ."

"Yeah, yeah, Paris, hotels, rats. What about the shower?" Roger asked, puzzled. "There's no shower in the small bathroom."

"Sorry." Barbara got up from the office chair. "You can take up to one shower a day. Your brother was in the habit of taking one at night. He'd go for a run, come back sweaty as all hell, and go straight into the shower. I like to wake up and shower before I start working, so the bathroom was never a problem."

"I can't stand running. In fact I can't even do it. One of my legs is longer than the other. It's a birth defect."

Barbara looked him over, from his hips down to his feet.

"And does that hold you back . . . a lot?"

"Either way, I'm used to showering every day. And I'd like to continue. Or is that unpopular in France?"

She stared at him and wondered how Roger and Marcel could have fallen from the same family tree. They were brothers but looked nothing alike.

"The hot water tank is the issue. We don't get any more than it gives. The building's utilities must date back to before the war."

"The Napoleonic one, I'm guessing."

One brother discreet, the other impertinent.

"I don't think they've changed anything in the building since my grandmother was born here. People tolerate it for the sake of peace."

Roger looked around. The apartment had personality—especially the living room with the grand windows. On a slight incline, like an observatory, the windows made the room feel different, picturesque, Parisian. The light of midday entered in rays, and between the February cold and the heat inside, the glass began misting at the edges of the wooden frames. The enormous cactus stood like the totem of the home. Roger plodded and strolled around the room, like a cat scrutinizing its surroundings without even knowing what it's looking for.

"What about the television?"

"My grandmother took it."

"There's no TV? Seriously?"

"She asked for permission from the retirement home to have a TV in her room. Who knows how many requests she had to make. But, in the end, she got it; if Mamie Margaux wants something, she gets it."

"Granny's frail, huh?"

The question surprised Barbara. It was never a question of whether Mamie Margaux was frail. She hadn't even thought about it in those terms. Mamie Margaux was in good health for an eighty-three-year-old. Her mind was clear, her pain in check, and she had a strong bite with dignified wrinkles. Above it all, she had the will to live. For her own sake and for all the life Damien hadn't been able to experience. And for the chunk of life stolen from Édith, her poor daughter. Because, even with all she'd been through, Mamie Margaux had no plans to surrender.

Once, a few days before leaving for the retirement home, she'd grabbed her granddaughter's hand at dinner and caressed it like she had when Barbara was little. Mamie Margaux told her that she hadn't yet heard the siren's last call. She knew that when the question arrived, the cursed question, the question posed in all uppercase—"WHAT AM I STILL DOING HERE ON EARTH?"—it would mean her first steps into the dirt. And once that moment arrived, the steps would become short, quick, and headed one way: toward death, with no hope for turning back.

Barbara and Mamie Margaux toasted with a glass of wine. Though the grandmother's eyes were losing their green, her granddaughter's still sparkled with the lush richness of forty—even more so when they tried to choke back emotions.

"To not asking yourself the fatal question, then . . ."

"And may it stay that way for a long time," said the grandmother, filling her gold-rimmed glass.

Spring had weighed heavily upon Mamie Margaux as she'd planned to leave her apartment—the one she'd lived in her whole life—since it had become a burden for her to climb the stairs. There was no other reason. She'd simply discovered what she'd long seen coming: that getting old was hard. When she turned seventy, the fifth-floor walkup became a big problem. The thought of returning home made her look forward to leaving the house less and less . . . When she turned eighty, that many stairs was torture. Once she realized she was leaving the house only when necessary—when whole weeks started to pass without her feeling the air of the street—she thought it was time to search for somewhere more comfortable. After so many years on the move, many spent carrying boxes up and down staircases as a retail worker, she'd finally let someone cook for her, care for her, pay attention to her when she wanted it, and leave her in peace when she wished to walk through the gardens of the Viviani Retirement Home. When she officially moved, she missed her red sofa, her collection of ducks, and the company of her beloved Barbara for the past three years. But when sadness reared its head, she'd think about that worn-out Himalaya of a staircase, each floor a base camp unto itself, and she'd let go of the nostalgia in no time.

"I'm leaving. Do you think it'll rain?"

Barbara approached the windows and studied the clouds while she tied her hair in a high bun.

"I don't think so. But it's Paris. You know . . . rats, hotels, and rain."

Roger zipped up his parka and slung the backpack over his shoulders.

"Can I say something?" He lightly lifted his pant leg up as far as his rigid jeans would let him. "Truth is, one of my legs isn't shorter than the other. I just can't stand jogging."

"A liar on top of it all."

"It was a joke, woman. Are jokes also against the house rules?"

"You know what? I don't like it either. At all. Running? It's not for me."

"It's a sport for people who weren't picked for any teams."

4

The Calm of Montmartre

The calm of Montmartre surprised Roger Narbona. He walked, climbed, descended, and cut through stone-paved streets, snapping three photos before rounding two corners and hitting a dead end. He didn't see a single person anywhere. It was like a city within a city. Where were the swarms of people from the Latin Quarter, the grand boulevards, and the Champs-Élysées?

Montmartre was altogether different. He wondered if the neighborhood had emptied for the weekend, if people had locked themselves in shelter from the February cold—oppressive and biting—or if he simply hadn't been warned that this was a bygone neighborhood.

Once he started feeling hungry for lunch, he entered the first place that looked authentic. Chez Richard was a small, long-standing restaurant on rue Véron. Under the red awning, the words "fifteen euros including coffee" were written on a blackboard in elegant and well-crafted handwriting. If they were this exact with the calligraphy, surely they'd be just as scrupulous about the quality and presentation of their dishes. His deduction was premature. The soup stock danced on one side of the bowl, the chicken on the other. The second course, the steak, was a rubber tire with a side of french fries. Those, at the very least, were well fried. Not at all oily, perfectly crispy on the outside and soft inside. How they were meant to be. The way his mother, the expert, made them, because she had to prove in some way that, even though she lived in Fontclara in the farmland of Empordà, she was a proud Frenchwoman.

"Fruit or cheesecake?" the lone waitress in the establishment asked Roger. She walked in a frenzy from table to table.

"Is the cake made in-house?"

"Yeah, of course."

"What kind of fruit do you have?"

"Apples and oranges." The conversation was starting to drag on a little too long for the waitress, her taut, white apron tied at her waist and falling to her ankles.

"What do you think?"

"I don't get paid to decide."

Roger looked up at her face. He was smiling, she was not. Her forehead dripped with sweat but her hands were too full to wipe it off. The restaurant had its heater on full blast, and she had to serve the dozen or so tables all by herself.

"I'll take an orange, thanks."

Just as the waitress headed toward the kitchen, dirty cutlery atop a plate of steak cartilage in hand, he called her back.

"Excuse me . . . Just a question." Roger wiped his lips. "Do you know why there are so few people in the neighborhood?"

She turned around and, as if to ignore him, continued onward. On her way, she said to someone, "Monsieur Richard, the guy at table seven."

"What the hell does he want?" The man looked in the direction of the new customer, who'd eaten his lunch with a Coca-Cola.

"He says he's got a question."

The owner, who hadn't so much as moved his mustache from behind the register the whole time, walked away from the counter and, dragging his feet, approached Roger's table.

Monsieur Richard was pudgy with a red neck, high cholesterol, and forty years of home cooking under his belt; and, best of all, he had an answer to Roger's question. He asked for permission to sit across from Roger, ordered Laurence, the waitress, to bring him a carafe of his "special" wine, and, once finished serving himself a glass, began to speak.

The older people had abandoned Montmartre. Because it was steep, because it was out of the way, because, in order to find a little bit of life—boulangeries, pharmacies, hair salons, pet food stores—you had to first descend toward Clichy Boulevard before climbing up the hill. The young people, meanwhile, couldn't live there because of the astronomical price per square foot. And if they *were* able to pay for it, they'd soon discover they couldn't park on the street, the buildings didn't have garages, and, even if they did, the garages were so damn narrow and shabby that it would be a miracle if they didn't scratch their car. *If you can afford to indulge your every desire, you should at least be comfortable. You shouldn't have to suffer to do jack shit,* reasoned Monsieur Richard, his toothbrush mustache bristling.

It was gentrification. An ugly word, an uglier concept.

Montmartre had slowly become a postcard neighborhood. It was rustic and pleasant in the black-and-white streets, picturesque and multicolored in the dozens of artists in place du Tertre and the eccentric clothing of the tourists who circled the vicinity of the Basilica of Sacré-Coeur—or the "Easter Mona," as the Narbona-Bazin family always used to call it, because it reminded them of the Catalonian holiday pastry. At the start of the twenty-first century, with its technological ambitions, living in a museum-like neighborhood made for more trouble than anything else. *Time doesn't just leave people in the past,* Monsieur Richard divined, signaling the end to the conversation.

Roger left a two-euro tip that the friendly Monsieur Richard and Laurence could split however they wished. Laurence hadn't stopped running around the entire hour that Roger had been seated.

When he exited the restaurant, he positioned the menu board into the camera frame. Like the majority of time he spent looking through the viewfinder, he let the camera lead the way. He had enough of an instinct to know when he was about to capture a cheap photo, devoid of sense or meaning, and would hold back the impulse. This way, he wouldn't have to delete the pictures later, which basically meant more free time.

He zipped his parka all the way to the top and strolled a while longer, wandering around identical-looking alleyways. In each one, he spotted something he hadn't seen on an empty stomach. He enjoyed meandering aimlessly and discovering untouched corners of the past. Not even a stray meow from around a distant corner could break his peace. But the cold was freezing his ears and cutting at his lips, spurring him to walk faster and faster.

He returned home once the streetlamps flickered on. As he climbed past each floor landing, he lowered his jacket zipper little by little. On the fifth floor, he felt around his pockets in search of the oboe key chain. He entered without announcing himself. Barbara's eyes were glued to the computer screen, and she barely greeted him.

"Holy hell, it's so cold," said Roger.

"What?"

"It's colder than Siberia."

"It's fine here."

"I meant outside." He set his camera bag down on the red sofa. "Is that normal?"

"It's Paris. It's February."

"Thanks for the information."

"They said it'll get colder. A cold front coming from somewhere."

"From the north, surely."

Extreme phenomena always come from above.

Barbara worked while listening to classical music. Some familiar piece. Roger had heard it many times before but couldn't put a name to it. Bach would be his guess. When you're not sure what you're listening to but it sounds really nice, say Bach. The cello suite played so quietly that Roger figured Barbara hadn't even heard it. He picked up his things, went to his room, and warmed his hands on the radiator. Then he put his butt on it. He took off his boots, grabbed his Canon, and stretched across the bed to skim through the photos he had taken of Montmartre. With the camera on his lap, he slowly surrendered to sleep. Roger hated naps. He thought they were a waste of time. Plus, once he woke up from them, he always felt bloated and like he couldn't relieve any of the symptoms. But night trains will topple even the bravest, and he offered up little resistance as sleep defeated him.

He was woken by a scream. He didn't know where he was, whether it was morning or afternoon, or where the cries were coming from. It wasn't just one, either. He got up and opened the window. It was a dark night, and the air shaft was emitting the same dreadful odor as when he'd first entered his brother's room. He brought his ear closer to the window to try to figure out where all the fuss was coming from. He thought he saw movement in the laundry room of the second floor. Or maybe it was the third. He definitely heard a woman cursing out her husband and his whole family, ancestors included. The man, if there was one, silently accepted the yelling. The tirade seemed like it would go on for a while, so Roger closed his window, hoping this wouldn't be his daily lot.

After the nap—he had no idea how long it had lasted—the room was no longer Marcel's. Roger had made it his own in just a few short hours.

Cold, he got to one knee and slid the suitcase out from under the bed to grab a thin sweater to wear around the house. But the suitcase resisted. He looked to see if it was jutting out into any of the wooden legs holding up the box spring. It didn't seem like it. He rested his other knee on the ground and leaned over to investigate. The Samsonite had gotten stuck between a leg and a metallic box. Even while splayed out on the ground, Roger couldn't fit his arm far enough to move everything at the same time. He stood, lifted the box spring and hoisted it over one of his shoulders, then, with one hand, nudged the suitcase while towing the box out awkwardly with his foot. The problem now solved, he put the mattress back into place, careful not to make any noise that might scare Barbara. The box was bright yellow, made of tin, and about twice the size of a shoebox. Based on the amount of dust gathered on top, it couldn't have belonged to Marcel. It must have stayed hidden there for a long time, perhaps forgotten, maybe even lost. There was a somewhat juvenile advertisement on the lid. He could make out the head of a Black man wearing a fez, red like his lips, holding a steaming white mug in one hand, and the words *"Banania le petit déjeuner familial."* It must have originally contained powdered chocolate separated into jars or packets. But Roger was fairly sure there was no longer any trace of ColaCao—or anything like it—left inside the tin.

Should he open it? At the end of the day, the only difference between snooping and investigating was perspective. And why not, if no one would know?

Before slipping off the lid, he gently shook the box to see if there was anything fragile inside. Nothing. It didn't weigh much, and he didn't hear any movement. He put the box on the bed and opened it with caution, making sure the dust wouldn't spread all over the duvet cover. Inside he found clippings. A wad of magazine pages, more photographs than articles. Pieces of pages carefully cut by hand. They hadn't been crumpled—just the opposite: the documents looked as if they'd been ironed. The person who had preserved them had good taste. There were pictures of Paris from a past time. Happy people stood in black and white. Elegant people with fancy hats, well-dressed workingmen, and a woman on a bicycle who looked like she'd posed expressly for the picture. They were images of serenity, of the happiness of the streets, of peaceful people filling tables on terraces. Then, among the clippings, he found a color photograph—a faint and faded hue—that emanated the same peacefulness.

Whoever collected the photographs clearly possessed solid judgment and a good eye. Roger hadn't exactly discovered a treasure, but, with an eye glued to the door in case Barbara should open it—he was sure she wouldn't, but without a latch, you never knew—he spent a good while discovering the beauty of a time period he'd never known. The fever of a long-ago Paris.

He returned the tin box back to its place and resolved to make the most of the photographs; all the while, Barbara continued to sit in front of her computer screen until eleven o'clock. She was wearing a blue muslin onesie that stretched from the hood folded behind her neck and covered her toes. The desk was British colonial, with a carpenter's trim work and several drawers. It faced the window, and the wood had become irregularly discolored by the sun. On top of the desk, next to her computer monitor, Barbara kept only a box, a plastic cell phone holder, and, at that late hour, an herbal tea whose scent filled the dining room.

"You know what surprised me about today?"

"Excuse me?" Barbara pretended she hadn't heard him.

"You're working." He pretended he hadn't noticed. "Sorry, I didn't mean to . . . What do you do for work?"

"What about you?" she snapped. Barbara relaxed. Her bad moods never lasted the whole day. "Foreign rights."

Roger sat down on the red sofa, eager to listen.

"International rights? For what?"

"For books, for authors. I make sure authors from our press are published in other countries and languages."

"Are you a literary agent?"

"No. A literary agent represents many different writers. I only sell—or try to sell, at least—writers from a single publishing house. I go back and forth to book fairs. London. Frankfurt . . ."

"And are they good? Your writers?"

Barbara faced him; she'd stopped turning her back to him for the very first time.

"Real *auteures*."

"*Auteurs*, you mean." Roger's French was impeccable, but he felt bad correcting a real Parisian.

"The three I represent, for your information, are three women, three novelists. And *are*"—she emphasized the syllable—"the best."

"It's a joke, come on." He saw Barbara's green eyes staring daggers back at him and tried to lighten the mood with a smile. "Tell me what you really think."

"If I didn't think they were the best, I wouldn't be able to sell them."

When Barbara smiled, Roger sensed a slyness. Perhaps her youthful aura had something to do with her front teeth, which had an elegant gap that Barbara showed little interest in modifying. Her hair, curly, dark, and unfettered, bounced around though she was sitting still.

Roger cleared his throat the way all Narbonas did before broaching a difficult subject.

"What kind of tea are you drinking?"

"The tin is in the kitchen. This one is . . . I don't know what I've made for myself today. Licorice, I'm guessing."

Barbara sniffed the mug to check. Roger continued on with his mission.

"You know what surprised me most about today?" The more eager you are to learn something, the harder it is to ask about it, he realized. "I've mentioned it before, and it's become even clearer now that I know what you do. I think it's strange there isn't a single book or photo in this entire apartment."

"You're thinking too narrowly. I have it all here." Barbara pointed to her computer screen. "It's more practical for work. I read it all from one place. Or, if I'm traveling, I read it on a tablet. I work with stories, not paper. I sell novels, plots, lives and personalities, writing styles, and feelings. When I moved here, I didn't have to bring a single physical book."

"I haven't gotten used to e-books. Not because I'm not a reader, but because I like touching the cover and knowing whether I'm on the right or left page whenever I grab a book."

Barbara stood and stretched her arms, arching her back like a cat shaking off its sleepiness. Too many hours sitting down, he thought. Yawning, she seemed to remember something.

"There actually is a book in the house. Just one, as far as I know. My grandma wanted to keep only one. Mamie Margaux's favorite."

Roger waited for her to fetch the book. Or, at the very least, for her to tell him the title. But Barbara went straight to the fridge, picked up an apple, washed it, and took a bite. Once he realized she didn't want to go down that road, he went straight to the point.

"And what about pictures? How come there isn't a single one in the house? It's weird."

"That . . ." She chewed the mealy apple in her mouth and sat back in her office chair. "There's a story to that."

Roger concealed his interest, donning a poker face. He didn't want to try his luck and blurt out something that would ruin it all. He yearned for that monologue—for an explanation he expected to follow—but also felt that, by feigning disinterest, he'd be more likely to entice the suspicious and discreet Barbara to open the floodgates. Even if slowly.

"One fateful day, my grandma woke up here, in her room, and said she didn't want to see any more pictures of herself. Just like that. I'm talking about a long time ago. She decided over the course of a single night. And, lo and behold, she immediately took down the three or four she'd had hanging. There weren't any more than that, but she took them all down. The ones with us, with my mother . . . family photos, all taken down. If she happened to be in the picture, she'd take it out of the frame and rip it up. No, sorry, I'm lying. She didn't rip them up. Maybe she hid them away, but who knows where."

"Wow, your grandma's quite the character."

"You've never heard of someone reacting like that?"

"I've heard of it, but why did she take them down?"

Barbara looked at the apple, checking to make sure there wasn't a worm.

"I guess"—she took a bite—"because of some bad experience."

Roger waited for Barbara to elaborate. He gave her the floor, hoping she'd keep unfurling her scroll.

But Mamie Margaux's granddaughter figured she'd said enough. She wasn't sure how he pulled it off, but she had somehow revealed more to that smart-aleck Roger, who'd spent only a couple of hours in the apartment so far, than she ever had to Marcel during their four months of silent cohabitation. Before saying good night, Barbara offered him one last nugget.

"You know the strangest thing of all?"

He looked at her expectantly.

"Since that day, my grandmother hasn't let anyone take a photo of her. Never again. Not once. By anyone."

5

A Sea Worth Gazing At

My grandmother is a duck.

The story of the day Barbara told everyone at school her grandmother was a duck would live in Hébrard family lore forever. She must have been seven years old at the time, and she'd made everyone laugh when she smiled and showed off the gap between her front teeth and chattered like a bird.

When her maternal grandmother was a kid, she had gone to see a performance of *Peter and the Wolf* from wooden seats in the main orchestra section. On the way to the theater, where her father worked, she was told that every instrument represented a different character and that she shouldn't worry: there'd be a happy ending. She went into it with the curiosity of a little girl who still believed everything her parents told her. She sat between her parents and fell under the spell of a distinct sound. She would never want to be Peter or the wolf. She knew that from the outset. She didn't like Peter because of the mop of bangs on the musician who played his chords. And being the wolf seemed even worse. He was the evilest of villains, with his French horn. Sitting there, dazzled by the spectacle and without even knowing who Prokofiev was, Margaux had a sudden revelation unlike anything she'd ever experienced. She wanted to be the duck. She knew immediately.

Margaux was hypnotized the moment she heard the very first notes of the duck's voice played aloud. She fell in love with the carefree sound of its gleeful music. She asked her parents what instrument it was, and, after skimming through the program in their hands, they responded, "That's an oboe."

"I want to be the duck. I want to play the oboe."

Barbara had heard the story so many times, complete with the same tone and pauses, that she had it memorized by heart. In speech class, when the teacher at school asked Barbara Hébrard to come up to the board and talk about an animal, she chose the story of her grandmother's musical revelation. With her hands in her pockets, she recounted for the class the adventures of Peter and the wolf. She told them her grandmother was a duck and that she played the oboe like an angel. Without even realizing it, she'd just told the story of the day that Margaux Dutronc decided to be one of life's side characters rather than the main one.

Mamie Margaux was simply Barbara's grandmother. She didn't need a more defined role. Barbara didn't think much about the label, as everything about her idol was perfect. She was flawless, and the feeling was unconditional. Mamie Margaux was young, fun, playful, and she knew how to spark Barbara's curiosity in, say, a Cubist painting, or a dramatic reading of a story, or the squeaking handle of the coffee grinder atop the kitchen counter on those occasions when she'd let Barbara turn it. Grandmother and granddaughter didn't see one another throughout the year as much as they would've liked. One lived in Paris, the other in Arles. One in gray, one in blue. It was difficult for Margaux to leave her apartment in Montmartre, where she'd spent her entire life. Barbara's parents, Clément and Édith, were always too busy to get in the car, leave Provence, and drive all the way up to Paris—a five-hundred-mile schlep—to see Mamie, who they already knew would be doing fine.

That summer, though, grandmother and granddaughter had completed a crash course of sorts. They spent two whole months together after Barbara's eighth birthday, less than a week after she'd finished the school year. July and August, all by themselves, in a hotel on the beach of Sainte-Maxime. It was the summer Barbara's mother couldn't get out of bed. Barbara always called it that because she didn't know what else to call it. Day after day, she'd noticed her mother acting sad and listless, lacking the energy or motivation to do anything. Édith had shut herself in her room and asked for the shades to be lowered, then, for weeks on end, wouldn't let anyone wake her or air out the room. A life full of darkness. Hardly a life. She only slept. She didn't want Barbara's father to wake her, either, not even at dinnertime. Only when the doctor stopped by and asked her how she was doing that day did she let someone turn on her bedside lamp, revealing her pale complexion. It was a bitter case of depression. There was no family history, as far as they knew. It struck quick as lightning.

When Margaux found out about the diagnosis, she packed two suitcases, loaded them up in her Citroën—her beloved Geneviève—and drove down to Arles to hug her daughter. She hadn't been able to muster much more. In the darkness of that room, she'd discovered a body that, now shying away like a wounded animal, had practically forgotten how to speak, much less smile. After a three-day uphill battle of trying to care for a patient who wouldn't let herself be cared for, Margaux made a proposal that sounded good enough to Clément, and Édith didn't have the strength to argue. Margaux didn't want Barbara to spend summer vacation shut up in the dark house. It wasn't good for her to see her mother struggle to get out of bed without understanding why. And nobody knew what to tell her when she asked about it. Somewhere beyond the evasion and vague answers—behind the rotting smell of half-truths—she'd begun to notice things being hidden from her. And if your parents and grandmother are hiding something from you, chances are it isn't good.

"I'll take her to a beach, a hotel, somewhere close to here," Margaux had urged without leaving room for an alternative. "For now, all of July.

She's a kid. She needs to experience the summer, sun, and sea . . . She can't see her mother like this. It's the best we can do for her."

For two hot months in 1975, they'd stayed in room twenty-one of a hotel in Sainte-Maxime on the Côte d'Azur. Margaux, having been to the Centrum Hotel before, was after some small-town peace and quiet, narrow streets, and a familiar beach. Sainte-Maxime didn't have the bustle of Nice, or the ambition of Cannes, or the luxury of Monte Carlo. It had none of the tourism of the more famous seaside locales, or the opulence of Saint-Tropez, which stood across the horseshoe-shaped bay, carved out over the years by the unrelenting swell. These were all places where they wouldn't have been comfortable. And Sainte-Maxime still had the air of Provence, along with an all-enveloping cheerful blue sky. In the evenings, a gust of refreshing cold air signaled the proximity of the Alps, sleeping over the sea.

Uncertain how long they'd be staying there, Margaux knew they needed to feel at home if they were going to have the vacation Barbara deserved. The Centrum Hotel wasn't luxurious, but Margaux had known that the hotel's owner would be absolutely tickled pink at having a little eight-year-old girl around. She'd also known that, if anything serious happened and they needed to head back to Arles, they could make it there in just a few hours.

The hotel was wedged between old, two-story seaside buildings, whose earthy colors were reminiscent of rustic Italy. From the terrace, which was more like a generous balcony, they could see the port near the entrance to a path that invited sunset strolls. Every so often, the city had installed stone benches in the middle of the boulevard for the casual observer. From their room Barbara and Margaux could see all kinds of people sitting there. There were vacationers who set their dogs loose and watched them from a distance, people exhausted by the journey from the other side of the Gulf of Saint-Tropez, and those wise enough to have discovered a great secret: that the Mediterranean Sea was a sea worth gazing at.

Grandmother and granddaughter had liked not having a routine. Besides the hotel's fully accommodated mealtimes, which were sacred, the rest of the day was at their whim. They made the most of it by starting early in the morning. Only the sun was up earlier than the pair, who slept side by side in a queen bed because there hadn't been any other options without a reservation, especially during the busy season of early July. Margaux liked going to the beach before the crowds arrived, and they would often set up camp near the water. With the whole beach to themselves, they could relax however they wanted. They played hangman in the sand and spent hours making sandcastles before the undercurrent of a wave washed over their fort. On some days, they would bring bocce balls with them; whoever lost the game had to be buried in the sand. And every morning, before going for a swim, Barbara would ask her grandmother to bury her like a mummy, with the sand packed firmly on top of her body. Margaux had of course been careful to leave her granddaughter's face uncovered, since Barbara was afraid of suffocating and didn't want to be left there. Once weighed down and completely rigid, she'd fight to break free from the sand armor with the sheer force of her arms, sometimes hurting herself in the process; then, once she was free, she would run toward the sea. The two of them, holding hands, would sprint headfirst into the water until one of them fell and took a knee in a sign of surrender.

Once the euphoric blue hour of cloudless sky arrived, when the horde of tourists finally ambled down to the beach, Barbara's grandmother pulled her in close and wrapped her in a towel so she could change into a dry bathing suit beneath it before returning to the hotel. They showered, relaxed on the terrace, and, while they waited for lunchtime, painted each other's nails and confided in one another, which made Barbara feel very grown-up.

After lunch, they would read a story and wait for the chance to ride Carole, the red bicycle that Margaux had rented for Barbara. "By the time you go back home, you'll be riding without training wheels," her grandmother promised her on their second day in Sainte-Maxime.

Barbara wanted it as badly as she feared it. It was time for her to learn how to pedal and keep her balance without any help. It was the goal of the summer, and every evening they would go down to the path and practice. At first, her grandmother held on to her with two hands, one on the bicycle seat and the other on Barbara's shoulder to help guide her and make her feel safe. After a few days—the first Sunday of the summer probably hadn't even passed yet—Margaux let go of Barbara's shoulder and kept one hand on the back of her seat. By the end of August, Barbara was already confidently biking in a straight line, but would repeat to her grandmother, "Don't let go of me! Hold on to me, okay? Hold on to me!" without realizing that she had already been riding for some time with her grandmother's hand hovering inches away from the seat. Once practice was over, Mamie Margaux revealed the miracle: her granddaughter had been riding solo for a while. Barbara could hardly believe it. She got back on the bike and started to pedal. Standing in place, her grandmother let her go, and, once she was around twenty feet away, Mamie Margaux called out to her, as if they were parting ways, "Come back soon, Barbara! Hope you make it in America! Don't forget about me!"

They'd celebrated the day with ice cream. Margaux, who had the biggest sweet tooth in the family, opted for a small cup of coffee ice cream and a plastic spoon. Barbara had earned herself chocolate ice cream on a cone, the biggest one. Afterward, her grandmother had lent Barbara her Jean-Michel to clean her sticky fingers, nose, and cheeks. Jean-Michel was one of those useful, all-in-one handkerchiefs that Margaux always carried in her bag. Much like her plumber in Paris, Jean-Michel fixed anything broken.

Mamie Margaux gave objects names. Not just the handkerchief, but Carole the bike, Vincent the pigeon, Benoit the stoplight. Geneviève was what she called her car, a small, white Citroën that she'd driven from Paris to Arles entirely in the slower right-hand lane. On the only day it rained all summer, she'd named their umbrella René. She referred to her bra as Georgette and to her bosom as Madeleine. Barbara would burst into fits of laughter whenever she heard it, and hoped that she'd have big boobs like her grandmother when she grew up. They were symmetrical, firm, and still perky, with lightly colored "buttons," as Barbara thought of them.

The oboe, however, was just a plain oboe. It didn't have a first or last name. Mamie Margaux had forgotten to baptize the instrument she carried with her everywhere.

One evening, at the hour when the facades of Saint-Maxime turned into pumpkins, Barbara opened the oboe case. She'd taken it out and was trying to assemble it when her grandmother yelled at her.

"Hey, honey! Don't you even dare."

The girl was a little spooked. She'd never been yelled at like that by her grandmother.

"I only wanted to—" A tear ran down her cheek before she could get out another word.

"Did you touch the mouthpiece? Did your lips touch . . ." Mamie Margaux signaled to the reed of the instrument.

"No, no . . ."

Expressionless, Margaux snatched the bell of the oboe, put it back in place, closed the case, and, with one foot on the mattress, placed it on top of the room's dresser where Barbara wouldn't be able to reach it.

"It's very fragile, you know? And I don't want it to get damaged." She pulled the girl closer and placed her in her lap to try to make peace. "Did you know that that oboe has a lot of history to it?"

"It's not yours?" she asked, sobbing.

"It's mine, but it actually belonged to your grandfather."

"Grandpa Dédé, the one I never met?"

"Yes. Damien. He played for a well-known orchestra in Paris."

"And what about you?"

"Me? I'm hopeless when it comes to the oboe."

"You play really well."

"I'm hopeless compared to him. Trust me. He was a musician."

The evening had ended happily. Whatever regret Margaux felt for being harsh offset Barbara's remorse for touching something that wasn't hers and angering her grandmother. All this and she hadn't even put it to her mouth! To return to more peaceful waters, they'd need to throw caution to the wind and become sweeter to each other than ever before that summer. It was an unspoken pact.

"Mamie, do that thing you used to do when I was little."

"What thing?"

"The thing where I dance on your feet."

"Oh, I don't think I can . . ."

"Come on, Mamie . . . Pretty please."

"How old are you?"

"I'm eight. You know that already!"

"Eight. Just think, we used to do that when you were three or four. Now I'm an old lady."

"Grandma, you're only fifty years old."

"Fifty already?" Mamie Margaux was appalled. "It's not possible."

Barbara grabbed Mamie's hands and tried putting her bare feet on her grandmother's espadrilles.

"How about we do this." Margaux slid Barbara off her feet and then hid her hands in her flower-patterned dress. "I'm proposing a pact."

Barbara, whose heart was racing, looked up at her with wide, round eyes, knowing that whatever Mamie proposed would be brilliant.

"If you tell me how many years there are between us, I'll let you climb up."

"Forty!"

"Forty-two, perfect. You guessed it."

Happiness was putting her feet on top of her grandmother's, holding hands, putting her head on Mamie Margaux's belly, and letting herself be carried.

"What about the music?" Barbara had asked after they'd begun dancing slowly and rhythmically. Her grandmother began to hum the first thing that popped into her head.

"J'attendrai . . . le jour et la nuit, j'attendrai toujours ton retour . . ."

Every forward step her grandmother took was a step back for Barbara. It was a fun game of pulleys, one of push and pull, up and down, here and there. When her grandmother exaggeratedly lifted one leg, the girl's knee rose up high and she'd start to laugh. Her mind on the dance, Mamie could hear Barbara but didn't pay much attention.

For Barbara, the two months of happiness with Mamie Margaux had flown by. She never found out that, before she went to sleep, when her grandmother said she was going down to the reception desk to ask for a bottle of water to keep on the nightstand, what she was really doing was calling home from the hotel telephone booth. Clément kept her up to date on her daughter's progress. It was slow but progress nonetheless.

At the end of August, when the figs were ripe in Provence, Margaux knew that it was time to return home. Édith had welcomed them on the street, all dressed up and with her hair done, with what looked like a forced smile on her face. Barbara had swung the door open and jumped out of the car, running to hug her mother.

"You've gotten so big!" Édith gave her a bunch of kisses and looked at her again. "Did you have fun, my love?"

"It was the best summer of my life, Mom."

"That's wonderful, honey. That makes me happy. I'm so happy that you're home."

"Guess what? I know how to ride a bike now."

The very next day—everything in order once more with Édith on the right dosage of pills—Barbara and her father began putting covers on her schoolbooks for the new academic year, and the routine of acting like nothing had happened continued. Mamie Margaux packed up Geneviève and drove slowly to Paris in the truck lane.

6

A Door Slammed Shut

Working from home had its upsides. Barbara didn't waste time traveling back and forth on a crowded bus, she didn't have to put on makeup, she could wear comfortable shoes, she could have whatever tea she liked, she saved herself from the biting cold of early March—the worst predictions said it'd only get worse—and she didn't need to talk about her coworkers' every ailment, worry, and sickness. There were also drawbacks. Sometimes the doorbell would ring, as it was now. Barbara had quickly learned how much of a pain it was if the doorbell of the Montmartre apartment rang when she wasn't expecting anyone and suddenly had to go open the door in the middle of a video call. This time, after the third ring, she hesitated. She didn't know if she should leave her chair in the middle of selling the rights to Anne Delacourt's work to a relatively interested Swedish publisher; she could say, in her best English, that someone would not stop ringing the doorbell, and that she'd go get it and be back in no time. She wasn't expecting a package. She wasn't expecting anyone. But whomever it was would surely get tired of waiting.

Barbara ignored the ringing for the time being. "Anne Delacourt is, day in and day out, Giresse and Trésor's star writer. Later on, I'll send you an Excel sheet with data that the Society of Editors collected.

Actually, I'll write down a reminder. Anne is one of the best-selling authors of the century in France. This novel may reach the top ten."

"We see. But . . ." The representative from the Swedish publisher, who was a couple of months away from retirement, stroked her chin, searching for the right words. "The topic worries us a little."

"What do you mean? Dystopian stories are selling right now. They're selling, and selling, and will keep selling. They'll be trendy soon, you'll see. One day, they'll make a television series based on Margaret Atwood's *The Handmaid's Tale*, a phenomenal book, and then everyone will want dystopian stories. And this is a good one, trust me. Delacourt is ahead of her time with this one; only she could have produced something like this."

"Yes, yes, we looked at the dossier you sent us, and we've read the book. We received a positive report on it. We like how she writes . . . short sentences, to the point." She scrunched her nose. "But the topic . . ."

"The topic? That's the best part. *Tomorrow* is singular. It's topical. Right now there are more mothers in the world serving as wombs-for-rent than there are mothers giving birth for themselves. It's a global shift. Surrogacy. This is a sharp yet elegant critique of consumerism followed to its ultimate ends. Children don't get kidnapped anymore—anyone can write that story. Children are being bought now. It's a world of wombs-for-rent. The poor half of the world gives birth to the children the rich half of the world want without having to put in any work. It's a staggering story."

The Swedish editor raised a finger so Barbara knew she wanted to interrupt.

"I don't know if that appeals to our audience."

"The reviews are unanimous. They're saying everywhere that Delacourt has done a meticulous job of addressing a subject that . . . that is delicate? Yes . . . delicate. But between the two of us, it's something only a woman could have written—a feminist woman with experience and a career like Anne Delacourt. That's why I find it strange that your Swedish readers haven't heard of her yet."

The steaming mug on the Swedish editor's desk fogged up her screen. She took a sip, buying some time to think.

"If we bought the rights, hypothetically, she . . . Do you think she'd come to Stockholm to do promotions and interviews? Two days, some touring—"

"Of course." She didn't let her finish. "Look, Anne is very much like that. Very normal. This novel was published in 2006, and the publishing rights have already been sold in thirteen different languages across Europe alone. Five or six of them have already been released, and the rest are being translated as we speak . . . even into Portuguese. And now you can have the distinction as the first Nordic country with *Tomorrow*. The first. Next month, I'll be meeting with Frode Arnesen, the Norwegian from Cappelen, who's coming to Paris for the same reasons, to consider purchasing the rights. Maybe it won't be a bestseller in Sweden right away—though I think it will be—but I guarantee it will be a long-seller, which is what we love most, right?"

"But does she travel or not?"

"So far, she's gone everywhere she's been invited. She travels everywhere in Europe. Sometimes I go with her. Her last trip was to Barcelona because she had a simultaneous release in Spanish and Catalan. They do it that way so that no one gets upset."

"We'll look at the numbers, Barbara, and think about it."

"You're going to sell so many books, we'll be deforesting the Amazon."

"Excuse me?" She raised her head as she was searching through the steam for the button to disconnect.

"Nothing. Nothing. It's just a saying."

The sound disconnected first, then the video. Once Barbara knew that all communication with Sweden had been cut, she buttoned up her pants and rushed to open the door.

There was no one on the landing. There was no sign of movement in the stairwell. There wasn't even a package on the mat. She pushed the intercom but gave up after her third hello. Whoever it was would come back.

Later on, she thought to call Jasper, in case it had been him and he needed something.

"All good here, thanks," he responded, a little bewildered, in his idiosyncratic accent. "I haven't gone outside today. I'm here with Hulshoff."

She felt a bit more at ease.

When Mamie Margaux still lived in the apartment, Jasper, who lived on the second floor, would sometimes come up to visit her. He never showed up unannounced. He had a well-mannered habit of calling ahead. Never wanting to bother, he'd visit only when Mamie was in the mood and invited him to join her for five o'clock tea. Jasper was a redheaded man born on the outskirts of Amsterdam. He'd come to Paris in the mid-1950s with his wife, Hilde, to work as a manager for a Dutch cheese business. The company had rented him the two-bedroom apartment for twenty-four months; now all alone, Jasper had spent the next fifty years—more than half his life—between those four walls.

After spending some time in Montmartre supplying red-paraffin-wax-wrapped Edam cheese all over France—and achieving quite the feat of selling foreign cheese to a country with twelve hundred of its own varieties—Jasper changed careers. He was named general director of a French company that exported Camembert all over the world. On an executive's salary with a twenty-year mortgage, he and Hilde were able to purchase the apartment they'd been renting. Other than Mamie Margaux, Jasper and Hilde were the longest-tenured residents of the building, photographed so often by the tourists who managed to look up from their own feet. The apartment building wasn't too dissimilar from the others in the area—whitewashed, with chipped walls on the lower levels and slightly irregular windows that had wood pleated shades. Its location at the intersection of three streets caused pedestrians to inevitably notice it. If you looked upward toward the attic's huge observatory windows, there was an illusion of a massive ship with a figurehead sailing above.

Jasper and Hilde never had children. They had cats, and always two at a time: one dark and one light. One for each of them. When it came time for the sad and inevitable moment of having to put a cat down, they began the search for another just like it. After Hilde died following a bizarre fall between the first floor and the ground floor, Jasper traded in the cats for a dog. He needed companionship and loyalty, and Hulshoff, a Labrador with a kind face who'd grown old with him, satisfied those needs.

On the April day Margaux had left for the retirement home, Jasper and Hulshoff saw her off at the doorway. Standing respectfully at one another's side, they waited as Barbara helped her grandmother into the car. Once she was inside, Jasper approached to blow her two kisses. Words couldn't explain the sentiment. The beginning of the last chapter in a person's life story calls for respect. And that implicit silence encompassed that respect. Everyone understood it wasn't a morning for words. Anything would sound too final. But even Hulshoff, who sat and watched the whole ceremony on his hind legs, sensed that his fifth-floor neighbor would never again climb those same stairs she once had so effortlessly. He might never see her again. Jasper would. He intended to visit her at the Viviani Retirement Home only from time to time, so as to not be a burden.

Roger returned home in the middle of the afternoon, after the glacial cold had frozen his fingers. He entered the apartment without announcing himself, unzipped his jacket, and messed with his hair with both hands. When he realized he wasn't alone, he greeted Barbara, who was picking up a catalog she'd left open on her desk.

"Maybe I should wear pants made for winter," said Roger, who was trying to warm his thighs by rubbing his jeans. "I've been freezing my ass off in these all day."

"Doesn't surprise me," said Barbara, grabbing Tuesday's edition of *Libération.*

"By the way, I've been waiting for a package delivery from DHL. It's already a little late, but I'm expecting them to come today."

"A what?" Barbara sat on the red sofa and began perusing the newspaper.

"A package. I ordered a lens from a catalog. A German lens. They're the best."

"Of course."

"They promised me it would be here today."

"I haven't left the house all day," she said, looking down at an interview on the inside cover.

"And no one's come by?"

"No . . ." She cleared her throat. "No one's rang today."

"That's strange."

"What is?"

"You said no one's come by, and I . . . never mind. It doesn't matter."

"What? Tell me," she inquired, without looking up from the newspaper.

"I got a call from DHL. I can even look up when they called. They told me they came by but no one answered the door. They asked me if I wanted them to leave it on the landing and I said no, because a lens like that costs a pretty penny. But obviously if you were home . . ."

"Well, if they did ring, I didn't hear it."

The mood in the house shifted.

"That's why I'm saying, it's really strange . . ."

"Maybe they did. But look, I'm in my own home. I'm not your maid, and I don't owe you any explanations."

"Come on."

Roger rolled his eyes, which he knew from past experiences annoyed people more than any bad word. When he didn't like something, when he was disappointed, when he caught someone in a lie, he would lower his eyelids slowly and condescendingly. He had noticed that the spontaneous and unrehearsed look sometimes irritated his opponent more than an insult would. He couldn't help but do it, even if people didn't like it, because it happened automatically.

"'Come on' what?" Barbara rebuffed. "What's wrong?"

"Well, I've been here for a week now—ten days to be exact—so I know you're not my maid. Or my mother." Roger grabbed his coat and headed to his room, grumbling. "Even though at your age, you could be."

"What'd you say?"

"Nothing."

"No, tell me. What'd you say to me?"

"That it doesn't matter. They'll come back and bring me the stupid package."

She got furious.

"Hold your horses, honey. You didn't just say that."

"And you didn't feel like opening the door when they brought what I ordered."

"I was working. I'm sorry."

"You see! I knew it. They did come."

"I was in a meeting."

"Of course." He rolled his eyes again in disbelief.

Barbara took a deep breath to try to keep her cool.

"How old did you say you were?"

"Thirty-three." He said it with some force. "And what about you?"

"Forty-one, and at forty-one, I couldn't be your mother, you got that? And if you're not comfortable in your brother's room, you know where the door is, because I'm all good here on my own."

The fight hardened like a callus.

"Can I say one last thing?"

"No," she said harshly.

"It doesn't seem like it to me."

"Seem like what?"

"Like you're all good."

Roger knew it would hurt her, because it was true.

For Barbara, there was no proverb to calm her aggravation. Paris was like a door slammed shut for her, the end of a past life. People came to the best city in the world for the lights, the paintings, the sky, the boulevards, the museums, the nights, the love . . . For her, it was the opposite. Paris was just her escape from the nightmare that was Maurice. It was distance from the anger, and it was the opportunity to process the sudden expiration of a marriage that had ended in the worst of ways. Leaving Arles and moving to the capital, to Mamie Margaux's apartment, was a chance to flee from the humiliation and to break away from her past, of course. She was starting all over again in her forties, when she'd least expected it, in a new place. At least she was lucky when it came to work. She really enjoyed selling the foreign rights for her authors. She liked it, and it kept her distracted. At least for a couple of hours, she didn't have to think about Maurice. Or about that fucking bitch. Because every single day, something became clearer: the only thing worse than him was her.

7

The Critical Moment

"And for dessert? An orange or an apple?"

There were few choices when it came to the fruit at Chez Richard. Laurence, the waitress with the long apron and melancholic eyes, already knew the answer. Roger opted for the orange by default. It annoyed him how, after eating it, his fingers would smell like citrus all evening, no matter how many times he washed his hands in the miserable bathroom of that neighborhood restaurant. When he put his index finger on the shutter of his camera to take a photo in the evenings, he was reminded of what he'd eaten at lunchtime. In spite of it all, he still preferred the orange to the apple. He'd grown tired of apples. He'd picked so many of them, carried so many boxes of them, and seen his parents grow so weary whenever a September storm ruined the golden apple-picking season that he no longer wanted anything to do with apples. Or his father.

Roger discovered that the best way to beat the cold in Paris was to walk. Every afternoon, a new exhibit. The city had so many of them that, instead of wandering aimlessly after lunch, he could choose an art gallery, a museum, or a photography exhibit. Every day, he ventured to a new one. That Tuesday, when the teasing sun and stubborn cold forced him to wear a scarf, gloves, and a wool hat, Roger went down to Beaubourg to see the recent acquisitions of Georges Pompidou. It presented just like that, with that ugly title. The "Recent Acquisitions." They comprised photographs the modern art center had purchased between 2003 and 2008. Roger enjoyed going back to the industrial-style building, which had a red-bellied glass serpent slithering up its eccentric facade.

The Pompidou Center had seemed like the epitome of modernity to Roger when he'd visited with his parents twenty years earlier so they could try out their new car, the only time the Narbona-Bazin family had gone to Paris. His parents were fascinated by the blue tubular machine. Marcel and Roger, on the other hand, were more entertained by the diverse fauna on the esplanade in front of the museum. During that summer of 1988, they saw specimens they'd never encountered before: bare-chested punks with colorful mohawks; Argentine jugglers wearing clown noses who held up ten chairs stacked on top of each other; human statues dressed as Charlot who were able to keep still without moving an eyelash for two whole hours; and all kinds of street musicians whose music overlapped, turning the square into a festive cacophony that the brothers from Fontclara, a hamlet with just fifty inhabitants and one Romanesque church, could never have imagined. They didn't have all that, even in Girona. Or Barcelona, which they visited from time to time.

Twenty years later, Roger had no one to talk to about all the oddities of life that passed before his eyes on that unchanged concrete plaza. But now peddlers dominated the square, selling sunglasses spread across blankets laid on the floor. They were certainly counterfeit designer brands, though the street vendors insisted they were real. Large groups of street vendors dressed in their traditional Pakistani garb could be seen selling small, plastic flying toys that would shoot into the air like rockets and drop down randomly onto the heads of tourists. Sometimes, if you looked lost, a pair of Jehovah's Witnesses would stop you and explain the virtues of their sect; although, in their fundamentalism, they didn't call it that. They called it "Christian confession." The jugglers with the chairs weren't there anymore. They'd all likely retired due to old age or lower back pain, or because they'd saved up enough to scrape by. There was still a punk or two left, but they'd since ditched the mohawk.

He paid the entrance fee to the photography exhibit and passed quickly through the bustle and into the silence of the museum. The escalator carried him to three enormous, dark halls that welcomed him with faintly lit images. He liked that there was a little bit of everything: Alina Szapocznikow's photo sculptures; Frank Breuer's warehouse logo, which had a distinct whiteness and aesthetic; and the old photo-booth strips of Max Ernst and Yves Tanguy that dated back to the Wall Street crash of 1929. The Pompidou Center had purchased them recently. There was also a black-and-white photograph that caught his attention. It was a Cartier-Bresson taken in Tokyo at the burial of the kabuki actor Danjūrō. The photographer had captured the critical moment of mourning for five women, two of whom smothered their sobs into their white handkerchiefs. A masterpiece. He lingered in front of the image for a while, motionless, observant. The excursion was worth it if only for that image. The emotion of the protagonists was contagious. It gave Roger goose bumps, but it was also the kind of photo he would never take—because he didn't know enough and because, since his father's death and the ensuing aftermath, he hated photojournalism. He should have rushed back into working for a newspaper and riding his motorcycle back and forth, documenting tragedy. But why would he want to preserve the tragedy of others when there was so much beauty to be photographed? How morbid.

He took the metro back home. With the heat at full blast on the public transit, he took off his wool cap and, had there been any room to, would've taken off his jacket. The trains were so packed during rush hour between the les Halles and Abbesses stations that he could barely lift an arm to grab on to the stainless steel bar when they stopped short. Roger wore his backpack in front to help guard his camera and lenses throughout the journey, including when it came time to traverse the infernal passages on the eternal walk to the transfer lines. When he was back in a train car, he placed his hand on top of his bag to protect it from being swiped. He didn't break contact with it for even a moment. In one way or another, he had to ensure it was still on him. He'd been warned that pickpockets made a fortune on Line 12 because of the gawking tourists. Once back on the street, he could breathe freely again. After fifteen days in Paris, the eighteenth arrondissement had already become home.

Bundled up, he made his way back up Montmartre using a shortcut he'd already learned. He made sure that the path from the metro exit to the house cut through streets that only locals, and few at that, ever walked. Sometimes he counted more cats than people. Even more so when the sun was beginning to set.

Out of nowhere, someone shouted: "Hey, photographer!"

It took Roger a minute to realize who the woman smoking under a streetlamp was. From the corner of his eye, he thought she might be a prostitute. The cabarets alongside the boulevard were full of them. When it got dark, two prostitutes would appear on every corner, as if they'd divided up the territory. But he hadn't yet seen any venturing up the steep neighborhood of Montmartre. It was a simple matter of supply and demand. It was harder to find a passerby to offer your services to on the solitary streets. It definitely wasn't possible up on the hill. Even less so when the cold made it inconceivable to stand and wait for a client willing to pay fifty euros for a blow job in the doorway.

"Come on, take a picture of me," the woman insisted.

Roger began walking toward her until he recognized her.

"Oh man. It's you. Did you finish your shift?"

"The lunch shift, yeah. I go back in an hour to start dinner."

"Richard exploits you," he blurted out. "And I think you start dinner early here in France."

"Are you Spanish?"

"Well, from Barcelona. Well, actually, from Girona . . . From near Girona. Well, from—"

She interrupted. "You speak French well."

"Because of my mother. She's from here, obviously. Well, not from Paris, from Bes—"

She cut him off again. "It seemed strange to me . . . with how hard it is for you Spaniards to pick up the accent." She didn't care where he or his mother were from. Wearing a jacket that covered her from ears to ankles, she leaned against a stone wall. "How do you want me to pose?"

"For?"

"For the fucking picture. Are you going to take it or not? You're a photographer, what with that thing hanging from your neck all day. You're definitely not a tourist with that big machine."

"Photographer . . ."

"I knew it since the first day you came to the restaurant."

"I am a photographer, or aspiring photographer, or—I don't really know what I am. But . . ." He pleaded for forgiveness with his eyes. "I won't take a picture of you."

"Excuse me?"

He cleared his throat so he could repeat it a little louder.

"I won't take your picture. Sorry."

"But . . . why not? It's only for me. Take it and send it to me. And that's it, man."

"I'm sorry." He shrugged his shoulders.

"What's wrong?" she asked, clearly hurt. "Am I not pretty enough to be a model?"

Roger moved closer to her. Once she was two steps away, he looked at her attentively. She appeared older and more vulnerable without the white apron. She seemed to be a worn, disillusioned woman. At around forty, Roger guessed, she had an altogether unfriendly air. If not cold, then sad.

"It has nothing to do with you as the model. You're . . . perfect. I'm really sorry, but I'm not going to take your picture."

"Are you an idiot? What's wrong with you?"

"*Désolé.* They're personal issues."

It dawned on the waitress that should the amateur photographer who refused to take her picture ever set foot in Chez Richard again, she would spit in his soup on the way from the kitchen to the table. It wouldn't be the first or second time she'd left a present for some deserving asshole. But the youngest of the Narbona-Bazin family, son of a farmer and a woman from Besançon, didn't want to seem like something he wasn't: an asshole.

"I'm Roger." He extended his hand.

"You're expecting me to kiss your ring now?" She slapped his hand away from her.

"It's cold as hell here. My apartment is just there . . . If you have an hour to spare . . ."

"Sure. Let's go up and fuck. Who do you think you are?"

"I wasn't going to say that. We can go up. I'll make you a café au lait and explain why I don't take photos of people anymore."

"Look, I don't have the time, and I'm not desperate enough to listen to you pretend to be an interesting artist. Suck my dick, man."

She threw the cigarette butt on the ground and stepped on it. When Roger glimpsed her worn-out boots in full detail, with their discolored leather and uneven soles from endless walking, he could have taken out his Canon and searched for the correct shadowing to take a nice picture.

"My name is Laurence," she said, with her hands in her pockets.

He took it as a sign of a truce.

"I know. I hear Richard shouting at you all day. Am I allowed to come back to the restaurant then?"

"Will your wife leave you?"

"No, I don't have a wife."

"Then come whenever you want." Laurence got close to his ear. "Want to know something? I'm dying to serve you soup."

8

An Air of Prayer

During the winter, family visits to the Viviani Retirement Home were restricted to the hours of 10:00 a.m. to 7:00 p.m. Barbara was used to being the first to arrive during those hours. On Tuesdays and Fridays, she woke early and, so long as she didn't have a meeting with an editor on the other side of the world, would go to visit her grandmother. Sometimes she wondered to herself how—at forty-one years old and after everything the two of them had been through—she still felt that same yearning to see and hug and hear her grandmother as she had when she was eight. It was hope sustained.

Prior to arriving at the retirement home, which was located on the edge of the Latin Quarter just fifty steps from the Seine, Barbara stopped at a long-standing pastry shop two blocks away from Square René Viviani to buy her grandmother a treat. If it wasn't a Saint Honoré cake, it was milk-chocolate cat tongues. Despite her age, her grandmother continued to indulge in her sweet tooth to the point of indigestion. She hadn't lost that wartime weakness for sweets. In times of hunger, sugar was a reward, a gift you could savor on your palate and make last.

Mamie Margaux had more of an apartment than a room. The only thing missing from the living quarters that would make her feel like she was still in a tiny apartment, albeit with medical assistance and hotel services, was having a kitchen with a stovetop. What she had instead was a microwave and an electric kettle sitting on a white laminate shelf. She had also negotiated for a mini fridge to be placed underneath. Some days, to avoid going down for lunch with the fellow residents, who she thought were in worse shape than she was, Margaux went out to buy ready-made food, heated it up, and ate it at the table she'd set up against the poet's window in her room. She was convinced she was the only resident who could come and go during visiting hours as she pleased. A week before checking into the private residence, she'd made the facility agree to sign a permission slip—a special kind of authorization that opened doors for her, quite literally. Margaux Dutronc told them that she was eighty-three years old, her head was clear, and, aside from the pain in her knees, her legs allowed her to walk a bit each day pain-free. She wasn't there, like the other grannies, to wait for the signal to take off from the runway. She left home to save herself the trouble of going up and down five flights of stairs, and it was precisely because she'd spent too much time shut in that she didn't want to miss out on an ounce of freedom. She was there in the interest of comfort, of adapting to her body and giving in to the whims of a timeline that sometimes felt like it stopped, then sometimes flew by. Margaux couldn't stand how so many of her fellow residents thought of themselves as locked up in the home, as if they were suffering a punishment for becoming a burden. Even the phrase made her shiver. Locked up. It wasn't a prison or asylum. She moved there out of her own volition, and she didn't want to become infected with resentment, which spread like a virus, permeating the dining room and the courtyard with the magnolia tree.

At ten on the dot, Barbara entered her grandmother's room and found her reading the newspaper, posture straightened, hair white, glasses clean, and pose dignified. She was leafing through the pages near the table that looked out toward the square. "At the poet's window." That's what her grandmother would call a large window with beautiful views.

"You still alive, Mamie?" Barbara made the same joke each morning she visited.

"Still am, my love," her grandma joked back in the same tone. "Good morning."

"Good morning."

Without taking off her jacket, a champagne-colored fake sheepskin, Barbara gave her grandmother two kisses.

"Your cheeks are freezing, sweetie."

"It's cold and dry today . . . It's Paris-Paris."

"And they say it'll get worse."

"Who says that?"

"The newspaper. But I don't know if these weather guys ever guess right."

Mamie closed the *Libération*. She folded it, set it on the table, and eyed her granddaughter from head to toe as she slipped off her coat.

"I brought you something new today. Let's see how it tastes." Barbara placed a small package on the table. "A Sacher torte."

Her grandmother's bony fingers struggled to undo the little pastry-shop bow.

"Sacher torte is the one from Vienna, right?"

"Yes. It's chocolate and peach marmalade."

"Put it in the fridge. Thank you, sweetie. I'll save it for dinner. That way I don't have to go down and eat with those cockatoos."

Barbara sat at the edge of the bed. "There's no need to—"

"You know Anine? The one whose room is next door, the one who's not all there? Today, she suddenly got it in her head to ask me in the middle of conversation, 'So what do you want to be when you grow up?'"

"Don't pay any attention to her."

"But the thing is she isn't just asking me, she asks all of us. She could be talking about anything at all, since she drones on and repeats herself a lot, and then, out of nowhere, she asks the question 'What do you want to be when you grow up?'"

"And how do you respond?"

"I change the subject. What am I supposed to tell her? That I'm already grown up, dammit? That I'm beginning to forget things too? What does Anine expect us to say? Nobody knows. Why does she ask us four, five times in a row? Nobody knows that either. *She* doesn't know, I'm sure; she's on the brink of—"

"She's older than you, right?"

"Anine? Not even. I'm two years older—but, poor girl, she doesn't function anymore. Her mind . . ."

"Not like you. You're a queen."

"I'm the best in this home. That's for sure." She showed off her best laugh. "All the doctors tell me so."

"I thought you were gonna say that all the grandpas in the residence talk about it. I've seen one wearing pajamas in the hallway who's handsome."

"Don't joke around, because there is one here who . . . would make you cross yourself."

"What?"

"No, no . . ."

"Say it, come on."

"'The Great Masturbator' is what the nurses call him."

"Oh, Mamie, I don't even want to know. Don't tell me."

Barbara was visiting with the intention of sharing Jasper's well-wishes. She'd run into him in the stairwell of the apartment building, and he'd vehemently insisted that she do so. At the time, she'd suspected that through some trick of the mind, he'd unfortunately guessed at her intentions: she'd pass the greetings along when she saw her grandmother if she remembered. But she let it go.

"How's my cactus?"

"Impeccable. Just the way you left it. Watching through the window all day."

"You're taking care of it?"

"It's in the same place, Mamie. It's perfect. Don't worry. It gets light, I water it only when the dirt is dry. I put in the clay that you left me, and I talk to it every day. I do everything you told me to do."

"It's heavier than a corpse, that cactus. The porter from the greenhouse who brought it up five flights must still be on leave. You should've seen how much the poor guy was sweating."

"Between the pot, the plant, and the dirt, that doesn't surprise me."

"I tried giving him a tip, and he said, 'I'd rather you let me sit for a bit.' And you bet he sat on the red couch, and I gave him a glass of water and let him rest until he recovered."

Mamie Margaux took out her hand cream from the nightstand and offered some to Barbara. It was a gesture both of them liked sharing. They did it unconsciously, having done it for Barbara's whole life.

"This one smells good." Barbara looked at the label on the tube. "Ah, L'Occitane."

"I think Jasper gave it to me."

"Oh, Jasper . . . I ran into him in the stairwell. I told him I was coming, and he sent his greetings."

Her grandmother didn't say anything. Both of them continued to rub their hands thoroughly. Mamie had not finished going through the apartment inventory by the time the cream had absorbed into their hands.

"And that guy? Does he still have the room?"

"Marcel? Yes. No problem."

"A lawyer, right?"

"Yes, yes. Discreet and . . ."

"He pays every month?"

"He pays rent on time every month. You don't have to worry about that."

She thought twice about whether she should get into the details. "In fact, he's just left for a couple of weeks, and he's sent his brother to use the room. Fine, but . . ."

"But . . ." Mamie knew how to detect any anger from her granddaughter, no matter how much she wanted to hide it.

"His brother is more of a loudmouth. Nothing serious, but the first few days he acted like it was his apartment. I had to stop him in his tracks, and you know, I don't like these things. It makes me uncomfortable having to say, 'It stops here, boy. This is not your house.'"

"I'm guessing he's young."

"Hardly. He said he's thirty-three. One time, I mentioned to him he's 'the age of Christ.' And can you believe he didn't know Jesus's age when he was crucified?"

"It's enough if the youth know who Jesus is at all."

"He's no dummy. He's plenty clever. He says he's a photographer. Or at the very least, he goes out all day with his camera and backpack."

"What kind of photographer?"

"I don't know. I haven't asked."

"Don't trust him if he's a photographer. Believe me."

Barbara stood up from the bed and approached the window, looking out onto the street.

"Is that the tree you were talking about, Mamie?"

"It's the oldest tree in Paris. Believe it or not, but there's a plaque out there that says it."

"Se non è vero, è ben trovato . . ."

"I'll tell you what it says. 'Robinia acacia, something, something, however many trees planted here next to the church of Saint-Julien-le-Pauvre in 1601,' I think."

"Let's go look at it, come on. Let's go out for a walk."

"Are you trying to kill me?"

"What do you mean?"

"From the cold, I mean."

"Let's go, come on. Look . . . the sun's shining out there, Mamie."

Convinced, Mamie Margaux and her granddaughter passed through the two tiled hallways that stretched between the rooms and the exit to the street. The Viviani was a home founded sometime around when man landed on the moon. It could have ended up a filthy and dilapidated center, but the new owners, the heirs of the founders, were careful about hygiene and had an obsession with maintenance. Every two years, they painted the building white from top to bottom. Every three years, they reupholstered the chairs. Every four years, they redid the lighting so it didn't look like a morgue waiting room. Inside, no one was forced to feel like they had to confront the ultimate question.

"Light, so much light, because we'll be in the dark soon," a nursing assistant had once told Margaux as she changed the sheets.

Barbara and Mamie went out onto the street, arm-in-arm. Each had their wool scarves wrapped up so high you could only see their eyes. Slowly, they approached the tree. The trunk was dark, wrinkled by the fissures of centuries.

"It's hard to believe it's the oldest in the city. I would've guessed I'd seen bigger or older ones, but I don't know how to calculate that." Barbara circled the tree. "It has a nice trunk. You can't deny that."

"A bit distorted, wouldn't you say?"

"A little skewed . . . but a mighty trunk. It has personality."

"At four hundred years old, who wouldn't?"

"It's pretty out here."

"Very. Dogs happily lift their legs here. Then they bow because they know it's a tree with history."

Barbara always laughed at every one of her mamie's fanciful ideas, as if they still were together that summer in Sainte-Maxime. They sat down on the only bench in the sun. Their bottoms freezing, they contemplated the tree that had outlived the Sun King, the Napoleons, Marie Antoinette, the Revolution, Hitler, and Sarkozy. With time, they'd had to prop up the heaviest branches so it wouldn't topple to the ground.

"History carries weight," the grandmother murmured with the ulterior motives of someone who hears the bell tolling every quarter hour.

A bicyclist, outfitted like he'd just escaped the final stages of the Tour de France, passed by the tree without even looking at it.

"Once the weather gets nicer, you know what you can do? You can come out here with the oboe and play in the square."

"Oh, honey, what are you even saying?"

"I'm not saying you should do it now. At the end of spring, in June, when it's nice . . ."

"What do you want? For people to throw money into my hat? We sure would make people laugh."

"I don't see why not."

"They'd throw tomatoes at me."

"You can do it on the 30th of May, an homage to my mother. She would have turned . . . sixty-three, if I'm not mistaken."

"Sixty-three on the 30th of May, yes."

"Yes, she died at . . ." Barbara counted on her fingers.

"Fifty-five. She'd just turned fifty-five."

Mamie Margaux knew it all perfectly. If you have to bury your daughter, the last thing you forget is her age when your world ended. You could've survived a war, you could've suffered never seeing your love again, you could've experienced many close deaths—deaths that are the laws of life and those that challenge any natural law—but if you have experienced the worst thing in the world, you remember it every day. Her age: fifty-five. The date: July 25, 2000.

"I think," said Barbara, looking for words that wouldn't hurt, "that you and I hardly speak about my mother."

"About Édith?"

"About both of my parents. About Édith and Clément. It's been eight years already. Almost."

"It'll be eight years in July."

"I don't know. It's a feeling. I'm not saying it's good or bad, Mamie, but maybe we've spoken too little about . . . I miss them so much. If they hadn't died at the same time . . . Do you know what I mean? Sometimes you don't know what's worse. At least they didn't have to miss each other. They went together, on a trip that my father dreamed about and . . . goodbye. But at the same time, throughout the years,

I think about it, and I think that when people go through an illness, the family can say goodbye. On the other hand, a heart attack, an accident . . . Maybe it's crueler for the living. Suddenly, it's good night. Everything is over, and everything is left hanging. There's no option that gives us closure. That much is clear. No matter how you look at it, it's a shit show, right?"

The grandmother had been staring at the oldest tree in Paris, bare from the winter, while listening to Barbara. She let a couple pushing a stroller pass by in front of them before saying her part.

"We hardly speak about it because we think about it a lot."

The subsequent silence, dense as the morning fog, had an air of prayer to it. Barbara laid her head on her grandmother's shoulder.

"You're right. We hardly talk about it because we think about it a lot."

Mamie Margaux slowly found her voice of serenity again.

"We're like a tree leaf. Every single one of us, a leaf. Beautiful, fragile, proud . . . imperfect too."

"Colorful."

"Yes, colorful. Or shriveled. Delicate . . . The tree is humanity. We each are one of the leaves. And we dance in the wind and need the other trees to live, and we hold on for the calm. Édith was one leaf, your father another. And Damien. And you. And I, holding on here. The game of life is designed so they fall one by one."

"What you're saying is beautiful, Mamie."

"It's a catastrophe," she said carefully, "when too many leaves fall all at once. The wars, the flu of '68, the crash of the Concorde. Your father's dream, you said it yourself. The trip he and Édith prepared for so long. The 25th of July, 2000. The dates. We'll start forgetting things, like that damn Anine, but we'll remember the damned dates. The dates and knowing what we want to be when we grow up."

"Mamie . . ."

"What?"

"Do you have a handkerchief?"

9

The Magic Word

Roger thought the soup at Chez Richard tasted better than ever. Hot, French, and with a touch of je ne sais quoi that gave it a nice consistency.

"Can I take your plate?" Laurence was carrying four dishes she'd collected from other tables in her left hand. She cleared away Roger's bowl and spoon to make the most of her trip.

"Excellent." He lifted the place settings to help her pick up. "Compliments to the chef."

"What chef?" Already carrying a full load, she gestured with her elbows. "Do you see a Michelin star on the door? There's no chef here. There are just two Korean women in the kitchen who make anything and everything. The meals all come out to fifteen euros—what do you think is going on?"

In addition to the stew, which contained a little bit of everything, he ate shirred eggs and an orange. For that price—a drink, two slices of bread, oily napkins, and a slice of Montmartre peeking out from behind the red curtains all included—he couldn't ask for more.

"Where's the boss?" Roger asked as he paid in cash at the counter.

"He's got a hell of a cold, he said. He must be down bad if he didn't come to manage every little thing."

"So you're running the ship."

"You can count on it." It was the first smile that Laurence had cracked in weeks.

"As the current boss, you might not have time to go out for a smoke between lunch and dinner."

"What's happening? You planning on taking pictures today? You've rethought it, huh?"

"No, no," he murmured. "I told you . . ."

"Does that offer to come over to your house still stand?"

Caught off guard, Roger reacted as seriously as possible.

"Yeah, of course."

"Write down your address." She placed her notebook and pen right in front of him. "I'll go."

"Ah . . ."

"You'll be there, I'm guessing." She gave him a threatening look.

"Of course, yes, yes."

"If you're not going to be there, don't waste my time."

"Well, I was going to head to an exhibition now, but I'll switch my plans. It's okay."

"That's how I like it," Laurence said quietly in a tone she hoped sounded rational.

"What time do you get out of here?"

She turned around to look at the big clock hanging over the counter, hidden behind bottles of Cointreau, Chartreuse, and Rémy Martin.

"I've got a good amount of time left. I still have to pass out some dinners. Pick up. Clean . . . There's still work left to do."

A change in plans indeed. Roger would see that afternoon's exhibition early and quickly. He searched for a metro station and went down to Saint-Paul in the Marais neighborhood. He rushed to the half-palace and half-magisterial hotel building that contained the Bibliothèque historique de la Ville de Paris, where a photography exhibition about Parisians under the Nazi occupation was being held. They had inaugurated the exhibition not even a week before, and he'd heard that there was some sort of controversy, but he hadn't followed the conflict. When he entered the

Bibliothèque historique—what Parisians, fond of acronyms, called the BHVP—he knew he couldn't dillydally. He left his parka and backpack in the coatroom, and he entered the first dark hall without reading the photographer's biography. He passed by the explanatory plaques and headed straight for the photos.

Right away, his eyes were drawn to a color photo of a woman holding an umbrella on a snowy bench at la Tuileries. It was the image of tranquility. It wasn't just the photo that emanated tranquility. The Paris shown, at least in the first gallery, was a serene one that didn't seem like a city suffering in the moment. You couldn't see the war. You couldn't see the occupation. German soldiers showed up only occasionally and only unexpectedly, as though they had simply wandered into the view of the lens. Among the photos, however, there did suddenly appear a perspective of the porches on rue de Rivoli lined with Nazi flags—the red drapes, the emphatic swastikas—on a blue-sky day. The streets were empty except for two workers riding their bikes. Further down was a photograph of a soldier descending the stairs of the Madeleine church, surrounded by all sorts of passersby, as if the uniform and swastika didn't make an impression on them. The majority of the photographs, magnificent in their perspective, modern in their framing, were of a happy city. They depicted children playing with elephants at the Vincennes Zoo, children skating beneath the Eiffel Tower, movie posters of big cinema halls as grand attractions, women sorting through tchotchkes at the flea market, men in tiny bathing suits soaking in the Seine at the pont du Carrousel. The exhibition also displayed the terraces of the chicest cafés, crowded with people on Sundays at Champs-Élysées or the Les Deux Magots café. Not a single empty table. Men in sport coats, ties, and fedoras with black ribbons on their heads. Dressed-up women trying to impress with fancy hats and brightly colored shoes. Roger discovered that in 1940, the penguin-like waiters had already begun wearing the same tight, white apron that Laurence wore from the waist down at Chez Richard.

The street markets were bustling with life. An absolute worldliness. The people who bought and sold, however, wore a different type of vestment. Flat hats intended for workers were widespread. Rather than sport coats and stylish vests, long, brownish coveralls were dominant in les Halles, as they didn't stain when carrying wooden boxes and wicker baskets full of food. The more Roger looked at the photos, without dedicating more than twenty seconds to each, the more he realized the grays and purples stuck out in that range of old green tints. But sometimes a somewhat sublimated red took charge. Nothing was aggressive; it was a simple color scheme with watery hues. At any rate, he thought it all had the discolored air of memory.

Memories don't blur with time—rather, their primary colors fade. Roger took out his cell phone and wrote down that idea, not thinking too hard of how it might come to use. After, he crossed through the two exhibit halls at a hurried pace and without stopping. They contained black-and-white photos. The images emitted more sadness and gravity, but they were just as poetic. Suddenly, a wall of photos of women on bikes appeared. Whether stopped or in motion, all of them had one thing in common. All the women, of which there were maybe thirty or forty, were looking at the camera as if posing. Smiling or not smiling, in their winter coats or a light summer scarf, blond or brunette, glasses or no glasses, they'd all become models for the photographer, who shot them from a low angle, as though he had gotten down on one knee to find the perfect proportions. Together, the cyclists were enchanting. As Roger was leaving, a single photo caught his eye. He recognized it, but he didn't know where from. He could have sworn it wasn't the first time he'd seen that gaze, those wheels, and that basket on the handlebars. He figured it must have been the picture from the exhibition posters on the streetlamps around the city, and he didn't give it any more thought. He looked at his watch and left.

At the exit of the BHVP, he picked up his belongings from the coatroom and saw next to it an exhibit catalog. It was too expensive, and he would have to wait in line to pay, so he grabbed the free pamphlet for the exhibition and went on his merry way. On the metro home, he read the pamphlet and learned the name of the photographer: André Zucca. In fact, just as he'd thought, all the images he had passed by too quickly were from the same artist. The black-and-white ones were his, as well as the color slides captured on paper. Between stations, Roger thought that everything he'd seen contained the thread of history. When he was two stops away from Abbesses, it came to him all at once. He knew where he had seen that black-and-white photograph of the cyclist, the image that had captured his attention right away. Of course. It was the same woman from one of the photos he had found, in a magazine clipping in the tin box beneath Marcel's bed. He was sure of it. As soon as he got to his room, he'd grab the Banania box and check, but he was sure of it. He didn't make these kinds of mistakes. Who was she? He had no clue, but he would bet his life it was the same person.

The doorbell rang while Barbara was in front of her computer. She had been studying an offer for the Bulgarian translation of Simone Sicilia's last novel. It was the last because it was the latest one she had written and, overall, because she would never write again. After finishing the manuscript and sending the proofs with red corrections to the publisher, she'd written a send-off on Twitter, placed a plastic supermarket bag over her head, and tied it tightly with two rubber bands, waiting for her final moment to arrive.

"Consumed by vengeance, I don't have anything left to say. I'll be living a new experience. I won't describe it for you." In ninety-eight characters, she'd shocked social media. Speculators considered this, that, and the opposite. It was her loyal fans, of which there were many, who guessed at what Sicilia had been hinting. When the police broke down her apartment door and confirmed her death, it headlined every one of the country's newspapers. Until the moment of her Tweet, the writer, a member of the '70s generation, had close to five thousand followers on Twitter. The next day, the number had multiplied by ten without her ever getting to see it. Giresse & Trésor rushed to publish the book posthumously. Once Simone Sicilia's *The Gift* arrived at bookstores in paperback, its success surpassed expectations. Everyone wanted to know to what extent her uncle, a well-known socialist mayor of a city at the foot of the Alps, had abused her since she was eight years old. The best-selling author described every single one of their decade-long weekly meetings at his city hall office. It was always when the blinds were closed, always following a similar ritual. At every meeting, there was a small gift. Pierre Sicilia denied it all right away, mourning the death of his niece. By the second week of the book's release, he'd resigned. By the third, he'd fled to Mexico, and all traces of him were lost.

The doorbell rang again, impertinently. Barbara cursed Roger for having forgotten his keys again. She got up, and without asking who it was, she pressed the intercom button to open the street door. She left the door of the apartment slightly ajar so the cold wouldn't enter and the warmth from the heater wouldn't escape.

Laurence was huffing and puffing when she got to the top. Even her coat was bothering her. Seeing the door slightly ajar, she tapped with her knuckles. She didn't dare enter without Roger telling her she could pass through. She knocked again three times, waiting for an answer.

Barbara wasn't sure why Roger was knocking if the door was open. She got back up in a swift movement to see what was going on and found herself face-to-face with another woman. They were both surprised.

"Sorry . . ." Laurence took a step back.

"Good afternoon," Barbara replied.

Laurence's voice didn't come out. She hadn't expected anyone other than Roger to open the door for her. Even less, a woman.

Barbara got straight to the point. "Do you need something?"

"I must have gotten the apartment wrong." She crumpled the paper with the address in her hand.

"It depends. Who are you looking for?"

"I don't know. Actually . . ." Laurence thought about turning around, but even fleeing would have required an excuse. "This is apartment five, right?"

"Yes, you can't go up any higher than this. But who are you looking for?" Faced with silence, she insisted, "Tell me."

"I'm not sure of the name."

"You're looking for someone, and you don't know their name?"

"He's a photographer." A timid smile took over her face. "A handsome Spaniard."

"If he's a photographer, he lives here."

"Ah." She opened her eyes wide like a scared dog. It was a way of saving herself from asking if he was around or not.

"He just left . . . Actually, he left in the morning, and he hasn't come back."

Barbara didn't know how to interpret the coagulated silence of the woman standing in front of her. A mystery lay behind her worn coat, sad eyes, and nose, red from the cold outside. They might have been the same age, but she looked much older.

Laurence didn't know how to get out of the uncomfortable situation. She had made an appointment with a customer, and she found herself petrified to be in front of a svelte woman with hometown advantage and hair worn the way she would've wanted for herself, the grace of curls that always looked like she had just woken up. At a loss for words, Laurence contemplated the woman who held the door open, and she envied those marked cheekbones and green eyes, which caused her to tremble. Why had the photographer let her come over for a fuck if . . . ?

Suddenly Barbara put two and two together.

"One thing, girl . . . What's your name?"

"Me?" She wondered whether she should give her real name. "Laurence."

"It looks like you have the wrong idea. The handsome guy from Barcelona lives here, yes, but he's not my husband. Or my boyfriend, or anything like that. He just lives here. He's got his room. And I've got mine. His name is Roger. Is that all better?"

"Hello!" Roger shouted from the entryway. He'd heard voices coming down the stairwell, and he'd guessed the scene right away. "I'm here now. I'm coming up, running. I'm sorry . . ."

Despite all the things he was carrying, he took the steps two at a time. Barbara returned to her office without inviting Laurence in, her sights set on the Bulgarian translation of Simone Sicilia's novel. Laurence remained at the open door, nailed to the doormat.

"Have you been waiting long?" It didn't seem like Roger intended on apologizing.

"I have to be back at Chez Richard at six."

Roger looked at the Casio watch on his right wrist.

"I got held up longer than I expected. *Désolé*."

He had learned that *désolé* worked for everything. It was a magic word. Not all languages have one that can save you. His mother had explained the luck of the French for having a word like that. You said it, and you were forgiven. You said it, and your conscience was clear. You said it and set back the counter to zero, and no one could chide you for anything.

They entered the apartment and closed the door.

To not disturb Barbara, who was working in front of the window, they went into Roger's room. Now that Laurence remembered that his name was Roger, Barbara, who had been so consumed in her own matters since she'd met Marcel's brother, realized he wasn't just a month-to-month renter but a person with his own life. A handsome guy, as the woman with the sad eyes had said, the woman who had not gotten the wrong apartment.

10

The Imminent and Unexpected Plundering

That night, they pretended nothing had happened.

After having two poached eggs for dinner, Barbara sat on the red couch with a blanket over her legs, put on her headphones, and propped her head up on a cushion. She listened to her music with her eyes shut so that if Roger left his room, he'd know she didn't want to talk. She liked the vaguely Eastern sounds of *Scheherazade*. Despite having listened to it so many times—she and her grandmother had listening sessions sometimes—she was fascinated by how a Russian like Rimsky-Korsakov could've translated an entire world of sultans and princesses into a score of his own melodies. Sinbad in *allegro ma non troppo*. Baghdad in *molto allegro* at the end of the performance. She and her grandma played a game of guessing which instruments were playing at any given moment—*now's the tuba, that's a clarinet, this is the harp*—and above all, they looked for the oboe. That is, the two oboes the composer had written into the piece, as if he'd known that Grandpa Damien would play one of them the day his orchestra performed *Scheherazade* for the last time, the last evening all the musicians played together before the drama started. The program, oblivious to the imminent and unexpected plundering of so many lives, said the concert at the Théâtre du Châtelet on May 18, 1940, would begin at six in the evening.

The recording Barbara listened to was much more recent. So often, her CD united the perfect acoustics of the twenty-first century, the digital sublimity right in the ear. Utter perfection.

That night, Barbara and Roger decided to pretend nothing had happened. Like Laurence hadn't knocked at the door, like Roger hadn't saved her from Barbara, like they hadn't rushed into his room, like the waitress hadn't slipped off her jacket, like she hadn't left it with her pain atop the chair in Roger's room and, in no time, made love without regrets. Like he hadn't asked her to please stifle her cries at the end, and like she hadn't felt like crying.

Once the waitress returned to Chez Richard to serve dinner, Roger left the room only to tiptoe to the bathroom. He didn't even turn on the light, just in case it might bother Barbara. He wouldn't have known how to act, whether it be out of a sense of responsibility or shame, if he ran into Barbara. It certainly wouldn't have been the time to say *désolé* either, which might be misinterpreted. Since he'd moved to Paris, he'd never witnessed his landlady bring a man home to the apartment. Or a woman. No one, actually. There hadn't been a single visitor in those three weeks. She was always in front of her computer, devoted to a job that made her happy, passionate even, but that absorbed her at all hours of the day. On an evening when Roger had ordered pizza, he offered Barbara a slice, and she explained her job to him. It consisted of, plain and simple, matching up an author's novel to a foreign publisher who wanted to publish it. Once there was mutual interest, she had to negotiate the price and royalty conditions and arrive at an agreement.

Roger returned to his room blindly, and, wearing only underwear and a shirt, he stretched out beneath the mattress to drag out the tin box. From the moment Laurence had climbed off him to lie at his side, curled up and breath faint, he hadn't been able to think about anything else. The urge to take the box out and go through the photos was stronger than he was, more tempting than the caresses after the explosion, the false appearance of happiness that lasts however long it may, sometimes a few minutes, sometimes a short nap. He had to confirm that the image he'd seen on the way out of the exhibit was the same one he remembered among the magazine clippings under the bed. He took out the box, put it on top of the warm mattress, and opened it. He moved the light from the nightstand closer to see it better, and he scattered the clippings. He went through the images, one by one, with the skill of a card dealer, dropping them on the comforter. He noticed that the tips of his fingers still carried Laurence's smell, as much as he washed them. He searched, shuffled, and looked at every picture, so full of detail, but he didn't know where to direct his attention. Maybe there were hints in the magazine text, rather than in the images themselves. Maybe in a photo caption or in the publication year, which, from what he could see on the top part of the cut pages, shifted between 1942 and 1943. Wherever there was a date, it pointed to those two years.

Suddenly, under a clipping of Marshal Pétain, the photo he was looking for appeared. The woman on the bike. Head-on, facing the camera, captured from a low angle, making the bike's front wheel look bigger than it was. He had no doubt. It was the same photo, the same girl in black-and-white he'd seen at the André Zucca exhibit. The beautifully weaved wicker basket in front of the handlebars made it unmistakable. He grabbed it and inspected it. She was more of a girl than a woman, now that he looked at it carefully. The image had a high-quality definition and played with the light professionally. Whoever the photographer was, he knew what he was doing. He mastered the diaphragm's shutter speed and apertures to transform a moment into a shot of resounding beauty. Those two-toned photographs, shades of gray between the whitest white and blackest black, defined the outlines, giving the portrait a nice clarity. The images didn't have the vague tonalities he'd seen in the seemingly amateur color photos hanging in the BHVP. He turned the photo around to see if there was anything written, but he didn't find anything on the back of the magazine clipping. No writing anywhere. Not even a hint. He spent some time reviewing the spread he'd created across the bed, and slowly he returned the pieces of the torn magazine back to the box of surprises. Excited by the discovery, still not knowing whether it was a treasure or a coincidence, he put the box back in its place. Under the bed, in the very back, against the baseboard.

After, he left his room to shower. It looked like Barbara had fallen asleep on the sofa wearing her headphones. Before lathering up, he waited for the water to warm. By the time he rinsed off, the smell of Laurence had disappeared forever.

"Good night," Roger called out as he went back to his room, shivering from the cold and trying not to leave any trace of water in the hallway.

"Night," she responded mechanically.

The next morning, something had changed. Barbara took an interest in Roger's job for the first time. After a breakfast of dry bread with cheese, he sat on the couch with his camera between his thighs to review and delete photos from the day before.

"You sure you're a photographer?" She approached him from behind.

"Why do you say that?"

"You've been here for a while now, and you haven't showed me anything . . . Not a single picture. I think it's weird."

Barbara sat on the back of the sofa.

"I didn't want to bother you," he said, without looking up from the small screen.

"That's what it is . . ."

"You're always so"—Roger noticed he had offended her and backed off quickly—"'focused' is the word. I've noticed you like to do your own thing, and I don't want to—"

"I like to do my own thing?"

"It's a saying."

Roger lifted his gaze for the first time and looked at her. She was wearing a tight, white turtleneck sweater.

"You know what I was thinking?" She nodded before responding to herself. "That I don't know anything about you."

"That's not true."

"Nothing at all."

"You know I'm Marcel's brother, that I take pictures, that . . ."

Neither of them finished his sentence. Barbara would've liked to tell him to be careful, that the waitress hadn't even known his name. Roger was on the verge of explaining that, even though he didn't really know how, he'd found himself in bed with the fifteen-euro-menu waitress. But out of shyness, caution, prudence, convenience, or who knows what, maybe because they didn't know each other well or maybe because they'd started to open up to one another—because being unfriendly all the time was exhausting—they both, again, decided to act like the previous evening hadn't happened. No one had seen anything. No one had done anything. Laurence? *Connais-pas.*

Seeing Barbara take a step forward, Roger made a suggestion.

"I want to show you something in the city. That's if you'd like to, of course."

"You're going to tell me about Paris?"

"That's not the plan."

"What's it called when men want to explain how life works to women?"

"A free orientation course?" He played dumb.

She couldn't help but laugh.

"I just want you to see something, nothing else. And maybe it'll be good for you to go out. You work too hard, Barbara."

"Who says I don't go out?"

"For groceries and things like that, yes . . ."

"And to see my grandmother at the retirement home, and I have meetings and I go to the press and I don't stop . . . It doesn't seem like I go out to you?"

"I didn't say that."

"Are you trying to control me?" Theatrically, she acted offended.

"Listen, Barbara. Let's let it go."

"Will it be worth it if I accompany you?"

"I'd like for you to come see an exhibit. It's photography in the Marais. If you want, come, and if not, I'll go back by myself. But before all the snow falls like they're predicting, I thought I could show you something. I honestly think you'll like it."

"Oh yeah? Why?"

"Because I have a feeling. An intuition . . . It blew my mind."

Barbara got up from the red couch, went to the desk, and grabbed the planner resting atop the bookstand like a centerpiece. It was big, made of black leather, and always open to the current week. She had written her appointments in pencil.

"In the Marais, you say?"

"Yes."

"At the Picasso Museum?"

"No. Close by, I think. It's at the Bibliothèque historique . . . the BHVP, I think, is what you say around here."

She flipped the page, circled a date, and turned back around.

"Something just came to me. On Friday I have to go to a publisher party around there. I think if . . ." She chewed like she had gum in her mouth. And in the end, she dared say it. "I go with you to the exhibit, and after you can accompany me to the party."

"Me? Is it a writer party?"

"It'll be fun."

"I'll be like an octopus in a garage. That's a saying here, in French, right?"

"It's a whole other world," she said apathetically. "You have to see one of these parties, even if it's once in your life."

"Oh, yeah? Why?" He turned.

"Egos in jackets, stuck-up authors who like and listen to each other, critics showing off, journalists who eat well for a night. You should see it."

"It doesn't seem like you think too highly of your world."

Barbara regretted these reflections. She walked it back.

"I say all that now, it's true, because I've spent years watching it, and now I'm familiar with all the fauna. But . . ." She bit the turtleneck and let it go. "I recognize that, in the beginning, these parties are dazzling. The writers say imaginative things, the editors are cultured, and if anything, everyone has a million stories, because they've met interesting celebrities. There are people you learn from and, more than anything, laugh with. You'll meet attractive people, you'll see. Attractive in the intellectual sense, I mean. Will you come?"

"And you?"

Barbara extended her hand. He put his hand in hers to mark his decision. There were four days until their adventure, an eternity.

"You think we'll be able to go? They say there's supposed to be the snowfall of the century."

"When do they expect it?" she asked.

"Next week. They don't know how to narrow down the day."

"Don't pay attention to it. The weathermen make more mistakes than the editors do with the manuscripts they're sent. With one big difference. Mistakes don't cost money for the wise guy who looks at a map and promises a downpour when it's hotter than hell."

11

Birds Love, and Give Gifts

On Friday, once the sun stopped beaming on the cactus, Barbara took a shower. She stayed there for a while. Beneath the flow of water, she collected her thoughts and what remained of the day. She took even longer drying her hair. She held up the blow dryer in one hand, and with the other, she dried her wet ends, which, like a clapper in a bell, insisted on ringing against her shoulder. After successfully clasping her bra, she went back into the bathroom to do her makeup. She had a vanity in her room, but with the light from the street in sharp decline, she couldn't see herself well enough to line her eyes. While Roger was grumbling around in the kitchen, she placed a drop of Mamie Margaux's perfume on her wrist and another behind her ears—a hazy scent with notes of lavender—the last touch before looking herself up and down to make sure she approved. She finally emerged from the cave to show off her look. Her burgundy cocktail dress was fitted, low-cut, and long-sleeved, and landed right above her knees.

When she came out of the living room, she ran into a Roger that did not look quite like Roger. He was standing impatiently next to the couch, looking impeccable.

"Wow. You clean up nice, man."

He kept himself from returning the praise. He didn't want to even the score with a compliment that might have been fair and well-deserved. But he was in a rush.

"I looked through my brother's wardrobe. He didn't have any decent clothing." He excused himself. "Luckily, Marcel and I are the same size, and I found this. Will I stick out much?"

Like a lethargic model, he stretched out his arms and let Barbara look him over with a glance. He had on a turtleneck sweater and a dark blazer. She looked at him without any timidity. Neither the colors nor the textures matched, but he had nice shoulders and gave off a sense of style, and she knew there would be very little lighting at the party.

"Very fitting." After three weeks of seeing him in jeans and lumberjack sweaters, she had feared something worse. "How should I say it? It's a very . . . Parisian outfit."

"It looks good on me, then?"

"It looks good on you."

"Thanks." Roger picked up her evening coat, and she understood they were in a rush. "Come on, we don't want them to close the photo exhibit on us."

"Ready for a double feature?"

"Ready. Excited to get there."

He opened the door so they could leave at once.

"I don't think I've ever seen you without your backpack," she said once they were on the fifth-floor landing. "Do you know how to walk without your camera equipment?"

"Yeah, I do honestly feel a little naked."

As they passed the second floor, Jasper opened his door to see who was clanking so loudly with their heels. The click-clack resounded throughout the whole stairwell. He saw Barbara and didn't hide his surprise. He'd never seen her wear such high heels, with tights that made her legs look strong and a snug dress the color of wine peeking out beneath the double-breasted coat she wore open. He couldn't stop himself from commenting on her elegance, something that might very well have been a genetic inheritance from Margaux, a family matter. Jasper, with Hulshoff as his inseparable witness, never missed an opportunity to give her grandmother little compliments, not even indirectly. He asked where they were going so nicely dressed, but right as Roger was about to respond, Barbara cut him short:

"A wedding. Good evening."

Out on the street, the temperature was plummeting faster than the sun. She hurried to fasten her black herringbone coat, which went down to her ankles, and once buttoned up, she slipped on her leather gloves. Roger wrapped the Cambridge scarf that smelled like Marcel twice around his neck. Slowly, they walked down Clichy Boulevard to catch a taxi. Between the cobblestones and the stilettos, it would have been easier for Barbara if she leaned on Roger's forearm. But she didn't dare grab on to him. She did, however, ask him to walk slowly. Alert, she concealed the dangers she saw all around without losing her balance or dignity. Walking next to her, Roger didn't for a moment think to help her.

"What must he think?" Barbara wondered.

"Who?" There was no one in the street. Roger couldn't make out who she was referring to.

"Him."

With her hands in her pockets to avoid them freezing, Barbara signaled with her chin to a bird flitting across the street.

"That one?" He hadn't even noticed the house sparrow, occupied with his own business. "What do you want him to think? The same thing as everyone else. 'What's for dinner?'"

"Don't be—"

"If there's one thing we have where I'm from, it's birds." He didn't think she could hear him with his mouth covered, so he lowered his scarf to explain himself better. "Empordà is a seaside plain, overflowing with fruit-bearing trees. It's a paradise for birds. A festival. I've seen people do all kinds of things to protect the apples from the birds . . . I mean, my father could have given a master's-level course on each bird species."

"Are they able to think or not?"

"Who? Birds?" He panted. "Birds think, remember, love, and give gifts."

Barbara raised an eyebrow incredulously. Roger was familiar with this response.

"Nests. Think of nests. They're complicated to build, right? They're not just built instinctively. There's so much intelligence that goes into each step of its construction, into placing branch by branch with a beak. Have you ever tried making a wicker basket?"

"Never in my life."

"Well, if it's difficult to do with hands, imagine having to do it with a beak." He pursed his lips and extended his neck like a blackbird. "I'm not sure if it's a crow, but there's a bird in Japan that throws nuts on the street so cars crack them when they drive by. Then it goes back to gather the pieces and eat them. Birds are cool. They kiss to console each other. And when their partner dies, they grieve. Some even get depressed."

"It's the opposite here sometimes. You get depressed if your partner takes too long to die."

"Humans, you mean?" He hadn't gotten the joke.

They lifted their arms at the same time to flag down an empty white taxi. Roger opened the door for Barbara to enter first. The gesture had the appearance of chivalry, even if it was more selfishness than anything. His legs were longer, and he'd fit better if he didn't have to sit behind the driver. Neither of them said where they were headed, and the driver of the Peugeot coughed to prompt them for an address.

"To the BHVP," Roger said, trying to make himself pass off as a local.

The chauffeur, who was from even farther away than Roger was, didn't understand a thing. He looked at them through the rearview mirror to check if they were messing with him. Or to read their lips so as to understand the destination.

"To the Bibliothèque historique . . . on rue Pavée," said Barbara. "In the Marais, please."

The barrier that separated the front seats from the back muffled any type of sound. It didn't look as though there was a hole. Tired of being robbed or out of fear of it coming to that, the taxi driver had installed a bulletproof piece of plastic, converting his Peugeot into a police car.

"And are birds happy?"

"I see you're fond of the topic."

"You're fond of it . . . You've poured more of your heart out in five minutes than you have during the three weeks you've been in the house."

"Happy? I don't know. I'm sure birds have feelings."

"And you?"

"Me?" He didn't know what she was referring to. "What about me?"

"Are you happy?"

Suddenly, he was hit by the dart he never expected Barbara to throw. Inside that taxi, closer than they'd ever been, knees pressed up against each other's since there was no extra room, and with the partition preventing them from clearly making out which neighborhood of Paris they were passing through, she left him speechless. What a question to ask. In his thirty-three years, he'd never thought about it. Was he happy? He simply was. Or acted like it. He moved forward without taking stock. These types of questions that came on their own only confused a person, in any case, when life was on the decline. Up to that moment, he was, he did, he located, he photographed, he classified . . . he lived. Each verb was a movement, an action. Stopping or thinking or settling the score were romantic ideas for another phase of life he couldn't even imagine. The time for taking inventory had yet to come for him, of missing people and places, of understanding himself, of melancholically comparing decades, of assessing the fears of old age, of resigning himself to a little arthrosis, of getting excited over something small and contemplating nature like it was infinite. But it wasn't yet time for the cracks to appear. He'd get to the age where he'd understand poets and buy comfortable shoes. As long as there was more future than past, he took being happy for granted. Shortly and simply:

"I don't have any reason not to be."

They passed the next few streets in silence. Each of them looked out their respective windows. To the left, Barbara saw the columns of the entrance of the Palais-Royal and the lights of the Comédie-Française theater, where she'd seen some Molière with her grandmother. To the right, Roger could make out the terraces of Saint-Honoré, with blankets on the chairs and a lit stove for every other table. Only the bravest dared sit there that Friday, March 28, which had already begun its countdown to the next day.

When the taxi pulled up to the last stoplight of the avenue de l'Opéra, Barbara whispered into Roger's ear.

"Do you think we'll make it there?" she asked, making sure the unsociable chauffeur couldn't make out her words through the rearview mirror.

"Why do you ask?"

"Haven't you noticed?" She lifted her finger to motion for him to be quiet. "It's shaking like a Chihuahua."

"Now that you mention it . . ."

"The car must be cold too."

"Maybe it's because of the diesel motor. Or the exhaust pipe is wobbling. It happens sometimes, if it's not properly clamped." Roger waited for the taxi to shift into first gear. "Listen to it now. When it moves, it doesn't make so much noise . . . right?"

"You know about cars too?"

"I know more about motorcycles."

"Racing motorbikes? Do you race?"

"Not at all."

"Do you race against the birds?"

"No." Roger laughed sincerely. "But I've ridden one my whole life. It's a passion. Have you ever been on one?"

"I wasn't allowed to ride them. 'You'll hear about it if we ever see you on a motorcycle.' My parents never let me get on one, not even as a passenger."

"And you listened to them?"

"Only child. What more do you want from me?"

"At some point, everyone falls off a motorcycle. I don't know anyone who rides that hasn't had . . . It's not even alarming. 'How many times?' we ask each other, and we already know what the other person is asking. Someone says, 'Three times.' 'Once for me.' When someone says, 'I haven't,' they better start praying . . ."

"I thought you were going to say, 'You better start shaking,' like this wagon we're in."

They laughed. The grouchy taxi driver reproached them with a fierce look through the mirror.

Roger had told her he didn't race, but each year he planned a trip that was sort of like a race. More tiring and riskier than a race. It was a bet against himself that he set every summer solstice along with three of his motorcycle friends. They'd start the longest day of the year at around a quarter after six with the sunrise at the lighthouse of the Cap de Creus, and hours later, they'd catch the sunset at the tip of Fisterra, the aim being to arrive there by ten in the evening so they would still have about fifteen minutes of light left. They traversed the whole Iberian Peninsula, from the easternmost end to the point at which the sun set, from the Mediterranean to the Atlantic, while there was still light out. They had to ride at full steam to cross the 832 miles before the sun was completely hidden. From coast to coast. From sun to sun. Roger shared this anecdote with Barbara.

"And then what?" Barbara asked.

"Then? Nothing."

"Men."

"What's that mean?"

"Just that. Men." She repeated the word in a more disparaging tone. "You do all that just for the sake of it? To say you did it, and that's it?"

That confused him.

"I don't know. We get there, and then we eat, sleep, and rest, and the next morning, we go back without rushing. We get there when we get there."

"That's good . . . Let's call it a tradition among friends. You say it's once a year?"

"Yes, some people meet up for a barbecue; we do this. For the last six years. The summer we buried my father, my friends saw I was sad, and they thought about doing this. We had fun, and it's become like an obligatory appointment with the motorcycle gang. Is there anything you do once a year with your friends?"

"Rue Pavée. The Bibliothèque. We're here," the taxi driver shouted.

Barbara insisted on paying. She took off her gloves to open her wallet, and Roger held them before they exited. The taxi driver grumbled, because they'd opened the door without looking and were inches away from hitting a Vespa.

Coats were more of a nuisance at the BHVP. They took them off and kept them in their arms throughout the whole visit. Roger even balled his scarf to fit into his coat pocket. There were people in the exhibit, but there wasn't a line to enter the galleries. The social media controversy and the mayor's unconvincing excuses had created a certain frenzy to see the city under Nazi occupation. But by the time they arrived, there were more people exiting than entering. Some were writing something in a gold book that had been placed next to the exit.

"What do you want me to see?" Barbara entered the exhibit decisively. "Just so you know, I hate surprises."

"We have to take a lap. They're photographs. Paris, as you can see. Paris during the four years of German occupation during the Second World War. There are some black-and-white photos, but the color photos have never been seen before."

"Have they been recolored for this exhibit?"

"No. This photographer was the only one who could take color photos. The only or the first. He had film rolls other people didn't. They're slides. Some two hundred and fifty, they say."

"They've never been seen before?"

"Not the color ones. They've arranged it by neighborhood. Each room is a different district of Paris."

Barbara walked slowly, a few feet in front of Roger. From time to time, she approached a frame, looked closely at some detail, read about the specific street pictured, and retreated to continue to the next photo, following the subtly marked path on the floor. Only sometimes did she call attention to something. "All the skies are blue," she said. "It doesn't look like Paris with these beautiful days." Then she pointed out, "The people are very dressed up, don't you think? It doesn't give the impression they're at war." She spoke, and Roger agreed. He didn't want to influence her. "Such beautiful women. The sunglasses look so modern. The terraces are bursting with people. Did you see Les Deux Magots café? Filled to the brim. How funny is this Mickey Mouse announcing theater-ticket sales? Look, there's finally a woman with a yellow star on her chest. There must have been many in the streets, but they hardly appear in these photos. And barely a Nazi soldier either. So few. All these happy people make quite an impression. I've never seen anything like this before."

"Now we're entering Montmartre," Roger noted like a docent.

"It's so lively on the boulevard de Clichy. The Cabaret de l'Enfer. The Moulin Rouge was a movie theater, did you see? 'Permanent spectacle,' it's written. And the Sacré-Coeur covered in snow. And do you see how smooth the streets are with the snow blanketing them? '1942,' it says. The streetlamps are the same ones we have now. Are all the pictures from the same photographer?"

"All of them."

"From the liberation too?"

"Yes."

"So much color, so much festivity, so many people . . . French flags, finally."

"'August 26, 1944.' It's written right there."

"Of course. August 26, 1944. They're beautiful. All of them. Wow . . ." She turned to look at Roger. "That's what you must say, since you understand them."

"Very beautiful."

"André Zucca?"

"Yes."

"An Italian last name."

"But he was from here. From Paris itself. He worked for the Germans. They hired him to take these pictures. Propaganda. But well-done propaganda. This is where the controversy of the exhibit originates."

"But this isn't the real Paris of the time."

"It *is* real. But it's just one part. He framed only the prints that showed happiness."

"Or normal life. And there was no normal." Barbara wasn't sure if they were supposed to move on to the next room or if they had seen what Roger meant to show her. "Is that it?"

"No, there's still one left." Roger pointed the way. "Here are the black-and-white pictures the photographer published in a German magazine. There are some really beautiful ones too. There's a collection of women on bicycles you need to see. Come on."

Once in the exhibit, he left her alone again. He stepped back carefully so Barbara could see all the women smiling at the camera from their bicycles. They all posed, comfortable in front of the lens. They were all splendid. They were a tribute to life. Leaning on the handlebars, their backs straight, a collection of hats and high heels.

"What a joke, pedaling with heels. They're even sharper than mine."

He didn't say anything. He let Barbara scrutinize the well-focused images, each one more beautiful than the last. In one, she noticed a woman adjusting her skirt, in another she liked the shadows of the wheel spokes projected onto the ground. She laughed at a three-year-old girl sleeping like a log on a bike while her mother walked beside it, hand on the handlebar, toward the Arc de Triomphe. If she had to pick one photo, she would've chosen the one with a dark, fuzzy dog sticking its head out of the front basket. In all the photographs, the city was but a sunny, peaceful, and docile scene. Out of context, no one would have guessed they were taken sixty years prior, even less that they were snapshots captured during a time of war and bombings. Roger let Barbara's eyes arrive at the photo. The one he had seen in the tin box beneath the bed. It was beautifully executed and impossible to ignore for too long. And now that he had it in front of him again, he was sure it was the same one. He had planned for his landlady to accompany him to the exhibit so she could have that image in front of her and really be forced to look at it.

"It can't be!" Barbara exclaimed.

Staying quiet, he walked up next to her to see her reaction.

She clasped her hand to her mouth and continued, "I can't believe it . . ."

"Believe what?" he asked innocently.

"That woman . . . Do you know who that is? You knew who I'd think it was . . ."

Not at all. That was precisely what Roger wanted to know. He got closer to look at the sign.

"There's only a date here. It doesn't have a name."

"I could swear . . . I could swear it's my grandmother. Mamie Margaux."

"Your grandmother? She was a girl here."

"What year is written?"

"'1942.'"

"A girl, yes. She was . . ." Despite her shock, she did the calculations quickly. "Seventeen. Eighteen at the oldest."

"Are you sure it's your grandmother?"

"Without a doubt."

"How are you so sure?"

"Because I know her. Look at her eyes. It's the same look she has now. And also because I was an exact copy at her age. Everyone has always told me, and I've seen photos from that time."

"And this one . . . Have you seen this one before?"

"This specific picture, I'd say no. Or I don't remember it at least."

Barbara hadn't taken even half a step back from the wall. Her eyes were glued to each fold of her grandmother's dress.

"This is one of those coincidences, one of the big ones," Roger said emphatically. "The kind that happen once in a lifetime. How exciting, huh?"

"Of course. Of course. I don't know how . . ."

"Honestly, she looks very happy. Like she posed for the picture." He treaded lightly but was clever enough for Barbara to catch his drift. "Does it make sense for your grandmother to be in this exhibit?"

"What do you mean?" Suddenly, her expression changed. "Do you think my grandmother was a . . ."

"I don't know. That's why I'm asking," he responded with a tone of false candor.

"Collaborator? That's not what we were told our whole lives." Barbara was confused. She became defensive of her family. "My family never fell for the Nazi games. Quite the opposite. Our history is altogether different."

As she insisted, she hoped with all her might that Margaux Dutronc's version of the war was as neat as the photograph in front of her.

12

Everyone Wants to Be in Manhattan

She didn't say no to the glass of champagne. As overwhelmed as she was when she arrived to the party, Barbara grabbed the welcome drink and didn't make it last long. Roger, on the other hand, walked straight past the waiter welcoming guests at the exclusive celebration with a tray in his hand, with the smile only money could afford. Anyone without an invitation wasn't coming in. Anyone who wasn't smiling couldn't work there. The hosts lived by the motto that a good mood was contagious. And it better not be fake.

The publishing party began on the red carpet of a postindustrial boat that was tastefully and expensively decorated, almost like they were celebrating the wedding of the center-back for the Paris Saint-Germain Football Club to the up-and-coming actress of the moment. The party was actually to celebrate Arthur Soto, one of Giresse & Trésor's authors, who'd won the latest Renaudot prize. He'd taken a trip around the world for three months, and when he'd returned, his editors wanted to throw him a party, and they weren't holding back.

"I'm not complaining, but—"

Barbara interrupted. "When a 'but' comes after a comma—because I heard how the comma fell—it scares me more than a hailstorm."

"No worries." Roger didn't want to let it go. "Without the 'buts,' then. You said, 'I'll go to the exhibit in the Marais because the party is right there. We'll come out of one place and enter the other.' Didn't you say that, or did I imagine it?"

"It was less than ten minutes away by taxi." Barbara left the empty glass on the tray of a waiter whose role was only to pick up empty cups and smile. "Everything is close by in Paris, but it's all far."

"Everything is close if you feel like it, huh?"

"It might be that, yes."

"What's wrong? We haven't even taken off our coats and you already regret coming?"

He didn't ask if she regretted going to the exhibit. Like the good Narbona he was, he preferred to change the subject.

"This neighborhood must be charming during the day."

"You'd get some nice pictures."

The Canal Saint-Martin was like a slice of Amsterdam in Paris. On one corner, near the dams and about fifty steps away from the swing bridge, there was an old, enormous, single-story factory that was rented out for ambitious parties, which starting at the turn of the century were called "events." And this was a chic event. It had embers of faint light, corners for sitting and drinking, decorations reminiscent of a bar in New York's SoHo, petals on the floor marking a path to the stage, and a band that played jazz classics. It was accompaniment music. The Martinican quintet—comprising four musicians and a singer shaped like a double bass with the finest timbre—also smiled at the guests when they looked at them from time to time. They had, too, signed it into their contract: *Play and show off your pearly whites.*

Barbara Hébrard from the foreign-rights department at Giresse & Trésor knew almost everyone. She greeted a newly arrived editor from Italy, a Hungarian translator living in Montparnasse, and Jean-Pierre Zanardi, an art gallery owner and close friend of Hayet Trésor, the co-owner of the publishing house. At the party, there was an elegance without ties, and an extravagance in red shoes; there were young, stylish people laughing their thanks to Éric Giresse, and an existentialist stowing away his pipe in the pocket of his blazer. The Dunhill bowl was hanging out of his breast pocket like a periscope for inspecting the party guests. Someone might have thought it was a camera recording everything for a social experiment. Everyone stood and talked. The prettiest of the women wandered. The cultural journalists—the selected few—followed the waiters' trajectories without being noticed. The sacred cows sat in the distant corner at the high court. The old guard, ready to impart and remove their literary blessing. With a caress and two adjectives, they could catapult a career. Using the same powers, they could damn an author forever with an unruly comment.

A woman Roger hadn't seen approached him from behind.

"Have you noticed? Everyone is happy at this party. Not a single one of life's victims."

He turned his head to see who was talking to him. He didn't recognize her.

She continued, "Let's get a little drunk, why don't we?"

"Of course," Roger responded, convinced she was confusing him for someone else. Just as quickly as she had appeared, she left. Silently, like a guardian angel. The back of her suit jacket featured a giant skull with wings.

"Do you know who that is?" Roger asked Barbara.

"She looks familiar. She's not from our publisher. I think she's a poet. A rich poet."

"How contradictory."

Without thinking, Barbara blurted, "What'd she say to you?"

"Nothing." It was too much work to explain it. "I didn't understand what she said . . . Now what's there to do around here?"

"Chat? Chat with interesting people. Listen to what they have to say about the literary world. Gossip a little, say hello, drink, laugh . . . and wait for the guest of honor, puffed up like a stuffed turkey. It makes sense that the author has a big head. It's an important prize. The Renaudot can change your life. And who knows? You can get a job from it, a whole contract."

They went to the counter, where the liquor bottles were illuminated by backlights. They wanted to see the spectacle up close. The bartender, his torso nude, prepared cocktails with catlike reflexes.

"Do you really think you need that much choreography to make a French Flamingo?"

"Sorry." She was distracted. "What'd you say?"

"Nothing." Again, it was too much work to shout to be heard.

She apologized again. "Sorry, my head is somewhere else."

He understood. "Still thinking about your grandmother's photo?"

"It's . . . I don't know. It gave me a bad feeling. It has me worried." She made a face. "Maybe I should have been excited to see her there, but more than that, it worried me."

"Do you want to go outside?" Roger asked with a long glass in hand. A Coke with Absolut vodka. She nodded.

At the back of the ship, there was a terrace with heaters so smokers could go out for a cigarette without infringing on the law. They could talk better there without the music.

"What's worrying you?"

Sometimes the simplest questions are the ones that bother you the most. It was difficult for Barbara to find the words.

"I'm not sure." She tried not to rush. She had time to figure out how she felt exactly. "I don't know if my grandmother knows that picture exists. I'm wondering whether I should tell her. What would you do?"

"You don't think she'd be happy to know?"

"At eighty-three? If you can't climb stairs and you're in a retirement home, would it make you happy to see yourself young and radiant on a bicycle?"

"Everyone's young at some point. Her included."

"But when your life is all in order, and you've closed chapters of your life . . . What right do we have to say, 'Hey, Mamie, have you seen this?'"

"You know her well. I can't say anything."

"I don't know if I know her well anymore."

"Why wouldn't she like it? It's not a torture session. It's a memory."

"Her photo in an exhibit on Nazi propaganda? After everything she experienced, after everything they did to my grandfather."

Without any greetings, three women Barbara knew, who'd come out to light their Marlboros, animatedly asked her to introduce them to her companion.

"Roger. Roger Narbona. From Barcelona."

He gave each of them two kisses, though they wanted to do three kisses in the French style. They all huddled around the heater. When they left its radius, the cold was cutting against their faces and hands.

"We were talking about birds," Barbara said, changing the subject. "You know a lot. You left me hanging on one thing . . ."

Roger couldn't think of what it was.

She continued. "You more or less said—don't pay any mind if I'm all over the place—you said that birds love, right? That they remember, they console each other with kisses . . . And then you said birds give gifts too. Is it true?"

"It's true. They give them to us. Of course they do. I did say that . . ." Roger felt the newcomers' six interested eyes on him, and he modulated his voice so it reached everyone. "Imagine a crow or a heron. If you feed them, they return to give you a gift. Look it up. It isn't long until they go back to the place where you left them food. And what do they do? They leave you a raspberry or something shiny so that you notice they've given you a present."

"Is it their way of thanking you?" the veteran literary agent asked, charmed by the explanation. Usually a city girl, she was suddenly interested in wildlife.

"Exactly." Roger had created some excitement. "It's proof that our brain and theirs are more similar than we ever imagined."

"Not long ago, I read something similar to that about the social behavior of birds and humans in the *New York Times*," remarked Soto's English translator, a woman with a profile that could be described as Egyptian due to her haircut, her bangs, and the darkness of her hair.

Suddenly, Barbara realized that her guest had captured the attention of a chorus of women. With a drink in one hand, he gesticulated with the other to the one Italian woman of the group and spoke knowledgeably. Marcel's turtleneck sweater and suit seemed like they belonged to him. Roger looked good in them and had a silvery voice; if he was timid—or ever experienced feeling so—he was hiding it well. He spoke naturally in impeccable French but with an accent that revealed he was not totally from there. Sometimes, he had to stop to search for a word he couldn't remember. In the midst of a Parisian cosmopolitanism that was so endogamous, someone new was welcome. And he was a new face. And young. And he made himself seen, with his lively, enchanting serpent eyes. In no time, the three women—a veteran literary agent, the pharaoh translator, and an aspiring novelist with the most eccentric hat at the party—encircled Roger. To not seem out of place, he showed off his best smile.

"So, are you an ornithologist?"

"No, the thing is . . . he's a photographer," Barbara chimed in to show that she knew him the best.

"What do you photograph? Sunsets?"

He took a sip as he thought of his response. He could pretend to be interesting, or he could tell the truth.

"You're thinking a little hard about it, man . . ."

He bet on both things, going for something in the middle. "I search for the fall in winter, the water in the desert, the music in the silence."

"That's beautiful," said the woman with her bra peeking out.

Someone sighed.

"And where do you look for love?" the pharaoh asked. All of them laughed nervously.

He calmly took it on, staring into the pupils of his audience, and said, "Ma'am, when I find love, I don't take pictures . . . I take videos."

"Olé," said the woman, all fired up.

"When you have good photos, bring them to me, and we'll set up a show." Madame Giroud gave him a card with her name. "I have a gallery nearby. If you'd like to see it—"

Barbara grabbed Roger's arm. "Let's go."

"But—"

"Let's go. It looks like the man of the hour has just arrived."

She led him out of the excited circle, and without dimming her smile, she reentered the boat. Inside, the atmosphere had become heavy with the egos, the alcohol, and the hypnotic vapor of jazz. Half an hour was always enough.

"Come on, I want to introduce you to the editors."

Éric Giresse and Hayet Trésor were a married couple around age sixty. They'd spent thirty years together and looked so much like each other that people in the sector thought they were siblings. *Twins,* someone at the party had said. They both had white hair, shaved by the same razor. They wore the same glasses, reminiscent of those belonging to an Industrial Revolution accountant. The same pinstripes that were on Hayet's blazer were also on Éric's. They even looked like they used the same teeth whitener. Both were super polite, amiable, and hospitable. Barbara had warned Roger that Hayet really loved men. And so did Éric.

Never having had children, the couple had poured all of themselves into their publishing house. They had founded it a couple of months after the death of Hayet's father. The senior Trésor—a last name, meaning "treasure," as in the kind that might determine the fate of some people—had made a lot of money for a long time in the paper business.

Once he and his tumor had been buried and the will had been read, his daughter was declared the universal heir. She'd thought such great fortune like the one that had rained down on her wouldn't run out, even if they started up a risky business. And she and her husband decided to open a publishing house. Giresse and Trésor had been born from a mission of only publishing what they liked. At first, they had to be novels that caught both of their attention. After some time, it was enough for only one of the two to be excited about a manuscript. As of the last nine years, ever since they hired a manager who had studied at a private business school and obtained a master's in publishing management from Utrecht University, they published whichever author could rake in the money. Luckily, the authors that Barbara represented sold well. First in France, then internationally. Anne Delacourt was close to twenty editions worldwide thanks to the dystopian surrogate revolution. When the suicide of Simone Sicilia became public, they sold more than two hundred million copies of *The Gift* in less than a week. It was also on its way to becoming an international success.

Arthur Soto, on the other hand, the honored guest of the party, was not represented by Barbara at the publishing house. Characterized by the marine-blue scarf he wore in summer and winter, the author had his own literary agent who looked out for his interests—whether they be material, immaterial, or even sexual.

To win the prize and become a Giresse & Trésor author, Soto had needed to write a story that the Renaudot jury voted for unanimously. They had highlighted three qualities of the novel: after years of too much commercial literature, it was a book about culture; it was meticulous in its characters; and best of all, it explored new narrative forms. They thought it was an achievement that, in a single paragraph of *Treble Clef*, there could be four distinct narrators, causing serious effort on the reader's part to distinguish who was speaking in any given moment. It wasn't easy, but the members of the jury, whom the publishers had also invited to the party in an almost suspicious collusion, considered it to be a literary evolution necessary to award and stimulate.

Microphone in hand and standing on a velvet platform, Soto described the plot of the winning novel himself. The party's guests encircled him, drawing close to the stage. The Martinican Jazz Quintet knew to go silent at the right time, and Soto explained that all fiction, whether from a book or a movie, had to be explained in ten words. He had counted them out.

"When Virginie gets pregnant, she has one wish."

"What's the wish?" a journalist, who hadn't taken off his hat all night, asked from the third row.

"Play piano," he answered shortly. Seeing the excited faces in front of him, he stretched himself further. "Before she was pregnant, Virginie had never played piano. Then, once she gives birth, she doesn't want to play ever again. This is the plot. If you want to know more, go out and buy the book. For the price of a sirloin in green pepper sauce at the Hippopotamus Steakhouse, you can buy the story of a woman, a piano, and so many more surprises. What more can you want?"

The crowd applauded him like they'd just seen Picasso paint *Guernica* right in front of them. The author, caught up in his sublime hour, jumped off the platform. If there had not been people in the first row, they would have had to pick him up off the floor. He was lucky they were able to grab on to him before he tripped. Someone, however, had grabbed him too tightly by the forearm, causing pain in his wrist.

"Is there a doctor in the room?" the singer asked into the microphone from the stage.

They used his blue scarf as an improvised sling.

The party lasted past midnight. Some people decided to continue it in private. Barbara and Roger ordered a taxi to take them back home. The dock at Saint-Martin was a bad place to flag one down, and the late hour made it even harder. Out in the open, the cold had started to become insufferable.

"Are you leaving already?" The guardian angel surprised Roger from behind again as he put on his jacket.

"We're leaving, yes," he said, signaling that there were two of them.

"Everyone in the world would love to attend a literary party in Paris, huh?" Roger couldn't say no to the woman, who continued whispering in his ear. "Well, everyone here tonight thinks Paris is too small for them. They'd rather be in Manhattan. Good night."

She stood on her tiptoes to give him a kiss before disappearing into the party, trampling winter leaves, the winged skull on her back.

"Good night."

"There are annoying people everywhere," Barbara said. "What'd she want?"

"Nothing."

"Sorry, it's none of my business. The taxi will be here in ten minutes."

Roger grabbed her by the shoulder, as if to protect her from the cold.

"Jesus Christ . . . it's been an intense night. Between everything."

"The party went on a little too long for you. I'm sorry."

"No, no . . . It's been interesting. Do you want to know what that woman said to me?"

"You don't have to tell me."

"She told me we make a good couple."

13

She Hated Surprises

Tuesdays and Fridays. Mamie Margaux marked down the two days her granddaughter came to visit her at the retirement home. They were sacred, invariable. After lunch on Sunday, while dozing off in front of the television to an episode of *Columbo*, she was told she had a visitor. She did not expect to see Barbara enter her room. Right away, she feared something awful had happened.

"It's nothing, Mamie. I just wanted to see you. Simple as that."

"But you came two days ago . . . ," she said, surprised.

"They say there's a spell of bad weather coming, and I felt like visiting. Does it bother you?"

"Me? Quite the opposite."

Sitting in the tall armchair, Mamie put a little spritz of fresh cologne on her temples and the nape of her neck to smarten up. Barbara approached the chair to grab her hands. She liked caressing her grandmother's fingers, warped by the oboe. Sometimes she traced a blue vein, the unavoidable furrows of age.

Seated next to one another, their teas steaming on the little table, they spoke for almost two hours. Before Barbara left, she passed along greetings from Jasper, the neighbor for whom not a day went by without a thought of Mamie, and she asked teasingly if Margaux knew what she wanted to be when she grew up.

"Now, don't you start with me too, Barbara, because Anine is getting on my nerves."

"She's still asking you?"

"Every day. Three times a day. Poor girl, her mind doesn't work anymore."

"And what do you say?"

"That I'm thinking about it, you know. What am I supposed to say? I ask for only one thing." Her grandmother became serious. "That I don't end up like her."

"I'm sure you won't. Your mind is very lucid."

"Bah, with this head."

"See you Tuesday, Mamie." She kissed her once on each cheek.

Before leaving the retirement home, Barbara buttoned up her coat and put on her wool cap. She crossed Square Viviani like she was being followed. She noticed how alone the oldest tree in Paris was, due to the inhospitable winter cold, and she ran home. She wanted to tell Roger about the conversation. She hadn't directly brought up the subject with Mamie. She hadn't told her she'd seen a photo of her. Nothing about the bicycle or her radiant happiness. She hadn't told her the name of the exhibition on the occupied city. She hadn't thought about hinting that she'd been a model for the Germans. She'd only asked if she could tell her again how she'd met Grandfather Damien, and, like a fireside tale, she let her speak, let her pour her heart out over a story Barbara had heard dozens of times since she was a child but that she liked listening to again. And, in that moment, she needed it. Now that she'd seen the picture of her grandmother, she searched for some indication, some hint, some inconsistency, some comment that could lead to the hidden side of her family's past. Suddenly, she sensed that Margaux's experience of the war was not the way it had been explained to her throughout her whole life. When the story is always told using the same words like they were rehearsed, when the same anecdotes are repeated like they were invented to make the story more believable, you start to become suspicious that something unknown is hiding behind it all. And that was the worst part: not knowing. She couldn't stand how, from one day to the next, a mistrust began growing within her. But there was a mystery eluding her, and she no longer had her mother to clear her doubts and set the facts straight, if her mother had ever heard a different version of the story. Forty-eight hours had not even passed since Barbara's visit to the exhibit at the BHVP, and now, she looked at her grandmother in another light. Her story, told in the same voice as always, no longer sounded the same. Barbara hurried home, half on foot, half on the train, to tell Roger about that uncomfortable feeling. The dilemma flustered her. But she finally had someone to share the anxiety with. Blessed news.

Floor by floor, she climbed up to the fifth landing, eager to chat and urgently needing to pee. But she knew she shouldn't run up those dilapidated steps if she didn't want to fall or have her lungs collapse early. She measured each step and took on each floor like a moving finish line. Between the second and third floors, she removed her wool cap. Between the third and fourth floors, she started unbuttoning her coat. On the last flight up to the fifth floor, she already had her key in hand. She hadn't peed since before she left the house, and the tea was starting to take its effect.

She entered the house and threw it all—coat, keys, cap, and bag—onto the red sofa and headed straight to the bathroom. The light was on. When she opened the door, she ran into a naked woman emerging from behind the shower curtain.

"Sorry!"

"Hello?"

Laurence was dripping from head to toe. She hadn't had time to grab a towel, and Barbara threw her a damp one that had been hanging behind the door.

"Can I know what the hell you're doing here?"

"He told me . . . You scared me too, you know? I thought we were alone," she said, excusing herself and wrapping the towel underneath her armpits. "It's just a shower. No need to act like that."

"But in my home?" Barbara asked emphatically, angry not only about the scare. Running into that woman again made her stomach turn. "In my shower?"

Barbara's possessiveness appeared twofold, emphasized by the fluorescent light. She was mad about the steamed mirror, the dark nipples pointing at her, and the violation of her most sacred space. Her whole life, there had been only two women who showered in this apartment. Mamie and herself. That's it. And she wasn't prepared for more. She hated surprises.

Roger, shut in his room, heard noises in the distance and guessed at the reason. He thought about going out to show face, but he would have had to get dressed, and he wasn't sure if, still erect, it would have made things better. It might have even produced the opposite effect.

"You're here again?" Barbara wasn't one for mincing words, having taken two steps back due to the lack of space in the bathroom. "Can I know where you come from, at the very least?"

"I was invited by . . ."

Roger. His name is Roger. You fuck him and you still don't know his name . . . She held back her thoughts. She only signaled the hall with an emphatic finger: "Go."

Laurence, on the short walk to Roger's room, left wet footprints on the tiles. Barbara entered the bathroom, threw the hand towel on the floor, put her foot on it, and angrily dried up the dampness Roger's unexpected friend had left. She slammed the door so it could be heard, bolted it, and pulled down her pants and underwear to sit on the toilet.

She remained there awhile, her head in her hands. She didn't even know how to handle the situation.

Roger didn't know how to act either. He simply asked Laurence to dress quickly, go out quietly, and leave, please. He told her he was sorry for the situation and that he'd go to Chez Richard for lunch on Monday.

On her way from the house to the restaurant, Laurence had never seen so much snowfall. The flakes created a curtain of ice crystals that pricked you from their heaviness.

The cold war that was established from that moment on in the Montmartre apartment could be won only with negotiation and diplomacy. But when an atomic bomb goes off in your house, there's always one side that's not ready to make things easy. And you have to respect the anger before moving forward. Despite the tension, Roger tried to fix things. In his own way.

"Désolé."

It didn't help that he left his room with the look of a priest. Frowning, Barbara didn't respond. She sat at her work chair and turned on her computer so Roger knew she was giving him the cold shoulder. Facing the window, she put on her headphones and worked for a couple of hours. She answered emails she'd left pending for the last few days. From time to time, interrupted by the dull roar of the storm, she looked up and stared at how the snow blew in front of her. She couldn't even see the building across the street. Always a fan of moderation, she thought that if that excessive snow fell much longer, there'd be less than forty-five minutes left in the world. And then, if this was the end, what did anything matter? The shower, Laurence, the bike, the war, and the history. And men. Men mattered even less. Bomb them. If everything was going to hell, maybe it was their fault. And, far from calming herself down, the pit in her stomach got deeper.

Roger decided to make noise in the kitchen so Barbara could hear his presence. They'd have to talk at some point. They couldn't keep the conflict going forever, nor could they continue to act like nothing had happened. But the more time that passed, the more Roger became angrier. He didn't understand why he was being punished with that childish silence. After all, he hadn't done anything wrong.

He decided to sit on the couch and wait for her to take off her headphones and let the screen sleep. Twenty minutes later, when she finally turned around, he was already waiting with words on the tip of his tongue.

"I'm sorry. I'm not aware of having broken any rules, but if I have to apologize, I'll apologize. I'm sorry."

"What are you talking about now?"

"You imposed them on me yourself on the first day. The rules."

"The fault might be mine, you'll see . . ."

"You said whoever cooks, cleans. Whoever spreads out, picks up. Don't touch the heater. Something, something, something."

"Very good. Nice memory. What else?"

"I don't know . . ."

"You only remember the ones that are convenient for you. The half bathroom, for men. Do you remember I said that?"

"Yes, but I can shower in the big bathroom. We agreed on that."

"You can. She can't."

"In the men's bathroom, there's no . . ." He dared to object. "I don't think it's such a big deal."

"And remember what you said when I finished reciting the rules? I sure do remember. That it was a monk's life. Frankly, hon, it doesn't look like it to me."

It spilled out. Barbara wouldn't put up with nonsense. The last thing she needed was for her not to be able to say what she pleased in her own home. On top of it all, Roger understood that their conversations couldn't continue to end like this. He lowered his voice but got straight to the point.

"You mean, if I understand correctly, what bothers you is that I brought her up?"

"I don't—" Barbara wasn't expecting this. "You know what bothers me? That you're all the same. You know when the last time I ran into a woman in my own bathroom was? It was at my house, and she was fucking my husband. They were lathering each other up. They weren't expecting me, and they didn't hear me arrive. What? That's funny, huh?"

From that perspective, this wasn't too serious. Roger thought it but kept himself from saying the words. Barbara picked up two mugs from the little table, carried them to the kitchen, threw out the tea bags, and washed them.

"Have you gone to see your mamie?" Roger asked without moving from the couch.

"I don't want to talk about it."

"Because you told me—"

"Yes, I went."

"And?"

"I don't want to talk about it."

"I was just asking in case you spoke about the photo."

"Good night."

She shut off the kitchen light, locked herself in her room, and, burying her head into her pillow, let herself fall into the bed. There are days that aren't worth getting out of bed for.

14

A Dull Snow

When they ran into each other in the living room the next day, they grumbled their good mornings.

Roger came out of his bedroom wearing his parka.

"Where do you think you're going?"

He was surprised by the question just as much as its formulation.

"Me? To the dry cleaners."

"I'd forget about that if I were you."

"Excuse me?" He still didn't know what she was talking about.

"You can't leave the house."

That put him in a bad mood. For however hurt Barbara felt, he didn't understand how, all of a sudden, she planned to forbid him from leaving the apartment to collect the pants he'd badly stained and taken to professional hands for cleaning the week before. He needed them. He'd come to Paris with very few clothes.

"Have you looked out the window?" Barbara asked, as calmly as a magician who knows his cards are marked.

Roger drew close to the window. At that point, a dull snow was falling like loose cotton balls lollygagging their way to the ground.

"There's a foot of snow. I'm not too scared to . . ." He made a motion to leave.

"A foot, you say? There's been almost five feet of snowfall in the span of only a couple of hours. Bertrand Delanoë's come out to warn Parisians of all types to stay inside."

"Who is Delanoë?"

"The mayor. He put out a message. Everyone to be shut in until further notice."

He looked out the window again.

"That's a joke, right?"

"No."

"Because of the fucking snow?"

"You can remove your jacket and take it easy. They said on the radio that there's never been so much accumulation of snow in the month of March in Paris proper since almost one hundred years ago. The strangest part is that it's so far into the year. Today is . . ."

"Monday, the thirty-first. Tomorrow, it'll already be April 1."

Roger didn't take off his parka. Moved to do the opposite, he angrily went to his room, stuffed his camera in his bag, put on his wool hat, and grabbed his gloves. He'd put them on once he was outside.

"I'm going to take photos . . . Today will be amazing with all the snow and empty streets."

"Pick up your pants. Don't forget to do that especially."

He closed the door and went down the five floors, convinced that if the day looked up and it stopped snowing, he'd get some special shots. The extreme cold and green-tinted light was a winning combination. When he got to the door of the building, he tried opening it but found it to be difficult. The exit door resisted. He put some force into pulling it toward him. After the third tug, he managed to open it. Before him, however, was a block of snow. So much had accumulated that it had reached the height of his shoulders. It was impossible to leave. There was no way of clearing the obstruction, or jumping over it. Where could he go? Behind that shelf of snow, there must be another one. Or more. All of Montmartre must be a sea of snow five feet deep, stretching from one side of the street to the other so there was no way of moving. The exit was completely barred. He took out his camera and snapped a picture of the door walled in by the polar whiteness. The snow in front of him was still clean, with a powdery texture. Once he took the picture, he returned to the apartment.

"You're back already?" Barbara asked as ironically as she could. "Are the dry cleaners closed on Mondays?"

"It's amazing. You have to go down and see it."

She had been waiting for him, feeling snide. "Or maybe you just weren't able to leave . . ."

"I've never seen anything like that before," Roger continued, surprised by what he had seen. "Did they say it'll last a couple of days?"

"It depends. First it has to stop snowing, and it shows no signs of stopping, and then we'll see."

"What'd the mayor say exactly?"

"To be patient, stay calm, make sure every family's groceries last, because they don't know how long it will be until we return to normal life."

"Are we in confinement?"

"That's the word he used, yes."

"But there must be some prediction, he must have given a hint as to how long we'll be . . ."

He walked up and down the apartment as though he needed to pee. He finally took off his coat.

"Get used to the idea that life has stopped. Nothing's happening. We're fine, the heating works, we have food."

"It's absurd." He set his parka on the couch. "There must be machines in Paris that get rid of . . ."

"At this thickness? Throughout the whole city? Impossible."

"I can't make heads or tails of this situation. We're losing out on days of our lives."

"Now, it'll just be—" She thought it was funny seeing how Roger took it so badly. He looked like a caged panther. "Look, it'll be however many days it'll be. Just don't think of tomorrow as April 1."

"No, it'll be March 32 if you like."

"Why not? Time has stopped. It's not too bad. Sometimes it's good for unexpected things to happen. Sometimes there are greater forces at work that destroy it all. You've never thought about it?"

"No." It was an offended and contrarian response.

"It's a good reality check. Springtime snowfalls are sometimes the worst ones. Sometimes nature puts us in our place."

"You're getting on my nerves." He threw himself on the couch, lazily, surrendering.

They spent some time in silence. Roger took his camera out of his bag and looked at the photo of the snow-blocked doorway he'd taken five minutes earlier. It wasn't much to look at, but he kept it to remember that historic snowfall. The snowfall of March 32, 2008.

Barbara sat in front of her computer, navigating through online newspapers. Each one reported the mayor's words across the front page. All the media outlets, every single one, printed photos by people from their homes that were being posted on social media. Other outlets published photo stories that were like postcards. Back when it was still possible to travel and the snow hadn't yet paralyzed the city, the newspapers had taken pictures of the frozen benches at the Tuileries Palace, the indiscreet footprints of a dog on the pont Alexandre III, the virgin snow covering the Rive Gauche on the Seine, or the powdered paddles of le Moulin de la Galette, unlike anything Renoir or Toulouse-Lautrec had surely ever seen. No wind could have turned the windmill blades weighed down by the heavy white. All of a sudden, the city of light, covered by snow, was a black-and-white landscape. "Hidden Paris" was the headline of the *France Soir*.

"In your experience," Roger asked like he didn't want to know the answer, "will we be able to leave the day after tomorrow?"

"I don't know. I've never seen anything like this," she responded without turning around. "Where I'm from, it snows maybe once every twenty years. And never to this degree."

"Of course."

"And maybe what you're sad about—" she started.

"What? Say it."

"What you're sad about is that you can't go see the waitress."

A low blow. He took it because he'd been expecting it.

"Hey, do me a favor. Let's make a truce. Can you look at me, please?"

She turned the chair so Roger was in front of her. She realized she'd taken it too far. She didn't know where that impulse had come from, but it wasn't the time to let go.

"What's going on?"

"I think I've already apologized. If we have to spend the next two or three days locked up here, let's play nice. This is my suggestion. I know we're in your house, and it's your space and whatever, but I can't go flying out the window."

"I think it's a smart . . . pact." Barbara couldn't stop herself from taking a jab. "Especially coming from you."

With a small smile that was more of an olive branch than a sincere commitment, the two entered an agreement.

It continued to slowly snow throughout the afternoon. Every time it looked as though everything that was supposed to fall had fallen, the snowflake factory would start up again. The gray sky did not foreshadow that the weather might change before the next day. Barbara sat on the couch to call her mamie and see if all was well at the retirement home. They, too, were up to the rafters in snow but had been advised not to worry. Everything was under control. Barbara explained that she had gone down to check on Jasper and to see if he needed anything. The man had made her look at his pantry, and she realized it was even fuller than her own. She didn't have to worry about him. He wasn't missing anything. He was prepared for war. They even shared a laugh, because Jasper had stocked up piles and piles of toilet paper just in case he needed it. Roger heard the conversation between Barbara and her grandmother from his bedroom. He didn't listen, but he waited for them to hang up to before he went back out. He had taken off his turtleneck sweater, and he had on a worn Harvard University T-shirt.

"Have you ever been?"

"Where?" Roger didn't know what she was referring to.

"To Harvard, man."

"No, no." He sat on the other end of the couch. "Someone gave this to me."

"The cold gets much worse there than it does here. These kinds of storms happen every year there."

"It's not for me, then."

"It's worth visiting. I went there once for a weeklong seminar on postwar plots in the North American novel."

"Fascinating."

"Very. Are you making fun of me?"

"No, no." Roger became serious. It was a trick he pulled not to burst into laughter. "You've read so many novels by so many people that surely you've read something that gives you goose bumps. I've been thinking about this for a couple of days. Why don't you write?"

Barbara became as still as stone. "Me?"

"Yes, of course. Your own works. I don't know. They don't have to be stories, since everyone tries that out."

"Did you know no one's ever asked me that question? What's more"—she took off her shoes and sat on her feet on the sofa—"I've never asked myself that question."

"And could you come up with a response?"

"Now?"

"No, I want it in two days. Yes, now, of course. Do we have anything better to do? There's nothing to do in this house. There's no television. Or books."

"Well, that's not true. I won't let you have this one. My computer and e-reader are full of books."

"Those aren't books, woman. I mean real books, made of paper."

"There's also one book made out of paper."

"The one that your grandfather gave your grandmother, it's true."

"I showed it to you, right? The dedication he wrote to her is so . . . Did you see?"

"You told me about it, but you never actually—"

Barbara placed her feet on the ground and started to get up off the sofa. Roger stopped her, putting his hand on her forearm.

"I'm going to find it for you," she said.

"After."

"So that you can see it . . ."

"Don't try to get out of this." He let her go, seeing that Barbara had sat down again and noticing they had never had such long physical contact.

"First, respond to my question."

"I need time to think about it, Roger. It's not the kind of thing you can respond to quickly."

"If there's one thing we have, it's time."

"That's true," she agreed, nodding.

"What do you think? In the middle of the twenty-first century, we've been given the gift to converse like it was five hundred years ago. Is there anything better? Is there anything more ancient? If we had a fireplace, we'd be like our great-grandparents." He rubbed his hands, pulled them apart, and clapped them back together to signal she was taking too long. "So?"

Barbara started to slowly gather her thoughts. She had no choice.

"I don't write because I don't have anything to say. I don't write because I wouldn't know how. I don't write because I'd rather read than write. I don't write because there are millions of people who already do it and do it well. There are probably two thousand people in France alone who could do it better than I could if I tried telling a story. I don't have an imagination, I don't have the skill for it, nor do I have the most fascinating people around me whose lives I can pull into a book that swings between reality and fiction."

"Uh, thanks . . ."

She didn't hear him. She'd been absorbed by the question. Now that she had started to reflect, she needed to continue the introspection.

"And I don't do it, most of all, because I'm conscious that in life, there are two types of people: main characters and side characters. And I'm the second kind."

"Don't undersell yourself."

"I'm explaining reality, the way it is. The main characters have titles. They're on the radio. They're interviewed. When they die, it's news. Someone even pays for their obituary. They're writers, but they're also politicians and businesspeople and singers. Sarkozy's wife—"

"Which one?"

"The third one." Her name was on the tip of her tongue. "The singer. Carla Bruni. She was a model. She's a singer. She's the first lady of France . . . At every point in her life, she's been the main character. *Chapeau* to her. But side characters have the role of existing; we're limited to knowing only who she is. Sometimes we buy her CDs, we hum 'Quelqu'un m'a dit' confidently, and, if we're lucky and well connected, maybe one day we see a fashion show at an elegant palace where she walks down the aisle. Suddenly, right when she's in front of you, she spins around and returns back where she's come from. That's it. You've seen a main character up close. This makes us side characters happy. Sometimes you run into a main character at a restaurant. Nothing happens. It's a spectacle. There are few of them, there are many of us. The majority of the world throughout all of human history are side characters. We're filler, we're trash . . . Our lives are assumed and managed. But we also have the right to be happy, god dammit. And sometimes we're happier than even the main characters."

"Happy? Of course. Look at you."

"Are you making fun of me?"

"No, no."

"What's wrong? I love the work I do. I'm in the book world, I'm lucky to sell the international rights for novels, and I'm happy. I'm sure I enjoy my job more than most writers who have long lines at book signings and full theaters when they present their latest nonsense. What's wrong, why are you looking at me like that?"

Roger had raised his brow, shocked.

"If you'll let me . . . Can I put in my two cents on the subject?"

"I have no choice but to say yes, right?"

"That's a rather conformist perspective on life. Because everything is predetermined, there's no reason to have ambitions . . . You've been given the role of side character, and someone else is the main character. Bad luck. The cards had already been drawn."

"It's not that. Do you want tea, Roger?"

"No."

"Sometimes, even normal people—because they work for it or play tennis well or because they write a dystopian novel that becomes a bestseller—from here to Melbourne, go from anonymity to stardom. And in that moment, we still prefer fairy tales, because a nobody has become the main character. That happens, and you know it does. You can't say it doesn't."

"There have been cases, yes."

"But it's so infrequent that, when it happens, you appear in the newspaper. Why? Because it's news."

He couldn't come up with a quick argument to refute her.

"Have you ever been in the newspaper?" he asked.

"No, nor do I need to be. And you?"

"I . . ." It wasn't the time for the long version of the story. He cut it short. "I worked in the news for a long time. I was a newspaper photographer."

"That's different."

"Of course. It has nothing to do with it. At the most, my name was printed vertically next to a photo, and that's it. By the way . . ." He needed to change the subject. "Speaking of dedications. You were about to show me something from your grandfather."

"Oh, now you want to see it?" She got up from the couch. "That's it? So, we're just done with the subject?"

"Come on."

"Thank you for the therapy, then. What'd you say about the tea?"

"No. No, thanks."

Barbara went to her room, which had been Mamie's room before that. In any case, the book had always lived in the same place. On the dressing table, in front of the mirror, as if every day it had been opened and read and reread until it was memorized.

She returned shortly with the volume in her hands.

"It's the last gift my grandfather gave to my mamie." She placed an old copy of *One Thousand and One Nights* in his hands. Roger took it carefully. The pages, some of the edges having been frayed, still held together from lack of use. The carefully sewn seams showed through the spine. "Have you read it?"

"Let's just say . . . *One Thousand and One Nights*?" He was on the verge of lying, but he figured he'd be caught and opted for the truth. "Not yet."

"It's the book everyone knows but no one reads."

"It makes me feel better that I'm not an exception then." He opened it to the middle, turned some pages, and breathed in the book's scent. "What's it about?"

"Oof, what a question . . ."

"Tell me like you have to sell me the rights."

She closed her eyes, thought about how to explain it, and began to thread together an appealing synopsis, as though it were a sale to a potential client. She did it passionately, like there was an editor across from her.

"Shahryar is the Persian king who, every morning, decapitates the woman he's spent the previous night with. He executes them, convinced all women will betray him like his first wife did. But there is one woman, Scheherazade, the daughter of a vizier, who, to avoid becoming the next victim, comes up with a genius idea. Each night, she tells him an extraordinary tale, but she does it with a catch. When the sun comes up, she leaves the story at a cliff-hanger so the king doesn't kill her, because he wants to know how the story continues the next day. Thanks to the suspense, Scheherazade is able to continue living this way for a thousand and one nights."

Roger let her finish, and he smiled mischievously.

"I'm sure all that rings a bell from school. Nice explanation."

"Thank you. Will you buy it or what? Do you want to publish the book?"

He hesitated. "You wouldn't be able to write a story like that now."

"Why not?"

"Everyone walks on eggshells these days. Maybe it could be written, but it sure wouldn't be published. A topic like that wouldn't be allowed."

"No, no. Literature is past all that. It's a form of artistic expression, and anything goes. Everyone must be free to write what they want."

"A serial killer who goes after women? Just picture it . . . No one would buy it from you."

"Quite the opposite. Look at it this way. It's a novel about the power of words. Scheherazade is able to tame the beast just by talking. Yes, the power of words. By speaking, people understand one another. It's a victory for pacifism. It's a book that transcends time."

"I don't know. I don't know . . . Maybe you're right, Barbara. You know more about all that."

He touched her forearm again. This time it was congratulatory for her convincing presentation. She slapped his hand off of her.

"Do you want to read it now or what?"

"The book?" He shook his head as if to say he had no choice. "Yes, the dedication. Can I read it?"

"That's why I brought it."

He moved his hand away to look for the page, dragging his eyes across the right-hand pages until he found it. It was there in front of him. Barbara watched how Roger's lips murmured what Grandfather Damien had written for Mamie in blue ink more than sixty years ago. The writing was clear, slightly shaky with nervously drawn letters. But the text itself, centered on the page, evoked a certain tranquility. Slowly Roger discovered each syllable as he followed them with his ring finger.

> *Margaux,*
> *My nights have been few. But in each and every one of them, the need to see your eyes has kept me alive. It's impossible to love anything more than I love you.*
> *Music and a thousand and one kisses,*
> *Damien*

15

The Sound of Temptation

The first thing Barbara did when she woke up, before washing her face, was look out the window. First, the monotone sky. The lead-gray of Paris had come to stay, and there was no way it would dissipate. The wind was no longer as strong as it had been days before, when the snowstorm looked like it would carry everything away. That Tuesday of confinement, however, had the air of a peaceful day without rain. The chimneys of the flat roofs of Montmartre, unaffected by meteorological predictions, blew smoke in all directions, defying the stillness of the urban landscape. Then, she looked down at the street. The snow continued to blanket it, and just looking at it made her feel cold. Without showering, she put on her blue onesie, which stretched from the hood to her feet, zipped it up all the way, and went out to make herself an avocado toast.

Roger had already made coffee for the two of them.

"You really woke up early today," Barbara remarked.

"Good morning, Barbara."

"I have a lot to do."

"Oh, really?"

"But I won't get any of it done. This weather is a drag."

"Be patient, kid. The bad mood won't help either of us out if we have to stay shut in here."

"I'll hand it to you on that for once."

"Last night, I put on the radio," she said, her mouth full. "They say it'll snow for days. You can take some interior shots. The apartment lends itself to that, don't you think? The giant cactus, the old radio. Who wouldn't want to photograph the attic apartments of Paris from the inside? The kitchen still has my grandmother's charm. I'm sure you've never photographed tiles like that."

"I think it's a big joke on my end. Not everyone is so lucky as to work remotely like you do."

Roger touched Barbara's waist with both hands to prevent himself from bumping against her as he passed behind. Having achieved this feat, he opened the fridge. The burst of cold on his face, he scanned the shelves, as if searching for inspiration.

"How many days do you think we'll last with what we have?" Roger asked.

"I'd say four or five, if no one takes it from us."

"That many? I'll make you lunch today. You'll be licking your fingers." Roger let the fridge door go and it closed by itself, airtight. "What time do you want food on the table?"

"What're you making me?"

"It's a surprise. You continue to work, and you'll smell it soon."

Once she finished her toast, Barbara headed for her desk, a mug of coffee in hand. She didn't have to turn on the computer because she always left it in sleep mode. Giresse & Trésor had sent a message to all employees warning them that the lifespan of their devices depended on the number of times they turned it on and off, and so they required employees to minimize the number of boot-ups as much as possible. Of course, they should turn off the monitor while their computer was asleep. She obeyed, and this way she was able to immediately open her documents and begin working. She prepared the portfolios for Simone Sicilia's posthumous novel to send to three Latin American presses that were interested in buying rights together. They represented three publishing houses from Buenos Aires, Lima, and Montevideo that were used to making a single business offer to translate and distribute a novel in their respective countries. If one of the three didn't agree, then, "See you later, it was nice knowing you." But Barbara knew that no one wanted to let Sicilia's *The Gift* go, because after the author communicated her suicide via Twitter, the book sold like hotcakes in every country it was bought and translated. The morbid interest in the story of a girl abused by her uncle, a well-known socialist mayor, written in first person out of spite, and a suicide involving a bag over her head as a metaphorical colophon to a story appearing in every newspaper made the book invincible. Who could suppress their curiosity when it came to a heart-wrenching story like that? In the document meant for the Latin American editors, Barbara added a list of the bestselling nonfiction books in every country that had published Sicilia's book. It was the leading title everywhere. A bestseller.

Roger closed the kitchen door and began preparing the tomato-and-onion sauté for his grandmother's macaroni. Now that he had all the time in the world and it wasn't the usual situation—boiling pasta in a sauce from a jar and then rushing off—he wanted to throw himself into it and cook with the love he'd seen his paternal grandmother, the Narbona, cook. Granny Maria. With her white-and-blue-checkered apron tied at the back, she began by grating tomatoes she'd blanched to peel more easily. When the tomatoes were ready, he peeled three onions, diced them really small, and threw them in a pan with some olive oil to brown. As the onion took on color—he noticed it with his nose before he did with his eyes—he added the grated tomatoes. The smell wafted through the whole house in no time. Granny Maria would have added botifarra sausage, removing the casing and sliding the minced meat into the pan, maybe with a bonus of four mushrooms. Roger resigned himself to the ground veal in the apartment fridge, originally destined to become a hamburger, and to half of the vacuum-packed duck magret that had been waiting for the right occasion. Once both meats were properly ground and fried, he added them to the tomatoes and onion, which was slowly disappearing into the sauté.

He stirred the mixture with a wooden spatula for seven minutes. Once it was ready, he turned off the fire, covered it, and let it rest until lunchtime.

"It smells really good," Barbara said when the chef emerged from the kitchen.

"It's good enough to make the angels sing. Does twelve thirty work for you?"

"Have you gotten used to eating on the French schedule?"

"We don't have anything else to do," Roger muttered. "The sooner we eat, the better."

At noon, he boiled a pot of water. At a quarter after twelve, he put in salt and the pasta. Three hundred grams of rigatoni with grooves that, according to Granny Maria, held the sauce and spirit of the cook better. Once he drained the pasta, Roger threw it back into the pot to mix it with the meat sauce. He poured it into the only casserole pan he knew to find in the kitchen, and he distributed the grated cheese (half a package of gouda) on top before putting it in the oven. In the three minutes it took to cook au gratin, Roger set the living room table with clean napkins. He even had time to open a bottle of red wine, a young Beaujolais he'd found in the pantry.

"Voilà." He placed the pan on top of the napkins and took off the oven mitts. "In my country, we say, 'To the table and to bed on the first call.'"

"That makes me laugh," she said, getting up from her office chair and moving to the living room. "Wow, rigatoni. It looks delicious. And smells even better."

"My grandmother's macaroni. As they say in Italy, *'la pasta non aspetta.'* Would you like me to serve you?"

"Well, since you already are . . . it should be nothing less than the complete service, shouldn't it?"

He served her a healthy portion. They each took a plate, and there was enough left in the pan for seconds. She filled each glass with wine.

"I think this is the first time someone has cooked for me in Paris. And you don't know how happy that makes me." She blew on the fork and tasted the macaroni. "Mmmm . . . So good. Excellent."

"Oh, come on, it's macaroni. It's no *nouvelle cuisine* . . ."

"If there was a survey with a good sample size and a low margin of error, and they asked you what you preferred, a familiar dish or the newest invention of the century, you know what would win, right?"

"If people were honest, yes."

"Then there you go. Congratulate your grandmother."

Roger raised both of his arms to the heavens the way he had seen Messi dedicate a goal to his grandmother Celia. They laughed at his homage to the original cook, and ate and went for seconds of Granny Maria's macaroni, and drank and talked.

"You're good at cooking."

"Only at basic things. But I do like it."

"Don't sell yourself short, because other people will. That's how life is."

Once it was time for dessert—he went in search of a banana, but Barbara was full—she asked him a question without any ulterior motives.

"Are any of your grandparents still alive?"

"Not anymore. Zero out of four. I'm not as lucky as you."

"Honestly, my mamie is worth four grandparents. You should meet her. Once all this is over, you should come with me to the retirement home."

"I won't say no."

"Something I regret—maybe not now as much because I'm older—but when I was little, I do remember how mad I would get about not having met either of my two grandpas. I saw classmates who had grandmothers and grandfathers, and I . . . It's the law of life, I guess."

"It's true. And your parents, are they fine?"

Barbara's silence was heavy. He didn't want to screw up.

"I don't think you've mentioned them once since I moved into the apartment."

"They're dead. Both of them."

Pure information. In five words, she had disclosed more about her father, her mother, and the precipitous end to their life stories.

"I'm sorry." Roger excused himself with a downward glance. "They must have been young."

"It was an accident. On July 25, 2000." After eight years, she could finally talk about it without getting emotional. "They were going on the trip of a lifetime. It was to celebrate my mother's fifty-fifth birthday, which was in May. They were both so happy planning it. They had saved for a long time. Every month, both of them put money in a piggy bank shaped like a convertible Ford Mustang, which they'd bought just for the trip. They spent a couple of years preparing everything, and look how things . . . It's a sick joke. Bullshit. At least they went together."

"A car accident?"

She shook her head. Roger realized she didn't want to talk about it. Just as he was about to change the subject, Barbara asked him, "Do you remember the Concorde accident?"

"Oof . . . It sounds familiar."

"They were going from Paris to New York to embark on a cruise across the Atlantic. Nothing big. In 2000, a nice round number. One hundred and nine people died. Not a single person survived."

"Shit. I'm so sorry for asking, Barbara."

"It's not your fault. It's okay." This time, she stopped a tear from rolling down her face with her finger. Then, she took a deep breath and continued. "The only fallen Concorde in history. It's bad luck, huh? A macabre lottery. And just think, the coincidences. One thing leads to another thing. Fatalities are like a domino effect when there are accidents like that . . . They say the investigation was clear, at least. When you think about it, there's hardly one cause for a tragedy. And you spend years and nights without sleeping, thinking about the what-ifs: What if the runway had been clean and hadn't blown out the tire; what if the remains from the wheel hadn't made one of the motor tanks explode? The plane would have taken off, and if . . . Tragedies are full of conditionals that have no turning back. And if . . . and if . . . Nothing. Everything goes to hell in one second."

"That's hard. Really hard for you."

"And for my mamie. My grandmother had my mother right after the war and had to bury her . . . Come on, it's the worst thing that can happen to you in your life."

"And a death like that. You don't see it."

She shot him a confused glance.

He didn't know how to continue. He tried the only way he knew how.

"What were their names?"

"My father's name was Clément. My mother's was Édith. Both good people. I can't think of a better summary of them."

"The parents of a daughter who, once she opens up, makes it worthwhile."

"Thank you."

Roger found himself indebted to Barbara. The time had come for him to share something about himself. About him and Marcel.

But he had to wait for the moment. That silence and retreat belonged only to Barbara and the memory of her angels.

He waited for nightfall to create the perfect conditions. He knew Barbara's habits before bed were the same every night. She'd sit on the red couch in the dim light of the living room and read from her tablet or e-reader or whatever the hell it was called, until her yawns got the best of her. Then she'd turn off the screen, say good night, and head straight to sleep. Before Roger detected the first signs of her sleepiness, he steeped two green teas and placed them atop the small table at the foot of the sofa.

"Wow. What's this?"

"I thought you'd like it."

He sat on the other side of the three-seater couch in the darkest part of the living room. He'd thought about how to begin his story. But in the hour of truth, it wouldn't come out. Barbara hadn't lifted her gaze from her book, and he felt sorry to interrupt her. But the words burned him more than the tea, and it was time to tell someone for the first time.

"This afternoon's conversation, while we were eating lunch . . . It's made me think of something."

He said it like it wasn't important. But Barbara knew Roger needed to speak based on his air, on his tone, on something—she didn't quite know what.

Roger had once thought it was a shame when the story of your father's death embarrassed you. It was even worse if what bothered you most was talking about his life. But he needed to do it.

"What'd you think about?" Barbara asked, turning her body to more directly face him.

The calm of the night and the tenuous light from the desk invited a slow confession in whispers, like someone who's not in a hurry to reveal a secret they've carried for a long time. Roger sighed and burned his lips with a sip of tea. When it all felt overwhelming, he moved the cushion behind his back and began to tell his father's story.

"Everything we now know about him I didn't discover myself. Marcel told me as he patiently and curiously put the pieces together. My mother preferred to keep herself in the dark once we buried my father in the Fontanilles Cemetery on a hot June day that felt more like early August. She didn't want to know anything more about that episode. She could guess how the story must've unfolded, but she put up a shield of ignorance to keep the memory of my father intact. I don't blame her. I can even understand where she came from. The local police advised me to let go of the case. Even though I worked at the newspaper at the time, they suggested I stay out of it. 'Let it go,' they told me, the way someone speaks about collusion. Maybe they talked like that because they knew there was something hidden behind that unfortunate end or because they saw me in a state of shock or because

I'd so unexpectedly come across his body. Whatever it was, I listened. I didn't want to involve myself in a familial disappointment that could drag us all down. Only Marcel, because he's a lawyer and it's a part of his character, wanted to know the truth. Due to his job, he has contacts with judges, he has coffee with prosecutors, and he's talked to the police and with everyone in the underbelly of those neighborhoods. He says that in the Empordà, which is a place where nothing like this ever happens, if you snoop around in every furrow of the plowed land and in every bale of hay, there hides a story no one dares even guess.

"My father's is one of those stories.

"Josep Narbona, the youngest of seven siblings, was a farmer his whole life. Day after day, year after year, everything appeared to be absolutely normal. He always looked like he was comfortable in his routine—which is notorious for seeming boring because it's repetitive and seasonal despite also providing security. *'When you have a routine, you always know what shoes you have to wear,'* he used to say. Throughout his life, Father didn't do much more than look at the sky, wear his mountain boots, and live according to the apple trees and their fruit. As a child during Franco's reign, he'd gone to school, to the one assigned to him, the one close to home. He went to Torroella, to the same grade schools his six siblings had attended, and he barely passed his lessons, without taking much of a liking to any subject. Maybe he was more into numbers than letters, but he wasn't more or less of anything, and it never crossed his mind to go to college. Or to go very far from home. His piece of land was his life. Again, he'd been prepared for that routine, and he never looked farther than that. If this is what life planned for him, a conformist by nature, then that's what he did. He was the type of person whose life had seemed to be determined for them at birth. Committed to work and to the land, he promised on more than one occasion that he'd never get married. The more you make these kinds of affirmations, the more likely people will remind you of them for the rest of your life. Everything changed the moment the French family came to the village. Their arrival shook Fontclara. First, there was a distrust of the Bazin family. What are they doing here? Had they lost something in this armpit of the world? Then, there was some spying on the family. What'd they buy? What'd they eat? How'd they dress? What was their daily schedule like? Did they go to church, or had they stopped? The cold and hardly cordial reception of the Bazin family lasted until the youth of the area met Fabienne, whose curls could be spotted from a mile away, and everyone wanted her to join their friend group. There weren't many girls in those parts, and the boys from Fontanilles to Palau-sator tripped over themselves to act cool in front of her. My father had always been pleasant, the kind to crack a joke. And they say he was more like that when he was young. At that time, he didn't speak French, but he would communicate in gestures to make Fabienne laugh. We always had a good sense of humor at home. My father was either telling a joke, or explaining a pun, or it was enough for him to fashion a towel into the shape of Napoleon's hat. It was always like that until the end, when everything went by the wayside. At that point, when my father stopped smiling, we should have noticed something was happening. And I'm sure my mom saw it; we guessed it, but no one dared ask if he needed help. None of us knew enough. We all know that fear is like a door with cracks in it."

Barbara reached for her mug. It had cooled down enough for her first sip. In the building across the street, a girl kissed her father good night and switched off the light.

"I like watching nighttime rituals."

In the swamp of his memory, Roger hadn't noticed. He didn't even hear her.

"Don't for a second think he was a careless father. Quite the opposite. When it came to education and discipline, there were always a lot of tickles and laughs, but when it was lunchtime, we ate. We ate dinner, after being called only once, our hands on the table and our backs straight, napkin on our lap, and we cleaned our plates without complaining, whether we liked it or not. It was the same with our grades at school. He'd sit in the armchair, the one in front of the fireplace. We'd bring him our report card, and he would look at it from top to bottom, reviewing the grades, subject by subject. Marcel's grades were usually better than mine. If we'd passed everything, he'd tell us he felt we could have done a little better. He'd return the report card, and that was it until the next grading period. That's how the trimesters went until final grades arrived, and then he'd limit himself to saying, clever as he was, *'It looks like we won't be repeating the grade.'* It was another way of expressing his satisfaction with normality. School was a process. Every year, it had to be taken care of without much consideration. Once, in the first trimester of junior year, I got sidetracked and failed three classes. My father looked at my report card, saw the failing grades, breathed in deeply, and just when I thought lightning and thunder and hail would fall on me, he looked at me, returned my report card, and told me to talk to my mother, because she could help me more than he could.

"But we weren't able to help him when he needed it. His tragedy didn't arrive from one day to the next. It began simmering, little by little, throughout the years. From what Marcel has deduced, it all started on a Thursday, the day when, come rain or shine, he'd play cards. The whole gang—all men, sometimes eight of them, sometimes ten, but my father always joined—had dinner and then started the game. They played botifarra, a game that's well-known there. I'm talking about the time around when my parents had just gotten married. My brother had probably not even been born yet when they started the Thursday meetups. You can just picture it. They smoked, they drank, they laughed, and they played for a couple of bucks. From what they've told us, their bets were always small. By the time Pep got home—because his friends always called him Pep Narbona—my mother had already been sleeping for hours.

"One Thursday, in the middle of a game of cards, one of them asked, 'Did you read about the casino they opened in Peralada? We should go there one day.' It must have been four or five years after the death of Franco, and with the arrival of democracy came gambling as a business. People no longer needed to travel to France to go to a casino.

Of all the friends in the Fontclara Thursday gang, only one man among them had gone to a casino, and only once. 'To Monte Carlo?' the group asked him. No. He didn't remember where he'd gone exactly, but he told them about roulette, *rien ne va plus*, and the blackjack table with the enthusiasm of a kid at a theme park. Suddenly, all of them were curious to check it out. If they hurried, Peralada was thirty minutes from the house by highway. They'd have to drive onto the national highway and, once there, drive straight down in two cars. The funny thing about the casino, which is still there, is that they built it in a castle. The fortification, which has a medieval air to it, clashes with the colorful slot machines ringing at all hours of the day. That jingle of money, after a short while, becomes the sound of temptation. The entrance to the castle, with its two towers, gave the casino an enchanting air. For them, it was like a red carpet welcoming them to a new world, a country of wonderments. The luxury, green carpets, the turn of the roulettes, the chandeliers, the dealers in tuxedos, the men in ties, the women in evening gowns. That place, which was far from his own, provoked a growing fascination in my father with his mountain boots. He returned home and recounted his experience. He looked like a kid who had seen his first skyscraper. He brought Marcel and me each a token as a souvenir. And he explained that things inside the casino didn't function with money but rather with those round and flat chips ornamented with a border that created addiction. As you might imagine, the ones he brought us weren't worth much. Twenty-five cents at the most.

"After that summer, the Fontclara friend group decided that, without telling anyone, they'd hold off on their game of botifarra once a month and head down to the casino instead. By the time Christmas came around, they were driving the two cars to Peralada two Thursdays a month. They almost never returned home before dawn. There were days my father would get into bed and, after an hour, get up to shower and go to the fields like nothing had happened.

"But things did happen.

"From what Marcel was able to piece together—the friend group had started talking in dribs and drabs, but eventually everybody speaks a little more than they would like—my father became a big fan of roulette. He ending up playing a lot of money every night. And every night, the chips became more and more valuable. He stopped exchanging money for tokens so he could let the bills rain directly onto the table. He became obsessed with a number, and he'd bet on fifteen, for example. And for seven, eight, or nine straight rounds, he'd bet it all on fifteen. He'd leave a five-thousand peseta bill on the table, and the dealer would know it was a bet on fifteen, odd, black. The ball would spin, and after several turns, it would stop on a number that wasn't his. One day, someone who was lurking near the roulette table and who had my father's number invited him to a game of cards. 'You like poker? You can win big,' he told him. And my father believed him. They took him to a back room, offered him a glass of wine, introduced him to some harmless-looking players, and began to play. From what his friends have explained to Marcel, they warned him not to do it. But the casino stopped the friends from entering the room just to observe. Nicely, but forcefully. What happened to my father, all alone, in there? No one knows. All the versions of the story agree that he was so happy at the end of the night that he asked to drive, and in an out-of-the-ordinary action, he didn't stop humming the caramelles he'd learned as a kid. They said that when they stopped for a piss on the side of the highway, the friends who'd stayed in the car went through the pockets of his blazer. The wads of bills he was carrying were so thick there was no way to button the pockets.

"That first day, he won the poker game. But it wasn't like that every time. Marcel is convinced they'd hoodwinked him from top to bottom that Thursday. They gave him a guppy as an appetizer, and he bit the ham. They'd nailed his palate. But that story, dear Barbara, I'll tell you tomorrow. Just like in your grandparents' book. Now we go to bed."

16

A Winning Streak

She called Mamie Margaux again to say hello and ask how she was doing. The Viviani Retirement Home had decided that no matter what, no one could go out to the therapeutic garden. Much less out to the street. It wasn't just a medical whim. The snow simply didn't allow for it. Maybe not as much snow had fallen in the fifth arrondissement as on the hill that was Montmartre, but it really wasn't a matter of comparison. There was no way to see from the Viviani ground floor how the oldest tree in Paris had held up. They could hardly make out the bell of the church of Saint-Julien-le Pauvre across Square Viviani, poking out from behind the shelf of snow mounded to the window. For once, "historic" was the adjective to describe reality without any sort of banal overexaggerating. In a city where in the last three hundred years, events with long encyclopedia entries had happened, "historic" was not a comfortable qualifier that worked for everything. Between revolutions, guillotines, and devastating wars, the Great Snowfall of the twenty-first century was a pause in time that didn't cause older people who had lived through everything to lose too much sleep.

"Be patient, Barbara," said Margaux, the telephone at her ear. "All kinds of things happen in life."

"I'm happy to hear you're taking it that way."

"We can't do anything about this. The snow, too, will melt."

"One day or another, that's true."

"Go down to check on Jasper, see if he needs anything."

"I was already thinking of doing that, don't worry."

"Make sure the snow on the roof doesn't weigh too much."

"I can't even put my head outside to see it, Mamie. How do you want me to climb outside?"

"But be on the watch that the ceiling doesn't start to cave in."

Barbara looked up with the apathy of God when he counts sheep because he can't sleep.

"The house is holding up for now. But if there is moisture damage, there's no one I can call."

"And don't eat too much over these few days, because you can't go out and burn it off."

"Mamie, please. What's gotten into you? I'm doing yoga, you know that. I haven't stopped. I do it at home now. I know the routines. I close the door to my room, and—"

"Your room? Why don't you do it in the living room?"

"Because I'm not alone."

"You'd have more space."

"There's plenty of space in my room. I lay the mat near the foot of the bed, and—"

"You're not alone?" Mamie elongated the question like she'd suddenly discovered something. "Who's there? The guy who rents the bedroom? Uh . . . what's his name? The one from Barcelona?"

"Marcel."

"And how is he? Because having to be shut up at home with a stranger . . ."

"Well, Marcel isn't here. His brother is here right now."

"Brother?" She dragged out her tone even more.

"Mamie, I've already told you this. I called to see how you're doing, not so you can tell me what to do. I *am* forty-one, you know."

"Don't be so sensitive. No one can tell you anything."

"Hey, I'm not asking you how many show-off widowers you're shut up with in your little hotel, am I?"

"What are you going on about? These old men stink when they get close to you."

"Be careful, woman, they'll hear you."

"Who could even hear me here if they're all deaf as a post?"

"Mamie, I think you're being a little loose-lipped. If there's nothing new, we'll talk tomorrow to see how things are going."

"They said on the radio that it's not supposed to snow today. It's the first day in who knows how many, they said."

"Good. Let's see if they are right, then. Kisses."

"Big kisses."

The day in that Montmartre apartment went by at a glacial pace. Barbara plunged headfirst into her work. She didn't stop working and making calls to editors in countries the snowstorm had missed by a long shot or, if it had hit them, who were shut in at home. Everyone asked her about the strange situation in Paris. They'd seen it on the news, and she responded with her mamie's words: *"The snow, too, will melt."*

Roger hardly left his room. It had been weeks since he'd become used to the stench that sometimes climbed into the open air like a bitter burp. With his laptop on his bed, he navigated through pages that could shed some light on André Zucca and the photograph clippings in his treasure box, the tin box under the bed. The story actually seemed less confusing than he suspected. But he continued without discovering what was happening in the picture of Barbara's grandmother, Mamie Margaux—so pretty, so young, so distinguished—that was hanging in the controversial exhibit. Judging by the internet comments, there was an ongoing debate about the insult of platforming Nazism sixty years after the occupation of Paris. "An Inappropriate Exhibit" was the softest term used on social media. Along with the rest of the paralyzed city, the BHVP was shut. In fact, all the libraries, museums, and public amenities had their blinds closed. No one was able to open them, just as no one was able to visit. Everyone was at home, and until when, nobody knew.

They agreed on the menu for lunch. Roger put on his apron and made a big plate of potatoes and vegetables for the two of them. They didn't feel like eating anything else. They finished the bottle of Beaujolais they'd opened the day before, cracked some nuts, and, once finished, returned to their own worlds. Throughout the day, neither mentioned Roger's father or Marcel. Barbara, who was anxious to know how the story continued, knew to wait until the night. Seated on the red sofa, each on opposite ends, with a nail-shaped moon spying through the window, she dared begin the conversation once the tea had cooled.

"We left off yesterday with your father at an interesting moment. He was winning money, a lot of money, at the poker table."

Roger was expecting it. The low light of the living room—only the reading light was on—invited trust. He undid a button on his shirt and ran a hand along his shoulder, searching for a thread of concentration.

He took a sip of green tea and began. "Practically without realizing it, Pep Narbona had entered into a dangerous spiral. My father waited for Thursdays to come so he could go to Peralada and play a game of poker. He'd spend some time at the roulette table, lose some money he'd never see again, and sitting on the high stool in the first row, he waited for the game to be announced. Someone would come look for him, he'd follow them discreetly into the back room, and once he passed through the door with the privacy sign, his Fontclara friends lost sight of him. Some days, the poker game lasted so long that they didn't even wait for him before heading home. My father knew to call a taxi to take him back if he finished a game and couldn't find his friends when the casino closed.

"One day, the taxi braked in front of the house when the roosters were crowing. My father asked the driver to park out on the stone path outside the doorway and wait for a moment. He didn't have a penny on him. The casino had emptied his pockets. He entered the house, opened my mother's bag, and took two bills out of her wallet, the price of the ride. My mother, who noticed everything, realized someone had gone through her things. At the very least, it wasn't the way she had left them. If she hadn't found the two bills missing, she wouldn't have said anything, but because money had disappeared without anyone letting her know, she tried to find out what had happened. She waited until lunchtime, and before we could finish the first course, she accused Marcel and me of having stolen one hundred euros in the form of two fifty-euro bills. It was either one of us, or both. She didn't suspect anyone else. Seated at the head of the table, my father continued eating his pasta soup and stayed quiet as a mouse. After, without getting flustered one bit by the incident and as tired as he was, he crossed his arms over the table and took a nap. We could yell, we could clink the dishes as loud as possible in the sink, we could raise the television volume, because once he ate, he slept like a log, his head on his arms. That day, not even the episode of Mother's missing money made him lose sleep.

"We don't know how long those poker games lasted. Years, probably. Marcel has slowly traced our father's running accounts and investments. In the last years, more money left than came in. Every month, he dipped into the well, and each time he got closer to running dry. When he ran out of personal savings, he dug into the company money. Narbona Fruits, the best in Girona, was a good business. They'd been lucky because of the apples, and they were even luckier because they hadn't had a bad year. But when Marcel asked for the books once my father was dead, he looked back and saw some strange settlements. Unexplainable movements. Consignments where they didn't belong. Just all-around disorder. Pep himself had set up a scheme so no one could tell he was playing card games to settle his debts.

"For you to understand what I'm about to tell you, Barbara, there's one thing you have to know. Before tourism discovered the Costa Brava and they built oceanfront apartments, Narbona Fruits had a nice tradition. Once the taxes were paid, the company directed part of its profits to buying a waterfront apartment on the beach of Pals. Every year, a new one. Instead of spreading dividends, they'd buy apartments to rent to tourists. In one building, my father's company ended up with all the ground-floor apartments and all the penthouses with the best views. Eight in total. But they were lost just as they'd come in, one by one. To everyone's surprise, the penthouses were sold first to make money he could keep on burning. But when it came to the ground-floor apartments, he gambled those in card games. And he lost them. And when there were no apartments left, he also bet a machine he used in the fields. And after, some piece of my mother's jewelry, one of those jewels from back in the day, art deco, with big stones you would have loved to see—because the more rural the farmer, the bigger the diamond. A way to demonstrate they weren't less than anyone—the real rural spirit.

"My father lost all of it. When it wasn't the fault of three jacks, it was because the four aces he wanted never turned up. He was convinced that everything the cards took, the cards would return to him. He just needed a stroke of luck. A winning streak. He thought fortune was like this: it could favor you just as suddenly as it could turn its back on you. He believed in chance. Wholeheartedly. But he was so blinded he didn't realize this was another thing altogether. They were fooling him, game after game, Thursday after Thursday. And even though his friends from town warned him and said, 'Pep, don't you think you're crossing the line?' 'Pep, maybe you should slow down.' 'Pep, this is snowballing. Don't you think you're getting into dangerous waters?' there he was, hard-headed, more stubborn than a mule.

"Around that time, I started to work as a photographer. That's one way of putting it. I had moved to Pals, to the town center, to work as an assistant at a longstanding store where they developed film and primarily took driver's license photos on the spot. When from time to time someone entered the establishment, which was run by a woman who was drier than day-old bread, the ritual always went the same way. 'Sit on the stool, button up, look in the camera . . .' You shoot, and they leave with four copies of a close-up. Using the paper cutter, I separated the images, cutting along the white mark like when you trim your nails.

I slipped the pictures into a sleeve with the store's name, and they'd go to the commissioner's office in Palafrugell to get their passport and go on a trip.

"One afternoon, around when it was time to close up shop, a man entered asking if we shot wedding photos. I didn't know the response, but I didn't say no. He explained that his niece was getting married, and he was paying for her wedding photos as a gift. He wanted a whole album, with pictures at the bride's house while she got ready, the godfather delivering the bouquet, the arrival of the car at the chapel of S'Agaró, the whole ceremony in full detail, the rice throwing, and after, the guests in the gardens of la Gavina, a hotel where the richest of the rich got married. I spoke to the store owner. She asked if I was brave enough to take it on, and I said of course. I ended up earning good money. Because one thing leads to another, ten days after delivering the album to his niece, the uncle returned to the store. Before thanking me for the project, he told me he was some head honcho at the *Diari de Girona*. It must have been an important position, because I didn't end up understanding him. He was the type to give you a business card with his name at the first hello to impress you, like they are someone worth knowing. But he did tell me he had come back to make me a proposal. His newspaper needed a photography correspondent in Lower Empordà. The previous one had left, and they wanted someone who was a short motorcycle drive away from taking a picture and doing all sorts of things. Someone who could photograph the lineup of the Palamós CF team or cover the fire in Montgrí and, five minutes later, be in Bisbal because the minister of health was inaugurating a primary-care center. I didn't have to think about it too long. I said yes to the head honcho. All of a sudden, I liked that bride's uncle a lot more. No one had ever entrusted me with anything. I left the little shop in Pals, where, honestly, I spent more time yawning than photographing. But working for the newspaper for two years had me on the brink of ruin. They reimbursed me for my transport and the motorcycle gas separately. To make anything close to a living wage, I needed them to send me on several small assignments every day, in a county where, nine months out of the year, nothing much happens. There was very little news. Even less news of interest. Local photojournalism is like that. For every somewhat brilliant photograph, you shoot loads of shit at a million never-ending events. You don't know how much mayors love appearing in the newspaper with their name in the caption. The smaller the town, the more columns they dream of appearing in. I can imagine the same thing happens here in France, but back home, the sheer number of speeches, municipal plenary sessions, inaugurations, and commemorations paralyzes the country. They don't have agendas for many of these events. In short, when I figured out the situation, I tried to turn my job into something more engaging. I sweet-talked the local police officers of all the bigger towns, the ones with at least a thousand inhabitants, into telling me first if anything noteworthy, anything outside the norm, happened.

"One afternoon, the newspaper sent me to the castle of Púbol because they were exhibiting a Salvador Dalí painting at the painter's museum and home. They'd purchased it, or recovered it, or whatever it was. The situation was that I was photographing the authorities in front of the oneiric scene, self-satisfied for having managed to bring the painting back home, and I noticed my cell phone vibrating in my back pocket. I didn't even silence the call. I let it vibrate while I met all those people who were so happy to be seen. The phone stopped ringing, and then after a bit, it started up again. When I had a chance, I stepped away from the group, and I got on the phone. The Gualta police advised me to head to the Ter River estuary, that I'd find content for the newspaper. If I hurried, I'd be the first one there. Where exactly? I didn't have to go as far as the beaches. I just had to follow the last stretch of the river. At the dike, he told me. You'll find it. He didn't give me any more clues. I'd never gone so fast on my motorcycle. I passed cars in a continuous line. I was aerodynamic. A Valentino Rossi of sorts. I felt important, like a journalist, for the first time. Starting at the Gualta cross, I guessed the rest of the way. At the plain, with the river always on my left side, I could already see the police car with the blue lights. I had it. I got off my motorcycle, took off my helmet, and prepared my camera. I let it hang over my jacket, and confidently, I went for my Pulitzer.

"'What's going on there?' I asked.

"'*Exitus letalis.*'

"I didn't understand.

"'A cadaver,' he clarified.

"The police officer who had called me pretended he didn't know me. The body was turned over, head in the water, feet floating. From where I stood, I couldn't see the body very well. The scene was hidden by reeds. To take the picture, I would have to walk into the marsh.

"'We can't touch him until the judge arrives,' the youngest officer said.

"'But maybe he's not dead,' I said.

"'Why do you think—'

"'How do you know? How can you be so sure?'

"I'd made them hesitate. I saw how they looked at each other, and without saying anything further, I guessed what they were about to do. Both officers walked with their boots into the water. They had decided to let the head surface. I was prepared. As soon as they turned him over, I would photograph nonstop. I put the viewfinder to my eye and my finger on the shutter. It was hard for them to carry the man's body, and it was as heavy as a . . . *One, two, three.* They coordinated their movements and turned him, and I began photographing. It was my father. His face had been disfigured by blows. There was blood everywhere. They immediately let him fall back into the water.

"'You convinced enough, man?' my police friend asked, drying his hands on his thighs.

"'Killed dead. That's a murder,' said the other one.

"'Are you okay? You've gone pale.'

"I sat on the ground with my face in my hands. I don't remember anything else. Only the horror of seeing my father, of seeing him in that way, and of having photographed him as if he were a piece of meat for the news. My father. I had said good night to him before bed, and the next time I saw him . . .

"'What's the matter? You've never seen a dead man before?'

"'They really roughed this guy up.'

"With my head between my knees, I was crying so hard that I had no air left.

"'It's no big deal. What'd you know him, or something?'

"I shook my head between sobs. Desperate. It was three days later—after the burial, the funeral orations, and the last 'Our Father'—that Marcel began to put things together. With time, patience, and perseverance and by speaking with everyone, he chased the truth. Our father hadn't known how to stop. Caught up in the game, his debts had hanged him. In the end, his Fontclara friends were right. 'Pep, this is snowballing.' My father had paid the price of not returning everything he'd owed. He'd lost it all, and he still owed a ton. And someone wanted to call in his debts. Who did it? Marcel hopes one day it'll all come to light. Poor innocent man."

"And what about you? What'd you do to your film?" Barbara asked, putting her hand on top of his.

"I blurred it. Immediately. When I got home that same afternoon, I grabbed my camera and opened it so everything would go black. I didn't have the gall to develop it. I didn't want to see my father's face destroyed again. I wish I hadn't seen it. I wish I hadn't gone. They would have killed him either way, but the memory would be completely different. He'd had a problem, and we didn't know how to help him."

"Oh my god, Roger." Barbara took her hand off of his, slid closer to him, and put her hand on his shoulder sympathetically. "You have no idea how sorry I am to know this whole story."

A new touch. Trust. All of a sudden, closeness.

"Throughout the years, you think about a lot of things. A lot. Addiction is one thing, an obsessive disorder. It's another thing for your father to be murdered."

"And for them to tell you to just let it go."

"Narbona Fruits." He smiled resignedly. "The best in Girona. And the rotten apple at home. And we didn't know how to see it. You know what the saddest part is? You ask yourself at what point your father went from being a hero to an obituary in an announcements page of a local newspaper."

"Don't get angry at yourself."

"It's easy to say, but . . ."

"The scars, huh?"

"They're always there."

"They stop hurting eventually, but they always sting to remind us of who we are."

17

The Lie of Valldemossa

Barbara and Roger resigned themselves to the isolation of the day and waited for night to come. They had created their own moment. One of them was there to listen to the story, the other to tell it. With both of them forced to stay inside, the hours waiting for confession passed slowly.

"If we had a television . . ."

"Do we need one?"

"Maybe it'd keep us a bit more occupied during the day," said Roger, who walked around the house wearing a Scottish rugby team jersey he'd found in his brother's wardrobe.

"If we had a television, we'd be hysterical," Barbara started. "The countdown to normality would never end. All day, specialists would be telling us theories to efficiently get rid of the snow. Each cleverer than the last. But in practice, not a single one of them would work, because nothing like this has happened in Paris. That's for sure; everyone would have lessons to teach. Everyone would know it all. And, all the while, they'd be instilling fear in us. They'd update us to the minute on the number of deaths due to the snow. They'd put a counter on the screen. People would begin to die of hunger because they've run out of food in their pantry. They'd tell us how many roofs have caved in per minute, how many homeless people have frozen to death . . . Every hour, they'd update us on the number of heart attacks they weren't able to assist because there was no way for ambulances to get to the victim's household. And every other hour, they'd repeat that the economy was plummeting. How great would that be, huh? Do you really need the constant catastrophic reporting? Would all that help the snow melt sooner? Are you interested in knowing that the GDP is plummeting further and further each day we're caged in at home?"

"You don't have a television, but it's almost like you do."

"So, we can't do anything? Then, let's have some peace and quiet. My grandmother said it yesterday when I called her: *Be patient.*"

"Lucky you," he said snidely, provoking her.

Barbara took a moment to react.

"What do you mean by 'lucky you'?"

"You have a job, and you can do it, because you're used to working from home."

"Look, I think a couple of days in the house from time to time without having to see anyone is good for you. If it were me, I'd make it a tradition. It wouldn't be so bad."

"Don't count on me. If this lasts a couple more days, I'll jump out the window. Why are you looking at me like that? You don't think I can? It's only five floors."

At lunchtime, Roger warmed up some fish *vol-au-vent* he'd found in the back of the freezer. He preferred not to look at the expiration date. Two per person, and that was that. In the afternoon, while the sun began to set, Barbara—on her second day in a row wearing that long, blue onesie—played music in the living room. Ella Fitzgerald's luminous voice singing "Summertime" in the midst of so much snow sounded more like a wish than an authentic contradiction. Barbara, carefree, hummed some songs Roger didn't know. Music and the Narbona family never went hand-in-hand. This proved even more so for jazz because of its unpredictability.

All of a sudden, midsong, Fitzgerald's liveliness went silent. The lights and music went out. They were left in the dark; the fuses in the house had probably gone out. The oven clock was dark, as well as the microwave's, and the fridge let out a sharp cry of surrender. The light disappeared like it was the end of the world, without warning.

"Shit."

Barbara turned on her cell phone's flashlight and went into the utility closet near the door. She waited for the circuit breaker to restart. But from what she could tell, the dials seemed to be in the right place. Nothing was out of order.

"Everything looks good here." She opened the door of the house to look out on the floor. The stairwell had also gone dark. "It looks like it's not just our apartment. The whole building is in the same boat."

Careful not to trip, Roger approached the window and looked out onto the street.

"There's no light outside either." He put his forehead against the glass. "I'd say the building across from us is the same. You can't see anything. Not a single light anywhere. From what I can see, at least three streets are in the dark."

"Are rue Chappe and Tardieu in the dark? As if things weren't bad already. A mass blackout." She let herself fall back onto the couch. "That's just what we needed. We can only hope it doesn't take too long to go back on."

"Weren't you the one talking about patience and calmness?"

Barbara threw a pillow at him.

After a while, the apartment telephone rang. It was a confused Jasper. He asked if the lights had gone out for her too. Barbara offered to go down to the second floor in case he needed anything. It wasn't necessary at the moment. She insisted he not hesitate to call should he need anything. The man was just worried about what would happen to the food in the freezer if the blackout lasted long.

"I'm sure it'll be short, Jasper. We'll be back up and running in no time."

Barbara could not have made a living as a prophet. The whole street was still in the dark three hours later. Based on what they said on the radio—thank goodness Mamie had still kept things in the apartment that ran on batteries—it seemed like the blackout had left the neighborhoods of Montmartre, la Villette, and a part of the ninth arrondissement in the l'Opèra zone without electricity.

The worst thing was that without electricity, there wasn't any heating.

They handled it well for the first hour. Then, they began to feel the effect of the two degrees the external thermometer read. Barbara walked through the apartment with a blanket around her like a cape. Roger, stone-like, said he was fine, until a shiver ran up his spine. "It's colder on the higher floors," Barbara lamented. In the end, she had to admit Mamie was right when it came to a phrase she'd heard her repeat plenty of times. Her grandmother had complained on more than one occasion about another reality, which was that the windows of old attic apartments don't close the way they should. So they had no choice but to accept the cold that froze them down to the bone, and cross their fingers that the electricity would come back again and they wouldn't have to sleep in cold sheets. Her grandmother didn't have a phrase about sleeping in damp, cold sheets, but she'd had a lot of experience doing it during wartime.

"If my father were here," Roger couldn't help saying, "I'm sure he'd bet the house on when the electricity would come back on."

"Is today the national day of dark humor?"

"You know what?" Roger said, wrapped in a blanket at the end of the sofa. "We look like two old people awaiting death, sitting here in the dark. Waiting for death to come collect us. The bus that won't come no matter how long we wait."

"You're a crackpot when you want to be. Have you ever been married?"

"What's that about? Are you seriously asking? Never . . . I'm too young to bury myself alive. I haven't run out of time. You're right about one thing, though." He wondered whether he should continue. "I've gotten to the age where I realize I'm better off dressed than naked."

"Oh wow." It was the last thing Barbara expected to hear come from Roger's mouth. "It wasn't like that until recently?"

"No. The other day, I was looking at myself and thinking . . ."

"Look, honey, don't be such a show-off. You're acting French."

"Well, on my mother's side, yes, there's something to that."

"How old did you say you were?"

"Me?"

"Yes."

"Thirty-three. And it's true. Until recently, I looked at myself, and—"

"Hold the phone, man. Don't be an idiot. Because if you're better off dressed at thirty-three, I should be wearing a giant coat that covers me to my feet so no one sees me."

"Come on. You look really good, Barbara."

They were silent. One for having said it, the other for having heard it. But they couldn't see each other in the dark. They could only make out an outline of discomfort.

"You know no one's said anything like that to me since long before my divorce?"

He thought about adding "I didn't mean to offend you" or "You really look good . . . for your age, I mean," but he held himself back. This wasn't the time to say either inappropriate remark. He tried to change the subject. It was called "thinking on your feet."

"Based on what you said the other day, it was a bad divorce, huh?"

"No. The divorce was fine. The marriage was what was cursed. Do you want me to tell you about it?"

"Barbara, I . . . The night has become gloomy. You said so yourself. We don't have anything else to do."

"It was good for me to tell you about my parents' accident."

"Whatever you need." With an argument like that, Roger had no way to escape.

"One second." Barbara had an idea.

She lit two candlesticks and put them on her desk. At least, in the flickering light, they'd become something more than two presences in the shadows. She curled up on the sofa with her legs underneath her, like a cat rolled into a ball. She wrapped herself in a second blanket and decided to tell the story where love and heartbreak were like two communicating vessels.

"I said my marriage was damned. If we were to think about it, maybe they all are, right? Mine was, for sure. The problem is I didn't realize it until it was too damn late. The most frustrating thing is . . . It all was, really. But when you row out, hoping to take the boat to port willingly and selflessly, and then you realize that he jumped ship, knowing that, when he wanted to, he'd rock it until he flipped it over. That will kill you with rage.

"When I met Maurice, I was running away from an absurd relationship. Alfred, who I had dated for two years, moved to Rome for work. He restored works of art, and if there's any city where there are Madonnas, saints, and sculptures ready for repair, it's that one. I figured he'd be there a couple of years. We saw each other less and less, our letters spread out over time, and slowly we realized the relationship wasn't going anywhere. I was the one who suggested letting it go, and honestly, he didn't put up much of a fight. I left happy. I had already met Maurice at some mutual friends' party. We agreed to meet for coffee near the amphitheater, and he seemed like a very neat guy, one who shaved every day and tied his tie in a thick knot, the English style, the way I liked it at the time. He looked like a new style of socialist secretary, far from the old way of doing politics. He looked like a secretary, but he was actually a peddler. And like all salesmen, he had a silver tongue, he was nice, and he knew how to win someone over with his words. He didn't pawn off an insurance plan on me, but after chatting for hours on hours, walking around the Camargue, he sold himself. And I bought him. Completely. Without even thinking twice.

"When she met him, my mother asked, 'You mean to tell me Maurice is the one?' Those maternal doubts, expressed in a contempt that could have been hidden, made me think he might be my soulmate. Mamie Margaux, who met him on the first Christmas he stopped by to say hello, winked at me midsnack to show her approval. I didn't need my grandmother's approval, but knowing he had it confirmed to me that I'd gotten it right this time. Because Maurice was macho, strong, brave, and robust. And a little bit of a show-off too. For example, my grandmother had always doubted that Alfred liked women. And now I can say she was right.

"I got married to Maurice—damn the date—the next spring. I don't like talking about it, but however things may be now, I felt like I was floating that whole day. I let myself be guided, and it was like I was on a soft cotton cloud. It was a sunny Friday, not a hint of wind. The day I'd dreamed of. We celebrated at a restaurant Maurice knew through personal connections near the mouth of the Rhône. Everyone said the location was idyllic, the food delicious, and the service impeccable. Waste of a party, waste of a dress, and waste of money that everyone spent. I'll just say, in a fit of rage, I burned the picture albums.

"At that time, everything was sunshine and roses.

"On my birthday, March 10, 1998, the first one since our wedding, he took me on a road trip. We left Arles and went up some paths near vineyards, and when it seemed like there were only about twenty minutes of light left, he stopped the motor. He told me not to move. He got out of the car—we had a Volvo with a big rear back then—and he went to the trunk. He came back with a bottle of champagne and two glasses. The champagne was cold, and surprised, I asked him how he'd done it. He told me there was a little fridge in the trunk, and I thought it was strange I'd never seen it. He'd borrowed it for the occasion, he said. And, caught up in the emotion of the moment, I forgot this detail that was probably the least of my worries. At that moment of toasting, amid the rows of grapevines, with an orange sky that exists only in Provence at the end of winter, Maurice was enchanting. He looked me in the eyes, kissed me on the neck, and whispered something I've never forgotten.

"'Think about something that made you happy today, think about something that's made you laugh in the last year, and think about a magnificent place you've seen in your lifetime.'

"I thought it was a splendid gift. The questions merited a bit of thought. I knew the response to the first question. That game, brought up like it was improvised, had made me happy on my birthday. It was original, personalized, and had me thinking. The whole situation, the champagne, the sunset, he in his most seductive pose . . . Sometimes the best gifts can't be unwrapped.

"What had been something that made me laugh in the last year? Him. It was him again. So many times. I could choose any of them. I went on about a night we'd gone bowling. And he, pretending to be a pro, had slid halfway down the lane. He couldn't stop rolling. His fingers had gotten stuck in the three holes, and when he went to throw the ball, he couldn't let go and followed with it, skating into the lane. The heavily waxed parquet flooring had done the rest of the job. When he got up off the floor, everyone who was at the alley, of which there were many, applauded him. And he got up like he was part of a show. He even waved like a gymnast at the end of an exercise, and I laughed so hard. I just couldn't stop.

"The magnificent place? I hadn't traveled much, and the Hébrards weren't the type to go to exotic locations. I chose Sainte-Maxime. The first summer I was alone with my grandmother in a hotel. The Centrum. One room for both of us. I was still a girl. One night, acting naughty, we ate ice cream for dinner on the beach. There was a stand that looked out on the sea. We stayed there for a while under the shade of the awning, sitting with our feet in the sand. It got dark, and we didn't need anything else. Mamie's voice, company before an impossible blue, salt on our skin, the absence of fear. If you asked me now what kind of ice cream it was, I couldn't remember. But I could tell you any flavor, and they'd all be true. That's the thing about half-remembered memories—we can put them together the way we want. And exaggerate them. Literature is full of stories like that.

"At that time, as a newlywed, I started my job at Giresse and Trésor. I worked out of the small office on the outskirts of Arles. I hadn't started selling international rights for writers yet. That came a little later, but it did let me earn money without the anxiety of looking at my bank account two times a week. Maurice and I split the rent for our apartment in half. We both agreed, and we did it the best way we could. If we split the painting, if we split the living expenses, then we could split the payment. That was my reasoning. He was the first one to insinuate that he could do it all on his own, but he must have seen my rage, and when it came to these matters, he never put up a fight or ever brought it up again. I liked that his family had money but didn't make a big deal of it. He was never ostentatious, however things may be.

"Maurice had an insurance brokerage. His father had started the business, and he'd taken it over. He had an office right in the center of the city. On the ground floor. They had about twenty employees on payroll, but he was the best one. He had a talent for selling you an insurance plan you didn't need: he insured your new car against all risks, he drew up contracts for your house, he sold you life insurance in case you died, or he made you sign up for funerary insurance so your benefactors didn't have to pay a cent when it came to burying you, incinerating you, or arranging the coffin, the prayer cards, the funeral vehicle, and the Bible verse. But Maurice and his father didn't make money with all that, which would have meant charging pinches of commission here and there; rather, the primary moneymaker, the rib-eye, was the business insurance. They went around selling policies to all the big and midsize companies in the area. There was a time when they covered around ninety percent of the big factories in the whole Provence region up to Marseilles. One thing was they never lacked money. I spotted it right away, but his dirty business was the full extent of the fine print. He always told me I was a person of letters, but he was even more so. Because when there's a fire, you have to read and reread the contract until you find the clause that can perhaps excuse you from compensating someone. 'That doesn't count. That's not covered.' I heard him say those two sentences most over the phone in our near seven years of marriage. Seven years of comedy. Our failure was clearly not covered by a policy either. It was stated but not signed. Go fuck yourself. Insurance for divorce doesn't exist. That's an insurance that is truly needed, but they don't do it. You see that only in the über-rich of Hollywood, who sign prenups just in case. As if love can be stamped onto a contract, right?

"I ignored my first suspicions of Maurice. Don't ask me why. I already had them on our honeymoon. Don't laugh, Roger, I see you . . ."

"I won't say anything . . ."

"We went to Mallorca for a week for our honeymoon. Seven nights in three different hotels. First Palma, then a hotel where all the stars hung over Cap de Formentor, and then to finish, a small hotel in Valldemossa, which is the one I liked the most. We had a suite that, if you looked out on the terrace, faced the fields of Chopin's house. Everything was well placed, in order, perfect. We arrived after lunch. Once there, once we were settled in and I had changed into something more comfortable to relax in the room, he said, 'I'm going out to stretch my legs.' It's true, he did ask me to accompany him. But now, after all these years and having rewritten the story a thousand and one times in my mind, I'm convinced he said it because he knew I would be too lazy to change. In short, he left for a walk. A long walk. He took so long I started to worry. More than worry; it's more accurate to say I become anxious. But I stopped myself from calling him. We hadn't strayed more than four feet apart since the wedding, and I didn't want him to think that, the first time we separated, even if it was for a little while, I was already trying to control him. I wouldn't have liked it if he had done that. And so, I waited. For a long time. After an hour and a half of me memorizing every molding on the ceiling of the room, I couldn't hold back anymore. I called him. I did it from the room telephone. It rang. *Doesn't mean anything,* I thought. *Someone's called him about some work matter, and he's had to help.* Fifteen minutes later—or maybe ten minutes hadn't even passed—I called again. I didn't want to call him from my cell phone, and I tried doing it again from the phone on my nightstand. Nothing. It kept ringing. I showered to rid myself of the bad mood that had set in, and I thought he'd come back when he wanted to. Right as I turned off the water, he entered through the door.

"'My love?' he shouted.

"'I'm over here.'

"I had showered with the sliding door open so the mirror didn't steam and—who am I kidding—so I could hear him if he returned while I showered. I waited for him to come say hi and give me a kiss. But he sat on the armchair next to the bed and turned on the TV. Wearing my damp bathrobe, I went over to sit on his lap.

"'I've been a little worried,' I said docilely.

"'About me? Oh, you're all wet, darling.'

"'You took a while.' I plopped a kiss on him. 'How far did you go?'

"'Not far. A walk around town, you know . . . It's beautiful, the whole thing. The whole place has all these colors and vegetation similar to the ones at home, don't you think?'

"Maurice said that. Maurice, who never again made another comment on the landscape. Never. In seven years.

"'I thought, where must my husband be . . .' I unbuttoned his shirt and ran two fingers along his chest. 'I thought, I hope he hasn't been kidnapped now that I've found the love of my life . . .'

"'That would be some bad luck, yes.'

"'I also thought, I hope work hasn't called him and is bothering him in the middle of his honeymoon.'

"'Me? No, no. What do you mean? I haven't spoken to anyone.'

"I pulled on a hair on his chest like I was playing. He was undaunted.

"'Oh, sorry!' I apologized innocently.

"'Someone did call me.' His reaction was delayed. 'A number from Spain, but I didn't want to answer. It must have been a wrong number.'

"'Of course.'

"Ten seconds later, which passed by slowly, like a Spanish procession, he returned the kiss and said, 'If you were so worried, you should have called me, woman.'

"He had the gall to say, 'If you were so worried, you should have called me, woman'!

"When we returned from Mallorca, all my friends wanted to see pictures from the wedding and asked me to explain the trip in full detail. The one I trusted the most was Mireille. More than trust, it was a real friendship. She was a former classmate who had gone through every year of school with me. Her parents were like my parents, and everyone said we looked alike. We weren't twins, but there was something to it. In the way we wore our hair down to our shoulders, in the way we laughed with our eyes, or how, both of us being the expressive types, we tended to speak with our hands. Sometimes doesn't it happen that best friends begin to resemble each other without pretending? It's true that after so many hours spent together as children and on several family vacations over the weekends, Mireille and I had become copies of each other. I knew that if I wanted to rid myself of my suspicions, I could do it only with Mireille. Only with her and no one else. In a moment of intimacy with Mireille, I hinted at it. She didn't let me finish.

"'Impossible,' she said. 'Get it out of your head.' And she said it so forcefully, I listened. 'You'll start off on the wrong foot if you begin with jealousy. You've never been jealous,' she continued. And she was right. I even felt guilty. 'Forget about this episode, for the love of God.' I listened. I didn't think about it again until, years later, the clues became evident. That had been the first lie. The lie of Valldemossa. There's always one that's the first. And then, it's hard to stop them."

"It must be addictive too," Roger said.

"In his case, I'm sure. The whole relationship was a lie. From beginning to end."

Roger waited to hear the inventory of lies up to the divorce. But it didn't happen. Barbara got up from the couch, carrying the blanket on her shoulders, and let out a yawn that dominated her.

"The breakup is for tomorrow, my friend."

"Come on. It's not even late yet."

"Do you understand how the king from *One Thousand and One Nights* felt now?"

"Hoodwinked?"

"Curious. You know what the book says? 'The arrival of dawn surprised Scheherazade, and then she went silent.'"

"Come on . . ."

Roger's protests were in vain.

"You did it to me too. And I waited."

"But Barbara, if you leave the story of your divorce on a cliff-hanger, you'll have nightmares. And in this cold. And as dark as tonight will be."

"'The arrival of dawn surprised Scheherazade, and then she went silent.'"

18

Robotic Love

Never had the people of Montmartre, la Villette, and a part of the arrondissement of l'Opèra wanted the sun to come out more. They'd spent the whole night without light, and those who lived in apartments where the heating depended on electricity were freezing. Dawn was expected to come at seven thirty, but any setback was possible in Paris during those strange, strange days. The day began with fog—impertinent and stubborn—and until the sun shone through the window and warmed them up a bit, they continued chattering their teeth. At least in rooms with windows, people could see, and there was a smaller risk of bumping into something in your path.

The light from the interior courtyard delayed in penetrating Roger's room. He was woken by the vibration of his phone, which he'd laid on top of his open suitcase on the floor. He'd plugged it in to charge, hoping that, during the night, electricity would have returned. It was the best way to test it.

When he opened his eyes, he hardly recognized himself. He hadn't worn socks to bed in years. But not even the bedspread and a blanket on top of that were enough. In fact, at midnight, he'd woken up to put on socks and the first sweater he could find in his brother's wardrobe.

He let the phone ring for a bit before it stopped. Seeing that it began again to ring thirty seconds later, he finally looked to see who was calling.

"Hey, toga man. Good morning. Can I know why you're calling so early?"

"Early, you say? It's eleven in the morning in Toulouse. Is it different in Paris?"

"What's up, Marcel?"

"Nothing. All good."

"You seem . . . euphoric."

"Yeah. The judgment's been called. Well, it hasn't been called, but it's been filtered down to me. That's France for you—money talks."

"And?"

"We won the case. And we don't even have to cover the costs."

"Oh man, that's great. Congrats. I'm happy for you."

Roger pretended to be happy without knowing what the case was about, who Marcel's client was, what they'd been accused of, or why the judge had taken so long. All he knew was that Marcel had called him one day to tell him he was going to Toulouse, that he'd be gone from Paris for a couple of weeks, maybe more, and that he was leaving Roger his room, which had already been paid for, if he wanted to come work on his photography project funded by the Girona art school.

Marcel continued. "You know what that means?"

"You'll get a raise?"

"No."

"They'll make you a partner at the firm?"

"For now, not that either. I wish. It means I'm coming back to Paris."

"When?"

"Tomorrow."

"No way, Marcel . . . Tomorrow? What world do you live in? Haven't you seen we've been locked up at home? That we can't even leave?"

"It's not that big of a deal."

"No. No. I swear. No one can go anywhere here. We haven't had power since yesterday. The snow is blocking the exits. It's incredible. Surreal. It's not that they're keeping us from leaving. There's no way of even trying. I'm sure you've seen it. There's no metro, no public transportation, no anything. Even if you wanted to, you can't come back."

"Roger . . ."

"What?"

"I know you as well as if I'd given birth to you, *tete*. You don't want me to come to Paris."

"That's not it."

"What's wrong? You haven't finished your work yet?"

"I've left one thing unfinished. That's true."

Marcel opened up a second line of investigation. "You're in love . . ."

"Yeah, with the cactus. What do you want me to—"

"But the room is mine, okay? By the way, is everything okay with Barbara?"

"Resigned, you know, just like everyone else. Locked up. No choice."

"Nice lady, too. She does her own thing. Doesn't bother . . ."

"Yeah." Roger was looking for the right word. "She's great."

"This whole time I've been staying at a hotel near the Palais de Justice in Toulouse. Three stars, comfortable, small. I can't complain. But I want to have my things, my wardrobe. What the hell. And I have to go back to work in Paris. Roger? Can you hear me?" he asked, noticeably confused by the silence over the phone. "Hello? Roger?"

"I think . . . Why don't you go see Mom for a couple of days? Until all this shit melts, and the mayor gives us permission to return to normal life. How long has it been since you visited Fontclara?"

"Listen, how about we do this? I'll get myself updated on everything going on in Paris. It's been days since I've even glanced at a newspaper, what with this hell of a judgment and final arguments, and I'll take a look at when I can head back. Keep thinking about what you want to do with your life. We won't be sharing my bed."

"Obviously not."

They hung up.

Shit.

He would have liked a nice hot shower to wake himself up and stamp out the cold, but the hot water tank was depleting, and this joke of a situation had gone too far.

He didn't tell Barbara about his call with Marcel. She'd heard on the radio that people would maybe be allowed to circulate the city in two days. Maybe. If it didn't snow again, of course, and if the temperatures rose a bit and helped melt the blocks of ice that turned blacker each day. "Maybe": the flake's adverb. And that is if the town hall finally managed to work the machines that clearly weren't prepared for precipitation of such great magnitude or duration, which had been punishing Paris in the middle of an era of human vanity. The extreme meteorological phenomenon had become a reality check for everyone.

"Did they say anything on the radio about when we'll get the electricity back?"

"Not until they fix the tower that fell."

"It's embarrassing. I thought these kinds of things happened only in my country."

"I'm worried about the fridge and the freezer. Either we eat everything that's been thawing or . . ."

"But how are we supposed to cook? We can't."

The very minute the domestic despair had set foot in Barbara's apartment, the lights went back on. Suddenly, like a miracle. The way angels arrive, without anyone hearing them. Suddenly, all the technology in the house was up and running. The oven, the computer next to the window, the phone chargers. The microwave clock, at 00:00, celebrated the return of the electrical current with intermittent flickering.

"I'm going to shower first," Roger said, pleadingly.

"I didn't know it was a competition. But I have to start working now that the computer is back on."

Roger conceded that he could wait. In the end, he didn't have anything to do. And plus, he knew the apartment was Barbara's, and he was only a tenant in the room, and for free, on top of it all.

Under the hot water, Barbara got rid of the cold that had settled inside her bones. She was in no rush to leave the stream of water rinsing out the soap and her ideas. She dried her hair with the blow dryer for a change, and, after three days of having not done so, she dressed like she was leaving the house, with black jeans and matching boots and, on top, a green button-down blouse. She let the back of the shirt hang low, like a loincloth over her pants. She tucked it into her pants from the front, casually.

She was comfortable around the house all day. It was only in the evening, once she lit the two candles and saw Roger sitting on the sofa awaiting the nightly story, that she took off her boots. Barefoot and massaging the soles of her feet, she picked up the narrative surrounding the events of her marriage with Maurice.

"Our apartment in Arles had four bedrooms. The one with the queen bed was the biggest and had one of the two bathrooms in the house. The guy from the real estate agency who rented it to us called it a suite: '3A has four bedrooms, one of which is a suite.' The advertisement made it sound nice. Maybe the space had its pretension, for sure, but for me, 'suite' was a word that had the connotation of a certain luxury. And our bedroom was a functional space, and that was it. We slept there, we showered there, we got dressed there, and with increasingly less frequency, we made love there. He preferred nights, and I preferred lazy weekend afternoons.

"The room in the back, the only one that didn't face the street, was the junk room. There we stuffed our seasonal clothing, suitcases, the ladder, the ironing board, and all the bulky things that would have been a nuisance anywhere else or weren't for everyday use. After that, in the two small bedrooms that were for kids if we ever had them, there was a small desk for each of us. We also split that in half. He wasn't the type to bring work home, but he did accumulate a ton of paperwork, which he had organized in different colored boxes to separate the receipts for the house, the car, and the bank statements he had saved his whole adulthood, just in case. The liar's little boxes. He had it all nicely labeled so he knew where anything was at any given moment. He never threw anything out. He stored his writings in a big safe in the corner of his desk. It served as a chest of drawers, on top of which he placed a framed photo of us next to one of his parents' fiftieth wedding anniversary. He was the only one who knew the combination to the safe. I remember he told me when he first bought it, and he showed me how to turn the lock however many times to the right until I heard a click and however many times to the left until I heard the final click. If I ever wanted to safeguard my nice rings, I would've had to ask him to open it for me. Looking back now, I very much doubt he would have let me see what he kept inside.

"My desk, on the other hand, was a refuge of half-read books. I had nice lighting, an ergonomic chair for people who spend hours in front of a screen, and a computer dating back to the fall of Rome. I didn't spend much time there, because I was mostly at the company office. When you begin working somewhere new, you want to immerse yourself in the business. You're curious about everything. You want to volunteer for any task, and you never leave on time. If there's anything Maurice and I had in common, it was that we were both in some ways workaholics, and we were lucky to be happy doing what we did. We were never in a rush to get home.

"Maybe I should have realized that was a sign. If you're not dying to go home and take off your shoes, say hi, and be with your partner, something is wrong. If you decide not to have kids—because, 'Barbara, we're fine the way we are'—that's another sign the road ends at a cliff.

I didn't know how to pick up on all those things at the time. That was one of his favorite phrases: 'We're fine the way we are.' He said it whenever we talked about taking the next step, going after it, because I was starting to get older . . . Just imagine it, I got married at thirty-one, and by thirty-three, I started to think I was getting too old to have a child. Today they'd practically give me a prize for having a kid so young. We didn't have one, because he lathered me up with another lie. It wasn't that we were fine the way we were, like he said, but rather that having a child together would have meant a permanent link to me. And he, from what I would see later, had ties somewhere else for quite a while.

"I wanted to discuss it with my friend Mireille. We agreed to go out shopping one Saturday afternoon like we'd done so many times before, and between the stores, I invited her for a Sacher torte at a pastry shop we loved.

"'Maurice and I are going through a phase right now that . . .'—I didn't know how to define it—'it's not boredom.'

"'Routine, maybe?'

"'No. It's a robotic love. I've been thinking about it, and if it's robotic, it's not love,' I said.

"'You're always playing with words and adjectives. You can tell you're well read.'

"'Yeah, I'm in the industry. But do you get what I mean, or no?'

"'From what you're telling me, it's nothing that hasn't happened to every couple in human history, Barbara.'

"'That's a shitty consolation, then.' She unsettled me, but I continued. 'So, it happens to you and Robert too?'

"'Oh, of course.'

"We were silent for a long moment. She ate, and I searched for the concept, looking out the window. I grasped it, more or less.

"'Everyone knows how that stuff works in marriages, Mireille. I watched my parents, until . . . In the end, I've seen so many couples who go from ecstasy to plodding along forever . . . and they resign themselves to it. I already know all that. I'm not naive.'

"'What do you mean?'

"'I think that Maurice and I have gone too quickly from passion to cohabitation, from love to friends, and from friendship to roommates.'

"'Roommates . . . with the benefit of sleeping together on weekends.'

"'It's not that.' I stabbed my fork into the slice of Sacher torte I was sharing with Mireille. 'I think there's something else.'

"And then, in a rampage, I shared the squash story. Ever since Maurice had taken the reins of his father's insurance brokerage, he'd decided that Fridays would be intensive workdays. They wouldn't stop for lunch, everyone would stay until three, they'd leave earlier, and that way, the employees could feel like they'd started the weekend early. It was a pact of good faith with employees; it's always good to keep them happy. That was Maurice's motto. Knowing I didn't leave work until seven in the evening, he took advantage of Friday afternoons to play squash. He was a good player for an amateur. He had a knack for sports. He'd taken tennis lessons when he was young, and when squash became a thing, he signed himself up, because he could play even when it rained due to it being indoors and, overall, because he always had the theory that you could work off all the week's stress after playing for an hour. Squash tests your limits. It's like an intense bomb to the heart. And, of course, you're able to de-stress and get rid of a bad mood by swinging the racket and slamming the ball against the glass. He always came home exhausted, and when he took out his dirty clothes from his bag, you could wring out his shirt and pants because they were absolutely soaked.

"'Eight days ago,' I told Mireille, 'I left work to take a couple of packages to the post office near the courts where Maurice plays.' Because it was Friday, I figured he'd be on the court from five to six, and I could surprise him. As much of a show-off as he was, I thought he'd be happy I went to see him play. I entered the club confidently without stopping at reception. The only person there was taking court reservations over the phone. I waved at her, but the woman didn't even see me pass. The eight courts looked occupied. There were four on the ground floor, and four more on the second. The ringing of the balls hitting rackets resounded throughout the whole space. Sometimes, you'd hear a shoe braking suddenly on the parquet floor or the yell of a player working his ass off to save a point. I did not find Maurice or anyone I knew on the bottom floor. I went up to the second floor. The lights of three of the courts were on. It looked like a men's club. There wasn't a single woman on any of the courts. It was 5:45 p.m. according to the digital clock in the hall. My husband wasn't on the fifth or seventh or eighth court. The sixth court was empty, with the door open and the fluorescent lights turned off. I went back down to the ground floor to make sure I had seen correctly and that Maurice wasn't playing in any of those four games. Then, I thought maybe they had taken the sixth court, he'd won the game early, and he was now in the locker room, showering after his victory. I waited for him at the bar. For fifteen minutes. Then for half an hour. I was there until seven. But no one appeared. I went back to reception. The woman was on the phone again, and I waited.

"'Excuse me, can I pay for Maurice Papin's court?'

"She looked at the map of the courts and reservations and stuck out her lower lip.

"'What court was it?'

"'I think number six. Court six at 6 p.m. Super easy. Maurice Papin . . .'

"'No.'

"'Or maybe it was under his friend's name . . . Maybe they paid already?'

"'No. Court six canceled today. They called to say they couldn't come.'

"'Oh, you're right, they couldn't come today. It's true. I'm sorry. Thank you so much.'

"'No problem,' she responded as she handed a folded towel to a member who'd just entered.

"At seven, I headed home like I'd come from work, and I tried to act as if nothing had happened. It was impossible. I was going crazy for an hour. He came home at eight, like he usually did on Fridays. He'd showered. He was wearing the same cologne as always, a l'Eau d'Issey for men I'd given him, which had a unique smell on his skin. The same one as always. Nothing more, nothing less. He told me he was hungry. Or starving, maybe he said, I can't remember. He always came home hungry from squash.

"'While you set the table, give me your bag and I'll put your clothes in the washer,' I told him.

"He gave it to me without hesitation. It was the same bag as always. A black Adidas bag with the handle of the racket sticking out. I had given it to him the year before for Christmas. I unzipped the bag, my pulse racing at two hundred beats a minute. I was overly cautious at the risk of my imminent discovery. I was the police about to seize ten pounds of cocaine in airport security. My excitement was at a peak. Anything could go wrong in a second. Once I took out the racket, I removed two crumpled socks. A damp towel. And a sweaty shirt, pants, and underwear. I sniffed them. They were soaked, but they didn't smell. I held the shirt up against the light. The sweat stains were, more or less, where they should have been if someone with Maurice's body had played squash at maximum energy for sixty minutes. Sweat on the chest, the belly, around the armpit. I put it all in the washing machine, and I turned it on so he wouldn't hear me cry.

"Mireille listened to the whole story without dropping her jaw. When I finished, she said, 'That's all weird, Barbara. Maybe they play at another facility?'

"'In Arles? How many squash courts are you aware of?'

"'I don't know.' And then she said something that made me think. 'Why didn't you say anything to him?'

"'Because I'm stupid,' I was going to say.

"'I don't know. I've been thinking about it all week. Maybe out of fear? Out of fear of losing the part of Maurice I still have. Of course, it must be that. Or out of fear of failing a common project we'd taken on, hoping it would succeed. Out of fear of knowing the truth. Out of fear of thinking I'm living with a liar who is so sophisticated he's created alibis with criminal precision. With the coldness of a serial killer.'

"'It's not that serious, Barbara,' she said.

"'No, of course not. I hope not . . . You know why I don't say anything, Mireille? Because I love him.'

"After that, out of a matter of survival, we continued at home as if nothing had happened. The opposite even. He went back to being affectionate and in a good mood, and doing nice gestures like he had in the past. Suddenly, he was lighting scented candles in the bedroom, or he'd show up at home with half a dozen oysters for us to share—with a bit of ground pepper, which is how I like them even if it makes me sneeze. I still had that nagging feeling, but I have to admit that when he wanted to, he knew how to act. He continued the weekly squash games at the exact same hour. One Friday, he came home with a black eye, because a ball had hit him right in the face. The blue faded slowly, and when I asked him what had happened, he made a joke I didn't like at all. 'My wife hits me,' he said, laughing. The second time I heard him say it in front of some neighbors on our floor, I asked him to please never repeat that. And he would laugh all over again.

"I don't know if it was two or three months after my conversation with Mireille, but Maurice began to behave unexpectedly. He started to act jealously toward me. Can you believe it? He'd say things he'd never said before. 'Where are you going today?' 'Who are you meeting up with?' "You're home late today, huh?' Suddenly, he started asking me about Samu. Obsessively. Samuel worked at Giresse and Trésor. His job had nothing to do with mine, but it's true that we got along and chatted and sometimes had dinner together. Some days, if it was nice outside, we'd go to the park for coffee before returning to work. He was a copyeditor at the press, and sometimes he wrote reader reports. They'd send him an original manuscript from the headquarters in Paris, and after reading it, Samu would write up a three-page report. He'd summarize the work, give his opinion with critical commentary, and at the end, in bold, he'd say whether he recommended it for publication. It was a poorly paid job for so much responsibility. A good report could make a new author happy. A bad report, however, could ruin the life of an aspiring novelist who gave up at the first obstacle. Samu, who was older than I was, was an interesting man with a good sense of judgment and who knew a lot of things. We got along well. And so what? I never thought about him as anything more than a work friend. But Maurice became obsessed with him. Or maybe he just made it seem like he was. That's what I thought later, when, on the very day, I put together the timelines of events over and over again. You know how Napoleon said the best defense is a good offense?

"It got to the point that one morning Samu came to work disoriented, nervous as all hell. He came over and said to me, 'I think someone's following me.'

"'Who?'

"'Someone. A private detective.'

"'What makes you think that?'

"Maybe he'd read too many novels, but the truth was that someone in a hoodie and Reeboks had waited for him in the lobby of his house, entered the same bakery as he had to buy coffee to go, gotten on the same bus, and gotten off at the same bus stop. Too many coincidences. And he didn't seem to be hiding himself.

"'Where is he now?'

"We approached the window and pulled back the curtain to look out on the street. If the detective was on watch, we'd see him from the first floor of the building. Right as we put our noses to the glass, the hooded man took out his cell phone and shot a burst of photos. Just as we moved back from the windowsill and let the curtains go, the guy sprinted away. We lost sight of him when he rounded the corner.

"'Am I right or not?' Samuel asked, trembling. 'What do you think he wants?'

"I couldn't tell him. I kept it to myself. I knew insurance companies tended to work with spies. It's pretty standard. I suspected it was a subtle sign my husband had sent me. It was a way of controlling me, of telling me he could know everything about me. I was simply waiting for the day Maurice lit the smallest ember at home in whatever absurd argument so he could use the picture he'd just taken like it was the winning card. *Here, here's the proof. The revelation.* And I'd feel bad, trapped, about something that had more to do with him and his perverse head than me. But the setup never arrived. Right as I expected the collision to come, something worse happened. I decided to meet up with Mireille to tell her about the new incident and my husband's strange and unexpected behavior. She was up to date on everything, and I preferred confiding in only one person.

"After listening to me, she told me it was all my anxiety. It was impossible for Maurice, the sweetheart, to hire a detective to follow my colleague, and she came up with a ton of arguments to get the idea out of my head. And then, it happened. My best friend, my childhood companion from whom I hadn't been separated since I was little, like two peas in a pod, told me to relax and suggested an exercise that would make me feel better.

"'You need to calm down and think. For example, think about something that's made you happy today. Next, think about something that's made you laugh in the past year. And then, think about the most magnificent place you've ever seen. Watch how it'll help.'

"I stopped to look at her. She met my gaze with the same imbecilic smile she'd had as she made the suggestion. Our eyes connected. I said, 'Yes, that's an interesting game. I'll try it. Thanks. Let's see if the whole thing passes altogether. It'll all be okay.'

"'You'll see that it will. Sometimes you make mountains out of molehills,' she had the guts to respond to me.

"Suddenly, I put it all together. That's how I felt. There was Maurice, and there was Mireille. My best friend and my husband. Both of them damned to hell at the same time. How had I been so dumb to not realize it? How had I been so mistaken, confiding in the person who had been tricking me for who knows how long? I looked at her, so sure of herself and her dirty little secret. I didn't know what hurt me more. There couldn't have been a better infidelity than the one they had pulled behind my back. I still don't know how I didn't strangle her. She was right in front of me, and I let her go. I preferred to wait for the right moment and prepare my trap so no one could ever again say it was all my imagination.

"Halfway through January, I told Maurice what I told him every year. I came up with a plan.

"'February fourth is Mamie Margaux's birthday. Should I go up to Paris alone, or would you like to come with me so we can make a trip out of it?'

"'You should go, my love.'

"'So should I buy a ticket for myself, then?'

"I asked him all this with my laptop sitting on the living room table.

"'Go for it . . . Tell her early February is a busy work season for me.'

"'The same excuse every year.'

"'It's not a lie.'

"'At least it's consistent, you're right.'

"I continued to search for a plane ticket from Marseille to Paris, looking for the cheapest flight.

"'How old is your grandmother turning?'

"'Now, it's better not to rush if I go by myself. I'll go one day, sleep at her house, and return the next. That'll make Mamie happier.'

"'Of course. Good thinking.'

"'I'll print my boarding pass so I have it all ready. I leave on the fourth in the morning, and I'll come back on the fifth after lunch. Okay?'

"'Whatever you want, my love.'

"'Yes, that's better. That way I can stop by the company's headquarters. It'd be good to show my face.'

"The printer spit out the two boarding passes. Departure and return. I picked them up and folded them.

"'Look, how nice. This is great.' I put them in my bag. 'I have the tickets now, and I was able to score window seats on both journeys.'

"'You really like to watch the clouds outside, Barbara.'

"'It makes me feel like my parents are nearby. You know I get on planes only when I need to.'

"On the fourth of February, I came here, to this apartment, to congratulate Mamie. When she opened the door, she put on the same show she did every year. 'What a surprise. You didn't have to come, you have so much work.' And then she hugged me and planted all the kisses she hadn't been able to give me in the last few months. She loved the plant I brought her—I'd bought it at the airport—and the box of marrons glacés that I knew she'd go crazy for, with her sweet tooth. She still loves them now. That day, as you might imagine, my mind wasn't on the flight or on dinner—we went out to eat bouillabaisse at la Mère Catherine—or on anything we discussed at the table. I wouldn't be able to repeat a single thing we said that birthday. I was just thinking about what time I'd make the call. Just before I left the apartment, sitting right over here—I remember it like it was yesterday—I called Maurice from my phone. He picked up right away. I told him that Paris was fantastic, that I missed him, and in a quiet voice, I suggested he congratulate my grandmother.

"'I'll pass her over to you.' And I gave the phone to Mamie immediately.

"Maurice did as Maurice does. He was charming. He excused himself for not having visited, he insisted he was sorry, and he commented I had told him that my grandmother looked younger every year. He lied, even about that. My grandmother returned the phone to me.

"'See you tomorrow, Maurice.'

"'See you tomorrow, little rat,' he responded.

"The balls. My flight from Paris to Marseille was at seven in the evening. I was returning that night. After an hour of a lot of anxiety, I was at the Marseille Provence Airport. After two, I was back in Arles. I parked under the house in no time, the scene of the crime. Ground zero. If I had schemed as coldly as he had, if I had concocted it like him, I had only one exit. Be brave. There was no turning back.

"I entered through the lobby, got in the elevator, and went up to 3A. Our house. Until that moment, it was our house. I put the key in the lock. The scent of candles in the room, lights unusually dimmed, and the sound of water in the shower. We know the sounds of our homes with our eyes closed. The door to the bedroom was half open. Before entering, I saw the bed was undone and a pair of women's shoes. I remembered them well, because we'd bought them together. I entered the 'suite.' I exhaled all the cold air in my lungs. I sat on the bed, and holding back my sobs, I heard them having fun. Two eternal minutes of torture. All my thoughts went rushing through my head. I concentrated the anger, the hate, the bile . . . But I waited for them to turn off the water so I could say one thing.

"'Maurice, Mireille . . . I don't want you to come out.'

"Silence.

"'I don't want to see you two ever again.'

"They didn't listen to me. First, he came out, shouting to the high heavens that I was supposed to return in the morning. Then, Mireille stuck her head out, depressed, acting as though she would cry like a martyr. She ran to put on her underwear. Too late. I got up and left the room because I didn't even want them near me. From the door frame, I gave them instructions with a force from an unknown origin. I'd never given so many commands, one after the other:

"'Get dressed, get out of here, and then, do me a favor.' Both of them looked at me fearfully. 'Think of something that's made you laugh in the last year. You'll see how it'll be good for you. But don't you *ever*, ever tell me how long you've been laughing behind my back, do you understand? I don't want to know.'

"'But—'

"'Shut up.'

"'Barbara, I—'

"'Shut up. You're sons of bitches, the two of you.'

"And that's how, on Mamie's birthday, my marriage ended. But whatever. The worst is that it also ended my trust in people, even people who seem like good people."

19

Stairs Don't Go Up or Down

How do you endure the unendurable?

That night, they went to bed early. In the coldness of their beds, they asked themselves the same question. He thought about Barbara's husband's infidelity and the tragic death of her parents. Ever since she'd told him, he hadn't been able to get it out of his head. A plane takes off, flying toward a dream, and while waiting for them to call and say, "We've just arrived!" the police ring the doorbell instead to give you the news that there's been an accident and there are no survivors. From everything to nothing in half a second. Without the chance to say goodbye. Without the chance to finish a conversation. Not a word of grace. Period. The two of them, but alone. A bloodcurdling end that no one deserves and that is painful to even imagine. Who went first? Did they realize their fates?

Two absences that all of a sudden hit you—mother and father—and weigh heavily on you. How do you suffer a blow like that?

The only way you can, of course.

Wearing a man's pajama set, Barbara thought about the murder of Roger's father with her head on her pillow and her eyes closed. A cruel punishment. The spiral of game, obsession, addiction, an unstoppable whirlpool—Pep Narbona's debts grew until he ended up like waste in an irrigation canal, his head underwater. How do you move forward?

The only possible way.

Living.

Living. People look down on gerunds. Barbara had argued about it once with the copyeditors at her company, but she maintained that when gerunds were used by themselves, employed in an isolated manner, they don't indicate present or past. And all you can do after a disaster is that: live. In the margins of time, accompanied by memories, wrapped in sorrow. Once the mourning period is over, if it ever passes, you get used to moving forward and taking the only path left for you as an opportunity. The clouds are like carriages that carry you, not a punishment forcing you to drag your feet.

Between all of it, Barbara was too agitated to fall asleep. The story of her marriage kept her awake. She had worked herself up all over again, like it had happened only four days prior. She got out of bed, pulled on her sheepskin socks over her pajama pants, and walked to Roger's room. She listened closely to hear if he was snoring. Like always, the door was closed, day or night. She knocked on it with her knuckles.

"Can I come in?"

"Hey . . ."

"Are you sleeping?"

"No." He cleared his throat. "Not anymore. Come in."

She entered and stood at the foot of his bed. Roger turned on the light on the nightstand—the insipid forty-watt light bulb—and sat up.

"Is something wrong? Are you feeling okay?"

"Yes, yes, but . . . Sorry if you were sleeping."

"I wasn't, Barbara, don't worry. It was a joke. How can I expect to sleep today? I was thinking about everything you told me."

"I need to talk, if it's okay. A little bit longer still." She tried to button her pajama collar. There was neither a button nor a buttonhole. "You've heard my version."

"Sit down."

"I want you to tell me what you think. Please."

"Sit down."

She sat on the edge of the bed, as if she didn't dare go farther. Roger propped up his pillow so she could sit more comfortably. He covered himself above the waist with the comforter.

"Me? How I see it?"

"Didn't you just say you were thinking it over?"

"Nothing specific, honestly."

"I'm interested."

"Well . . ." Roger was stuck between a rock and a hard place. "It's hard to say. I don't know Maurice. My mother always used to say something: 'Judge not, that you be not judged.' She says it, but it was originally said by some saint . . . When it comes to infidelity, I guess everyone knows their own." He hesitated, not knowing what he was trying to say. "Actually, this is what it must have been like forever."

Male avoidance. The more real a conversation is, the more lost Roger became. She noticed it immediately.

"Look at me," she said, interrupting him. "I don't want compassion. Who do you think I am?"

Roger covered his nose and snorted under the blanket.

"Well, what stings to me," Roger tried again, "is Mireille's high treason, Betrayal with a capital *B*. For your best friend to do that to you. Fucked over, in the biggest way."

"I appreciate your honesty." She breathed in deeply. "I've spent plenty of months without knowing who to talk to about it."

"Has she tried . . ."

"To contact me?" She leaned over and put her head against the mattress. She sat up again. "By all means possible . . . Calls I've hung up on? A few. Two letters I've ripped up without reading. One day, she even stood at the bus stop in front of my door waiting for me to leave the house. She told me she wanted to explain herself. That she had the right to it. She asked that I please listen. I walked fast, her on my tail like a pest, begging me to give her five minutes. In the end, after ignoring her, I stopped suddenly, and I told her to get out of my face and to leave me alone forever, or I'd make sure to tell Robert, her husband, everything I'd discovered regarding her and Maurice."

"Did you do it?"

"I was tempted to on more than one occasion."

"Do you think her husband was in the know, or was he clueless?"

"Maybe he was suspicious. For my part, I don't think he knew anything." She smiled for the first time that whole night. "Directly."

They didn't talk about Maurice anymore. Or about Robert. Barbara didn't know if the couple was still together after her subtle revenge. She was done with them. She had gotten out burned enough. They talked about Mireille. Mireille and all the anxieties it had stirred up that the person who knew everything about her, who'd shared so many things with her as a girl, was the one to betray her while looking Barbara in the eyes and then laugh with her like there was nothing wrong, like she wasn't fucking Barbara's husband. She'd stopped expecting much from men. But Mireille, who'd traveled across half of Europe with her via Interrail the first time their parents let them travel alone, Mireille who'd smoked her first joint with her, whom she'd shared her most intimate secrets with at every age, who'd secretly accompanied her to the gynecologist when Barbara had contracted a vaginal infection from somewhere, who'd even consoled her when her parents died. Poor Édith and Clément had known Mireille very well. And loved her. Years ago, she'd slept over at her house plenty of times. If her parents had ever discovered that Mireille, her best friend, who'd gone with her to try on wedding dresses, turned out to be her husband's mistress . . . She couldn't count the number of times she'd processed the whole scenario from beginning to end like it was an old silent film, and she'd come to the conclusion that Mireille and Maurice had been involved even before the wedding. In fact, if she ever found herself face-to-face with Mireille again, she'd ask her a single question. Only one. The call. The long call Maurice had made from Valldemossa during their honeymoon in Mallorca. "Was it to you?"

Barbara was sure of the answer. It was precisely that intuition that caused her so much suspicion. If you can't trust the person you believe in the most, then what do you do? And since experiencing his father's death, Roger agreed with how painful the retroactive discovery can be. Because if it's difficult to find out your father is a compulsive gambler and has debts he can't pay, it's even worse to find out he's been beaten to death, and to look back and replay the last few years of his life, when the man had pretended to be one thing and turned out to be something else completely. And he added that you can't trust the world anymore when your best friend and husband are the ones who've really fucked you over. It's hard to lose the two people closest to you; it's even harder to realize you no longer have a safe place. Everything comes crashing down. So long to a friend, her husband could go to hell, and that's when all the doubts come flooding. Roger said he understood that feeling of defenselessness. Barbara discussed a subject never mentioned in the newspapers, of being able to trust people again after an experience like that. And she said that, in the end, stairs don't go up or down on their own; everything depends on us. And she told him about Simone Sicilia, how she'd been abused by her uncle, how she'd revealed it all in a book of revenge before killing herself. He asked if the book had been edited by Giresse & Trésor, and Barbara responded that it had, and he asked that she please share it with him because he wanted to read it.

"Roger. Can I ask you for one thing?"

He was silent.

"I don't want to sleep alone tonight."

He stayed quiet. He had to process if he'd understood her. Her eyes, eager for companionship in a way he'd never seen them, answered him. Roger pulled aside the comforter like a father letting his child in when they have a nightmare. As flustered as he was, he managed to say only one thing:

"On one condition. Don't bring the sheep into bed."

She laughed nervously, took off her sheepskin socks, let them fall discreetly to the floor, and surrendered to the comfort of warm sheets in no time.

She was the first one to wake up. The ray of vertical light streaming through the crack in the door was enough for her to guess the time. In fact, she hadn't been able to sleep through most of the night. It wasn't her bed, it wasn't her pillow, and she still didn't know how she'd even dared ask him to share a bed with her. Sometimes, when she turned, she'd open an eye and stare at Roger sleeping only inches from her. Little by little, the shaft of light outlined his silhouette, sketching his features. He hadn't shaved for a couple of days. The beard growing in was dark with prickly hair and matched his thick eyebrows. The joyful skin of his early thirties didn't contain a trace of wrinkles, nor did the area around his eyes. His breathing, calm, emitted the tranquility of a nonsmoker. She was in no rush for him to wake up. She liked looking at him and thinking that, without the confinement of the snowstorm, she would never have gotten to know so well this guy who'd shown up to her house only a few weeks ago with the entitlement of a karaoke bar owner. The 32nd of March had let them fill their days with conversations and moments that, under normal conditions, wouldn't have fit on the calendar.

Roger opened an eye.

"Good morning," Barbara said first.

"Good morning," he responded, clenching his eyes shut. In the nebulousness of his first waking moments, he had to think. What was Barbara doing in his bed? "Everything okay?"

"Mm-hmm," she replied.

After that guttural affirmation, she thought Roger would go back to sleep. She didn't want to bother him. She observed him for some five minutes, which passed as slowly as a turtle. When her heart had had enough, Roger woke up on his own, serene, like he'd been listening to rain. Barbara, leaning her head on her hand, her arm propped up by a pillow, waited with words on the tip of her tongue. She'd had time to think about it.

"It's been a year since I made love."

The sentence came out how she wanted it to. Blunt. Informative. Without sounding like a complaint or a desperate cry. She said it, counting her words, and let her tone do the rest.

"I don't do favors, Barbara." Then, dropping the bad joke, which had left her cold as stone, Roger wriggled over and kissed her on the lips. "I do it only when I want to. And I would love to do it right now with you."

The second kiss was longer. By the third, they were holding each other's faces, looking at each other closely with surprise, and letting their eyes laugh. And by the happiness of unexpected things that accelerate the booming of the heart, they didn't rush things under the sheets. Every piece of clothing they removed was a respectful game. All clothes off. Until, body against body, they wrapped their legs around each other and felt a new warmth. Then they hugged each other. Chest against chest, Barbara and Roger sealed a shared happiness. They needed to feel protected in each other's arms, and they made it last. Slowly, they let touch guide them down the path of desire.

By the time they melted into each other, it was noon. Once they were finished, they stayed in bed, stretched out, looking up at the ceiling and caressing each other with the door open. Surrendering to a situation that was unthinkable only a week before, they gave in to sweet dreams and short phrases. She had put on the pajama shirt without buttoning it up. She berated him for teasing with "I don't do favors," which he could have kept to himself in that moment. He ribbed her right back. He teased her about saying "It's been a year since I've made love," which had sounded like a cry for help. They joked in whispers, as they acknowledged that on the day they'd met, Barbara had thought he was stuck-up, and Roger admitted he hadn't understood how his brother could live in an apartment with such an uptight woman.

"You know what I'd love right now?"

"We don't have it," she responded, no intention of moving.

"A glass of milk with Banania."

"Really? You like that banana mush?"

"Isn't it like a chocolate milkshake?"

"Why do you think it's called Banania, smarty-pants? Oh, of course, you're the king of apples, and you can't pick out a banana."

"Listen—"

"In any case, I don't think we have any in the house."

"Are you sure?" He carefully ran his finger over her nipple.

"Oh, Roger, what's gotten into you . . ."

"Shhh." He put the same finger over her lips. Barbara pretended to bite him.

"Where are you going?"

Roger climbed over her and jumped up from the bed. He slid on his underwear from the night before and his pajama shirt, and he stretched out on the floor next to the bed.

She asked, "Can I know what you're up to?"

He was already face down on the ground with half his body beneath the bedspring. He stretched his hand to touch the box with his fingers. Using both hands, he dragged it out.

"I found a treasure . . . Close your eyes. Are you ready?"

"Oh . . ."

"Close them. I don't know, maybe you already knew what was under here."

"Under the bed? No idea."

He put the tin Banania box on top of the bed. "You can open your eyes."

Barbara opened them, not knowing what she'd find. "Banania!" She laughed. "Is that your brother's?"

"I don't think so. You've never seen this box before?"

"Never."

"You don't recognize it?"

"No." She touched it and shook it. "I thought it'd be heavier."

"Open it."

She took off the lid with the caution required by surprises. Immediately, she let escape an "oh." And another. It was in front of her, and she could hardly believe what she was seeing.

"It's Mamie's picture!"

"It's your grandmother, right?"

"The same one we saw at the exhibit."

"Yes or no?"

"What a coincidence. The same bicycle, the same pose. And of course, it's this one . . . How can it be? What is all this?"

Barbara realized that, under the picture, there were several black-and-white photograph clippings. All of them seemed to have come from the same magazine. Who were all these people?

"Your grandmother never told you about it?"

"Never. I'd remember."

"And what about your mother?"

"Not at all. But my parents never lived here." Suddenly, she furrowed her brow. "Wait, what were you doing going through things that don't belong to you?"

"I thought," he replied cheekily, "it was my brother's box."

"Of course. And—" All of a sudden, she came to a realization. "Now I get why you were interested in me seeing the exhibition of . . . What was the name of the controversial photographer?"

"That's the least important part."

"You'd already seen that picture. You'd seen it here first . . ."

He raised an eyebrow playfully and defiantly. "You think I'd do something like that, Barbara?"

"You're a trickster." She pinched his thigh. "Did you see it here first, or not?"

"I can't answer without the presence of my lawyer. My lawyer is my brother, and right now, he's at a trial that, by the way, seems to have gone well for him."

"What else do you know about these clippings, about this story?" she said, disoriented by the picture she was holding of her grandmother. "Have you researched it?"

"These are all pictures from the war. Basically the years of Nazi occupation in Paris, so . . ."

"Starting from the summer of 1940. When Mamie wasn't a grandmother, or mother. When she was . . . what? Fifteen or sixteen years old. Seventeen, maybe."

How do you endure the unendurable?

Behind those magazine clippings were the most sinister years of the war.

Margaux in black and white. Jovial, despite it all. Elegant and pretty on top of the bike. Lit up by someone she knew. That museum picture, so well-defined, hid a story.

The story of Mamie Margaux and the love of her life.

Only she knew it.

Margaux

20

The Echo of Boots

The convertible parked at the door of the Théâtre du Châtelet without screeching. Five German soldiers in uniform from head to toe jumped out of the car. They had a mission, the determination to carry it out, and the explicit orders not to be unpleasant toward the musicians. To get from the Conciergerie to the theater square, they needed only to cross the Seine River through the pont au Change. They could've arrived immediately if they had walked, but they preferred showing up in a car. It was imposing, scary, and gave the order an official air.

The concert rehearsal continued, indifferent to the ruckus in the streets. Before lunchtime, the orchestra followed Schubert's score and Maestro Delphin Moureau's baton. He was a conductor restrained in his motions but expressive in his facial expressions. The seats on the main floor were empty. In the penultimate row, Ferdinand napped in a wooden seat, accompanied by the notes of Symphony no. 8. He'd walked there from his house through the deserted city, and just like he had done every day to make the walk feel shorter, he'd counted the cars scorched by the entrance of the Wehrmacht to the city and abandoned in the mass exodus in the days that followed. Four months had passed, and no one had taken away the scrap metal. In fact, some of the automobiles still slept belly up. Counting—abandoned cars, swastikas hanging from the streetlamps, women waiting in a line in front of some establishment with their ration cards in hand—was one way, like any other, of distracting himself and not thinking about the horror they'd been forced to live through. Or of surviving.

Finally, Ferdinand had walked up the right bank of the Seine and arrived at work. Once at the theater that Tuesday, he'd followed the same routines as always, far from the world of threats, death, and bombs. He'd put on his khaki coveralls and started the workday much earlier than the musicians, who'd shown up loaded with their instruments. With the whole theater to himself, he could make noise without anyone shooting him mean looks. He'd changed the burned-out light bulbs; he'd steadied the conductor's platform, which the conductor complained had been "dancing"; he'd gone back and forth all day, and the moment he'd been able to sit down to listen to the orchestra, he'd fallen asleep. Since the time of sirens and planes had begun, Ferdinand had slept with his ears open. Sleep is never completely deep during times of war. This time, because he was the closest to the door, Ferdinand was the first to notice the noise, the murmur coming from outside. All of a sudden, he heard it quickly approaching. A knock on the door, some footsteps, and some running, all of which weren't good signs. The echo of the Nazi soldiers' boots. He'd heard them for months, and he never heard that clomp-clomp without a shiver running up his spine. In no time, there were five soldiers behind him. Ferdinand stood up reflexively. The conductor noticed the violinists sitting closest to him were looking toward the back of the room from the corners of their eyes. Continuing to move the baton in his hand, he turned his head to see what was distracting his musicians. He guessed where all the ruckus was coming from. When he saw the uniforms standing at the back of the room, belt buckles shining, he went back to concentrating on his orchestra. He continued conducting like nothing had bothered him, neither him nor Schubert. The soldiers didn't want to interrupt the rehearsal either. Without being told to do so, all of them let the music prevail until the first movement ended, as a well-placed compromise between the soldiers and musicians. The conductor took a seat, and it was finally then that the rhythmic steps of the boots began advancing up the aisle of the main floor. Onstage, the musicians let their instruments rest. The conductor, with his white eyebrows, approaching seventy years old, wiped his forehead with a crumpled handkerchief before returning it to his pocket.

"Sir, how can we help you?"

"That wasn't Mendelssohn, was it?" asked the only official wearing a peaked cap.

"No, sir. Schubert, Symphony no. 8."

"Sounds good."

"Thank you. Many hours of—"

The official, who barked in an angry French, was not there for conversation. A soldier with a soft cap took out a folded paper and handed it to the official.

"There are more people here than last week." His gaze swept across the orchestra. "There aren't any empty chairs today."

"I can't make bread without flour," responded the conductor, not in the mood to agitate anyone.

The official put on his reading glasses. "I will list one by one the names of those who were in this orchestra the last time we came. You know how it works. When you hear your name, stand up." He began reading the typed list from the very top. "Delphin Moureau?"

"Present. I'm sorry if I don't stand up. For a while now, I—"

He was cut short by a glare.

"Are you the conductor of the Pierné Orchestra or the class clown?"

"Sorry, sir." He understood that now was not the time to act brave and dropped his baton on the music stand.

"I don't want you to respond. Don't say anything. When you hear your name, get up and stay quiet. Understood? Archambault." A bassoonist stood up. "Beaulieu. Bélanger. Chastain. Cornett . . ."

They stood one by one. A violinist, a clarinetist, a cellist, a timpanist—all stood when they were called and remained standing. The officer kept them in alphabetical order.

"Daniau. Fontaine. Forestier. Herzog." No one stood. "Herzog?"

"He's not here," said the conductor.

"Herzog?" the official asked again, like he'd only heard a buzzing in his ear. "Herzog, oboe? He isn't here?"

"Your men took him away," responded the electrician from the back of the hall. "Seven days ago."

The five uniformed men turned all at once. The officer, a question on the tip of his tongue, narrowed his eyes to see who'd spoken.

"And you . . . Who are you?"

"The electrician." He stood up as well. "The electrician for the Châtelet."

"Name?"

"Dutronc. Ferdinand Dutronc."

"A friend of Herzog?"

"No, sir. I knew him here, of course."

"Are you also Jewish?"

"No."

"Anything more to say?"

"No, sir."

"Then be quiet. Ferdinand . . . What was it?"

"Dutronc, sir."

Using an uncapped pen that a soldier rushed to hand him—everyone has a role in a war—the officer wrote down the name Dutronc at the very top of the list and continued down the alphabet. Hidalgo, Jordan, Lefebvre, Martinez, Mirailles. With each name, he made sure the musicians placed their instruments on the chair and stood up in the resigned manner of people who have lost.

There were still some men left sitting in the middle of the orchestra once he finished the list. The officer counted them in a quick glance.

"Very well. I see there are seven recruits left, conductor."

"May I speak?"

"If it's to say the flour thing again, I understood it the first time."

"I mean, if you may permit me, an orchestra needs all its musicians. Schubert composed for a fixed number of violins, percussion, and woodwinds, and . . . if the musicians leave Paris or if . . . I have to look for others, you understand? I need fifty-four musicians. The concert is next Sunday."

"Symphony no. 8?"

"Yes, sir."

"We'll come."

"It would be an honor to play for you."

"You don't know how happy I am, conductor, that Paris has welcomed us warmly—"

Suddenly, a metallic plate crashed to the floor. The bang scared everyone. One of the soldiers drew his hand to the holster of his gun. Mirailles, the cellist, turned white as paper. No one was in the mood to laugh. The officer asked the seven musicians who hadn't been on the list to stand up and identify themselves. He required them to go section by section. The wind instruments were the last ones standing.

"My name? Damien Devère."

"Is that a clarinet?" The officer pointed with his pen.

"No, sir. It's an oboe."

"It's the second oboe," the conductor clarified.

"So you're taking the place of . . ." The officer looked at his list. "Herzog?"

"I don't know. I'm guessing that I am, yes, sir."

"Did you know him?"

"I don't know him, sir."

"Aren't you a little young to play in an orchestra?"

"I'm twenty-one years old, sir."

The conductor intervened once more. "May I say something?" Looking down, he waited for permission. "I could say that, due to the circumstances, there really isn't much of a selection. But I prefer to tell you the truth. Devère is very good. He's been with us for less than five rehearsals, and . . . He's surprised us all, because, as young as he looks, he's a virtuoso."

Damien was scared the officer would make him play. He'd really hate to have to demonstrate his skills in front of everyone. It was a cursed trauma. During his musical beginnings, when he hadn't yet switched from the flute to the oboe, he'd hated when his parents forced him to perform a small concert for the family's Sunday dinner. But he avoided the danger. It looked like the officer was suddenly in a rush.

"You already know the rules. You can play, you can rehearse, you can have concerts, and you can continue with your musical lifestyle, but not a single Jewish person is to be in this hall. Not onstage, in the orchestra, or in the theater." He pulled off his glasses and stowed them in a pocket. "What time is the concert?"

"At four in the afternoon, sir. As always."

"We'll see you on Sunday."

The farewell—"We'll see you on Sunday"—was more informative than threatening. But then the echo of the ten boots resounded up the aisle to the exit of the hall. They didn't need to mark their steps to show who was in control. Their pride went nicely with their uniforms. The orchestra members took a while to react. No one said anything, no one sat back down, and the instruments continued resting on the ground or on top of the chairs. The conductor, the first to take a deep breath, gave everyone a ten-minute break. Once they determined that the soldiers had left the theater, the majority of the musicians took advantage of the October sun to go outside for a smoke in the square.

"Damien Devère?" Ferdinand with his cleft chin had waited for Damien in the aisle. "I want to introduce myself. I'm Ferdinand, the electrician."

"I heard. You were brave, sir."

"Or irresponsible, depends on how you look at it. Ferdinand Dutronc." He extended a strong hand.

"You took a gamble." Damien clasped his hand, musician's fingers in the electrician's.

"I didn't say anything that wasn't true."

"Maybe, but whoever goes against them . . . So, they took Herzog away?"

"It's a tragedy what they're doing with the . . ." He didn't dare say the word. "You should've seen them last week. They took him and four more like him away. Herzog was a veteran of the orchestra. A good man, a father of three, but poor people—a last name like that rats him out."

"I'm sorry to be taking his place."

"You go your own way, boy. Like everyone else. It's war. You've done well for yourself. Are you going out for a smoke?"

"No." He excused his blunt reply. "I need to keep my lungs clear. I have companions who smoke like chimneys, but it's better not to when it comes to playing."

"Of course."

"But if you're going out, I'll accompany you."

"It's not necessary. I appreciate it. Would you mind it if . . ." He took out a pack of cigarettes from the pocket of his buttoned coveralls.

"Go ahead."

"I smoke four a day. Can't afford more."

Ferdinand lit a cigarette on the main floor, and the two crossed the lobby to the street. Damien, a mess of curls on his head, was quite chatty. During the ten-minute break—which lasted exactly ten minutes, because Moureau was a man of stubborn discipline—he said it was an honor for him to join the Pierné Orchestra, which had been lucky to be one of the four great companies the Germans had permitted to continue with programming. There were many other orchestras and bands that'd had to dissolve, and many musicians, of all ages, were looking for work anywhere they could find it. He was fortunate they'd hired him from his first audition, because he had several colleagues who'd just left the conservatory or had long careers who were now offering private lessons at a discount to earn some money. "Everyone's looking for work," he said. Things were becoming scarce in every way. It'd been only four months since the Wehrmacht had entered Paris, and the situation became more difficult with every day that passed. Week after week, things got worse. Everyone said it, without fearing the Germans understood them, and it was true. The tension of the early days was gone, but every morning the city was emptier. Emptied of people, food, life, and stores. Between those who'd closed their blinds, those who'd fled—to the south, toward the fields, looking for unoccupied territory—and those who didn't have enough for food, establishments became fewer each day. Ferdinand listened, nodding his head in agreement. "The day will come," Damien said, "when they'll sell us cuts of meat that look like matchbooks." He said he and his family—father, mother, and a younger sister—lived two blocks from les Halles, and there was still movement at the market. They were lucky—he emphasized "lucky"—they could still maybe find a bit of everything.

"I live on rue Chappe, up in Montmartre in the eighteenth arrondissement. A lot of people there have fled to the countryside. There are abandoned homes, whole buildings where no one lives. Sometimes, these days, you see a family return who'd left during the occupation. They'd packed everything in a few hours and left loaded up like mules. Some even took their queen-size mattress . . . And now you see them coming back little by little."

"In les Halles, there are also people who . . . Actually, I can't say it too loud . . . My parents and sister fled the day before the Germans entered, but once they saw they had nowhere to go, they came back to the apartment to hold out. There's no other choice."

"There's more life at the foot of the Montmartre hill. There are the Clichy cabarets, the brothels of Pigalle. That's the kind of meat they want. They go crazy, these soldiers, like they've never seen nipples before."

"They have to demonstrate their power, I guess."

"Yeah, with our women."

With a shout, the conductor had everyone in front of the music sheet right on the hour. He didn't make a speech. He limited himself to raising the baton to call for a serene silence. The concentration. The magic of the moment before the music. Once he resumed the rehearsal, he managed to make the Unfinished Symphony fill the hall in the way it more or less sounded in his head. Serious and mysterious in the beginning like the human soul, delicate and in spurts in the final coda. He couldn't perform miracles. With seven new musicians, what more could you expect?

The concert on Sunday went the way the conductor thought it would. The strings were better than the winds, more concentrated in the end than in the beginning, and because the hall was full, any out-of-place note went unnoticed. He hoped the audience hadn't perceived the early entrance of the clarinet, and based on his experience, he was convinced that only the true lovers of music would have noticed the viola had been out of tune during the second movement. The local audience, satisfied by the appearance of normality, applauded madly. The German officer and his soldiers, who had occupied the very best rows on the main floor, left proud, believing the show had been performed especially for them. Plus, the fact that a German composer was being played in France was an honor of conquest.

Ferdinand had seen the concert from the drop scene. Due to the absence of a stage manager—he'd disappeared from the grid with the occupation in June—he took it upon himself to lower the curtain after the last applause. While the musicians gathered and debriefed, he went up to Damien Devère, who at that moment was putting his oboe back into its case.

"Congratulations. A good debut with the Pierné Orchestra."

"Honestly, it's such a strange feeling. But it sounded good, yes. The conductor just came to shake my hand. That's a good sign, right?"

"The best. Moureau tells it like it is."

"Did you like it?"

"I don't understand music."

"A way of saying you didn't feel it."

"The very opposite. I would've liked to have brought someone today."

"Your wife?"

"Better. My daughter. She . . ." He doubted whether to continue. If he stayed quiet, the story would have ended there. "She also plays the oboe."

"Oh, really?"

"Well, she'd like to. Actually, she was asking me . . ."

"What is it?" Damien smiled. Ferdinand had taken a stand against a German officer with decorated lapels, but he was nervous to speak to him?

"She was asking . . . It's nothing. If you maybe could give her a lesson. She'd be so happy. We'd pay you something, of course . . . What we can, you know we're all—"

"Oboe lessons? I've never thought about it." *But why not,* he thought. "How old is she?"

"She must be around . . . sixteen. Her name is Margaux."

21

You Would Think He's Louis Armstrong

Damien and Margaux met the traditional way the next week. Margaux's father, Ferdinand Dutronc, the Theatre du Châtelet's electrician and odd-jobs man for the past seventeen years, made the introductions. He waited for the orchestra to finish their Saturday morning rehearsal before meeting Damien at the main lobby in front of the coat-check hangers, and he said the sentence he'd practically memorized.

"This is my daughter, and as I mentioned after the concert, she's got a strong hankering to learn to play the oboe."

"Did you watch the rehearsal?" the musician asked before he gave the girl three kisses.

"Yes, of course. It was fantastic." She had turned her enthusiasm into formality. "It's a pleasure to meet you."

"The girl's not too old to learn the instrument, is she?" her father asked in the way that fathers who talk too much do.

"Late? It's never too late to learn anything," Damien assured. "We have a family friend in Britain, where we spent summers before everything started, who bought a trumpet when he was fifty years old. He bought it for himself without ever having touched a trumpet. If you closed your eyes and heard him now, you'd think he was Louis Armstrong."

Father and daughter laughed without knowing what he was talking about. Having had essentially a week to think about Ferdinand's offer, Damien continued: "The problem isn't that you're . . ."

"Sixteen years old."

"Perfect. The problem is whether I know enough to teach you." He hugged his oboe case close to him. "Yes, I play it. I've never spent more time with anyone or anything than my oboe. They hired me here because the circumstances are what they are, and it's an honor to be a part of the Pierné Orchestra, but . . . I'm no oboe professor. I've never given classes before. I've taken many, that's true. I've had some very good teachers too. But when it comes to experience, I have none at all. Of course, if you're willing and you want to, let's try. There's always a first. We're living in novel times, huh?"

"Of course," Margaux replied.

"Everything is different. We have to adapt to the new circumstances, and we have no choice but to do things we never thought we would," said Ferdinand.

"Good. If you want me to teach you, I know it'll be worth the effort. And I think we'll succeed."

"Me too," she said, fascinated by the enthusiasm the young man radiated when he spoke.

"No need to discuss it further," said her father, who had previously agreed on payment for the first-time teacher. Every private lesson would cost him seven francs and a piece of fruit. Whatever he had, whatever he could get depending on the week.

Once they sealed the deal with a handshake, Ferdinand returned to the stage to fix a small lamp on the conductor's music stand. It wasn't just the whim of some fussy bigwig. The maestro had complained that the light bulb would sometimes go out on him. It would flicker, and if the notes on the music sheet shook, then good luck. "They look like ants running in circles," Delphin Moureau said, never losing his sense of humor.

When Margaux and Damien were alone, they sat on the bench at the entrance of the theater, and he asked, "So why exactly the oboe? Why not the flute, the bassoon, the clarinet?" Overcoming her embarrassment, Margaux confessed the event that had made an impression on her maybe a little more than a year prior in that same theater. Her father had asked her to accompany him to see a work by Prokofiev. He was sure she would like *Peter and the Wolf*. And he was right. She didn't know what she was about to hear, and the surprise that each character had its own instrument sounded like a world of fun. It was original. She watched the performance, her mouth agape, and she wondered how the composer had known to match each sound with each character. The clarinet for the cat's footsteps. The delicate flute for the birdie. The timbales were the surly hunters. The beloved grandfather moved to bassoon notes. The three trumpets were the dangerous wolf, so sure of the power of his canine teeth. And Peter, daring Peter, would always risk it all to the plucking of strings. But what she liked the most by a long shot was the duck's voice. The sweet sound of the oboe contained so much love in itself, held so much beauty when it appeared on stage, that she became emotional. It was the first time music made her cry. There, glued to her wooden seat, Margaux noticed the special connection between her and that instrument. Since that morning of enthrallment, she'd become a nuisance at home. Quite a nuisance. There wasn't a day that passed when she didn't tell her parents she wanted to play the oboe. Months went by, the Germans entered Paris, the Luftwaffe rained bombs down on them, family friends started exoduses toward unknown places, and she still maintained her obsession. In the end, her father found someone who promised to teach her how to play.

In the span of a few weeks, Damien Devère had accumulated a couple strokes of luck.

The Germans had set his mother free after detaining her in a random street raid; he'd been hired in a famous orchestra; and now an opportunity had presented itself to bring home more money and a little bit of fruit in exchange for private lessons.

He'd been able to join the Pierné Orchestra thanks to a school friend, Imtold Lefebvre. They knew each very well, and their schoolboy years had bonded them so much that the outcome was clear in no time.

"The Pierné is looking for an oboist. Would you be interested?"

"What do you think about it?"

"One of the two we had . . . You know how things go these days. They're not allowed to even play anymore, what with the Jewish Statute. Are you interested?"

"Yes. Very."

"Honestly, I already talked to Delphin Moureau about you. He's a good conductor. He's set in his ways, but he's got a good baton."

"If they hire me, I won't let you down."

"Like hell they won't hire you. We have concerts scheduled. We have the Unfinished Symphony eight days from now, and between the members who've left and the members those sons of bitches have taken, we're completely handicapped."

Damien Devère and Imtold Lefebvre had gone to school together for many years, and during a couple of school years, they'd shared a desk. At that time, Lefebvre was a little different from the rest. He played the violin from an early age. He was the only boy in the class who played an instrument—at a school that was all boys—and when he went to class with a case bigger than he was, his classmates were intrigued. He opened it, took out the violin and the bow, played three notes in secret, and became a hero. But everyone watched how he struggled during gym class. The teachers also knew what a terrible experience it was for him. They forced him to do somersaults with not an ounce of compassion but rather the pedagogical certainty that what doesn't kill us makes us stronger. Barking imperatives, his teachers told him how he had to first curl up and then push with his feet to complete the somersault. But Lefebvre couldn't do it, as frozen as he was. It was even worse to those miliary ticks. Sometimes he even trembled. It was then that the teacher, without any consideration, grabbed him, placed him in front of the mat, made him crouch, supported him from the back of the neck with a hand, put the other arm behind his knees, and on a count of three, helped him somersault. If he got up with his legs twisted, they forced him to do it again. Again and again until he stood up straight, martial attitude intact and spirit crushed.

The suffering of the schoolboy years, marked by short pants, ended when the weak boy placed his violin on his shoulder. At fifteen years old, he was already performing concerts in the small halls of Paris. He played Saint-Saëns's Rondo Capriccioso and left everyone astounded by his virtuosity. Soon, he made a small name for himself in the city's musical circles. So much so that when Delphin Moureau had a free space in the Colonne Orchestra, Lefebvre scheduled an audition with him. Moureau said, "Today you'll play Mahler's Fifth with the whole group," and after listening to Lefebvre play, he said, "You start Monday." It's true that he put both his hands on his shoulders, looked him in the eyes, and warned him he'd be the youngest of all the musicians.

"There's no showing off when you're in an orchestra. Only contributing. Everyone in service of the score. Understood?"

And Jean Lefebvre had agreed. Jean was his name. Imtold was the nickname his friends had given him. It had stuck with him even at home. Sometimes, he signed unimportant documents that way. "Imtold L." It bothered him at first that they were making fun of him, but trying to stop it would have been worse. What would he have achieved from getting angry? He had to admit he had the obsession—he'd call it a habit—of beginning his explanations, anecdotes, and gossip with the unavoidable "I'm told." It's true, he was always careful not to reveal his sources. He couldn't remember a single time he'd betrayed the person who'd told him a secret. That was another thing. He never revealed anything to do with his own life.

During the previous weeks, ever since Marshal Pétain's speech asking the French people to collaborate with the invading forces of the Third Reich, Imtold Lefebvre had to share the rumors he'd heard. So as not to put his foot in his mouth, he shared information only with those he thought, like him, resisted the idea that the occupation of half of France would be forever and the new European order was definitive.

"I'm told Hitler came to Paris in the morning. He was only interested in seeing the inside of the l'Opèra and then immediately left. Like a dog pissing to mark his territory." "I'm told the Germans confiscate cameras. Did you know that? We're not allowed to take pictures now as an occupied country." "I'm told these *Kartoffeln* sack the apartments of Jews, Americans, and British, and remove any art they find. They use the Jeu de Paume as a warehouse. They take the good art back to their country." "I'm told Radio Paris—what a disgusting station—settled in on 116 Champs-Élysées." "Be careful, friends, because I'm told there are people who counterfeit bread ration cards. I'm told who's trafficking these cards." "I'm told our conductor, the maestro Moureau, has a lover. And I'm told it's not exactly a woman." "I'm told." Imtold Lefebvre. If he hadn't been the violinist for the Pierné Orchestra, he would've been a good journalist. Or a top spy. When anyone whispered this to him, he simply smiled.

Damien explained to Margaux that Imtold had always been that thin, that the lack of cheeks underneath those bony cheekbones was not a consequence of the war. At school, he ate like a bird. On more than one occasion, Damien, who was always a small boy, ate any plate from the school mess hall that Lefebvre didn't like. In exchange, Imtold asked to copy Damien's math homework. Margaux listened and laughed but had only one thing on her mind: to find out the day and location of her oboe lesson. Out of a sense of security, she proposed holding them at her house. One afternoon a week, once she got out of school. If her father wasn't needed at work, he would be home by the time the lesson started. Her mother wouldn't come back until the Galeries Lafayette closed in the evening. She was a shop assistant at the building on boulevard Haussmann in the ninth arrondissement, a fifty-minute walk from their house.

Michelle had started as an apprentice in the perfume section and, over the years, had moved up to the women's clothing floor. She sold haute couture to the neighborhood bourgeois just as she sold ready-made dresses, the everyday street wear of Paris. Since June, however, the store had lost almost all its clientele. Loyal and lifelong customers had stayed in the city but had locked themselves at home, frightened and with very little desire to expose themselves. If a client did go out, she no longer wanted to spend money on dresses and skirts. She had to save for whatever might happen and had to make do with the clothing she had at home. This order traveled from person to person, from house to house. From what Michelle said at dinnertime, only German soldiers entered the Galeries Lafayette since the start of fall. Never by themselves. They came in pairs and sometimes in groups. They climbed one staircase, went down another, and looked at everything. They were all fascinated by the number of products they said they'd never seen in their country. They bought them, wrapped them, and packaged them to mail home. Even food. Michelle, who had opinions about the Germans but maintained a perennial smile behind the counter, said that despite everything—and she emphasized "despite everything"—these people behaved politely in her store. They didn't seem like scum in there. They asked, they made themselves understood, they inquired regarding the prices of things, they paid the marked price in francs without haggling, and after everything, they said *merci*. Many times, in French and in their native language. When they left, packages in hand, it didn't feel like they were murderers.

The day Damien and Margaux met each other, Imtold Lefebvre ran into them chatting at the entrance of the theater. With his violin case under his arm and an exuberance unbecoming of a classical musician, he told them he was going to the Rive Gauche. "I'm told they've opened a German bookstore for only German soldiers. I can't believe it."

"Where'd you say you're going?"

"To the corner of boulevard Saint-Michel and place de la Sorbonne. I want to see it with my own eyes."

"Imtold . . ." Damien knew his friend better than anyone else.

"What's wrong?" he asked, not stopping in his tracks.

"Be careful. Don't make them angry."

"Me? Don't worry about it."

"Remember you can't win the war by yourself."

22

A Miracle Around Every Corner

Luck.

Michelle's colleagues at the Galeries Lafayette spoke about it often during the long hours no one passed through the shop. On the women's floor, the shop assistants, with their blue uniforms and their hair pinned up according to the employee manual, chatted because, in some way or another, they needed to kill time. Chatting helped distract them from the misery of the streets, the heavy sadness, and the uncertainty that had suddenly invaded their families. They spoke of chance and concluded it had a crueler side to it during times of war. Between life and death, there is sometimes a very thin thread of fortune. Loss had reached everyone, but tragedy clung tighter to some more than others. Michelle was the first to recognize she was fortunate her husband hadn't been recruited to go to the front. At the Châtelet, he, in his electrician's uniform with a handful of almonds in his pocket, could act like the war lived only in the margins of his workday. Ferdinand had been left alone during the Germans' visits to the theater. The husbands of three of Michelle's colleagues, however, had left home because France called them to stand up against the devil. There are levels even of bad luck.

Nathalie—foulards, scarves, and accessories—knew her husband had been sent somewhere close to Tours, and sometimes, maybe once a week, she received a letter written in soldier's ink. Nathalie figured he was telling her lies to keep her from worrying. At the end of every letter, which seemed shorter every week, he ended with a great truth: "I love you." And she became just as emotional when she read every letter. What a strange combination yearning and fear create when they mix.

Marion, who was in charge of intimate wear, didn't know where Romain was. "Join the front" was the slogan men repeated to one another before June. And Romain, a coward of sorts, wasn't brave enough to hide himself. He thought it would be worse to escape and resigned himself to his fate. It was clear what it would be. He put on his military outfit, looked at himself in the mirror in the foyer of the house, and with the cries of a small child, he collapsed to the floor, saying he didn't want to go. He had a hunch the Germans would enter whenever they felt like it and that they would triumph the way they had at Verdun in 1916. He saw the big wave coming to swallow them up and knew it was impossible to escape it. He was convinced that he, weak of body and spirit, wouldn't make it to Christmas, and he started crying again. Marion's words of hope didn't console him. Nor did her caresses. When the soldiers passed by to pick him up from the doorway of his house and loaded him onto the gray truck, he didn't have the energy to even raise his hand and wave at his wife, who was still cheering him on and saying, "Everything will be okay, Romain. You'll see." She hadn't heard any news since he'd left six months ago. *"Pas de nouvelle, bonne nouvelle,"* Marion repeated in front of her coworkers to avoid tormenting herself.

Without a doubt, Marthe had been the one who suffered the most with the Nazi occupation. She'd become a widow only two months after getting married. She'd mourned at work, and it turned her stomach when she had to attend to the swastika-clad soldiers, who acted friendly while placing an order for a skirt for their wives. She could've vomited on them. Her husband, Frédéric, may God forgive him, hadn't resigned himself to the idea that Hitler's assassins were the new overlords of Paris. What were they trying to prove with the daily martial parades down Champs-Élysées from the Arc de Triomphe to the place de la Concorde obelisk at noon? Why did French boys everywhere all of a sudden want to be German soldiers when they played war?

One August night, Frédéric left the house, defying the 11:00 p.m. curfew. Even though Marthe had asked him to please not violate the orders of confinement and to stop acting like a hero, he insisted he needed to get some fresh air. He said, "I'll go only as far as les Invalides, and I'll turn back. I won't run into anyone." They kissed, and she never saw him again. What had he done? What was he carrying? Who had he run into? Why hadn't he returned that night? She would never know. At the first hints of light, Marthe went out in search of him, hoping for a miracle around every corner that never materialized. She wasn't able to find him. The nightmare continued, and she cursed herself for not having stopped her hero. As if the three days of worrying over Frédéric's disappearance wasn't enough, the way she'd found out about his death was even more devastating. On her way home from the Galeries Lafayette, Marthe saw her husband's name, Frédéric Rameau, on a poster hanging on a streetlamp near the German Kommandatura on the avenue de l'Opéra. His name was in the middle of seven others, all men. The sign was in German, and Marthe didn't understand what it said. She didn't want to ask the men in green uniforms acting as guards five doors down with their cigarettes. She stopped passersby, each in their own world, coming and going from the Palais-Royal. Disoriented, she asked all of them the same question:

"Pardon me, do you speak German?"

Some said no, others didn't answer, some even turned their heads away, which was a way of saying, "Don't get me involved in this war."

"Pardon, do you know what it says here?" Marthe asked the question again. "Pardon, do you speak German?"

She continued to ask. Men or women, she grabbed them by the elbow. Even more desperately each time. A pedestrian, a big man who'd avoided running into her, looked at the notice as he continued to walk.

"It says . . ." With one glance, he'd seen enough. "That they'll be executed today."

She never found out what had happened that night. No one told her how they'd arrested him. Or if he'd resisted. If he'd tried to contact her. She didn't even know what happened to the body of her beloved Frédéric, blown to pieces by the bullets. The absence of details is another form of torture during war.

In spite of her despair, Marthe hadn't missed a day of work, due to the absolute madness of having to pretend like nothing had happened and so that they wouldn't implicate her in who knows what charges. Upon discovering the news, her boss patted her on the back and asked her to please fix herself up because she was looking pale. It was a company order. "Put on makeup, be as pretty as you can, and most importantly, smile at everyone no matter who they are. People are having a hard time out there. Every client who steps inside our store should enter a small oasis. Misery, hunger, and emaciated faces have no room here."

Michelle, Nathalie, Marion, and Marthe dressed up every day. Then, when fall began to turn into winter, Marion showed them a trick for saving on tights. She took off the uniformed pumps and placed her foot on the top of the stool behind the counter.

"What color would you like your tights to be?" Marion asked.

"Nude," said Michelle.

"So what you do is grab black eyeliner, and you'll have them in no time."

Carefully, Marion took off the cap and drew the straightest line she could muster up the back of her leg from her heel to the fold of her knee. She stood so they could see.

"Compare one leg to the other. Doesn't this one look like it has a tight on it?"

"Definitely."

"And if the tights are supposed to be black?" Nathalie asked, not so convinced by this invention. "Your leg would look white, and you'd have a black line on your calf."

"Girls, I also have a trick for that. Smear a little bit of Elizabeth Arden lotion to darken your legs, then draw the vertical line, and you have black silk tights. Impeccable."

"Of course, these tights won't rip."

"Not a run in your tights, I guarantee it. Cheap and, listen, they'll last you your whole life."

"That's until you take a bath."

"You're a good saleswoman, Marion."

All four burst into laughs and began to fantasize what color they'd paint their legs for different occasions. Once this was all over, of course, because no war lasts forever.

Damien arrived at Montmartre, his shirt sweaty. As bundled up as he was, the walk from the Châtelet had taken its effect. He double-checked that the building on the corner of rue Chappe and rue Tardieu was the house belonging to Ferdinand Dutronc's family.

He rang the doorbell for the fifth-floor apartment. After a couple moments of silence, he heard someone shouting to him from the sky.

"Damien. Up here."

He looked up, and despite the darkness, he saw Margaux leaning out the window, waving to him discreetly.

"Is it locked?"

"Yes, yes," he responded after pulling at the door.

"Give me a second."

She disappeared inside and immediately returned with a rope. With the skill of having done this many times before, she snaked it down the building's facade in a zigzag motion. A key was tied to the very end.

"You're lucky your father is a handyman," Damien shouted as he waited for the rope to reach him. "It's the fifth floor, right?"

"The very top floor, yes. I'm sorry."

Damien climbed the steps two at a time. Following an afternoon of rehearsals and traversing half of Paris, he still had some energy. It was the hope of a new challenge. He was about to give his first oboe lesson to a girl who'd hardly even held one before in her hands. On the way to Margaux's home, he came up with twenty different ways of starting out. Once he was upstairs, he chose one.

"Close your eyes."

Sitting at the table where she ate dinner with her parents every day, Margaux listened to him. Damien placed the case in front of her, opened it, grabbed his new student's hands, and put them on the pieces of his treasured instrument.

"Let's see how many parts you find."

"Oof. This one is . . ." She felt a round-necked tube.

"Try doing it carefully. I'll hold it. Come on."

"This one is longer, right?"

"Correct. The lower body is the longest. Don't open your eyes. I'm watching you."

"No, no."

"You've got one left."

"This one . . . it's the shortest. Could it be?"

"The upper body. Yes, ma'am. Don't open them yet." Damien put the instrument together in no time. "Open your eyes."

"Oh!" exclaimed Margaux.

"That's the oboe."

"It's a work of art."

"People see it like this, as one piece, but it's important you know it comes in three parts. The upper body, the lower body, and the bell that rounds off the sound, which is the first part you took out."

"It's fabulous."

"We wouldn't be able to clean it if it didn't come in three parts. And it's essential to clean it after playing. This is all wood. If we don't open and dry it every time, the moisture in our breath can damage it right away. The wood can rot, and . . . And this oboe should last for several years, maybe for my entire life. Here, do you want to hold it?"

She didn't hide her joy at having the oboe in her hands. She held it with the same care as she would a baby who belongs to someone else. Damien showed her how it functioned: his right hand placed under, supporting the weight of the instrument, and his left hand over the oboe to play the keys at the very top.

"There are twenty-three keys. And each finger is used . . . except for one. Which one, do you think?"

She thought about it.

"The thumb, this one." Margaux wriggled her right-hand thumb.

"Exactly, because it stays underneath and holds up the oboe. So now," Damien said, surprised at how he was shaping up to be as a teacher, "do you think the instrument could be played this way? Would you be able to play it?"

"Me . . . ? Oh wow . . ." She looked at the instrument from top to bottom. "I don't know. It's missing . . . the little tongue. So that it plays."

"Brava, Margaux! There's a fourth part, which is the smallest and most important of them all. What you call 'the little tongue' is actually the reed." He took one out of the pocket of the case. "This is for you. The reed is the primary element. Without it, the oboe couldn't be played. It's the link between you and the oboe. It goes in like this, see . . ."

Damien grabbed the instrument, and with the steadiness of a surgeon's hand, he inserted it into the socket. Only the tip of the reed stuck out.

"You can put it in your mouth. No one's used it before you. One second—" He stopped her suddenly. "My first piece of advice is to always hide your teeth. My second piece of advice is to round your lips into the shape of an *m* . . . Very good. Now, little by little, pinch your lips halfway up the reed."

"Like that?"

"Perfect. Pinch the reed without completely closing your lips, so sounds can go through. And now release some air. Can I show you a trick?"

"Of course."

"Try to blow out air in a very thin, concentrated, and tubular stream, and it's also important to do it with a lot of velocity; if not, it won't play."

She tried it. Margaux couldn't do it at first. She moved the chair back to be more comfortable, concentrated hard, and tried again. Her heart was beating quickly like she was going in for her first kiss. Still, she continued once more to channel the air precisely.

"Blow the air with more velocity. Try orienting it more."

Suddenly a sound escaped. The first sound was the antithesis of music. She withdrew the oboe from her mouth and laughed shyly like she'd performed a grand concert. Damien stood and shook her by the shoulders to congratulate her.

"You can now say you've played the oboe."

"Oh, of course," she responded sarcastically.

"The distance between what you've heard and Albinoni's Concerto no. 1 is not so vast."

After, they took the reed out, left the oboe on the table, and spent the rest of the afternoon working on a single thing: practicing with the reed. Each used their own reed. Damien would make a sound, and Margaux had to copy him. Sometimes it was low, sometimes it was high, one would be short, and one he'd hold for a while to see how long she could maintain it without getting dizzy. When a ridiculous vibration or a screech that sounded like a balloon losing air would escape, they laughed. Margaux never would have thought the delicate piece, smaller than a cigarette and resembling a toy whistle, was what made the instrument she'd fallen in love with play.

By the time Damien left the apartment, Ferdinand still hadn't arrived home. Halfway down the stairs, he crossed paths with a woman going up, and he said good night to her.

"Good night," she responded. "There's so little light in this stairway."

Her open coat revealed the sight of her blue uniform. From that, he knew she worked at the Galeries Lafayette. He guessed she must be Michelle, Ferdinand's wife. It was the first time he'd ever seen Margaux's mother. They bore a strong resemblance. If he squinted, he could see what Margaux would look like when she got older. All of a sudden, Damien knew all the members of the Dutronc family.

Violin case in his lap, Imtold Lefebvre waited for the darkness of night. He'd left the rehearsal, said goodbye to Damien, who mentioned he was heading to Ferdinand Dutronc's house, and walked all the way to place de la Sorbonne. It wasn't far from the theater. Once there, he sat on a street bench in front of the German bookstore. Throughout the afternoon, he observed the little movement there was on the corner of boulevard Saint-Michel. In over an hour, he'd seen only two soldiers and a man of around sixty enter the bookstore. Just by looking at the man's rounded figure, Imtold guessed he was a Pétain supporter, a slave to the conquerors, a traitor like so many he'd begun to see settling for the status quo. He'd likely entered the shop to buy a German book, despite not speaking the language, that would serve as a sort of safe passage if he ever ran into problems. The pair of soldiers left after ten minutes, each with a volume tucked under their arm. Once they were on the street, the taller one let out a large belch and mentioned he'd let a friend from the regiment borrow the book.

"Borrow? I'll rent it out," the other said, waving the air with his hand. "I bought it to conduct business."

Imtold didn't see what he'd bought, but he'd studied long enough in Leipzig to understand what the pair of *Kartoffeln* had said. They were the last two people to leave before a blond man—practically albino—turned out the lights, exited the shop, lowered the blinds, and, using a key, locked the bookstore with its two-window displays on each side of the door. Imtold had monitored for enough days to see that the shop windows, same as the store, displayed only German books. To annoy people. To serve as a reminder that the tables had turned in Paris. To demonstrate they'd conquered the cultural capital and were pissing all over it. To show they were the owners of the world. These were the thoughts that gnawed at Imtold and his roommate, Samuel Bardollet, who'd also spent time surveilling movement, but from the other side of the square.

When the city was silent, when the blond manager had certainly arrived home, when he confirmed there was not a soul left in the square, Imtold made the signal Bardollet was waiting for. He whistled the first four notes of Beethoven's Fifth, and his friend knew the party had begun.

"You or me?" he asked, sitting on the bench next to Lefebvre.

"You place it, and I'll keep a watch. We settled on that, didn't we?"

"Yes."

"So don't change the plan now."

"Is it ready?"

"What do you think?"

"Are you nervous? What's wrong with you?"

"No. But stop nagging me, you hear?"

"You think it's time?"

"It's now or never, Samu."

"If they catch us . . ."

"There's no danger now. Do exactly what I said. We haven't done all this so that now . . ."

"Understood. I'll place it, activate it, and leave toward Vaugirard."

"And I'll head behind the university."

"I'll see you at home."

"Good luck, friend," Imtold Lefebvre said, before opening his violin case.

Samuel Bardollet took out a small explosive. With the nimble fingers of a violinist, Imtold Lefebvre stripped the wires and twisted it with another wire he'd frayed at home. He had a bomb in his hands in no time.

"Now, be careful," he said, handing the explosive to Samuel as carefully as someone passing a crying baby.

Imtold closed his case, stood, and, pretending like nothing had happened, walked with his back toward the bookstore.

"Run, Samuel, run . . ."

Short-legged Bardollet approached the store, his heart beating a million miles a minute. He placed the bomb at the foot of the door, calculated that he had a twenty-second margin, and ran like he was possessed. He ran and counted. *Nine-ten-eleven.* He had enough time to leave the square and get to Vaugirard. When he was around *sixteen-seventeen-eighteen-nineteen*, the sharp din of the explosion threw him half a meter off the ground.

The sound of glass shattering echoed throughout the whole neighborhood. Only one of the windows remained intact. The door and the other three windows were blown to pieces. Immediately, all the dogs in the area began barking.

Mission accomplished.

"Those sons of bitches can go fuck themselves."

He didn't think anyone had seen him.

Luck.

23

The Notes Don't Lie

Damien prepared his lessons before showing up to the Dutronc household. He set himself an objective, and once he defined it, he looked for the easiest and most entertaining way to teach it to Margaux. Nothing was complicated with the amount of enthusiasm the girl put into things. But everything required time. One day, before beginning the session, Damien asked her to imagine a small child.

"When he's a year old, he doesn't get up and start walking out of nowhere. First, he crawls, then he holds himself up, then he falls on his butt. A day comes when he takes two steps and teeters until he's able to walk a little better each time. It's the same thing with the oboe. First, you tremble, because you don't think you can do it. Then, you stumble. But it all comes together, little by little. It's the same with any instrument. There's a process. You don't go from amateur to expert like flipping a light switch."

Another day, as he unloaded his oboe pieces from the case, he told Margaux to let go of her romantic notions, because there is no inspiration in learning. There is only work.

"Do you want me to share the real trick to playing the oboe? Hours of practice."

And Margaux, whose eyes crinkled when she laughed, responded that maybe one day there'd be a pill you could take to play an instrument. You'd go to the pharmacy and say: "Here's my prescription. The doctor said if I take it three times a week around dinnertime, I'll be playing the violin by next month. If I switch it off with another pill at breakfast and lunch, I'll be playing the violin and viola. And by the end of the year, I'll know how to play the pas de deux from *Swan Lake*, and the audience will cheer me on."

Another day—they enjoyed these meetings more and more each time—Damien told her to pretend he was performing Rimsky-Korsakov with his best students at the Saint Petersburg Conservatory. He'd gather the students and give them a preview of how the year would go. "In the beginning, I'll speak, and you all shall listen. After, I'll speak less, and you will all begin to work. In the end, I won't say anything, and you'll be working tirelessly."

"Which stage are we at?"

"Which do you think?"

"Where you speak less, and I"—she brought the oboe to her mouth—"work harder and better."

Once they finished chattering, they set to work. They sat next to one another so Margaux could more easily copy Damien's gestures than if she were looking at him head-on, like in a mirror. She paid attention to the way he placed his eight fingers to draw out B-flat major, the lowest note. He watched her closely. He corrected her air flow. He helped her find the stability to prevent air from producing variations in sound. He insisted she put adequate pressure on the reed with her lips. He interrupted her when he thought the sound was weak, lifeless. They repeated three notes, again and again, until she was the first to notice that it came out the way it was written on the sheet music.

"The notes don't lie, Margaux."

"But they don't always sound the same."

"Because the sound that comes out of an instrument is always the effort you muster out of yourself."

"I have to speak . . . through the instrument? Is that it?"

"Exactly. I once had a professor born in Kyiv who snatched the oboe right out of my hands and said, 'In a low register, you have to believe you are a bassoon. In a middle register, you have to believe you're a clarinet. And in a high register, you have to believe you're a flute. You imitate other instruments and, unconsciously, your sound heads in that direction.'"

"Maybe I should sign up for lessons with that teacher. I'll learn faster."

"But you won't have as much fun."

Margaux didn't want to admit he was right, but she turned red. She wasn't aware her face revealed how pleasant those hours they spent together were.

"Come on, let's not get distracted," Damien said when he noticed her head was in the clouds.

Conscious of her hand placement, he was exacting. She was like a sponge. She absorbed everything after the first explanation.

"The left-hand pinky manipulates five keys. Stretch that small finger farther . . ."

"Your fingers are longer," Margaux protested.

"Hardly. You also have to be able to reach it easily."

"Let's see something . . ."

Margaux placed the oboe on her lap and gave him her palm so they could compare finger length. She demanded Damien place his hand against hers. He didn't resist his student's game.

"Don't cheat," she insisted, making sure there wasn't even half a millimeter of space between the base of their thumbs.

They put their hands together. Hers were colder.

"I could chop off the piece of your finger here, and you still wouldn't have an excuse."

"Why are your nails so round? Let me see . . ." Margaux suddenly took his left hand and opened it wide.

"Do you know how to read palms?" Damien muttered.

She didn't respond. She examined those four lines on his palm whose purpose is unknown. To start conversations, perhaps. Margaux looked at the lines closely. She inspected his palm like someone looking for a shortcut on a treasure map.

"Congratulations, Dami. This is your life line." She followed it with her finger, tickling him. "Do you see how long it is?"

"Honestly, does it matter how long your life line is when you're in a war?"

He'd said the word.

The lessons, the oboe's vibrations, the hours they spent together were an oasis. Both of them were isolated from the world. From the fifth floor, you couldn't see the German soldiers, heads held high like they owned the city. Even when they leaned out the window, they couldn't see the fear, the low morale, the ration lines, or the hot water bags the elderly kept in their beds to endure the cold of winter. And despite it all, seasons passed, from the summer skies of truce to the tortured grayness of January. In between, there was everyday misery and the dragging of feet. Every month was the same story. Retaliations. Punishments. Arrests. Deportations. The four seasons. The prisoners of spring were maybe already dead by fall. Who even knew about the men who'd enlisted voluntarily or by force? Who could know what had happened to the soldiers who'd been imprisoned? They didn't talk about it at Margaux's school, and everyone acted like nothing had happened at Damien's orchestra. They argued about musical scores among themselves. During a rehearsal break once, someone said they'd heard Beethoven's Fifth Symphony as a kid and that it stayed with him for the rest of his life. Someone else added that Beethoven was the most temperamental of the geniuses, in stark contrast to other composers who were more reserved. They spoke of music, always of music, never about the character of its creators. Still, someone else responded that Ravel was like a clock, where everything ticked with an unusual precision. And whenever anyone dared compare French and German music, there was a stinging discomfort, and someone would change the subject right away. Just in case. Especially because the Pierné Orchestra knew how the Germans acted. They would always be the Colonne Orchestra, but they had been forced to change their name out of necessity. Édouard Colonne was Jewish. There were lines you couldn't cross.

The Montmartre attics weren't just an escape. It was paradise for the two of them. After a year of adjusting to a more limited lifestyle, she tried to play the duck's entrance in *Peter and the Wolf.* She'd spent days secretly rehearsing it so she could surprise her teacher. She invested several hours of practice. Her parents chided her, "This song again?" And she repeated it and persevered. That is, until the evening came that Damien and his artist's curls climbed up the five flights, oboe case on his shoulder, and suddenly Margaux greeted him with two commands that were unusual for her.

"Sit and listen."

She took all the time she needed. She searched for her concentration and the duck's voice. She closed her eyes to internalize it. She softened the reed with her lips. She began playing, and the music flowed.

It was a lethargic duck. The lower notes of the score presented him that way: lazy and gloomy. Later, however, when the wolf eats him and the duck revives, Margaux knew to draw out the same melody but with a different hue. She knew how to change the oboe's character. He became a sharp and happy duck. She was able to describe him the way the composer had imagined, and it felt like a miracle to her while she played.

Damien was fascinated. He hadn't expected the small concert Margaux had secretly planned for him, never having mentioned it to him. He was even more astounded she'd missed so few notes. He didn't even want to tell her. It was the moment to applaud her for having dared to play it and for having been able to differentiate between the downtrodden duck and the revitalized duck.

"I didn't expect this, Margaux. Brava."

"What'd you think?" Her heart raced.

"Impressive. Really."

They stood from their chairs and hugged. Margaux, oboe still in hand, wrapped her arms around Damien's waist. He squeezed her in his strong arms. The fact that her hair brushed his cheek didn't bother him. They were happy. They stayed that way for a while. She would have liked to live in that embrace.

On the walk home, Paris didn't feel as tired or as tinged with solitude. At once, the building facades regained the serious elegance of his city. He walked down boulevard de Magenta and thought about Margaux's hopeful eyes as she awaited his verdict regarding her private concert. He couldn't believe she'd grabbed his palm with the excuse of reading his life line. He liked how decisive Margaux Dutronc was. How she had slowly become that way, either as they began trusting one another, or as she'd grown older. She'd turned seventeen in February, and she was already a woman. When they hugged, he felt her close. Both emotionally and physically. He liked to think of what they did afterward. They sat back down and, each with their own oboes, played the duck's melody at the same time, in synchronicity, like two instruments in an orchestra. They played with one eye on the score and the other on one another's laughter. He would never forget this afternoon of new feelings.

"Damien? Damien Devère?"

Someone shouted after him on a shadowy corner. He'd only barely heard the man's voice, but he couldn't see him with how dark it was.

"Who's there?"

The man took two steps forward.

"You don't recognize me?" he asked, his voice subdued. "Are you pretending you don't know me or something?"

Frightened, Damien approached him to look him in the eyes. His face was familiar.

"From the orchestra, I'm guessing . . ."

"Hot."

"Mirailles, maybe?"

"Hotter, hotter."

"Cello, right? Now that's it."

"Michel Mirailles. They call me M. M."

"You're kidding me. At school they called me Dédé."

"The youngest and best-looking of the orchestra. Here you are . . ."

"Sometimes I sign my name as D. D." As he got closer, he noticed that Mirailles's breath reeked of warm wine. "What are you doing around here?"

"Waiting for curfew. When it's time to go home, don't worry, I'll be there."

"Sleeping off the hangover."

"Who? Me?" Mirailles had to make an effort to keep himself up straight. "Come on, buy me a drink . . . There's still a bar open two streets up from here."

"I know it. It's full of green uniforms until the witching hour."

"So what? They won't do anything to you. They're like dogs. If you don't say anything to them, they don't bother you."

"I'm going home, Mirailles."

"Come with me, come on. They won't bother you." He tried grabbing his hand, but Damien shook himself loose.

"I'm heading home. I haven't seen my mother all day."

"Of course. You're a kid who still lives with his parents."

"With my mother. My father—"

Mirailles grasped his face to shut him up.

"Look at what fine skin you have."

Once he had Damien trapped, his mouth in the shape of a circle, he kissed him on the lips.

"What the hell are you doing, man?" Damien stepped back and pushed him away. "Are you crazy or something?"

Damien looked around, worried someone had seen the kiss forced upon him. If he'd known how to, he would've punched Mirailles. He wiped his mouth with his shirtsleeve. He was a bundle of nerves.

"If anyone saw us, we'll be dead by tomorrow. You're a jerk."

"Don't worry about me. The Germans won't hurt me."

"How are you so sure?" He continued to wipe his mouth.

"I know it . . ." Michel had said too much and corrected himself. "I know it. That's all."

"Good night, Mirailles. Go home. You're wasted."

"Wanna know something?" He grabbed him by the collar so he wouldn't leave. "They used to call me M. M. for Michel *Marieta*. Faggot."

"Well, congratulations. I don't—"

"But you—" He was about to say it, then he stopped. "You're so cute, Dédé."

"I'm what?" He wasn't going to let Mirailles get away with anything else. "'But you'? What does that mean?"

"Everyone in the orchestra knows. Everyone talks about it."

"About what?"

"That the conductor, the great Delphin Moureau, hired you for the orchestra because . . ."

"Say it."

"You had your way with him."

"Me? What you're saying is absurd, Mirailles. You're really drunk."

"They said you played it good . . . That oboe."

"That's not true!" he shouted angrily.

"Everyone knows Moureau likes his boys young and skinny."

"I don't know anything about that. He's never put his hands on me. Not the conductor, or anyone else."

"I have," Mirailles said proudly, raising his finger.

"You're an idiot. And stop drinking. *Auf Wiedersehen.*"

He said it that way to make it hurt, and then he ran quickly home.

The next day, Mirailles didn't remember anything at the noon rehearsal. He found it strange that when Devère squeezed through the music stands to find his place in the center of the orchestra and he said good morning to him, the oboist didn't even acknowledge him. He just shot him an angry glare. Somewhere deep down, he had the sensation of a vague and remote nightmare in which Damien Devère appeared in some way, but even if he was promised the end of the war, he wouldn't have been able to remember where they'd run into one another or what they'd said.

Damien clearly did. From *a* to *z*. So much so that, during the rehearsal break, he approached Imtold and said, "Tell me everything you know about our cellist. Everything."

Like always, Imtold Lefebvre was well-informed. Even if he wasn't, he pretended to be. He recited it with a credibility that provoked an "amen." On more than one occasion, they joked that he'd chosen the wrong career. "You'd make a better living on the radio than with your violin."

"About Michel Mirailles, you mean?"

Once Damien assented, Imtold began recounting everything he'd heard from his various sources. He kept it all stored in his head.

"I'm told he's the type who can't keep his pants on. He doesn't like to sleep alone, and he doesn't have a wife or a girlfriend. I'm told you won't find him at One Two Three, the brothel on rue de Provence that's overrun these days. I'm told he's a drunk and plays better during evening concerts than morning ones, because his hangover is still dragging out. I believe that one."

"Me too," added Damien.

"I'm told he's been seen at 52 Champs-Élysées, which is where the headquarters of the Propagandastaffel is located. I'm told they have about fifty offices all over the occupied zone, but where does Goebbels go when he comes to Paris? To 52 Champs-Élysées. He's even got an office there, because it's a key location. It's where he manages the organization of the whole department of propaganda. I'm told nothing happens unless it's approved by Colonel Schmidtke, Heinz Schmidtke. I'm told that's where they decide the programming for Radio Paris, and they say which artists can play and which can't. That's where they control the newspapers that have surrendered to the Germans. *Le Matin*, the

Paris-soir . . . That's where they censure and go after people. They don't let anyone publish anything that attacks Hitler or hurts the Wehrmacht. The newspapers are printed in French but written in German. I'm told they're the ones who prohibit our theaters from playing American movies. And the British ones too. I'm told nothing gets past 52 Champs-Élysées. They're a well-oiled machine. A weapon of war. So, I'm told that one morning, Michel Mirailles was seen entering the Propagandastaffel, and then two weeks later he started writing opera criticism under a pseudonym in *Je suis partout*."

"What's *Je suis partout*?" Damien asked.

"The magazine that's everywhere. The weekly that outs Jews and communists between art and culture reviews. It was already a fascist media outlet before the fascists arrived."

"It's like *Signal* then? Nazi propaganda?"

"Worse. There are days they publish the names of Polish, Czech, and Romanian Jews in Paris, and they print their addresses so they can be hunted down."

"What pseudonym does Mirailles use?"

For once, Imtold Lefebvre rolled his eyes as if to say, "Now you got me stumped." He knew it, but he couldn't remember. It was on the tip of his tongue, but it wasn't coming to him. It made him so angry not to be able to answer a question that he shut his eyes so hard his eyelids hurt, and with one last effort, he blurted out a name like a snake spits out venom. "Jean du Silence."

24

Desire, Reality

Whenever Margaux left the house, her father always said, "Be careful." Her mother used to say, "Be smart." One appealed to fear, the other to responsibility. It seemed like they had divided the roles, but it had never been that way. They were two spontaneous sentences that, slowly as Margaux grew older, had become familiar crutches without the three of them realizing it. "Be careful" and "be smart" were, in the end, the subtle formula each of them found to say "I love you" without it being too apparent. When Margaux walked down the street by herself, it was always with her mother or father's permission. Oftentimes with permission from both. If she had plans to do something during the day that went beyond her routine of coming and going to school, she'd have to notify them of it in the morning. There was no way to notify them later, when Michelle was behind the store windows of the Lafayette or Ferdinand was fixing the electricity at the theater. One Saturday morning, while Michelle was in the bathroom, Margaux entered and closed the door so her father wouldn't hear them. The conversation wasn't going to be easy. She'd turned it over in her head so many times she didn't know how to bring it up. She took advantage of her mother putting on her eye makeup inches away from the mirror to let it fly.

"Tomorrow afternoon . . . First of all, tomorrow I'm seeing Damien."

"I didn't know you had class tomorrow."

"No, no . . ."

"On a Sunday? He must have a concert."

"Not in the afternoon. If they're playing, it'll be in the morning."

"Your father would know."

"Of course." She didn't know how to say it. Margaux was slightly taller than her mother when she was barefoot, and she had to look down at her a bit. "We're not doing a lesson tomorrow, Mama. Actually, Damien . . . he asked me if I could go to the movies with him."

"To the movies?" She looked at her daughter, confused. "In Paris? At your age? You and the oboe teacher?"

"Oh, Mama, he's not just any teacher . . . It's Damien. He's been coming for more than a year."

"But you're going to the movies? I don't understand."

"He said he'd pay. Don't worry about the money."

Michelle stopped doing her makeup, stepped back from the mirror, and looked into her daughter's eyes.

"I don't like it. It doesn't look good to me. It's not about the money, which is also a factor. You haven't missed out on a thing from not going to the movies. I don't have anything against the boy, but . . . Why do you have to go to the theater by yourselves?" She turned back to line her eyes. "I don't like it."

"Mama, please. I never ask for anything."

"I don't like the idea of you going. I already said it."

"We've spent the last two years locked up at home. I'm seventeen, and we're going to the boulevard des Italiens . . . We'll meet at Le Camèo. I'll get there on my bike. We'll see the movie, and I'll come straight back."

"So, you already know what you were going to see."

"We agreed on it yesterday, yes. I wouldn't have any way to tell him . . . You already know."

"I don't know. I don't know at all."

"Please, Mama. I'm asking you, please . . . Come on. Just once."

"Exactly, because it's the first time you've ever asked me something like this."

"You said it yourself. I'm asking, not telling you."

"I should hope so."

"I could have done it without letting you find out. On another day, while you and Father are at work."

"Don't break our trust."

"I won't break it, geez. That's why I'm telling you."

"I . . . I don't know what to say right now."

Michelle breathed in deeply. All this was new, and she had to tread carefully. Maybe it was time to trust Margaux. Even if her daughter was taller than her, she was still her little girl. There was no reason something should happen to her. The city had been quiet for months. There hadn't been any cases of girls going out by themselves, and . . . Either way, the theaters were open and had become a great distraction for the conquered. It was a new way of trying to forget their circumstances. It wouldn't be for very long either . . .

"Mama." Margaux kissed her sweetly on her cheek. "I'm asking for what I want most in the world."

"Be careful, young lady," Michelle said, without softening. "Don't step out of line on me."

She had to stick to her principles. She didn't know if Margaux was ready to go out with someone, but, as her mother, she sure wasn't. Her legs suddenly started to tremble. She knew she should stand her ground in saying no but was starting to waver. At the same time, she hadn't communicated that in specific words. Giving in didn't have to look like surrender.

"What would you go see?"

"Damien suggested *The Wrong Man*. The orchestra conductor recommended it to them."

"*The Wrong Man*? I haven't heard anyone talk about it." She looked at herself in the mirror and saw her mother thirty years younger. "I hope you both like it."

"Does that mean it's a yes?" She was happy. "Mama, you're letting me go?"

Her mother closed her eyes to express reluctant permission.

"What will you wear?"

"I was thinking . . . I'll show you right now."

She ran off to her closet and came back with a checkered skirt and two blouses, one with a high neck and another one without lapels. Her mother had seen enough with a quick glance.

"You should dress up more. Just a bit dressier, Margaux. Tomorrow is Sunday. And it's got to make the Germans itch to see that, despite everything, we're still the most elegant in the world. Fancy, fun hats, the latest shoes. They must be dying of envy. They should know they haven't totally conquered us. That's the motto."

"What motto?"

"The secret of all Parisian women."

"Do women talk about this with each other? I don't believe it for a second!"

"It's true. But we don't need to talk about it. We look at each other on the street, and we all agree. We wink at each other. It's the secret password to communicate that they'll never be able to take our glamour. It's a way of rubbing it in their faces. So, they realize they'll never be able to have it all."

"Mama, the stories you come up with. They're soldiers. Who believes they care about all that?"

"I'm telling you I see it every day at the store. It affects them more than you think. They wish their women had our style, the way we wear things here." She murmured something Margaux didn't understand. "I think that . . ."

"What'd you say, Mama?"

"Nothing. It gets so hot when both of us are in this small bathroom."

"That wasn't it."

"I was thinking you can grab something from my closet if you want. We'll take a look tomorrow, if you'd like. Let's see, I don't want you to look too grown-up, though . . ."

"We don't want Damien to get scared, Mama."

"Or for him not to recognize you."

"Can you imagine? That would be awful."

"That's impossible. Oh, lady." She grabbed Margaux by the waist and shook her little girl. "You've gotten so big!"

They laughed together.

"What's going on in there?" asked her father from the winged armchair, as he moved the dial on the radio.

"Nothing. Your daughter's just gotten so big."

That Sunday, as she helped her daughter dress, Michelle became an accomplice in the teenager's anxieties. There was a war outside, Europe was an immense battlefield, but that afternoon, Margaux's world didn't encompass that. It was all Damien, the theater, and *The Wrong Man*. In fact, the movie was the least important detail of them all. She didn't want to say it out loud—all three of them knew it already—but it was the first time she was going to the movies without her parents. She also didn't say that, for the very first time, she wouldn't be sitting in the middle seat. It was—and this was a big deal for her—her first date with a boy. But she didn't want to repeat it to herself because just the thought of the word "date" surprised and disturbed her. A mix of fear, hope, and butterflies wriggled in her stomach. She became even more anxious when she wondered whether she'd know how to act at every point of the date. What are you supposed to say? How are you supposed to behave? Where did you learn all of this, and how come no one had told her about it? She was so anxious she wasn't even hungry at lunch.

She tied her hair in a high bun so her face could be seen. She curled her eyelashes to highlight her big eyes. She'd slipped on a dress she borrowed from her mother, who'd convinced her it was the one that complemented her complexion the most. It was a springtime, knee-length, green dress with a moon pattern. When she looked in the mirror, she knew it had to be that dress. None of the others she'd tried on looked as good on her. She put on a maroon coat that resembled a cape over the dress along with a small matching hat she wore aslant to keep from crushing her bun. Everything was well thought out. Everything had a reason. The heels too. It'd be more comfortable to pedal with laces.

At the door of the apartment, her mother looked her over one more time. Then, she grabbed her by her shoulders and gave her a kiss, the kind for special occasions.

"Be smart," she said in a trusting voice.

The click-clack of her heels on every step, going five floors down, was the echo of rushing to make it on time. The Dutroncs stored their bikes behind the building's entrance. It didn't bother anyone, and they trusted no one would take them. There was only one woman left in the whole building, and she lived on the third floor; she'd become a widow after the event at Tours. Since the start of the exodus that first June, it was very quiet in the stairwell. Too much so, her father said sometimes.

Margaux stretched her dress out under her jacket, got up on the bicycle seat, put her feet on the pedals, and let the wheels glide down the stone streets of Montmartre without pedaling. The clattering was quieter from Clichy to the boulevard des Italiens. The path was instantly level. She had to apply more force, but the stones weren't as uncomfortable and her breasts didn't bounce as much. Her desire to see Damien was greater than anything else, but she didn't want to go so fast as to catch the attention of some corner patrolman thinking she was fleeing a scene. She didn't want to go faster than necessary, more than anything, because the last thing she wanted was to arrive to her first date sweaty. At three on the dot. At the door of the movie theater.

Damien—dressed in gray with a vest and a skinny tie—was already waiting for her under the sign of Le Camèo. There were the gigantic, vertical red letters, and there he was underneath them. Like the movie theater was pointing at him.

"I think this is the first time I'm seeing you without your oboe case."

"I think it's because it's maybe the first time I've left the house without my oboe in years." He extended his hand to help her dismount the bike. "Two kisses, right?"

"Three. It's still France."

She secured her bike to a streetlamp. Damien had already bought the tickets and was carrying them in the pocket of his sport coat. While they waited for the doors of the theater to open, they distracted themselves by looking at the movie posters hanging in the window. They more or less killed time like the dressy people around them were doing. Some men stuck out their cigarettes and neared the sidewalk to ash it with a flick of their fingers.

"Did you know the movie was German?" Damien asked.

"Me? How could I . . . We'll still watch it, right?"

"Whatever you want."

"If you've already bought the tickets, we should use them."

"Can I say something?" He thought about saying it either way. "You look very beautiful, Margaux."

"Oh, really?" She laughed sincerely. "That's so nice."

"I've never seen you look so elegant."

"Did you see?" she said, turning on one foot.

They were the third in line to enter the theater. It was dark and smelled like dry velvet, a projector ventilator, and patchouli water.

"You choose. Where do you want to sit?"

Margaux contemplated the sea of empty chairs. There were three whole rows in the middle of the floor reserved for the Germans. The sight of them was enough of a reminder of who had the power in there as well.

"Better to be behind them than in front, don't you think, Damien?"

"Yes, wherever you want. But hurry, people are coming in and . . ."

"Oh." Why couldn't he choose? "Well, these two are fine, I guess."

"Here in the corner?"

"You don't think so?"

"Anything is fine with me."

"Too far back?"

"Behind everything, you mean?"

"Calm down," said Margaux, sitting next to the wall. "You don't have to watch the orchestra conductor today. Are you nearsighted or something?"

"Me?" He felt attacked.

"Are you nearsighted and didn't tell me?"

When they turned out the lights—oh, the most holy feeling—she inched closer to his seat and whispered a confession into his ear.

"I won't have to take off my hat sitting in the last row."

This ensured she wouldn't block anyone. Only she knew how many pins held the hat to her head and how impossible it would be to put it back on again. A woman sitting two rows ahead, the type of person who loved to shush, turned and silenced them.

"Shhh!" Her threatening finger, perpendicular on her lips.

For a while, they were as quiet as death. When she was with her parents at the theater, no one ever had to scold her. Maybe that's what growing up was. Challenging, bothering, testing the limits, sitting next to the boy you liked, feeling a new feeling, and then, all of a sudden, a grumbling lady turns around to ruin your mood.

The Wrong Man was the story of a boring couple. Margaux and Damien were so preoccupied with watching each other from the corners of their eyes that it was hard for them to follow the couple's misadventures. Attention was at an all-time peak in that theater. If there had been a fly, everyone would have heard it. For their part, they lived on the sidelines of the screen.

That Sunday afternoon, they were on the verge of writing the first page of their own screenplay. Both of them noticed it—in their breathing, in the silence, in the latent tension—but neither of them dared move history forward. Until. Until. There's always a moment in which a single gesture leaves an impression on an entire life. Magic.

In the middle of the movie, Margaux took her right hand off her lap and let it fall, lifelessly, in the space between the seats. She wasn't looking for anything. She just hoped. Damien, who'd spent some time with his arms folded across his chest, took a while to unwrap them. He didn't want to make a false move. But his heart accelerated the way it did right before the start of a concert. He moved his toes around inside his shoes as a trick to distract himself and prevent his mouth from drying up. A friend from his orchestra had given him this advice to combat nerves some time back, and once the moment had come, he put it into practice. Slowly, he let his left hand fall into neutral territory. Without turning away from the screen, they found each other. Margaux let her ring finger run twice over one of his to greet him. He thought carefully before reacting. He returned the gesture with the same light touch. One finger, gingerly, over another finger. It was a way of saying, "Yes, it's me. I'm here." Margaux, catching on quickly, knew it was her turn in that game. She next touched Damien's warm hand with all her fingers just as subtly and respectfully. Suddenly, with their gazes forward and their arms down, hidden under the chairs, their hands found each other. First, they interlaced their fingers and were motionless in their secret. They made it last so as to enjoy the moment, to still their emotions, and to make sure what was happening was real. Desire, reality. After a while, once they actually clasped their hands, placing their palms together, they finally looked at each other. Illuminated by the light of the screen, they communicated with their eyes. Their looks said the same thing. Happiness, satisfaction, fear. Complicity for the first time. The effervescence of love, absolute and surrendered. There didn't exist two happier people in Paris in that moment. They didn't let go of each other's hands until a second before the lights switched on.

They remained in their seats as the audience, comprising some seventy people, filtered out through the center aisle of the theater, and they discussed the movie, the wait to exit feeling eternal in their excitement. Damien didn't stop moving his toes so his mouth wouldn't dry. Absorbed, Margaux looked straight ahead as though the movie was still playing. She wasn't too sure why she had to put on a front.

"Are we the ones who are in the wrong?" he asked, as the two last audience members passed by them.

"Wrong about what?"

He inched close to her slowly, certain they were both dying with yearning.

"About this."

Their first kiss was short. Short but sweet. The second was more intentional. Seeing that Damien had closed his eyes, Margaux copied him. *It must work that way,* she thought. She discovered that, in the dark, she was more aware of his tender and extremely fine lips. She realized what an interesting and pleasant feeling it was to have a tongue play with your own. They were like a cat and a mouse in there, and eventually they found each other to make peace. They closed their eyes—now she understood—to savor the world that instantly opened up before them. They kissed each other wholeheartedly and lost track of time. He put his hand on the back of her neck, and she did the same, searching for symmetry. Give and take. The charm of doing things evenly.

"Let's go."

"One second," Margaux said, looking for his lips again.

"I'm scared they'll lock us in here." He took a moment to stand up, as the erection under his pants would be visible to everyone. "Come on, let's go."

"You're like my father, man. Always rushing to leave everywhere."

They breathed deeply and stood up. Before reaching the lobby, they hugged. She stood up on her tiptoes for their first standing kiss.

At the exit, they were blinded by the afternoon sun. On the street, the Germans were making a racket and greeting each other with the sounds of their boots, that obsession of theirs. People walked in all directions, and another line had formed down the boulevard for the six o'clock showing, soon to begin. The Dutronc bike had gotten lost within the line, and they had to ask permission to move through and unlock it.

"So now what, Margaux?"

"What do you mean?" As mixed up as she was, she didn't understand if the question referred to the next few minutes of that singular Sunday or if he was waiting for a response about how those kisses had changed her life.

"Do you want to do something?"

She liked seeing how, in the light of the street, Damien's eyes shined just the way hers must have been.

"I promised my mother I would come back while it was still light out."

"It's early, Margaux."

"But it's the first time I've ever asked to go to a movie, and . . ." She ran her hand over his shaved chin. "It's a good idea for me to return home if we ever want to do anything again, don't you think? I'd rather go home."

"I'll accompany you some of the way back, if you don't mind."

"Why would I?" She playfully poked at his belly. "What are you saying? Why would I mind?"

They walked up the boulevard without touching. They let their hands touch only accidentally. Holding on to the handlebars, he walked her bike, and she walked happily at his side. The nerves of the journey there were forgotten. Now there was just complicity and jokes on the walk and in their spirits. The infinite winding staircase of first love. Always up, always turning around the same axis without there ever being a hint of an end.

"Don't accompany me any farther, Damien. You're walking too far from your neighborhood. I'd spend the evening with you, but . . ."

"When will we see each other again?"

"When's our next lesson? You are my oboe teacher, remember?"

"Teacher of what?" he teased. "And to think it's all thanks to *Peter and the Wolf*."

"Can I kiss you, Dami?"

"Here? On the street?"

They looked around. Spotting only an old woman sitting in a doorway, they didn't stop themselves from doing what they desired.

"See you Tuesday, then."

"I really, really, really can't wait to see you at my house, Damien."

Letting go of each other's hands was like climbing a mountain. Margaux put on her coat, stretched the dress over herself, and mounted the bike. The breeze grazed her face. She pedaled happily, with the sensation of remembering every touch and movement before her first kiss. And the feeling of those lips and his tongue inside her mouth. She never would have thought she'd be so good at it without asking anyone for tips. And on her first try. She should have opened her eyes to see his face. That way, she would remember how Damien looked in that exact moment. She pedaled and felt radiant. Her fresh face, the new vibrations, her heart pumping.

She slowed down as she reached Notre-Dame-de-Lorette. An old barricade forced her to move in zigzags to avoid the sandbags and stones. She dismounted to move slower. A man wearing an armband she couldn't identify raised his hand to stop her.

"Ma'am. Just one moment."

Margaux hesitated to stop walking. The man had a nice face, spoke French, and had a camera hanging from his neck.

"What a beautiful Sunday afternoon," the man said. "The sky, the sun . . . You're so pretty with your hat and bike. Would you let me photograph you? The light is so perfect right now. You just have to make the most of it."

"A picture? Of me?"

"If it's okay with you."

If only it were all that easy, she thought.

"Here?"

"Here, you're slightly backlit. Let's switch places. You go over there."

Margaux turned around.

"There you go."

"It would be perfect if . . . I don't want to bother you, sorry."

"What? Say it."

"If you got up on the bike, it'd look so pretty."

He didn't have to say it twice. She mounted the bike, placing one foot on the sidewalk to hold herself up and the other on the pedal.

"Where should I look?"

He put his eye to the viewfinder of the Leica.

"Tilt your head slightly to the left. As if I weren't here."

"Like this?"

"Exactly. Smile a little, girl, it's a wonderful day."

Of course, that street photographer didn't know the half of it. Margaux didn't have to force her smile.

"Now?"

"Ecco qua."

He had it. The photographic composition dreams were made of. Frontal, looking at the camera, with the lower perspective that made the front wheel look bigger than it was. The wicker basket, so nicely braided, in front of the handlebars. In the background, the lights and shadows on the building facade. At the forefront, a girl of categorical beauty. Paris, elegance, despite everything. One more for the collection.

25

I'll Search for You in the Rain

They understood each other with a look. It came with the job. The violinist Imtold Lefebvre—always one eye on the score, the other on the conductor—was used to living with his sights set sharp. He and Samuel Bardollet knew right away they'd go back. They decided on their next goal as soon as Imtold mentioned he'd passed by the German bookstore on the outskirts of the Sorbonne, as soon as he explained it'd reopened under the name "Rive Gauche" and that people came and went like nothing had happened.

"Should we do it again?"

"Why not?"

"We'll blow that bookstore up as many times as they reopen it. Who do these rats think they are?"

Bardollet didn't leave the house much. Just for the essentials, and that was it. Even when he dared go out, he refused to wear the damn symbol identifying him as a Jew. Before taking a wrong step, he calculated the risks, planned the route, and as lanky as he was, he tried to go unnoticed and not give anyone the opportunity to become suspicious. No longer with a salary from the factory and having to hide at home for the past two years, Samuel had converted the dining room into a modest and rudimentary workshop where he forged bread ration tickets. Not even the experts could tell the difference. Later, he'd leave, a package tucked under his arm, sell the cards on the black market, and return to his shelter. It was a matter of survival. Imtold, despite his nickname, guarded his roommate's secret. He didn't tell anyone. They were risking too much.

"Once we blow up the bookstore again, maybe we should do something with Maurice Chevalier," Bardollet said, the parts of the explosive device laid out before him like an unsolved puzzle.

"The singer? What'd he do?"

"I can't stop hearing him on Radio Paris."

"Radio Paris ment, Radio Paris ment, Radio Paris est allemand." Imtold sang the lyrics the resistance had invented using the traitorous radio station's signature tune. He continued. "Chevalier is already one of them. I think he spends the whole day at the radio station. He sings live. Maybe we should punish—"

Bardollet raised his hand to stop his friend from saying anything else. "We twist the cable this way, right?"

Imtold lowered his face to look at it closely. With his expression of ignorance and his demeanor that of a slacker, he was like a medical student faced with his first patient in the operating room. "I wouldn't know how to do it, Samu. You're the expert."

"The thing is, I don't remember right now if—"

"You make sure it doesn't explode before we want it to, dammit."

"I can think of more heroic ways to die in the middle of a war. Do you think we moved this one last time," Bardollet said, pointing to a red wire, "underneath the other one?"

"How would I know?"

"If this explodes here, you're right. We won't appear in the history books."

"We won't even appear in some amateur novel."

"Don't make me laugh, dammit. This is fragile."

Samuel Bardollet handled the bomb with a gentle touch. Slowly, he put two and two together. He was much less doubtful than he seemed.

"When do you want to do it?" Imtold asked.

"Tomorrow," Bardollet responded, concentrating and not looking up. "We said tomorrow, right? Once they close the bookstore. Do you have a concert?"

"Rehearsal. For Rimsky-Korsakov."

"A Russian?" asked Bardollet, surprised. "They let you play Russian composers?"

"The conductor is good with those lowlifes. You know how Delphin Moureau can be . . . Slick as an eel. He knows how to stay in everyone's good graces."

"And the *Kartoffeln* want to show they're not bad people, that life is normal here. They may be sons of bitches, but they're clever."

"So, tomorrow?"

Imtold extended his hand so Samuel could shake it.

"We'll do it again," he said, with the courageousness of brave men. In response to the gesture of complicity, he shook his hand slowly, careful not to incite an unexpected detonation.

"I hope it will stop raining by then."

"Of course, I hope so too. I hate running down the wet cobblestone streets."

A naked poem. The treasure chest. The infinite moment. The hand game. The light of dreams. The voice of a man. Sine qua non. A party in a forest. Choosing a lipstick. Dressing as a fairy. Repeating your name twice in a row in different intonations. The smell of wet grass. Watching, silencing, loving. I'll search for you in the rain. Every word, a star.

Margaux had written fifteen ways of knowing you were in love in her yellow notebook. Every day she saw Damien and spent time with him—however long it was, she enjoyed it until the last second—she would lock herself in her room afterward and express her feelings that day. She put the way he made her feel through a filter, and after she sifted through the essence of it, she dipped her pen in the ink and wrote in beautiful handwriting. She wanted to keep it short. If it could be said in three words rather than four, then so be it. But she felt so much with so much passion, and everything was so novel that sometimes it didn't come out right. In their every-other-day meetings since that first kiss, they'd pushed the oboe to the side. Everything was fire and laughter. Margaux's parents, unaware of what was happening in their house, continued to pay the young teacher. The boy charged them the same fee because of what they would've said and also so as not to raise suspicions. Seven francs and an apple. What more could you want? There were days, though, when the couple became so excited while talking that Margaux curled up on Damien's lap to kiss him. Then, they didn't even end up opening the case. The days on which they set up the oboe and placed the reed to play had started to run dry.

"Can I read it to you?" she said, taking the intimate notebook out of her drawer.

"Read what?"

"What you inspire in me. Every time I see you, I write down my thoughts." She opened it up to a specific page. "Or would you rather read it yourself?"

"No, no."

"Ready?" Margaux let a silence fall between them.

A naked poem.

A treasure chest.

She read it aloud slowly.

The infinite moment.

Damien savored every concept. He guessed at what had inspired every image. Sometimes, he nodded his head like he had correctly ascertained where his beloved Margaux's feelings came from, the girl who had shaken him to the point that he didn't know where north, south, his head, and his heart began.

"Now it's your turn."

"What is?"

"To say what you're feeling."

He looked at her tenderly. Then, seconds later, he scrunched his nose. He didn't want to improvise with any metaphors, or be short and corny. He didn't dare to. He grabbed his oboe, softened the reed with his lips, and let the music rescue him. His eyes closed shut, and he played with all his heart. The melody was a sea of calm. Margaux also closed her eyes to allow herself to be transported. Once he finished his solo, they synchronized their return to reality.

"What was that? It's so beautiful."

"It's a gift."

"For me?"

"For both of us. We just started rehearsing Rimsky-Korsakov's *Scheherazade*, and I love it. This is the second movement; it's a treat for the oboe player."

"Yeah, I heard that." She was entranced. "It's beautiful. It draws up visions of distant lands."

"Listen to these notes," Damien said, before he repeated the beginning. "It's a musical trip, right? The bassoon draws its musical theme from Prince Kalandar, and then the oboe enters and responds to it this way. It's the same melody as the bassoon's, but it has a fresher sound, more colorful."

"You're always one for 'more.'"

"Playing it makes me happy. I'm in dialogue here with the harp, you should hear it."

"It sounds peaceful."

"You recognized that. Wonderful. It's beautiful with a whole orchestra."

"How nerve-racking, everyone concentrating on you in that moment. I'd die. Of embarrassment, I mean."

Damien played the whole melody again. Then, he interlaced it with his passages from other movements of *One Thousand and One Nights*. "This is Sinbad's boat," he explained. "Here, I play with the flute, clarinet, and the cello." He instilled all his enthusiasm in his descriptions. "But in the third movement, I overlap my voice with that of the violas, and I promise it's extraordinarily beautiful. It's the moment for the young prince and princess."

"It's the two of us."

"Not exactly. I hope we have a better ending."

Margaux snatched the instrument out of his hands and placed it carefully on the bed. She sat in front of Damien and kissed each of his eyelids.

"Your eyes are so beautiful I could poke them out," she teased.

"Yours are even more so, Margi."

"Now . . . now can I tell you that I love you?"

"I'm sure it can't be as much as I love you."

"How can you say that?" She kissed him playfully all over his face. "How can you say that, Dami? I'll always love you more than you love me."

"How can you measure that love? By the two times you say my name in different intonations?"

"Don't laugh at me, you idiot."

"I'd love to hear you say my name in different intonations . . ."

"For the sake of your vanity?"

"Out of curiosity."

"Well, you'll have to hold on, big head."

Their lips. Their mouths. The scent. Watching, silencing, loving. They were there for a while. First on the chair. Then, they moved the oboe and lay on the bed. The game of hands. Slowly, Margaux unbuttoned his shirt. From top to bottom. She took her time ruffling the hair on his chest. Her slender finger played with it. She liked trying new sensations slowly.

"What are you going to write when I leave today?" Damien asked, his torso naked.

"I have to think about it."

"Can I write it for you?"

"In my notebook?" She suddenly wasn't sure if this excited or saddened her.

He sat up and searched Margaux's dressing table for a piece of paper on which he could write his prediction. Using a pencil, he wrote down a word, folded up the paper, and placed it beneath her pillow.

"Open it when you go to bed tonight. We'll see if it's the same word you write in your notebook."

"Are you betting it will be?"

"If you guess correctly, it's eternal love."

"I don't believe you."

"I'm a man of my word."

"Give me a hint."

Damien thought about it. "It's a single word. Just one."

That evening, Margaux used up a whole candle, her notebook at her side, waiting to fulfill the test of distilled love. Finally, when her parents insisted she go to bed because she had school in the morning, she made her decision. She dipped her pen in the black ink, and, using her best calligraphy, she wrote down a single idea. A unique word. The essence of the day. After, nervous to reveal the correct answer, she ran to put her hand under the pillow. She found the paper Damien had written on. She opened it. A single word.

Scheherazade.

The same word she'd written in her notebook. Scheherazade. Eternal love. She'd won.

"Go to sleep, Margaux, please," her mother shouted from the next room.

In the morning, on her way to the Galeries Lafayette, Michelle sought shelter under a doorway. Her umbrella wasn't enough. The wind turned it inside out, and she was soaked halfway up her calf because of the deluge of water that was falling. Angry thunder made the streetlamps and facades tremble. Its hoarse echo enveloped everything. There was the feeling that each thunderclap groaned closer and closer. But the storm couldn't last all morning. As much as the black sky fought to remain, it ended up surrendering. It knew well enough that riots don't last more than fifteen minutes in Paris. You just have to be patient and wait. She stayed there, glued to the doorway, watching how, right before her very eyes, the raindrops created bubbles in the puddles. Once the storm calmed slightly, she continued on to work, careful not to slip.

"Twenty minutes late, Mrs. Dutronc." The floor manager, the nasty "Monsieur Mustache," was waiting for her, his finger on the face of the clock.

"What could I do? In a downpour like this."

"Dry off and change, and don't let this happen again."

"Shut up, idiot," she murmured, careful to ensure he couldn't hear her.

She put on her blue uniform, fixed her hair, retouched her lipstick, and went to her floor. There was a strange silence between Marthe, Nathalie, and Marion that was an unsettling novelty.

"Good morning," Michelle said.

Practically no one responded. Why on earth were their faces so serious? Yes, she'd arrived late. One day. She didn't see why it was such a big deal that they had to treat her so coldly.

"Why are you looking at me like that? Can you tell me why?"

They continued looking at her with disgust. Just in case, so they knew she wouldn't be walked all over, she said, "We've all been late before, and that's no reason—"

"What's this?" Marion interrupted her.

She threw the magazine in her hands on the glass counter, open to an exact page. To shake off all the anger directed at her, Michelle pounced on top of it with an open hand, like she was trying to kill a fly. Her eyes could not avoid the picture in the magazine.

"It's Margaux!" she blurted with the spontaneous happiness of seeing her daughter on the family bike, photographed beautifully in black and white.

Marthe, Nathalie, and Marion looked at one another and exchanged an offended look as if to say, "She's making fun of us."

"We already know it's your daughter. That's why we're asking you, Michelle."

"What's she doing here?" Marion asked.

"You're about to tell us you didn't know," Nathalie said incredulously.

"Know what?" Michelle was still astounded. "That she'd appear in this magazine? I didn't even know she'd been photographed."

"She didn't tell you, your own—"

"My daughter? No."

"Do you expect us to believe that, honey?"

Michelle couldn't stop looking at the picture. She recognized the jacket, the hat, and her daughter's sincere smile. Margaux was truly splendid. She knew, without a doubt, when the photo had been taken. Two Sundays ago. She had no idea, though, who could have taken it. She didn't think Damien had a camera. And if he did, she believed even less so that he'd dare take it out on the street. If he were seen with it, it'd be taken from him, and as prudent as he was, he would never risk it.

She looked up from the magazine and saw her three coworkers, with whom she'd never had problems, looking at her with anger in their eyes.

"What's wrong?" she asked defensively. "Yes, it's Margaux. I think she looks very beautiful."

"But don't you see where the picture has appeared?" In a fit of anger, Marthe closed the magazine and thrust the cover in her face. "*Signal*, the Nazi magazine."

"What's your daughter doing here posing for the Germans?"

"I don't know anything about it . . ." Michelle's shoulders shrank with every accusation. "Do you really think . . . It must be a misunderstanding. Margaux isn't involved in any of that."

Marthe laughed falsely and spoke like Michelle wasn't there.

"Who does she think will believe that?"

Nathalie addressed her directly, fixing the lapels on Michelle's blue uniform in a maternal gesture, and after, as calmly as she could, she asked the question that had been burning inside her for a while. "Let's see. Your husband didn't have to go to the front. Now your daughter appears in this German magazine, and who are you? A spy?"

"Please, Nathalie, how can you say that? Stop making up stories. I think everything must have an explanation."

"No!" Marthe interrupted her. "Some things don't have explanations. Or justifications. Because these sons of bitches killed my husband, and I don't know where he ended up and maybe I'll never know. And because Marion—this woman standing directly in front of you—because her husband was recruited to the war only two months after they got married, and she's never seen him again . . . and you, the Dutroncs, strolling around Paris as if nothing is happening."

"We knew there were things going on . . . We knew you had the ration card for big families. People are going pale with hunger. Our meat portions have gotten smaller. Meanwhile, you have double the rations of milk and meat. Grifting for two whole years. Calling in favors from the Germans."

"What did you do it in exchange for, Michelle? Did you think we didn't notice?"

"We're not stupid."

"This is just what we were missing. Now your daughter acts like a model for them."

"The bicycles. People used them to flee into exile, and you use them to pose nicely in front of that trash."

"Here." Nathalie angrily ripped out the page with the photo and thrust it to her. "Take your daughter."

"Collaborators are disgusting. Dis-gust-ing."

Michelle begged for mercy, overcome by another storm that could carry everything away.

"Would you listen to me for a second?" she said, her lips trembling.

"No."

"But—"

"We said no!"

Marthe's spittle landed directly on her cheek. Michelle was so shocked she was late to react. Once she wiped it off with her sleeve, a thread of tension led her to hold Marthe's hard gaze inches away from her.

Michelle collected herself. "You should apologize. For what you've done and said."

"On top of—sorry, *what*?"

In a furious rage, Marthe lunged at her. She scratched Michelle's face, and Marion and Nathalie had to hold back her arms to stop her. Meanwhile, Michelle curled up on the ground and covered her cheeks with her hands to protect herself so they wouldn't continue fighting her and because, just like the scratches, their accusations of selling out to the conquerors hurt. She hid, because deep down, she started to doubt whether the Dutroncs were doing something wrong. Her three coworkers suddenly thought they were traitors. Who else thought that? Truth hurts, but this was all a lie. The Dutroncs, she and Ferdinand, did all they could, like so many others. She, a spy? They didn't do anything but serve, stay quiet, and obey.

"What's going on in here, ladies?" The manager with the wilted mustache broke them up. "For the love of God . . . What must our clients think?"

"But no one's come in all morning," Nathalie responded unenthusiastically.

"Work and be quiet, all of you. And you." He pointed at Michelle with his chin. "Do us the favor of washing your face."

Michelle grabbed the page with the picture, and looking at the floor, she headed to the dressing room in the employee bathroom of the Galeries Lafayette. She inspected her wounds closely in the mirror. It came to her quickly—when they asked her at home about the scratches on her cheek, she'd say a cat had attacked her on the street. In the shriek of the storm, a black cat had emerged out of nowhere, jumped on her, and ruined her day.

26

One Night, Maybe Two

Imtold woke early and, without changing out of his pajamas, began playing. The violins in Rimsky-Korsakov's *Scheherazade* contained passages with very delicate phrasing. It was a beautiful but complicated melody, like all masterful works performed for the first time. He practiced to find perfection. He tried over and over. He didn't want the conductor to have to stop the rehearsal again to ask him to concentrate on his left hand. Once was enough humiliation for him.

In the room next door, Samuel slept as best he could. Despite trying, he hadn't gotten used to his roommate's tendency to practice his violin at all hours of the day. The music kept him up more than the anxiety of knowing he had a job to complete that evening. He'd emerge from his cave, meet with Imtold in the place de la Sorbonne, and once they made sure there was no one left in the German bookstore, they'd drop their gift off at the door and run away, one up Vaugirard, the other behind the university. Half an hour later, they'd meet at home to celebrate with a glass of wine and pretend nothing had happened. They had repeated each gesture, each movement, a dozen times. The synchronization was crucial. So was the superstition. If things worked out for them the last time they tried, on the night it rained cats and dogs, they'd repeat the pattern.

The first thing Samuel did when he woke up was curse the sound of the violin chords. After, he splashed his face with a little water and looked out the window. Paris had woken with a clear sky, a sophisticated blue. Not even the birds dared to disturb the suspiciously calm scenery. A hole in his stomach, he opened the bread box with the hope of nibbling on a crust, even if it was stale. He found the same thing there that he found every day: nothing.

Resigned to a breakfastless morning, Samuel turned to speak with Imtold, who'd come into the kitchen. "Two days ago, someone told me about this kid. You know the youngest of the Bailocs? He's three years old, and he thought an orange was a ball. He'd never seen an orange. It was the first time."

"I get it. Good morning."

"Good morning." Samuel adjusted the sheet music on the music stand. "By the way, you got it right the first time you played."

"Thank you."

"It sounds so good, there's no need to play it again."

"We have a concert next weekend."

"Seriously, Imtold, you've got it down. Trust me, don't practice anymore. Don't think about it anymore. You don't need to."

"You're sarcastic this morning." Imtold set his violin on the table.

"Be careful," Samuel warned with a small laugh. "Don't confuse your cases."

Inside Imtold's old violin case was the explosive Samuel Bardollet had carefully prepared the last few evenings. An explosive device he'd whipped up out of anger that had been brewing for months, since the Vél d'Hiv Roundup. Practically overnight, almost all his Jewish friends had disappeared. They hadn't taken just men, as they'd done during the initial years of the war. Women, children, and whole families too. Thousands. People ripped from their beds, arrested, and driven to the velodrome in the fifteenth arrondissement, where they waited for five days without food or water. After . . . No one in Paris knew where they took those people. Not even Imtold had a guess.

Samuel had escaped, because, in his handiness, he'd built a hiding place on the roof of the building. He'd taken advantage of the angle created by two chimneys to set up a minuscule refuge where he could hole himself up if things went south. He knew he couldn't stay in that shoebox for too long. He'd suffocate to death. But he had to risk it. The alternative was always worse. And when the moment came, his secret corner saved his life on July 16, 1942.

He had decided to set the lair up the day Imtold had arrived home with a green card he'd picked up on the street. By the middle of the first May of the Nazi occupation, not even a year since the invasion of France, Jews had not yet been forced to wear the yellow star on their clothes. In the span of a few days, the French police had circulated a note that spread across the whole city. It was a green card signed by the French police inspector asking all foreign Jews who'd come to Paris as refugees to report to the Gymnase Japy for a routine check, with a blanket and a day's worth of food. According to the note, they'd receive documents there, and their status would be legalized. If they didn't comply, they could face "severe sanctions." Many guessed it was a ruse due to those two words. Many others fell hook, line, and sinker for the trap. It was the green card raid.

"If they truly did that to the Czechs, the Polish, I'm sure they'll come after their own one day or another," Samuel predicted. "To them, we're Jews, and that's it. They don't care where we came from."

"Of course, it's true, Samu. So true that we have no idea where they took those poor people. They may have deported them back to their countries."

"You don't believe that, my friend."

The next morning, scared he'd be hunted like a rabbit, Samuel began building his hiding place on the roof of the house. Only half a man could fit in there, and he couldn't spend too much time inside. He didn't care; that small space was enough for him. There were advantages to eating so little food and being able to bend like a contortionist in a circus.

They reviewed the plan again. Once Imtold finished his rehearsal of *Scheherazade* with the whole orchestra in the afternoon, Samuel would wait for him at the door of the Châtelet. He'd go there with the old violin case containing the bomb. Imtold would emerge from the theater, his own instrument case in hand. Slowly, the two "musicians" would walk together toward the place de la Sorbonne. By the time they'd arrive, the German bookstore would already be closed. They would wait outside on the corner bench to confirm that detail while pretending they were chatting. There would be no rush. They couldn't rush these things. The moment they knew no *Kartoffeln* or passersby were around, Samuel would approach the window closest to the door, open the case, and, in less than seven seconds—he had calculated it precisely—activate the bomb to go off thirty seconds later. Case in hand, he would run toward Vaugirard. Imtold, acting uninterested, would begin walking in the direction of the university. They'd meet at home, no matter what. If a problem came up . . .

"Everything will be fine. There won't be any problems. We know the plan well," Imtold reassured Samu.

As credible as Imtold could be, he also was human and thus was capable of making mistakes.

Yes, Samuel picked him up after rehearsal. Was he carrying the case with the surprise inside? Yes. They walked toward the square, and the bookstore lights were already turned off. They sat on the bench, as they had planned, and when the moment presented itself, they stood. Samuel walked to the window next to the doorway, and Imtold, humming quietly to calm his nerves, headed toward the university. Samuel opened the two locks on the case at the same time and, hands sweaty, activated the explosive before counting to seven. At that exact moment, the door of the bookstore opened.

"Halt! Halt!" shouted the German soldier.

Samuel began running in the direction of Vaugirard. The soldier, who was trailing from the bookstore, shot at him as he fled, hitting Samuel in the leg with his second burst of shots. Limping, Samuel managed to make it a few feet before the second shot hit him in the back, causing him to fall. Injured, Samuel was left face down. Everything after happened quickly. That same soldier approached him and finished him off with two shots to the head. Just as the blood started pouring out in streams, the bomb burst all the bookstore windows. Hugging his violin case close, Imtold turned the corner behind the Sorbonne with no choice but to run up a couple of streets. Fear pumping in his body, he decided he couldn't return home. But until when? He'd think about it when he could. Right now, he just had to flee.

The Gestapo jumped right on the case. They called in the soldier who shot Samuel to the general station the morning after the attempted bombing of the bookstore. He went to 84 Avenue Foch with the violin case that had flown just a couple of doors down in the blast, and reported the events. He said he'd seen only one person, whom he'd killed as he attempted to escape, and that he himself had been lucky to follow him. If he'd stayed inside, guarding the bookstore, he'd be dead.

The head of that department of the Gestapo was in a very bad mood. He had two scientists from the laboratory come down to investigate the case with a magnifying glass. The only name they could find was the luthier's written on the old label. Not much of a clue. They also had photos they'd taken of the unidentifiable dead man once they'd removed him from the street. And they guessed that, in some way, the resistance had emerged from the music scene. In Paris, this information was the same as no information. It was like a needle in a haystack. The head of the department was not one to mince words when it came to giving orders:

"Look for the resistance and inquire about it everywhere. Turn over the conservatory. Interrogate everyone who enters and leaves the Jeunesses Musicales. Don't leave any leaf unturned. There must be some benefit to having infiltrated every orchestra. There aren't so many. This is the moment they should help us. Someone must know something. Should there be any doubts, you know what to do. Don't rest until you bring me the group behind this. I want them all. Do you understand me?"

He gargled and spit on the boots of the five soldiers standing in front of him. They stomped their heels, raised their hands, hailed the Führer, and bravely got to business.

Everyone runs in war. First, there's the exile. The desperate escape to some unknown place out of the need to get out before it's too late. For those who stay, there's the refuge, the rush to shelter themselves when the sirens ring. Everyone underground—the sooner, the better. The sprint to the bunkers, caves, and metro stations. It didn't matter now. Jean Lefebvre, the violinist of the Pierné Orchestra, known as Imtold for his gift of discovering a million and one rumors and spreading them even further, couldn't run. When he felt the soldier's hand on his shoulder, he knew it wasn't worth trying. He found himself with both hands behind his back within seconds. A man wearing green had snatched his case. He was only two streets away from the theater, but he hadn't managed to make it to the rehearsal.

"What's in here?"

"My instrument," he responded coldly. The six soldiers that circled him were unsure. They were about to leave the case on top of the car hood until one of the soldiers, the one who had the most braids on his lapels, advised them not to do so with a sharp look. They opened the back door of the vehicle, put a hand on Imtold's neck, and pushed him into the car. Two soldiers sat on both sides of Imtold, and the door closed. As soon as the car took off, they blindfolded him with a scarf and said, "Don't worry. The journey will be short." He was scared they'd take him out soon, but the journey was literally only a minute. He knew where they'd taken him. Across the river, to the Conciergerie, which had been converted into a Nazi prison.

They forced him out of the car, swearing at him. With nothing more being said besides at the opening and closing of doors, he sensed they were crossing halls. They dragged him, blindfolded and handcuffed, down a set of stairs without warning. They sent him down the last flight rolling.

Two brawny men picked him up by his armpits. Since he'd been blindfolded, his hearing and touch had been forcibly sharpened. A door creaked in front of him. They roughly took off his handcuffs and pushed him into an abyss, then closed a metal door behind him. Three locks slammed shut, each one sounding more definitive. Punishment, execution, death.

Before he dared do anything, he waited a bit, quiet, with his back against the first wall he could reach.

"Hello . . . ?" he said, his voice thin, to see if anyone would respond.

The silence was absolute. He slowly untied his blindfold. That didn't help much. The basement didn't have any light. The cell was damp, without even a bull's-eye window or a crack of light peeking out from under the door. Absolute blackness, as though he'd been killed already.

He spent hours on the cold stone. He had no way of knowing how many. One night, maybe two. At some point, sleep, fear, and savage hunger took over him. As he nodded off, the sight of Samuel Bardollet came to him. Samuel running, Samuel shot in the back, Samuel lying on the ground, and the soldier approaching him and causing his head to explode with two bullets. And the trickle of his friend's blood that must have pooled on the cobblestone. When he felt a little braver, he stood and looked for a hole in the wall where he could peek through and ask for help . . . Nothing. From time to time, he heard shrieks from beyond the darkness.

"Jean Lefebvre?" someone shouted from the other side of the door.

"Yes . . ."

"Put on your blindfold. Tell us once you're ready."

It wasn't easy for him to tie it. His fingers trembled due to nervousness, hunger, and weakness. The door opened, and they grabbed him by the arms.

"We're going on a trip," they told him in bad French.

He barely made it up the stairs. He detected light from the corners of the mask. They went up two floors, sat him down in a chair, and took off his blindfold. The sudden brightness hurt his eyes. It took a moment for him to adjust. Once he was able to focus, he saw a beefy, bald man wearing Gestapo pants and boots sitting in front of him. On his torso, however, he wore a sleeveless shirt that outlined his pecs. At a glance, his arms resembled those of a champion weightlifter. The man looked above the prisoner's head, as if there was someone behind Imtold waiting to give the officer permission to begin his interrogation.

"What's your name?"

He didn't respond.

"Tell us your name."

"You already know it."

"We want you to say it." He looked over Imtold's head again.

Imtold felt a sudden, hard whip lash on his back.

"Now, tell us your name."

"Jean."

"Jean . . . Looks like you're slowly regaining your memory. What else, Jean?"

He shook his head. And instantly he received another lash.

"Don't be so stubborn." The officer was poking fun at him.

"You already know my name," he said again, concealing the red-hot burning of the wound.

"Jean Lefebvre. Now tell us the name of your companion."

Imtold waited for another attack from behind. Just when he thought it wouldn't come, the angry lash reached him.

"Are you refusing to speak?"

Another lash.

"Your friend is already dead. You can't do anything for him now."

The pain made him lurch forward onto the ground. The torturer let go of the whip and returned him to his chair. The brawny interrogator was in no rush.

"We've been to your house. Did you live together?"

He didn't confess. He received another lash.

"Samuel Bardollet, your roommate, was Jewish. Scum . . . Are you a Jew too?"

He shook his head.

"And so?" The officer was acting patronizing. "Why this hate for the Germans?"

Imtold looked into his interrogator's eyes. He didn't just have the arms of a weightlifter. His nose also looked like it had been flattened by punches.

"Where else did you plan on placing bombs?"

Silence.

"Where next after our bookstore?"

Imtold pursed his lips. A blow to the back. The interrogator raised his hand to stop the executioner from giving out any more lashings. He stood lazily, approached Jean Lefebvre, grabbed him by the neck, and hoisted him up off his seat.

"Do you know who we are?"

Imtold didn't open his mouth.

"A Frenchman like you must know who died in this same building, right next door. Are you familiar with the name Marie Antoinette? Tell me, have you heard of it?"

He limited himself to agreeing by looking down.

"Do you know how she died?" The officer pressed his Adam's apple with his two pincerlike fingers. "The guillotine was a great invention."

He let him go. Imtold crumpled onto the chair. When it seemed like the interrogation was over, the officer punched him so hard his teeth cracked, and he was knocked to the floor.

Then, everyone disappeared, and they left him alone with a swollen face and a burning back.

A couple of hours later, the bald interrogator who gave commands and the soldier who complied returned. The interrogator had gotten cold and put on his uniform shirt on top of the one he was previously wearing, but he left it unbuttoned. As soon as he spoke, the smell of wine filled the air.

"Jean Lefebvre . . . I did tell you we've been to your apartment, right? We found a lot at your house. And there were a couple of things we didn't like too much. It's really disgusting to counterfeit bread ration cards. Don't you think it's unpatriotic to take advantage of your fellow man's hunger?"

Imtold listened and didn't speak.

"Who else helped you with your attacks? Someone like you, who takes advantage of his own people? Tell us. You didn't do all that by yourselves. Who else was there? Where did you meet?"

The quieter he was, the more lashes he received. But he kept his pride.

"You should cooperate. It doesn't make sense to harbor more people. When you hide, where do you hide?"

Imtold suddenly realized they had changed their strategy from the afternoon. They were no longer asking things they knew. They weren't warming him up anymore just to bully him and make him sing. Now, they didn't even touch his hair.

"We also found all kinds of sheet music at your house. It turns out you're a musician. From the Pierné Orchestra. A violinist, right?"

Imtold panted to avoid saying yes.

"A beautiful profession. But you must know something . . . It's a shame, but while we were searching your apartment, your violin fell and broke. I suppose it wasn't one of those really expensive Stradivariuses. From what they tell me, it's in pieces. I'm sorry."

Irony as torture.

"Let's see these violinist hands."

The interrogator extended his fingers so the violinist would copy his gesture. Imtold reluctantly did so. The soldier with the whip instantly handcuffed him again and placed a table between the interrogator and his victim. He grabbed him by the wrists and placed them on top of the white tabletop.

"A nice violinist manicure. Such perfect fingers," said the interrogator. "Now, tell me, who else was with you and Samuel?"

Imtold closed his eyes with the same force he closed his mouth with. The interrogator suddenly ripped out one of his nails. Imtold's screams could probably have been heard from across the Seine.

"Who else was part of your crew?"

He ripped out another nail. The ring finger.

"Who helped you escape?"

He moved to the next hand. The other ring finger was left raw.

"Give us a name."

The officer played things symmetrically. Now it was the index finger.

The violinist's shrieks bothered the interrogator.

"A name, you son of a bitch."

When he'd furiously extracted eight nails, he closed his own fist and, like a hammer, he forcefully smashed each of Imtold's fingers, breaking them one by one.

He didn't say anything else. The interrogator and the soldier left the room, and they never came back. They let Jean Lefebvre die alone, without anyone knowing his fate. In the following days, the rumors of Imtold's disappearance spread throughout the whole orchestra. There was a different version for every tale. Most likely, none of them were true.

27

That Old Way of Loving

Dear Margaux,

I'm writing to you from home, my heart full of fear. With the way things are shaping up, I'll make it out. Everything happens so quickly, and I fear I may not be able to tell you how much I love you again.

The news flies these days. And, unfortunately, our orchestra is in the midst of a storm. Today, I found out they arrested Imtold Lefebvre on his way to the theater, and what will happen after this, only God knows. However, I worry it won't be good for me or for us.

Imtold is my friend, and based on the way he disappeared, I'm beginning to think I'll never see him again. It's really cruel imagining what has happened to him. And how all of a sudden, I'll never see someone who's been by my side my entire life. He was a school friend who became an orchestra friend, and it saddens me knowing we may never play together again. I hope I'm mistaken, but . . .

It terrifies me most to think about how his life may have ended.

I introduced you to Imtold the day you and I met near the door of the Châtelet. Now, the wagging tongues in the orchestra, which do exist, say that Imtold was a member of the resistance. They say Imtold and a friend of his I didn't know blew up a German bookstore that was—and still is—near the Sorbonne, twice. I didn't know. I can't believe it. But the conductor, Delphin Moureau, told us the Germans hunted down Imtold's friend, a guy who made bombs, and wounded him, and instead of finishing him off, they tortured him until he confessed what they wanted to hear. I have no idea if things went that way. No one knows anything for sure. Truth is scarce during times of war. The reality is that Imtold's been swallowed up by the earth.

As you can imagine, I have nothing to do with all this. What happened? I don't know how to tell you. We move in uncertainty in this damn city, ever since the devil arrived in a sidecar. All I know is that Imtold stayed at my house for three days. Hiding? He never said that. The week before, he asked me for a favor. He explained that he couldn't return to his apartment, and what else was I supposed to do? I told him yes, of course, he could stay the days he needed to. He would have done the same for me without thinking twice or asking me why. Not everyone becomes selfish in war, like they say. There are people who help. A lot. And they do it with their hearts, risking themselves for good people. And Imtold was a hell of a good person. And friend.

If I'm writing to you, Margaux, my Margaux, it's because I'm scared. Very scared I may be next. Why? Because you see how the cookie has crumbled. Because everyone listens here and everyone talks. Because, in order to save yourself in this world, you betray your neighbor, your acquaintance, if you need to. And we all fall like flies.

Hitler is the devil, and it feels sometimes like this will have no end. We Frenchmen have lost, and the Vichy government surrendered to save their own skin. They surrendered in the name of the homeland and gave the country as a gift. I don't understand it, but I do see an end to all this. The BBC, which you know I listen to sometimes, says it will, that there will be a day the nightmare ends. But if this international assistance is to come, I hope it doesn't take too long, because this has been very difficult and long.

It might be too late for me.

What's my sin? Nothing, dear Margi. I haven't done anything. And you know that. We musicians who've been able to play in big orchestras are privileged. We haven't had to go to the front, and despite everything, the Germans respect us. You know I live for music and for being with you as long as the situation allows it. This is the first time I've ever been in love. And the last. I never would have said that love could create these feelings. Every day we're together, I hear the angels and archangels sing. Every day we're together, my happiness is so great that not even Ravel could describe it in musical notation. Every cloud over our heads disperses when you look at me, dear Margaux. Your laughter is my salvation.

You're very young, you are. You have your whole life ahead of you. Don't let these people run it. Go your own way. Always go your own way. Try to be happy. Better said, be happy. Do it, even if it's for me.

And whatever happens, never stop playing. You play so well. Every day, you get better, my little duckling. The notes will never betray you, remember?

Take care of your father. He's a good man. You ought to know he has everyone in his pocket at the theater. Mr. Ferdinand endears himself, because, even in these times when everyone's days are gray, he never says no to anyone. Maybe we should all try to act like him. Being on good terms with everyone, never looking for problems. That's human. What's so bad about our natural instinct to ensure conservation? We still don't know who will be writing this episode of history in which we're caught up. We don't know how all this will be judged, but in the day-to-day, our situation, the situation of the good-faith Parisian, isn't about cowardice or bravery. There are many nuances between the German collaboration and the active resistance. And this is perhaps where the majority of French people who still live in occupied territory try to be. Whatever way this ends, don't ever scold your father for anything. He undoubtedly did what he had to do. He searched for the best thing for you and your mother. Whatever they say, he's in an understandable position. Adjust to the situation, strive to live, move forward, and wait for better times to come. Survive, yes, this is the sacred verb of our times. Survive with the hope that this Nazi nightmare cannot last forever. Not even Hitler will be eternal. There will be a time when this world of fear, hunger, and sirens must end in some way or another.

It comforts me to think that, for every sheet of paper we rip off our calendars, an end may grow nearer.

And when the day comes, when the barbarism ends, I'll want only to be with you. To live it. So that the two of us, if you're willing, can start a family. This is a wish of mine I never expressed to you, and I'm taking advantage of the moment to tell you.

My most beloved, I'm getting ahead of myself, don't you think? And I don't know if this is the right place or time to say these things. But I'm writing in spurts because my heart is dictating, because I have nothing to lose, and because I'm picturing your beautiful eyes reading these lines. I assure you that if I could have one wish from the magic lamp in One Thousand and One Nights *right here and now, nothing would make me happier than to know there's a future in which you and I light a fireplace, waiting for the moment a baby calls us father and mother. Can you imagine how talented our children would be at playing the oboe? Or maybe they'd want to play the bassoon to annoy you?*

Margaux, my duckling . . . Don't ever be ashamed.

Allow me to say it to you one more time. It's impossible to love more than I love you as I write this letter that I hope you won't need to read. You are my life.

I love you with that old way of loving.

With all my heart, without holding anything back.

D. D.

P.S.

I hesitated to write you this letter. Once I wrote it and without even daring to reread it, I really questioned whether I needed to get this to you. I hesitated again out of fear. Out of fear that it would weaken you to read it. Out of fear that it could end up hurting you. If anyone finds it, I wouldn't forgive myself if this letter incriminated you in something you had nothing to do with. I've questioned everything, in short, out of fear this might be the last time I could "talk" to you. Nothing in this world would make me angrier, dear Margaux. If that were even the case, I've wondered if this silent goodbye would be easier for you. I don't know. Everything is so complicated and strange that it's too hard for me to think with so much fogginess around me. Forgive me, in any case. Sincerely, it's come out of me like this, with my heart.

I hope to have wasted ink in vain and that you and I can see each other again. If not tomorrow, then the day after. At the moment, I have only written the words. At every event that life brings us, you must play the music.

Always yours.

Damien folded the three sheets of paper and placed them in an envelope. He didn't list a sender. On the outside, he wrote only one thing.

For M. D. (in case of emergency)

Once he checked the clock, he realized he had to run. The rehearsals before concerts were sacred, and Moureau would get irritable if all the musicians were not in front of the music stand, their sheet music ready, ninety minutes before doors opened. He knotted his tie, dressed in his dark concert outfit, and ran his hands through his hair in front of the mirror to loosen his curls. He didn't like how they'd bunched up on his forehead.

With the letter in his jacket pocket, his scarf wrapped around his neck, and the oboe case in his hand, Damien walked toward the theater to the rhythm of the *molto allegro* of the second Rimsky-Korsakov movement. Anxious about Imtold's disappearance, he had the feeling on his way to work that this wouldn't be just any Saturday. He looked from side to side when he turned every corner, waiting for a green uniform to ask him where he thought he was going. He feared that, in an ambush, a patrolman would surprise him, shout at him to halt, and ask him, "Are you Damien Devère?" And then it'd be lights out, good night. Only Germans had access to gasoline over the past few months, and there wasn't a single vehicle that wasn't driven by a swastika-clad uniform circulating the Parisian pavement. The few women who walked toward the ration lines dragged their feet. The dejection and hunger deteriorated them week after week. Despite everything, they'd go anywhere they needed for two potatoes and a head of cauliflower, and they were resigned to stand and wait however long they had to.

In front of the Hôtel de Ville, a stone's throw from the Châtelet, Damien realized that the sole of one of his shoes had opened from the front, like the mouth of a whale. He was right at the theater, and he approached slowly, trying to hide his torn shoe. He didn't have any others. The poster in the doorway announced the concert of the day in large writing. *Scheherazade.*

He traversed the lobby, entered the dressing rooms, and popped his head onstage. A couple of his companions were already tuning their instruments in the hall. The percussions and the strings said, "Good afternoon," and Damien mechanically and halfheartedly responded. The busy wind instruments returned the greeting with their eyebrows. Trying not to bother anyone in the narrow slalom between the music stands, he arrived at his seat and left the oboe case on top of his chair. Far from that madhouse, Ferdinand, knee on the ground, made sure the conductor's platform was leveled. It had become an obsession for Delphin Moureau, because he didn't want it to look like he was conducting the concert during an earthquake. When Ferdinand looked up, he saw a pair of shoes.

"What's broken now?" He looked up farther to see who was standing there in front of him and found Damien before him. "Oh, hello, boy."

"Good afternoon, Ferdinand. When you're done . . ."

"Right now." He shook the wood with both hands. "Now the conductor can jump and stomp, because this thing won't budge, even if he dances a fandango."

The electrician huffed and puffed as he got up. He had started to need to leverage himself with two hands on his knees to stand up.

"Do you have a minute?"

"I even have two," Ferdinand responded, not guessing what Damien had in mind.

"Let's go to . . . ," he said, gesturing toward the theater wings. "There's too much racket here."

Once he had Damien in front of him, the electrician realized this wouldn't be any ordinary conversation. It was enough just to look at him to pick up on it.

"What's wrong with your eyes?"

"Me?" Damien replied innocently. "What's wrong with them?"

"It looks like you've seen a wolf."

"The truth? That's why I wanted to see you. I might be in trouble."

That's when Ferdinand became alert. "What happened?"

"They caught Imtold. One of the violinists."

"I know who he is."

"They arrested him."

"I know. And?"

"I could be next, Ferdinand. I hope not, but I could be the next one. I have this hunch—"

"All right now. Let's not get flustered too early. You? Why you?"

"I swear I have nothing to do with the German bookstore. I haven't done anything, not a single protest, but . . ."

"But?"

"Imtold was my friend. And he stayed at my house. Not long, just a few days. But he stayed at my house."

"*Merde.* Who knows?"

"I have no idea. But for me, all this . . . Everyone is a potential spy in this city these days. Everyone knows something, gossip spreads. If more than just you knows something, you've already lost. One rumor is enough to . . ."

The electrician shuffled the almonds in his pocket. "I know what you mean." He took a deep breath. "I'll do what you need me to."

"I'm only asking for one thing, Ferdinand. Just do one thing for me, understand?"

"D. D . . . I . . ." He took his hands out of his pockets and opened them. He begged for forgiveness with his eyes. "Don't ask me for anything that—"

"I won't compromise you. Don't worry. I won't get you involved in any problems. God protect me. This isn't going in that direction. But please promise me that . . ."

"Tell me, then."

"That you'll do me this favor."

He took the letter out of his blazer pocket.

"This is for your daughter." He held the envelope like it was burning him and placed it in Ferdinand's hands. "It's for Margaux, but safeguard it for me, please. And don't give it to her. Never give it to her. Never in your life. Do you understand what I'm asking you?"

"I don't think I understand what you mean," he said resignedly.

"Protect it. Let her read it only if something happens to me. Only if they arrest me or if I disappear, or if . . . Only then can you give her the letter and tell her about this conversation." Damien's eyes were misty, and he tried to hold his tears back. "Please. Can I count on you?"

"Why don't you send it yourself? You can still send letters."

"I don't think I'll be able to send anything from where I'll be."

"Don't assume the worst, Damien."

"I'm not. We're already in the worst possible situation." His nerves made his voice higher pitched. "Can I count on you? Do you understand the mission?"

"Fine." He tapped on the letter with his finger. "You put it here . . . 'For M. D. in case of emergency.'" He placed the letter in his pocket.

"Ferdinand, my friend . . ." Damien struggled harder not to cry.

They hugged each other like they never had before. Resting his chin on the electrician's shoulder, the young man held back a sob to say, "I really love Margaux. I really love her, you hear?" and he felt Ferdinand hug him tighter. The electrician hugged him tightly like he hadn't hugged anyone throughout the whole war. He hugged him tightly to seal the pact. He hugged him tightly to let him know he was part of the family. He hugged him tighter and tighter, because he was afraid that this goodbye, disguised as courage, would ruin his daughter's happiness. And suddenly he understood what it would mean to give her the letter in his pocket.

Damien dried his eyes with the sleeve of his blazer and entered the hall. Once he was at the door, Ferdinand shouted, "Boy. I don't know if I should tell you now."

Damien turned around. "What is it?"

"I also had a surprise for you." He didn't know how to say it. "My daughter is coming to the concert."

"Now?"

Ferdinand nodded.

"But . . . I asked Margaux not to come. I told her there weren't any tickets left today. That—" His shoulders drooped. "Oof."

"I'm sorry. I knew it would make her happy. I told her if she wanted to listen to the concert, she could stay with me in the drop scene. She won't be able to see it, but . . ."

Damien forced a smile. "You did well, Ferdinand, don't worry. I'm happy to know your daughter will be here. I'd like to see her. I'll play better than ever. Today, we will revive Scheherazade. It'll be a great concert. You'll see."

"I'm sorry, Damien."

"On the contrary. Thank you so much, Monsieur Dutronc."

Ninety minutes before the concert, a visitor knocked at the door of the conductor's dressing room. Delphin Moureau told them to come in as he hummed the final movement of *Scheherazade*. Two German officers walked in with determination, followed by two soldiers who looked like they meant nothing but business.

"Do you know why we're here?" the officer in black asked nicely.

"To wish us the best of luck with our concert, I suppose."

"Well, of course, *Herr Dirigent*."

"But it'll be hard for it to sound the way you would've liked," said the officer in green, who was clearly not visiting the theater for the first time. "We heard you lost a violinist this week."

"No doubt. If anyone knows that, it'd be you, since you do the head count every week."

"What was his name?"

"Who?"

"The violinist."

"Lefebvre. He appeared as Jean Lefebvre on your lists, because that is his Christian name, but everyone here called him Imtold. He was a very good violinist."

"You'll miss him."

"Of course. An orchestra is like a clock. If there's a hand missing, the clock will continue to tick, but it will stop telling time."

"Is it so noticeable to have one fewer violin?" the officer in green asked, the only one playing along with him.

"That's something you, someone with such musical sensibilities, surely know how to judge."

"I see you never get nervous, *Herr Dirigent*."

"Should I be?"

"Sir, you have a concert in"—the officer looked at his clock—"an hour and a half. Well, that is if you end up conducting this concert, of course. May we sit?"

They didn't wait for permission. The two officers grabbed two chairs, turned them to face Delphin Moureau's stool, and took a seat. One of the soldiers, the one whose face was half dark like he'd injured his skin in a fire, went out the door, locked it, and stood guard from the outside. The other, a dunce, kept watch from inside the dressing room.

"Do you know who Denise Landau is?"

"No, sir."

"Are you sure, *Herr Dirigent*?"

"I believe so . . ."

"Well, that's very strange, because she knows who you are. In fact, she knows a lot about your life. She's come to see us, and she's told us things . . . about herself. But mostly, about her husband and you. Or, sorry, maybe I've gotten the last name wrong. Maybe you know her as Denise Sully. They have that tradition here in France too, huh? Where the woman takes the husband's last name when they marry? Answer when I ask you something. Do they do it or not, *Herr Dirigent*?"

"Yes."

"Very good. Let's continue. So you know who Denise Sully is?"

"I don't know her personally."

"You're right. You're a real gentleman and haven't had the pleasure of meeting her. That's something she told us herself, that deep down *Herr Dirigent* is a coward. The person you know very well, whom you know in the most intimate way that we don't dare say, is her husband, correct? Does the name Jean-Clair Sully ring a bell?"

"I know him, yes."

"I'm happy to hear you're starting to remember."

"But I haven't seen him in a long time."

"How long?"

"A long time. Since the war started, we . . ."

"What?"

"We haven't seen each other again."

"That's not exactly what his wife said. She told us, in all the nasty details she could have kept to herself, that you and Jean-Clair are lovers. She tells us you see each other twice a week, and that these meetings continue to this day. She tells us she was suspicious her husband had another woman in his life and didn't stop until she uncovered it. And what'd she find? A double serving of surprise. Her husband's mistress wasn't a woman but a man instead. Can you imagine how poor Denise felt? She discovered the affair was with a well-known man. A prestigious man. A famous orchestra conductor, who it turns out has a Rimsky-Korsakov concert this afternoon in a hall full of German soldiers ready to applaud once the performance ends. But you know what's wrong? We Germans don't clap for faggots. We are, as you say, cultured people. We know men love women, and everything else is depravity and sickness. This is the problem. Are you one of these homos?"

"I . . ."

"Why's your lip trembling? Are you going to deny it now? Are you a homo or not? If you have a lover who's married to a woman, then what happens? Are we to think that maybe you're bisexual like Jean-Clair Sully? It doesn't surprise me that France loses its wars when it has people like you. You're in the wrong century. This isn't Rome or Greece or any of those bacchanals those people had. Do you know what we do with faggots? We send them on a trip. We isolate them, like the Jews, so they don't mix with the normal population, because you know what, *Herr Dirigent*? Everything is contagious. Bad things are even more contagious. You're like a virus that spreads, and no one knows how. That's why it's better to start from the root. Cut it in one fell swoop."

"What do you want from me?"

The officer maintained a stubborn silence before responding.

"Names."

Someone called at the door, and the soldier with the burned face entered.

"They're calling the conductor to the rehearsal, sir."

"Tell the orchestra it may be a while. Tell them to keep tuning and to start from the beginning."

"Yes, sir," the soldier obediently responded, before leaving the dressing room.

"This depends on you, *Herr Dirigent*. We want you to name names."

Delphin Moureau cursed himself for not having fled to Switzerland when his lover had told him everything was ready for an escape, without the risk of getting caught. He lifted his chin, and he tried to keep his dignity. "Where is Jean-Clair?"

"Are you asking if he's on vacation?"

"I want to know if he's okay."

"You're really in love, aren't you? His wife told us you two were really head over heels."

"Please don't joke."

"Don't what?" The officer in green poked Moureau's cheeks forcefully. "You're not embarrassed to be a homosexual? Someone so great, so famous, so disgusting . . . What an example for the people."

"Let it go," the official in black intervened.

The officer in green obeyed him immediately, tried not to become irritated, and continued the game in his error-riddled French.

"Where is Jean-Clair, you ask. Look, Denise cooperated. She came motu proprio. She told us what was going on, and we made a promise: she tells us who her husband has been with, and we let her husband get back on the right path. You understand how that works?" He flicked the conductor's chest hard. "Do you understand or not?"

"What names do you want?"

"The ones that will allow you to conduct the concert today. The alternative wouldn't be good for anyone."

The conductor lowered his head for the first time. The officer took the opportunity to suggest a pact.

"The names. That's easy. If, after, you correct your behavior, and we don't find out about any more sadomasochistic episodes, you can conduct the concert next Saturday and the Saturday after that. It just depends on you."

"But I don't understand what you want me to tell you. Whose names? For what?"

"The names of the people who helped Lefebvre bomb our bookstore. You must know his friends."

"I don't know anything about that."

"We heard you knew Lefebvre very well. He's been in the orchestra for a long time. That doesn't mean that you and he . . . ?"

"Please . . ."

"Did he hide at your house?"

"No, sir. He's never come to my house. He was just a musician in the orchestra to me."

"He wasn't a faggot like you, you mean."

The conductor put his head between his legs. The head officer let him be for a minute. When he grew tired of listening to him cry, he put his hand on the conductor's shoulder and reminded him of the proposal in a whisper.

"Just one name, *Herr Dirigent.* Just one, and you can conduct the rehearsal and the concert on Saturday, and we'll never bother you again. That's the deal. That is . . . if you keep your dick in your pants."

"Just one?"

28

Everything Is Today

The main floor of the Théâtre du Châtelet filled within ten minutes. The German soldiers, who occupied the first rows and the lateral boxes, sat, took off their caps, and spoke in low voices as Damien's oboe played a note for the rest of the instruments to tune to. Sometimes, a soldier let out a laugh, the Saturday afternoon kind, when obligations give way to a truce. In the last rows of the stalls sat those who entered peacefully, who wanted a peaceful afternoon, who wished for the music to distract them for a couple of hours, and who wanted to avoid a confrontation with anyone. The women had dressed up to the best of their abilities. There were some who'd made dresses from the clothes of men who would never return. All of them had learned to make the most of shirt pieces and old sheets. Going to the theater, for a performance or a concert, was an occasion to demonstrate a certain firmness. But it was also the occasion to show that whatever the situation may be, they were women, they were French, and they wanted to have fun. It was a way of saying that not all was lost to the German superiority. They could have Paris, all of France, and half of Europe, but they would never be able to take away their air, elegance, and good taste.

Every five minutes, Ferdinand Dutronc opened the service door on the side of the theater, checking it wouldn't close on him again and peeking out onto the street to see if his daughter had arrived. The third time he wedged the door open with his foot, he saw Margaux walking quickly on the quai de la Mégisserie. She was wearing a black jacket and a knee-length checkered skirt that mixed gray with yellow.

"Come on, honey, we're running late," he shouted from a distance.

"I had to walk around, because they cut . . . There were two burned cars."

"It doesn't matter, Margaux."

"But Papa—"

"Hurry up, girl. They're about to start."

He let her in and shut the door to the street. She knew the way. As a child, before the nightmare started, she had accompanied her father to work many times. She liked the theater drop scene. The smell of wood and turpentine, the darkness, the electrical boxes, and the counterweights on the hundreds of wires meant to lift and lower the set. What satisfied her the most was that her father had a solution for everything. Everything he had to fix was a challenge he could overcome with a little skill and time. A handyman like him never faced the same challenge twice in the theater.

"Where do I go?"

"Grab that chair and sit here between the wings."

Between the curtains, Margaux tried different positions to find out where she could watch Damien best. Once she located his profile, she tried to greet him discreetly. Softening the reed with his lips, he hadn't noticed her. Margaux didn't know how to grab his attention, but, as focused as he seemed, she didn't want to bother him the moment the lights went out in the main hall. He looked nice in his black suit, white shirt, and bow tie. He looked older, more serious, more important. Even more handsome.

Suddenly, the conductor bumped into her. As he passed, he hit her funny bone.

"Hey, girl, you're being a nuisance here."

Delphin Moureau let his bad mood dissipate, forced his best smile, and entered into the spotlight. The musicians stood to greet him onstage, and the hall applauded them all preemptively. When the conductor turned toward the audience to bow, he located the two German officers sitting in the fifth row. The one in green and the one in black. Center aisle.

He faced the orchestra again, hoping to feel more at home. With a wet finger, he made sure the pages of the score would turn. He did not hurry to begin. It was his way of reclaiming power and concentrating all eyes on him. He closed his eyes to inhabit the spirit of Rimsky-Korsakov. He picked up the baton with his right hand, and he raised it high enough so the musicians became alert. From that moment onward, not even a fly could be heard in the hall.

The first note came from the trombones, magisterial and peaceful. Right away, with the first violin solo that introduces Scheherazade, Damien's gaze wandered in a quiet moment to the emergency light on stage right. There, between the wings, he discovered Margaux's loving eyes watching him. With a twinge of his heart, he returned his gaze to the score and the conductor, who was gesticulating more today than he had in other concerts. That Saturday afternoon, Delphin Moureau hardly waited to work up a sweat. The conductor didn't look at the oboes, not even by chance, throughout the whole performance. He kept them in front of him, directly in the middle of the orchestra, to evenly distribute their sounds throughout the theater. He didn't give them a sign or an entrance. Moureau's gaze, protected by the violins, looked past the oboes and fell on the percussion section. Damien, waiting to read, play, and draw out the perfect sound, saw the baton out of the corner of his eye, but at no point did he notice Delphin Moureau ignoring him.

At the end of the third movement, Damien, who was dedicated to playing the music of the young prince and princess, straightened his neck to look at Margaux. Not having taken her eyes off him once, she blew him a kiss that he received instantly. His hands occupied, Dédé caught the kiss with his lips midair and sent it back with a loving smile. He played the last movement of *Scheherazade* earnestly. The vibrato left the oboe with the timber of an enamored soprano. Never in any of his rehearsals had he managed to draw out a sound that so resonated with him. He was the instrument, with his spirit serene.

The clever audience didn't applaud until the end of the concert, and when they did, it reverberated throughout the hall, sounding professional, rhythmic, and very German with its exact length and lack of passion. Standing next to her father, Margaux clapped enthusiastically.

"How lucky is it that I came, Papa? It was one of the best concerts I've ever heard."

"I'm so happy, Margi," said Ferdinand, still clapping the third and final time the conductor came out to greet everyone.

Once the hall was silent, the dance began. People paraded in the street, soldiers chatted in the hall, and the conductor hurriedly slipped back into his dressing room. The only thing he told his musicians was "Thank you, all"—which was routine—and he disappeared. The performance of that Rimsky-Korsakov deserved kind words, even if it was a brief, warm elegy. But Delphin Moureau exited as the orchestra members began packing their instruments and discussing the notes they'd missed.

"Today's audience won't have noticed."

"They come here like they're going to see the circus."

"Let's see if we get a review in the *Je suis partout*."

"Do you think we might? I didn't see any critics in the hall."

"They don't have to come. These people write what they want. They do the same thing with the war . . ."

Damien took apart his oboe and wiped the inside with a cloth to dry the wood. He grabbed the upper body of the instrument, held it up to the light, and looked through the hole like a pirate looking through a telescope. He glanced to his right to make sure his lover was still there. Then, he put the lower body and bell inside the case. Once he closed it, he saw Ferdinand in his uniform holding his daughter by the shoulder.

Margaux pretended like she was applauding him at full speed, her hands together at her chin, but without making any noise.

"I'm coming." Damien moved two chairs to clear his path and walk toward the Dutroncs. At that second, someone called to him from stage right.

"Damien Devère?"

He stopped and turned on his heel. Between the curtains stood two German soldiers.

"Come here, please." The man with the burned face was authoritative.

"But—" With his hand, Damien signaled he was going the other direction.

"You're Damien Devère, are you not?"

"Yes, yes . . ."

"Please do us the favor of coming with us. Accompany us, please."

He questioned whether he should take a step forward or backward. Margaux noticed his anxiety, and she moved to walk onto the stage.

"No, Margaux." Her father grabbed her arm, holding her back.

Damien lowered his head and resigned himself to slowly walking toward the soldiers.

"Dami, don't go," Margaux shouted.

Her father continued to hold her back with both of his hands so she wouldn't escape.

"Who is she?" the man with the burned face asked. "Do you want her to come with you?"

"No, no . . . She's just a girl," he responded in a low voice so she wouldn't hear him from the other side of the stage. "Just a family friend."

"And that?" the soldier asked, pointing to the case Damien carried in his hand.

"My oboe case," he responded, making his way closer to a possible abyss.

"No need to bring it."

"I bring it with me everywhere."

"You won't need it where we're going."

He lifted his eyes to hold the soldier's gaze. The man with the burned face had hatred in his eyes.

"Damien!" he heard from the other side of the hall.

Margaux's hoarse cry resounded throughout the whole theater.

Her desperate howl coincided with the moment they forced that Pierné Orchestra oboist to abandon his instrument on the last chair of the stage. It was the instant Damien noticed the silent soldier was forcefully grabbing him by the wrists. It was the moment Ferdinand, who understood like no one else the gravity of the situation, hugged his daughter with all his might and said, "My love. We'll get past this. I promise we'll get past this." She barely heard what her father was saying. She had just witnessed Damien's arrest. She had him in front of her, and they hadn't been able to say goodbye. He hadn't even turned around to look at her one last time. But why hadn't he done so? In her seventeen years of life, Margaux had never cried so much.

Her father waited some time to give her the letter. He couldn't find the right moment to disrupt his daughter's mourning. He feared she'd become even more consumed by the matter if she read what Damien had written. He watched her whimper through those first few long weeks. For all the years she lived, she would never experience such pain again. Ferdinand knew it, because parents are experts in two things: the trajectory of life, and their children.

A devastated Margaux had returned home and placed the black oboe case on top of the chest of drawers in her room. In the following days, she sat on her bed and spent hours looking at it, as if it were a picture you carried with you forever. At times, it was a totem of hope. At times, it was a prayer altar. Absentmindedly, she contemplated the case Dédé always carried in his hand. He never let it go for the world, and she hoped it was an amulet of good luck. She only prayed that one day her love could put together his oboe, blow the reed, and draw out that calm and loving music only he could. With its perfect sound and temperate spirit. Sometimes, she shut her eyes as furiously as a clenched fist and wished for it with all her might.

Ferdinand didn't know what Damien had said in the letter he kept hidden, but he could imagine. Words of first love that are never forgotten. A declaration of love for good measure. Maybe thoughts of a short life expectancy, because in times of sirens, death, and misery, who thinks five years into the future? In war, no one asks how the day has gone. Everything is today. If you've made it to the next night and things are the same as they were the night before, you can be thankful. Ferdinand had thought at some point that, with the young musician's sensibility, the letter would be sheet music with an unedited and dedicated composition Margaux could play now that she was pretty good with the oboe. He'd been tempted to open the letter, read it, and seal it again. In his handiness, he could do it without anyone noticing. But he didn't dare. If Margaux ever caught him, she wouldn't forgive him.

As time passed, he safeguarded the letter, but Damien's words repeated inside his head. *"Never give it to her. Only if they arrest me or if I disappear."* To give it to her or not. He had promised to follow the instructions. Had they arrested him? Yes. Had he disappeared? No one might ever know what the Germans were doing to Damien. Everyone had heard stories of families, neighbors, and good-faith people who'd been arrested or who'd disappeared, and weeks went by without any news. The earth swallowed them up. The more he thought about it, the less obvious it became what he should do.

One night in bed, tired of being alone in his distress, he decided to mention it to Michelle, who immediately became alert.

"What happened?" she asked.

"Damien . . ."

"Do you know something?" She turned on the small lamp on the nightstand.

"No, no . . ." He cleared his nose with a handkerchief he'd kept scrunched up under his pillow for some days. "Damien asked if he could speak to me the same day of the concert, before he was arrested. Right before the concert. He took me away from the orchestra, and he gave me a letter. A letter for the girl."

Ferdinand opened the nightstand. He took out a letter, and he gave it to his wife regretfully.

"What does it say?" Michelle brought it up to the lamp. "'For M. D. (in case of emergency).' What does that mean?"

"Ah. That's what's keeping me from sleeping. Damien asked me to never give it to her. Only . . . only if they arrested him or if he disappeared."

"You have to give it to her, Ferdinand. I don't know what you're waiting for."

"I'm confused. What do you want from me? The kid hasn't officially disappeared."

"Who knows where he must be right now. What they say about the trains is terrible."

"And if they let him go? If he returns tomorrow, but I've already given her the letter?"

"For the love of God, Ferdinand." Michelle shook her head.

"What's wrong? Why are you looking at me like that?"

"You're so naive sometimes. I can't believe you think that . . . In these past three disgusting years, how many people have we known who've been arrested like Dédé and who've never been seen again? How many, Ferdinand? Tell me."

"A million."

"You have to give her the letter."

"But—"

"Tomorrow."

He took a deep breath, frightened.

"If you don't do it, I will." She put the letter on top of her nightstand and turned off the weak light bulb. "Good night, love. Now, try to sleep. You've already kept me up long enough."

Michelle couldn't believe that two "Our Fathers" later, Ferdinand was already snoring like the letter didn't exist, like Margaux didn't exist, like they hadn't arrested Damien, and like Imtold hadn't disappeared. But she could not fall asleep. Two thoughts kept spinning in her head like two obsessions where one took over the other in a loop that never ended. Damien's letter and the photograph in *Signal.* The letter that Ferdinand hadn't given his daughter. The magazine photo of the girl on a bike she hadn't shown anyone. Not Margaux, not Ferdinand. She should have explained how she'd discovered it, what her coworkers at the Galeries Lafayette accused her of, but she wanted to save her family from the stress. It was not fair for them to hear her say these things. And of course, a cat hadn't scratched her face. Everyone protects their silence for survival. And the more she thought about it, the more serious the letter became, the bigger the photo grew in her mind, and for all her tossing and turning, she didn't know how to position herself. The worry lasted until the first movement of the sun.

29

The Presence of Absence

She read the letter every day. She pictured the circumstances in which poor Damien had written it. How scared and cornered he must have felt to say such profound things with a steady hand. Soon, she knew snippets by memory. Whole fragments Margaux had traced with her finger. When she read them, they furrowed within the folds of her brain. There were days, in the lackluster mood of the Dutronc apartment, when his frightened words came to her without prompting. She would say them to herself, and she'd hear Damien's voice.

> *With the way things are shaping up, I'll make it out. Everything happens so quickly, and I fear I may not be able to tell you how much I love you again. If I'm writing to you, Margaux, my Margaux, it's because I'm scared. Very scared I may be next.*

On a day that had more sun than rain, she hardened her heart and grasped on to the most helpful sentences of the letter:

> *You're very young, you are. You have your whole life ahead of you. Don't let these people run it. Go your own*

way. Always go your own way. Try to be happy. Better said, be happy. Do it, even if it's for me.

Not even Hitler will be eternal.

And when the day comes, when the barbarism ends, I'll want only to be with you. To live it. So that the two of us, if you're willing, can start a family.

Margaux, my duckling . . . Don't ever be ashamed.

You are my life.

And then came the end of the letter. With those two words that tormented her.

Always yours.

It sounded like a formality, but she was convinced it wasn't. After a whole letter full of heart and bravery, Damien wouldn't have said goodbye in such an ordinary way. It wasn't his style. There was a middle ground between politeness and sending her off with the same expression he could've used with any ordinary friend. Or maybe he couldn't continue his honesty and it was his way of saying "I give up"—Margaux eliminated this option out of all of them. "Always yours" had an intention that obsessed her. The "always" as an adverb held the feeling of eternity, which on the one hand she liked, but on the other hand, when taken as a goodbye, it terrified her. She even looked for the entry in the dictionary to see if it had another possible meaning. "Always" combined all of what's past with what's to come. And this was when she began to obsess over an idea, one that didn't let her live in peace. In this future, this "always" from this time forward, would she be with or without Damien? With his return or just his memory? The love would be the same, but life wouldn't. "Always yours" was, in the end, a way of giving her an order: Resist.

First, she counted the days she hadn't seen him. Then, the weeks. A month after his arrest, she thought for the first time that she'd never see him again. The presence of absence at all hours was crueler than anything else, maybe even more than death, but she didn't want to think about that. Every time the madness attacked, she banished it immediately. She kept her worries "on a short leash and muzzled." She'd always heard her father say that, and she tried to practice it herself. In the battle against sad thoughts, however, she was used to losing. No one could say that she, a girl, hadn't struggled. Only two words, seemingly so simple—"always yours"—and she hadn't stopped thinking about it for several dark weeks.

In all that time, Margaux didn't touch the oboe case. She didn't try putting together Damien's instrument, instead waiting for him to be the one to return and touch it. But the months blurred together, news never came, and there were no tears left for her to cry. The days were sad. The nights long. She slept, as teenagers do, but her nightmares consumed her. There were bad ones, and there were worse ones. Every night, old ghosts. Wicked soldiers with the skin of Barrabas stood before her and knocked the heels of their boots like the shriek of a Romani dance. Soldiers pulled Damien by the hair and pushed his head into a bathtub of cloudy water until he drowned. Spiders crawled up her legs, and she didn't have the energy to brush them off. Her whole body itched, and she scratched until she drew blood. And then she'd wake up sweaty and with an inconsolable sorrow. Her lover's face faded a little more each day. In her dreams and her memories. She couldn't handle it. And she cursed herself for not having a photo of him. She remembered his black curls, his smiles, his astute eyes, and the taste of each kiss on her lips. But each day, the outline was more faded, and details began to disappear. This loss of definition was a slow torture for her.

She still had, of course, the time they'd spent together. The oboe, the music, the classes, *The Wrong Man*, and the day they'd told each other the most loving things.

"Have you ever swum in the Seine?" Damien asked her after a lesson.

"In the Seine? You're crazy."

"You couldn't guess how many people are on the bank of the river past pont du Carrousel on the nicest of days."

"Germans, I'm guessing."

"I don't know. I don't think so . . . From the little clothes I do see when I walk past, they don't look like uniforms. When I walk to the theater, I see them swimming, and I want to join."

"The water must be cold."

"Some people swim, and some chat or sunbathe. Do you have a bathing suit?"

"Me? Here?"

"Do you have one or not? Look how beautiful this afternoon is. We still have three hours of sunlight left. If we run now . . ."

"Seriously?" Margaux needed to know if Damien was pulling her leg.

"Do you have a bathing suit or not?" he asked again with a sneaky smile.

Margaux ran to her parents' room, and she tried on one of her mother's two-piece bathing suits that she liked. It fit her like a glove, and she left it on under her dress.

"And what are *you* going to wear?" Margaux shouted hoarsely from her parents' bedroom.

"That's my problem. Hurry up."

"You sound like my dad, always in a hurry."

They rushed down the five flights and left Montmartre on their bikes, pedaling next to each other until they made it to the river near the Louvre. They biked along the bank, and before crossing the bridge, they dismounted and left their bikes next to a tree. Holding hands, they descended the stairs leading to the basin. The blessed beach with its hard stones.

"I didn't know this existed," Margaux said.

The men who'd been there the longest—at a glance, there were three times more men than women—had turned the tree bed farthest from the river into their own plots of land. They'd laid out a towel and lazed around in the sun. In the water were a few people who were fussing, and others who suffered the cold in silence.

"Are you going to swim?" Margaux asked.

"I'm going to dive in headfirst."

"Damien, please. That's very difficult."

"Should we sit here?"

Margaux took off her dress and discreetly made sure her breasts remained inside her bathing suit. Her matching bottoms had the same tiger print as the top.

"Do you like it?"

Damien had no choice but to look her over. He'd never seen her with so little clothing.

"It does a lot for you," he said nonchalantly, as he finished unbuttoning his shirt.

"Well, I stole it from my mother. Don't tell her."

"Who? Me?"

He left on his underwear. Tight, black boxers. They were, more or less, similar to the bathing suits belonging to a majority of the men on the beach. Some spoke German. Others, who weren't as blond, refrained from saying anything out of caution or because they were by themselves. Margaux and Damien weren't the only couple. Maybe the youngest, yes. And like the rest, they did what all lovers intended on doing there: talk.

The stone ground was red hot, and in order to avoid burning themselves, they shared the only towel they'd brought with them. A white one that Margaux had grabbed from the wardrobe at home, one she didn't think anyone would miss if she didn't bring it back. They sat next to each other, their thighs touching, with a view of the swimmers and passersby on the opposite bank of the river. Beyond them, the gothic crest of Saint-Germain-des-Prés peeked out, aligned with the dome of Saint-Sulpice in a distant plane. Behind them, the sun informed them it had yet to retire but hinted that they should leave nothing unsaid, because once the golden hour passed, it was time to go. This was the custom.

"What are your favorite views of the city?" Damien asked.

"Oof . . ." Margaux had never thought about it. "From the top of Montmartre, maybe, because those are the ones I've seen the most, or from the top of the tower of Notre-Dame. I went up once with my parents. Maybe it's the memory that makes it beautiful to me."

"I don't think I've ever been to the top of Notre-Dame."

"You should hurry to see it. You never know when they'll drop a bomb."

"Notre-Dame? It's indestructible, Margaux. There's no one who can bring it to the ground."

"What about you? What's your favorite view?"

"This one. With you."

"I like hearing that, but—"

"But it's true. Here, with this downward perspective. Sunken, hidden by the river. There's a point of humility to the city. If you look at it from the Sacré-Coeur, you can see so many things at such a distance that you never end up knowing where to look. From up there, you have a bird's-eye view, a view of superiority, of total domination. I prefer this. A discreet Paris. Life in its details." He looked at her from the side. "Don't you think so?"

"Yes, perhaps . . ."

Margaux ran her hand on his thigh to swipe off an ant. Now that her hand had landed—his thigh was hairier and stronger than she'd imagined—she let two fingers walk down his knee, tickling him and moving back up.

"Sometimes I wonder what Paris will be like when they're not here," he said.

"Who?"

"These little Germans," he whispered.

"Do you think they won't be here forever? I don't remember what the city was even like before."

"You're so young."

"And you're stuck-up." She checked him with her shoulder.

Damien looked at her defiantly. When she turned to face him, he gave her a quick kiss. Not wanting to be taken for less, she returned the affection. They had never kissed in front of so many people. It felt like no one was paying attention.

"I was thinking, Margaux . . . What if they never go away? And if the occupation is permanent? Would you come with me?"

"What do you mean?"

"Let's escape. Let's flee, you and me. I think I have a way to . . . I've thought about it many times, and I have a plan. I know how to get to Toulouse without them catching us. And once there, it's whatever you want."

"Dami, my love, have you thought about me and you . . . ?"

"We'd live as musicians. They'll want us somewhere. And if not, we'll do something else. It doesn't matter what. I'm only interested in who I go with. And it's you. I look ahead and I see that all the hope we have here is crippled. We can't do what we want, we aren't free, and we have a life to live. The future sounds good if you're in it, and I want you to be there with me."

"I want it too, Damien . . . But escaping is risky."

"It's worse to stay here."

"Oh, my . . . I'm getting overwhelmed. Leave when, how, in what way? It's easier said than done."

"Imtold knows the way. You know who Imtold is, right?"

"Yes, Dami." She laughed. "Don't ask me again. You've introduced me to him three times."

"Would you come?"

She took her time to respond. "Swim and I'll tell you."

"Swim with me, and it'll be true."

He stood. She accepted the challenge.

"But don't dive headfirst. Everyone goes down that ladder."

The ladder wasn't far from them. They had to walk around two people who were sunbathing and a group that was making a ruckus as though happiness were possible. Damien kicked up some trousers that were left scrunched up, and he began to descend. The ladder didn't have a handrail, and every step was slippery with moss due to the wetness. When he had one foot in the water, he turned. Margaux watched him from a distance. There was doubt in his eyes. Curiosity and a certain dread. It was a first step. She went down to Damien, who took his foot out of the water. Before saying anything, they hugged.

"Is it cold?"

"No. It's freezing." With a caress, he moved two strands of hair out of her face. "What are you saying, Margaux?"

"That I'd come. I'd come, and I'd live with you, wherever it is. I only want to spend my life with you and to . . . You can just imagine. To know what it's like to have you hug me and make me yours. I'm dying for it, Damien. I promise you, and I know you know it. But I can't leave. I can't leave my parents here. They don't have anyone else. They've done everything for me, and I can't bear to . . . I love you so much. Like crazy. And if this lasts longer and we're not fine here, we'll flee from this nightmare later, but now . . . You understand, right?"

He nodded, hiding his lips.

"I'll take charge of it. I love you too. And we'll always do what you want to do." He was convincing. "But now?"

"Now what?"

"Now you'll swim with me."

"No, no, no . . . Please."

He'd already grabbed her hands, and they both jumped into the water screaming and laughing. After some time spent dipping their heads in the water, chasing each other, and pretending to drown each other, they didn't find it as cold anymore. Or that's what Margaux remembered now, as she lamented that her experiences with Damien were slowly losing color, like an old photo. She was too young to look back. At eighteen years old, it wasn't her time to be nostalgic. But her memory preserved each moment, each gesture, and all the small words from that evening on the Seine, where they stayed till the sun said, "Until next time."

Since Damien's arrest, Margaux tried not to pass by the Seine. When she had no other choice but to cross it, she looked at the river out of the corner of her eye and promised herself she would never swim in it again for all the years of her life. Those waters that ran silver would never be for her. She didn't want to pollute a place where she'd been happy. The two of them, happy. Just thinking about the word made her anxious. She felt bad for having had fun. Regret for the good times. She felt guilty for the simple fact of trying to live during a war, to live without harming anyone, betraying anyone, to live with a hate toward the German uniforms, to live clinging to her homeland and her family at their Montmartre apartment, and to live missing Dédé. She'd spent so many months without him.

Not even Hitler will be eternal.
And when the day comes, I'll want only to be with you.

She still had the letter memorized and could recite it with her eyes closed. She spent so many hours in her bedroom, whole afternoons there without leaving.

One evening, she opened the door and went into the dining room, shouting. Her parents, who were lying on the red sofa, became frightened.

"What's wrong?" Michelle, whose head had been on Ferdinand's shoulder, stood.

"On the radio, they said that—it can't be true, right?"

"What station?"

"On BBC, Mother. They said the Jews aren't being taken to labor camps in Germany. There's a place, I wrote down the name . . .

Auschwitz or something. They say they suffocate two hundred people a day in gas chambers there. I can't even imagine it."

"Holy mother—" Michelle covered her mouth with her hand.

"They're only telling us that to scare us, Margaux," Ferdinand said tepidly to calm everyone down. "It's impossible."

"What's a gas chamber?" Margaux asked.

"How do the BBC people know . . . ," her father trailed off.

Margaux looked at the paper on which she'd written "Auschwitz." She'd taken more notes in the corner with her pencil.

"It apparently comes from a newspaper written in the south, *Les Étoiles*, a secret newspaper."

"I haven't heard of this newspaper."

"It's run by writers, it says."

"Just picture it . . . Who do they think will believe that?" Ferdinand tried to dismiss the story. "Writers from the south and the resistance . . ."

In a fit of rage, Margaux threw her pencil against the window. Her anger provoked an unexpected rebound.

"Will you listen to me?" She was surprised by her own shouting, but she couldn't stop. "Do you want to come down to earth? And what if Damien got on one of those trains? And if hours from now—"

"Margaux, please, I'm sure they don't do all those things."

"And Damien isn't Jewish, honey," Michelle added.

"So what? What's that have to do with anything? How many people do we know who've been arrested and who've never been seen again? You don't have to be Jewish to know how these things go."

"We shouldn't think the worst, Margi."

"Why? Why do you say that? What do you know? You, who've lived here your whole lives, always here, in your house, acting like nothing's happened. It's been eight months since they took Damien. Eight, and here we are, acting like life continues. So, no, do you understand? No."

"Margaux," her mother said, trying to console her daughter with a caress.

"Leave me alone." She wasn't up for speeches. "You work at the store, helping Germans with a smile, like they're good people," she said, looking at her mother. Then, turning to her father, she continued. "And you go to the theater to service everything and make sure nothing is needed. Do you plan on doing anything at any point, even if it's just for me?"

Ferdinand acted like the man he was. He was offended. He huffed like a hippo, went silent, and left the dining room for his bedroom. Michelle, who was just as hurt as her husband, tried to talk.

"You can't scold us. We don't deserve that, Margaux. Everything we do, we do for you. If we've made a mistake, I don't know what it was. Stay or leave, what should we have done? But now that we're here . . . We moved so that you have a school and food and so you could be happy despite . . . You wanted the oboe, you got the oboe."

"Happy? You're joking, right? Without news of Dami in eight months, happy?"

"No one—"

"Can anyone put themselves in my shoes?"

"And can you put yourselves in ours, baby? No one likes the occupation, Margaux. No one. But there's a moment where you have to say to yourself, 'This is the way things are,' and you just have to get used to it. There's no other choice."

"Mama, please."

"Please what? You have no idea how upset your father and I are to see you like this. We don't talk about anything else. Your father—" She questioned whether she should continue. "The other day, your father said that if he knew where Damien was, he'd ask to switch places."

"You don't believe—"

"Margaux, stop pushing my buttons."

"Why? What'll happen? You'll tell one of those Germans you know to come find me?"

Michelle looked at her daughter. She should have slapped her with all her might, but she held back. Instead, Michelle went to the bedroom, opened the drawer of her nightstand, and grabbed the clipping she'd been hiding there.

"What are you doing?" Ferdinand asked, sitting at the foot of the bed with his face in his hands.

"Nothing."

She went back into the living room, shoved the image right in front of her daughter's nose, and spoke to her in a different tone.

"It doesn't seem like you're having such a bad time, does it?"

"Is that me?"

"It's you, all right."

"Where'd that come from?"

"You were radiant."

All of a sudden, Margaux's legs quaked. "I remember this day perfectly," she said, bluntly. "I knew they'd taken my picture, but that . . . Where'd it come from?"

"It's from the Nazi propaganda magazine. It's all over France, all throughout Europe. *Signal.* Every fifteen days, there's a new edition. Some really beautiful pictures. And you're the most impressive of all of them, posing like a model."

"How could I have known, Mama? That man didn't tell me the photo would appear anywhere."

"No one knows anything when it's inconvenient to ask."

"Please . . . He asked me if he could take my picture, said the lighting was nice, and I . . ."

Margaux couldn't stop looking at herself in the photograph. So dressed up. It was true. It had turned out nicely. Despite the fight with her parents, she looked herself over and thought she looked pretty. She almost didn't recognize herself so happy. It was the day she'd gone to the movies with Damien, not long after they'd parted ways. How could she not be delighted? In the photo, not even an hour had passed since the miracle of her lifetime. Her first kiss.

30

The Best Day of the Century

Everything ends. Hardly ever is it so sudden. In April, the antiaircraft sirens interrupted a Pierné Orchestra concert. They had just played a couple of bars from the third movement, and alarms began to sound from afar. First came the audience's shock, after the doughy looks of the musicians. The Allied air force had been bombing the area surrounding Paris, and orders had been to take shelter as soon as possible once the sirens went off. The conductor, guessing at the hall's anxieties, made a final gesture with the baton and left Wolfgang Amadeus hanging. Delphin Moureau turned to the audience. Conscious there were just as many Germans as there were Frenchmen in the hall, he made a measured speech:

"Ladies and gentlemen, the alarms instill caution in us. It might perhaps be good for us to leave calmly and seek shelter. Best of luck to everyone. As the maestro Mozart said, 'No one knows how many days are allowed him. We have to submit to the will of Providence.' Thank you for coming."

When he looked back to pick up the musical score for Symphony no. 31 in D Major, half of the musicians had already left with their instruments in tow. Ferdinand hurried them to the basement of the theater. Others preferred to run to a metro station or try to get home and at the very least await the bombing lottery with their wives and children. In the bowels of the theater, some musicians crossed their fingers, others listened closely to try to hear the first plane before anyone else did, and still others prayed that the explosions would miss them by a wide margin. Those who'd escaped the Luftwaffe bombing four years earlier prayed that, in order to make it out of this one, their saviors would appear from the heavens to save them.

"These people make a lot of mistakes. You mean to tell me these pilots are English?"

"They seem more like Spaniards."

"The other day, they tried to blow up a railway junction, and they took down two buildings with people inside."

"If they're supposed to save us, we'll be waiting forever."

"But what do you want? Better these guys than the Germans."

"It was much worse then. Or did you forget, my friends?"

In the middle of the argument, the lights went out. The light bulb gave a flicker of warning, and suddenly, the bunker descended into pitch black.

"Ferdinand?"

"Dutronc? Are you here?"

"Yes. Of course."

"Do something . . ."

"Fix this power outage, man. Don't leave us in the dark."

"Boys, I fear this isn't limited to the theater."

"You don't even have a flashlight on you."

"I carry only a handful of almonds in my pocket. Don't you know that?"

"They must be hard as rocks. They're the same ones you've had for years."

"When you finally eat them, you'll have shits like a sheep."

"Can you all be quiet, holy hell," someone who wasn't in the mood for jokes shouted.

They spent hours locked up, until the lights went back on, until the sirens stopped ringing, and until some time had passed since a bomb hit. By the time silence fell, there weren't any almonds left in Ferdinand Dutronc's pockets. It was how he calmed his nerves, hoping that Margaux and Michelle were together somewhere safe. Sometimes, some of the musicians who were sitting on the ground whistled a melody, and someone had to guess what piece it came from. It was the game they played at every bombing.

"*Music for the Royal Fireworks* by Handel?"

"Handel, yes. Not the work."

"*Water Music.* The first suite."

Once it had been guessed, everyone came together to hum it at half volume. The murmured tune brought them so much peace. In the hall, they were an orchestra. Underground, they were a heart.

A few months later, Michelle's coworkers at the Galeries Lafayette said, with a renewed enthusiasm, that what had happened in Normandy in early June was a blow against the Germans. The proof was that Radio Paris didn't talk about how thousands of North American soldiers had landed. Maurice Chevalier continued to sing all day—sometimes an Édith Piaf song would play—they discussed the vast cultural agenda of the city, they praised the German excellence, but they were silent about what had happened on the Atlantic Coast, under lock and key.

"Do you think they're coming to save us?" asked a salesgirl, her arms folded.

"They say they are on the BBC. And there are more Englishmen than Americans."

"But Normandy is really far. Do you know how many hours away it is from Paris?"

"The Germans have gotten nervous, that's for sure."

"They hardly come by here. They don't buy anything anymore."

"And they're in a grouchy mood." Marion became serious, raised her chin, and imitated a haughty grimace. "You just have to see them in the streets."

"They don't show up on the steps of the opera every day."

"Don't get your hopes up. The Wehrmacht . . . What I'm trying to say is the Wehrmacht continues to parade down Champs-Élysées every noon like nothing is happening."

"They'll be fleeing like rabbits."

"They've been saying that for a while, but they're not moving from here now."

"There better not be a single one of these dogs left."

"Nathalie, woman, they'll hear you . . ."

"We thought the Allied bombings would be our salvation, but—"

"Let's trust in them a little more, dammit. They say Dunkirk is important."

"The boys. Watch the boys in the street. The ones who play war games. Who do they want to be? Germans? They're the good guys to them. The ones who win."

"Because they haven't seen anything else during these times, jeez . . ."

"You listen to English radio. What does Churchill say on there?"

The chatting at the counter lasted until the angry mustached manager told them playtime was over. He'd had enough gossip, and they shouldn't get too hopeful. The Germans weren't going down without a fight.

But one thing did change with the general strike in mid-August. No one saw a big difference in the day-to-day, but there was a renewed air in the city. The fear of the Germans seemed to suddenly dissipate. As if their guts had grown larger, the police officers, the postal workers, and the heartiest in the city became emboldened. Barricades, planted left, right, and center in all the most strategic locations, hindered the movement of the Germans. But the Germans' best weapon was their ability to endure, reorganize, and counterattack cruelly. When the resistance couldn't hold back any longer, General Leclerc's armed troops entered Paris through Porte d'Orléans. The republican Spaniards of the "La Nueve" division entered through Porte d'Italie. Eisenhower, the hero of D-Day and H-Hour, also sent the Fourth Infantry Division of the Allied troops to the center of the city. There was a sense of victory when the Allied forces arrived at Hôtel de Ville on August 25.

The bells of Clignancourt began to ring. Soon, those of Saint-Sulpice, Saint-Germain-des-Prés, and Notre-Dame followed. In every church, even more joyously. The ringing of freedom moved from the neighborhood to the streets to the cul-de-sacs of every arrondissement. People knew what had happened right away. They didn't have to turn on the radio or listen to speeches. The joy surpassed the proclamations. Citizens celebrated by shouting in the courtyards. That August, women peeked out of wide-open windows and shouted as they hadn't for four years. They liberated themselves in a way they had maybe never done before. They went down to the street without grabbing their keys and sang and danced. On the path to the city center, as if they knew there would be a big party in Hôtel-de-Ville, people hugged neighbors, acquaintances, and people they'd just met. A sincere smile was enough to merit three kisses. Eyes were the password of victory.

No one knew anything for certain, but everyone put in their two cents.

"They say they've surrendered at Gare Montparnasse."

"They haven't had time to flee."

"It seems like they've arrested the German General Staff."

"Hitler ordered all the bridges on the river to be blown up, but they didn't make it there on time."

Everyone had their own rumors, that was for sure.

That Friday afternoon, French flags appeared everywhere. No one could have guessed that they'd had so many stored in the backs of their closets. The streets were blanketed in three colors: the blue of sky, the white of peace, and the red of blood spilled over the four years of a nightmare that had finally ended. Children clambered up walls and gates with feline agility to untie the red and black swastikas. Out with all the standards. By the afternoon, they'd rid the squares of swastikas entirely. In the buildings where officers had set up shop, no one could be found. In the hotels they'd made their own—Crillon, Le Meurice, Raphaël, George V—one could catch only a glimpse of Nazis in their rapid escape. The general enthusiasm didn't take long to mix with that of the soldiers who'd liberated them. They greeted, applauded, and received them like heroes, and suddenly, the soldiers' weariness became nuanced. Their feet, sweltering inside their boots, seemed to not burn as hot. Women climbed up on the trucks full of soldiers and celebrated. Babies held up from their bottoms by their mothers wanted to climb the tanks as if they were fair attractions. Champagne also appeared everywhere, and whoever had it in hand drank straight from the bottle. In the improvised festivity, they passed it from one person to the next. Everyone shared in the ritual of winners. No one refused anything.

Michelle and Margaux left Montmartre, and, holding hands, they went to search for Ferdinand at the theater. Their feet raced down the sloping streets. Liberty made them run. The Châtelet, however, was at the center of the action, and it was difficult for them to get there. Not even a needle could fit between place de la Madeleine and place de la Concorde. The closer they got to city hall, the more people there were. They avoided the hundreds of bags of dirt that the resistance had positioned as barricades in the last weeks. On their journey, they sang "La Marseillaise" a couple of times and shouted, *"Vive la France,"* at the top of their lungs. When someone said, *"Vive de Gaulle,"* they joined in. When they heard, *"Vive la liberté,"* they echoed *"Vive la liberté."* Margaux arrived at the theater with a flag in hand, the contagious excitement from the street, and a latent, deep-down thought of Damien. Did he know that Paris had been liberated? Would he return to the city? Was her love very far? Was Dédé alive or dead? After so many months without any news . . .

The mix of emotions vanished when she hugged her father. Mother and daughter had entered the theater through the back door, and they found him toasting with three of the Châtelet's workers, who, sitting on the backs of their chairs, discussed the small battles the resistance had fought.

"Look who's here," said one.

"A surprise for you," said another who was facing them.

Ferdinand Dutronc turned and saw radiant Michelle and Margaux before him. Smiles, hugs, and teary eyes. His wife was wearing a beige blouse with pointed lapels, and his daughter was in a blue dress with a white-moon pattern. They were the most beautiful women in Paris. The three hugged, put their heads against each other's, and stayed like that for a bit. They cried and laughed at the same time. The father, in order to hide his shaking, passed his hand through the hair of the two women. Together, they exorcised four years of misery. They'd been living lives that didn't seem to be theirs. And they'd made it out. As a family. For that reason, they laughed and sobbed in a circle without holding back.

"Let's go into the street, Father. Take off your uniform. Today's not a workday. You have to see all of it."

"Come with us, Ferdinand," Michelle begged, her eyes pleading in a way meant for special occasions, as if to say, "Today is a day we'll always remember."

They walked among the crowd. They held hands so they wouldn't lose each other. Margaux felt happy walking between her father and mother, like she had when she went to kindergarten. Everything made them laugh. Some men took off their ties, others threw their hats in the air. Many women removed their shoes and walked with them in their hands like they were carrying hunting trophies. Someone gave Ferdinand a small American flag, and he waved it before throwing it up and catching it midair as he had seen in Sienna the one time he'd traveled to Italy. A British soldier carrying a cask had put his feet in a fountain and wouldn't leave, claiming it was the best day of the century. In a patchy French, he tried to speak to a statue, not realizing it was made of stone. "*La meilleure journée* of this century," he repeated, the woman ignoring him. He spent a while hugging her, and he still didn't notice the coldness of the breasts he peeked at from the corner of his eye. Everyone around him was laughing. No one wanted to pull him out of his fantasy.

"They say de Gaulle will speak from that balcony," someone said.

They looked for a place, even a remote corner, where they could watch the general's face. The crowd fell as silent as a morgue, listening to him. A sea of people, so quiet and attentive, waiting for words they'd prayed to hear for four years.

"Paris has been insulted. Paris has been destroyed. Paris has been martyred . . . But Paris has been liberated!"

Once more, the excitement, the shouts, the party, the ruckus, the songs, the champagne, and the bottles of wine passed from hand to hand. Michelle and Ferdinand went home. Margaux, who'd run into old school friends, asked to stay. No matter what, she wanted to celebrate a little longer. It was the party of all parties. And for once, her parents didn't know how to say no.

"Where are we going?" Margaux asked her friends.

"To look at the soldiers," Amélie, her redheaded friend, responded. "They're from the Fourth Infantry Division."

"What does that mean?" asked Camille, her hair braided down her back.

"That they're to die for."

On a night of firsts, it was difficult for night to approach. Night didn't arrive in Paris with its effervescence of joy. Paris had a lingering light that late-August Friday. The party, colored by the stripes, the stairs, and the tricolor flags, didn't have to have an end. Amélie, Camille, and Margaux followed the hubbub. The more there was, the better. The friends were excited. Soldiers had broken the lines and descended from their trucks and cars, quenching their thirst at whatever café had something to drink. Victory was celebrated everywhere. Places that had been full of Germans only the week before now greeted American soldiers with flattery and glasses of wine. They waved them in and invited them to all types of liquor until it ran dry.

"Should we go in here?" Amélie had always been the most daring.

"What do you mean? There's so much smoke," complained Camille.

"Exactly why. The more smoke, the better."

They hadn't gone down even three steps before they penetrated a wall of fog that prevented them from seeing past their noses. The atmosphere was thick, the music loud, and shame had been left at home. A woman passed by, her breasts loose. The woman, who was around their mothers' age, couldn't stop laughing, while a soldier, a cigarette between his lips, tried to aim the smoke at her nipples.

"Are you sure we can enter?"

"Margaux, we're already inside. Walk forward and don't turn back."

They acted casual, and once they were at a counter with high stools and they drank what they were given, it got hotter. None of the three had tasted anything that burned so much. When their glass were refilled, Amélie drank, Camille hesitated, and Margaux stopped.

"You're not going to drink that?" a soldier asked, coming up from behind them.

"Do you want it?" Margaux replied, sensing his presence from the corner of her eye.

"It's a day of celebration." The American, who was speaking French with a Texas accent, took the glass from Margaux and drank it in one gulp. *"Vive la France."*

"Vive la France," shouted the three friends, laughing. They found themselves surrounded by two more soldiers.

"How nice. We have the whole army for our choosing," said Amélie, before grabbing on to the only soldier wearing a hat.

"Le jour de gloire est arrivé," sang Camille. And without waiting a second longer, she launched herself into the arms of the soldier that looked the youngest to her.

"And you?" asked the American who'd drunk from Margaux's cup.

"I . . . I haven't drunk as much as they have," she responded, faced with a new situation.

She looked at him, and she thought he was polished, with the appearance of a good person. His skin had been bronzed by the sun, his cheeks weren't carved out by hunger, and at some point, he'd found time to shave. They looked at each other without saying anything. If he hadn't turned thirty yet, he was close. Slowly they let their eyes smile. There wasn't enough light to see the colors of their irises, but they could read each other's intentions. Their eyes talked on their own.

The soldier grabbed her hand with confidence.

"Come with me."

When Margaux got down from the stool, she noticed the soldier was more than a foot taller than she was. They crossed a dark hall where all the couples kissed desperately, with a cigarette consuming itself in their hands. At the end, a heavy curtain was drawn. There was a counter holding eight cups, and a sofa that could seat four people. He fell on top of it, spreading his legs and extending his arms in wait for the girl to launch herself on top of him. Margaux closed the curtain, searching for as much privacy as possible. Once she was on top of him, she nibbled at his lips.

"Are you from Paris?"

"If I say yes . . ."

"What?"

"Will you think of me as a war trophy?"

"Absolutely. I'll think that I was lucky to meet the most beautiful Frenchwoman in the country."

Margaux kissed him again. She put her heart into it. The glasses of wine from the party had created a fun fog. It freed them from fear and prejudice. And that polished American, who looked like he'd been plucked out of an office and not a war, excited her with his interesting personality. His shirt smelled of tobacco and gunpowder. She liked sniffing the hairs on his chest. How she loved that game. Without waiting for his permission, she unbuttoned his shirt and ran her hands down his chest. Suddenly, he grasped her butt under her dress. With his fingers, he searched for the edges of her underwear and smoothed out any wrinkles he found. The more kisses there were, the more excited his fingers became. Slowly and delicately, he found what he was searching for. He woke her up carefully, and he stayed there for a moment with a cautious touch. It felt like magic for Margaux, whose eyes were closed.

"Do it slowly, Yankee," she whispered, kissing his eyes.

"Are you scared?"

"Me?" A second and a half later, she responded, "No."

The doubt, however, had remained on the couch. The American realized he was likely ten years older than her. He looked in her eyes to calm her nerves.

"You're never too young or too old to make love," said the American in a scratchy but academic French.

It wasn't the moment to speak anymore. She unbuckled his belt like she had done it many times before, pulled down the American soldier's zipper, and in two yanks, removed his pants. Next, she moved her skirt back, and she let the soldier shimmy her underwear down to her knees.

"Slowly, you hear?"

The response was guttural. He knew how to hold back his passion. The up-and-down movement of his hips was smooth. The battering ram knocked at her door elegantly. It didn't try to push it down forcibly. It was necessary to persevere and enter with a welcoming permission. Margaux pushed her chin into his neck and felt how naturally she explored an unknown path. The sliding inside her felt less rough each time. With more wetness came more pleasure. With each jerk, more music. From the beginning to the end. She couldn't say in how many places she felt it. In no time—maybe it was an instant or a whole minute—an explosion invaded her whole body. Finally, the soldier's panting launched her into a new type of enthusiasm.

They stayed quiet, fit together like a single body, until they regained their breath at the same time. Neither was in a rush to measure their heartbeats.

"Are you okay?" he asked before pulling away.

"Very," she breathed deeply. "Very good."

Just as Margaux was about to explain how she had given him a gift, the American asked her a question.

"What's your name?"

"Michelle," she responded immediately. She said it confidently.

On her way home, a little before the sun emerged, when the party and hangover had transformed the street into a portrait of drowsy shadows, Margaux wondered why she hadn't told him her real name. And even more so, why'd she suddenly said her mother's. And what was his name, the soldier from the Fourth Infantry Division? It didn't matter. Maybe it was better that way, now that it was starting to become a foggy memory.

31

They Could Die of Jealousy

Post festum, pestum. Margaux had heard the Latin phrase in school, and she hadn't forgotten it over the years, with its elliptical verb resembling a curse repeated here and there throughout different moments of history and geographical locations. *After the party comes the plague.* This was the case, too, in Paris in 1944.

The months after the city's liberation were not easy for anyone. Every person had lost someone—the count of men who wouldn't return was in the thousands—and while everyone wanted to go back to the normality before the occupation, the weight of the absences was heavier. Paris couldn't be fixed overnight. It was hard to recognize the face of liberty after years of imprisonment. Hunger continued to be something that needed resolving. Stores slowly raised their blinds, but food was still scarce, and pillaging in the street was widespread even without Germans to blame. Life was being rebuilt from a moral poverty. Everything involved reproaches and mistrust. Envy and revenge. Traitors were hunted down. It was a wild purge. With and without trial, all were executed: the traitorous militiaman, the Gestapo informer, the collaborator who'd ratted out his neighbor as a member of the resistance, or the poet who'd written in favor of the Vichy puppet government. Every day, there was a new case.

"Today, I watched how they made a line of women parade around naked." Margaux arrived home in disbelief. "There's maybe thirty of them in the middle of Rivoli. And people were spitting and insulting them. It was . . ."

"Don't look at those kinds of things," her mother replied.

"I asked, 'But what did these women do?' And they told me they'd gone to bed with the Germans."

"Yes, what do they call that, Ferdinand?"

"Horizontal collaboration," he responded, without looking up from the newspaper.

"That. Horizontal collaboration. It's a good name."

"Mama, please."

It wasn't an easy autumn for the Dutronc family either. Days passed, and the hope that Damien would return vanished slowly. Margaux had been thrilled at the departure—or surrender or defeat or whatever you wanted to call it—of the Germans. Her parents tried bringing her down to earth, but she refused to sit around twiddling her thumbs. The first few weeks, she moved heaven and earth to find anyone who might know anything. The name Damien Devère didn't appear on any of the Red Cross lists. The Gendarmerie—who didn't encounter a lack of women looking for husbands, fathers, and brothers—didn't know a thing. They were overwhelmed by the avalanche of fruitless searches and were in the worst of moods.

Margaux endured the suffering alone. Her parents had their own problems, and they had just enough to save their skin. A couple of days after the liberation, Michelle was fired from the Galeries Lafayette. The whole sequence of events took place in less than a week. First, they fired the floor manager. The angry mustached man had a lot of sympathy for the Nazis. Over the four years, he'd laughed along with them, and Marthe, Nathalie, and Marion decided to inform on him. A resistance cell waited for him at the door of the store and shoved him into a truck, and despite his shrieks that this was some kind of mistake, they didn't care to know anything about misunderstandings. Revenge moved them more than truth did. The smallest denouncement was enough to make the charge.

After, Michelle's coworkers went after her. They accused Michelle of being a collaborator. She and the whole Dutronc family. They were still angry that Ferdinand, unlike their husbands, hadn't enlisted for the war. He must have had some contacts so he could stay at the theater. They also hadn't forgotten what had happened with the girl, Margaux, modeling for a German propaganda magazine.

"You're all a disgrace."

"They should shave your head and make you walk through the city so everyone knows what you are."

Astounded by the anger of her coworkers, Michelle defended herself as much as she could.

"I didn't suck up to the Germans."

"We can't know that for sure."

"Listen," she begged. "How many years have we worked together? You know me well. I'm not capable of anything you're saying. We survived at home . . . Survived and nothing more. Is that our sin? I'm really very sorry for everything you and your husbands went through, but it's not our fault. We didn't—"

"She's right, girls," Marion jumped in in a spell of sympathy. "We can't accuse her of things we haven't seen."

"But we don't want to see your face here ever again," said Marthe, feeling the need to emphasize the extent of their forgiveness.

They refrained from accusing her of anything they couldn't prove. Their magnanimity was limited to sending an anonymous letter to the company headquarters in which they expressed doubts regarding Michelle's behavior, and before the good name of the galleries could be stained, management had called her in and told her she needn't return the next day.

There were also some shocks at the Théâtre du Châtelet. The conductor of the Pierné Orchestra had disappeared in mid-September, and no one knew anything. His lover's wife, who'd already marked Delphin

Moureau as a homosexual to the Germans, had now denounced him to the resistance as a collaborator. At every turn, the sycophant's rancor had made her play her cards with the sole objective of saving her marriage.

Over the past year, Ferdinand had watched the disappearance of Imtold Lefebvre, Damien Devère, Delphin Moureau, and other musicians in the orchestra who he'd not had ties with, because no one can be friends with a hundred people at the same time. It was not the electrician's problem whether a conductor, an oboist, or a violinist were missing. After all, there were a thousand and one virtuosos in the city looking for work, and they'd find another conductor to rehearse Debussy's Symphony in B Minor. What worried him was that, in the theater and orchestra, there was someone pulling the strings, calling people out, or exempting them based on convenience. He had the feeling—and certainty—that it had happened when the Germans were in the city, and even now that none were left. The rat was inside the house, and he feared that, depending on how the wind blew, it would be his turn next.

But it was Christmas Day when a cold front settled in the Dutronc household. Margaux, who'd been a bundle of nerves over the past few weeks, thought a lot about whether or not she should say anything during dinner. At the end of the day, there was never a good time to disappoint your parents. They'd decorated the apartment like they hadn't in recent years, and her mother prepared the chocolate log so they could lick their fingers. She didn't want to ruin their appetites, but she knew the surprise and the fuss that followed would create a memorable "before" and "after" of the day in their house. In fact, she couldn't wait any longer to share the news. As hard as she tried to cover herself with a towel when she walked from her bedroom to the bathroom, as much as she dressed in baggy clothing, her belly would eventually be noticeable.

Before picking up the dinner plates, Margaux decided it was time. She grabbed her mother's and father's hands and mustered the strength. She tried to be tactful and soft, but the words were what they were:

"I'm pregnant."

The news left the family silent. Michelle and Ferdinand immediately understood, but it took them by such surprise, in its unexpectedness and strangeness, that they were still as stone. They'd never thought their daughter would confess something like that to them.

"Impossible," said her father.

"Are you sure?" asked her mother.

Margaux nodded, chewing on her upper lip. The silence hung heavy throughout the apartment once more. Her father took a deep breath and let go of her hand.

"How embarrassing, how embarrassing . . ."

Michelle's world came crashing down. "I'm sorry." Margaux tried to look into her mother's disdainful eyes. "I'm so sorry."

"Who's the father?" Ferdinand slammed his fist down. "Is it a German?"

"No, no. I know it's not." It was the one question Margaux hadn't expected from him.

"It can't be the Holy Spirit's." Her father stood. He couldn't stand the tension. "Are you sure it's not a German?"

"Papa, please, it's—" She tried to keep her voice from shaking. "It can only be an American soldier."

"An American, how great."

"The night of the party. We got carried away, and—"

"The fucking party!"

"Jesus Christ, Margi." Her mother touched her hand. "How did this happen?"

Margaux shrugged her shoulders, looked down, and remained there for a moment in penance. She waited for her parents to have it out with her. But Ferdinand didn't say anything else. He counted on his fingers, confirming there were four months in total between August 25 and December 25, and with a jolt, he grabbed his jacket and scarf and made to leave the apartment.

"My love, don't leave," Michelle reproached. "Not now. Let's all talk about it, please."

"I need some fresh air," he responded, like he hadn't heard her. He slammed the door. As he walked angrily yet lethargically around Montmartre, he decided he would never tell his daughter he loved her again. And by God, would he follow through with it.

Her mother, on the other hand, improvised a speech whose direction she wasn't sure of. She spoke about this. She cursed that. She swore this. She damned that. And everything revolved around her disgrace, what people would think, the obstacle in front of them, how a fatherless child would survive, how she'd been so thoughtless, the bad luck of getting pregnant her first time—if she was to believe it—her ruined reputation, the black cloud that hung over the family, the fact they'd just emerged from war and now had to return to the bunkers to hide their shame, how she'd been able to be so shameless, what Damien would think, poor Damien . . .

"Don't go there, Mama." Margaux stopped her. "Don't you dare."

"I'm sorry, my love. I don't even know what I'm saying." She wiped a tear with a kitchen rag. "I don't know what's going on, I'm confused. I'm sorry . . . I feel like I'm sleepwalking. Don't listen to me."

"Of course I'm listening to you, Mama."

They hadn't let go of each other's hands the entire time. Even if they were hot or sweaty, Margaux needed contact with her mother now more than ever.

"It's such a big surprise. So . . . I guessed as much. Now I'm putting together that something wasn't right . . . but pregnant? I should have seen it, I'm so stupid. Oh lord, it's so confusing, Margi."

But she didn't just need her mother. She would have also liked some understanding. She took a deep breath, and carefully, she dared to say: "I didn't think you'd congratulate me, Mama. But I did think you would think more about me and less about what people might say."

"What do you mean?" Her mother knew perfectly well what she had meant and more.

"I expected my father's reaction. Swearing, two words, and then he flees. But you . . . I wish that at some point you had looked down and asked me, 'Margaux, how are you? Are you okay?' One question. That's it. Simply, 'Are you okay, my daughter?' Just that."

She started to cry. Her mother remorsefully joined her. They got up without letting go of each other's hands and hugged. Their legs failed them, as emotional as they were. They let it all go, noisily and in thick tears. They emptied themselves until the last sob. All at once, however, a weight had been lifted for Margaux. Perhaps the worst was over.

In her fifth month of pregnancy, she managed to go outside without feeling ashamed. If someone liked her belly, that was all well and good. If someone grumbled about it, they could go to hell. If someone speculated about it, they could die of jealousy. In the sixth month, her father began to speak to her again. He still wouldn't tell her he loved her, but Michelle and Margaux were convinced his view would change. Once Ferdinand could see himself as a grandfather rocking a baby, maybe he'd be happy to show off his grandchild to everyone.

In the seventh month, Margaux was dying to see her baby's face. If it was a boy, she'd name him Damien. If it was a girl, Édith maybe. Deciding by herself had its advantages. She didn't have to agree with anyone.

In the eighth month, each of her legs weighed a ton, and it was difficult to move around the house. She went up and down the five flights only when necessary. There were long spring days on which she heard more from the radio than anything else. Sometimes, she listened to music she couldn't dance to, other times news that sounded a little better every day: French troops crossed the Rhine and entered Karlsruhe. Soviets advanced toward Bratislava. The United States Air Force conquered Hong Kong. Daily attacks were waged over Berlin and Hamburg. British troops isolated Holland from Germany. American troops liberated the concentration camp of Buchenwald, near Weimar. By mid-April, Hitler seemed to be cornered.

A week later, on a Tuesday when her mother had gone down to try to buy some fish and her father had gone to work, Margaux was napping in her room. She laid on her side, her belly resting on the mattress, which was how she was most comfortable. She also thought it was the posture in which her child moved the least. She was so comfortable that she'd fallen fast asleep. When she heard her name from afar, she didn't know whether it was day or night. She didn't know if she'd dreamed it or if she was really hearing it. A couple of minutes later, she thought she heard her name being called from the bottom of a well again. Sometimes, the man who was shouting called not only for Margaux.

"Ferdinand?" There was a pause. "Ferdinand? Michelle?"

The protagonist in her dreams knew the whole family . . .

"Hello?"

That voice . . .

"Margaux? Hello?"

The shouts were coming from the street.

"Hello, is someone there?"

She got out of bed and went to the dining room to figure out where the shouts were coming from. The window was half open, and she opened it up all the way. Carefully, she leaned out the window to look down on rue Tardieu.

A man looked up. He was completely shaved.

"Damien? Is that you?" She began to cry. "Damien!"

He blew her a kiss before he said anything.

"I'm here, Margaux. We won!" He raised his arms and repeated, "We won!"

"Damien . . . my love. You're alive . . . You're alive!"

Margaux put her hands to her head, and with her palms, she wiped the stream of tears that confirmed the law of gravity.

"Throw me the keys, and I'll come up."

"The keys?" Margaux was confused. "Is it locked?"

"Yes."

"No, no . . . I'll come down and open the door."

She went down the five flights as fast as she could, propping herself up on the railing. With each step, she experienced a mess of feelings, just as rash as they were contradictory: Damien wasn't dead, how happy she was to know this. But as soon as she opened the door, Damien would see . . . But Damien had gotten out—how happy and unexpected . . . But when Damien hugged her, he'd feel her belly . . . And Damien, so skinny, where had he been? How would Damien take the news that she was pregnant? But Damien had been revived, thank God. Whatever happened, there was no other option. He would have to handle it the way he handled it, there was no hiding it.

She opened the door and threw herself around his neck.

The hug. Everything was concentrated in that hug. Peace, fear, nerves, desire, anxiety, thankfulness, suffering, hope. Condensed love in a wordless reunion. She didn't say, "You're a skeleton, Damien. You don't have any curls left." He didn't make any indication of Margaux's state, like it wasn't real and nothing was happening.

They went up to the apartment, she walking slowly in front of him.

"I'll tell you everything, Dami. But first I need to know everything about you. Where were you? How'd you get back?"

"I've dreamed of coming back to this apartment so many times. The first oboe lessons . . ."

"The house is the same, you'll see."

"And your parents?"

"They're fine, they're fine, thanks. They're not here."

"That's why no one heard me."

"I was sleeping because . . . because this weighs me down, you know?"

He continued to act like he hadn't seen her swollen belly. Once upstairs, they hugged again without kissing. Damien didn't dare, and Margaux didn't feel it was appropriate. It felt wrong without updating him on how she'd gotten into this situation.

"But tell me, tell me about you . . . I need to know it all, from the moment they took you."

Eyes feverish and sunken to their sockets, Damien sat down to recount a story that had ended in Buchenwald only ten days prior. The beginning, however, felt like so long ago, and he wanted to tiptoe around it.

When they'd arrested him, after the concert at the theater, they'd taken him to the prison, where they hadn't even interrogated him. There'd been so many people in the same cell, and they treated them like animals. Then, they took them to a camp in France, out in the open, with a barbed-wire fence. A week later—or maybe it was two—they loaded the prisoners in a wooden wagon, and he went on a horrible trip to Germany by train. What happened next was worse. Someone explained that they were three hundred kilometers away from Berlin. When they arrived, they told them the name of the place no one on the train had heard of before: Buchenwald. After a year, or maybe more, everyone who was left would never be able to forget it. Damien tried to tell it all with the same naturalness as always, but his face had lost its shine. Sometimes he coughed and had to stop recounting his story, which expressly omitted all the terrifying details. He didn't want to even think about them. Why did he have to explain how pigs in the SS stables were fed better than they were? What would he have gotten out of telling her how they'd executed his friends? He spent more time, indeed, talking about the last few hours he was in Buchenwald. The prisoners' revolt, the Germans' anxiety, and the escape before the Sixth Armored Division of the United States Army had freed them. On the truck back to France, almost all of them still wore their striped uniforms. Near Fontainebleau, having had to walk the last few kilometers, Damien and two other men were seen by a woman near the highway. She made them come into her house so they could shower, and she gave them clothes to change into. She also gave them a suitcase and packed pants and shirts into it for them, because she didn't have any men left at her house. They'd all died during the war.

For months, Margaux had pictured Damien in one place and in a specific way. Now she knew the reality clashed entirely with her fantasy.

"If I'd had a way, I would have written to you from there," said Damien. "But I didn't have a pencil or paper or any way to—"

"You don't have to excuse yourself. I know your letter by memory. The one you gave my father when you saw things were heading south."

"You can rip it up now."

"I won't ever do that."

"Maybe"—he tried not to look at her belly—"maybe words of love don't have much meaning anymore."

"Oh, no . . . Damien . . . Let me explain. Please."

"You have nothing to explain. I told you to go your own way. And you listened."

"Let's stop with the sarcasm, Damien. Let me—"

Margaux didn't know where to begin her story. She had to tell him it wasn't a betrayal, not to jump to conclusions, that it had all been an accident. But he got ahead of her.

"I thought about you every day. Always."

"Even if you don't believe me, Damien, I also—"

"You gave me strength, you know? When I thought I couldn't bear it anymore, when I saw friends from my barracks die, I thought about the day you read my life line. Remember what you said?"

"That it'd be long."

"That it'd be long, yes. And that gave me the strength to continue. I thought about you. Your face came to my mind, and I was convinced you couldn't be wrong." He coughed. "My friends dropped like flies, from typhus, from hunger, from things you don't want to even know about . . . Every day, there was someone who didn't come back. But you said I'd live a long time, so I had to resist whatever it may be."

"Oh, Damien."

"Even if it was just to see you one last time."

Margaux grabbed his hand and kissed his palm. His skin was gray and dry, his fingers like bones. She gave him another peaceful and sweet kiss on his hand, searching for that familiar smell.

"Do you think I can play the oboe with these hands?"

She didn't hear the question. She couldn't continue to act like nothing had changed. It was time to confront it.

"You haven't asked me who the father is."

He was silent.

"Why haven't you asked me yet?"

"Do I have a right to?"

"Of course you do, Damien." She sighed deeply. "The father doesn't exist. There is no father, believe me. I don't know his name. I didn't want to know. It was the night of the liberation of Paris . . . Do you know anything about that day?"

"No clue."

"The city was madness. The party lasted two days and nights. It was at the end of August. Everyone was hugging everyone. It's not an excuse, I know. I met an American soldier. One night. Just that night, and goodbye."

He stared at her. "Put that way, it's—" He stopped.

"Say it. Don't feel bad."

"A child of happiness."

"Dami . . . I'm so sorry . . . I thought, I'm sorry, that maybe you—"

Damien shut her up with a finger to her lips.

"These last few years have been so horrible that a new life must be welcomed."

"Damien . . ."

"And even more so if you're the mother."

"I love you so, so much. I'm so sorry."

"Can I kiss a pregnant woman?"

"It's what I want most in this world . . ."

Slowly, they moved closer together. Damien's lips were dry, but he hadn't forgotten his passion for Margaux.

"I've missed your eyes, always so beautiful," he said.

And she pretended and responded that his were the same too. And they found each other's lips, and they didn't know how to process that this was truly happening to them. They sat on the sofa. Margaux stretched out her legs to reduce the swelling. Damien, exhausted, fell asleep with his head on a pillow. Margaux observed him. Gaunt and sickly, with bony cheekbones. In just a year, he'd aged eight or ten. From the grimace he made at times in his sleep, it looked like he was having a nightmare. When he woke, he didn't know where he was. A warm cup of coffee waited for him on the table. Margaux held the oboe case on her lap.

"I didn't open it. I haven't touched it in all this time."

Damien grabbed the case and left it on the table as if he didn't care about it at the moment. He was thinking about something else.

"Margaux, is it true that you're alone?"

"Of course, it's true."

"You haven't fallen in love with someone else, and you're scared to tell me?"

"No, no, no. I promise that everything happened like I said it did. I don't know who the father is. I know who it is, but I don't know what his name is. I won't look for him, and he—"

"Margaux." He didn't need to hear anything else. "Listen to me for a second."

"Go ahead, Mr. Devère."

Damien put both his hands on her belly. "I want this to be my child."

"Are you telling me this honestly?"

"I'm serious. Our son. If you want that, of course."

"Or daughter. I have a hunch it'll be a girl."

The child had to say its own piece.

"Did you feel that?"

"It kicked, didn't it?" said Damien, admiringly, because he'd never felt life knocking at the door.

"That means yes, that nothing would make her happier. And I want it, of course. Everything about today feels like a miracle, Damien. You're alive. You're here. You're with me. I can't believe it. Maybe it's moving too fast. It caught you by surprise, and . . . What happens if a couple of days from now, you regret this?"

"Margaux. That won't happen."

"You're not doing it out of pity? Are you sure?"

"I'm doing it because I love you and because I want to."

"Damien . . . How can you be so generous with me?"

"Because I want us to do this together, if you're willing, like the family we're meant to be."

"You don't know how much I've suffered, how much I've missed you, how I thought you had . . ."

"And look. I've been resurrected," he said, bursting into a laugh. "I was supposed to surprise you, but you're the one who surprised me."

Margaux grabbed his hand and put it back on her belly so he could see how a life yet to come was moving.

"When she's born, my hair will have grown some, maybe not the curls from before."

"If she's a girl, her name will be Édith."

"I like it," said Damien decisively.

"Édith Devère. It sounds nice." She proudly caressed her belly. "My daughter, let me introduce you to your father."

32

Afternoon of the Faun

He didn't open the case until he was alone.

He did it slowly, fearful about something he wasn't sure of. Of the oboe not being there, of the wood cracking, or of something having broken. Even of not knowing how to play it anymore. The oboe was the same. Intact. He found it just as he had left it after *Scheherazade* in the theater at the time of his arrest. It was true that Margaux—out of superstition and in order not to further weaken it—hadn't dared to open the black case during his long absence. She'd guarded it like a token of love.

In his imagination and when hunger had prevented him from sleeping, Damien had played an oboe for the bunks in the barracks, surrounded by men with parched skin and spirits. The music in his head had been one of the disciplines he imposed on himself so as not to go crazy in that camp of terror and death. It was comforting and lifesaving. There wasn't a day he hadn't imagined practicing his oboe. He started with Bach's cantatas, continued with Richard Strauss's *Don Juan*, and ended where he could before the shouts of some Nazi—those damned dogs—ruined his private concert.

He took out the three parts and put them together. It looked new with its sparkling-clean keys. He caressed the wood and inserted the reed carefully, sliding it into the reed socket like the instrument was a virgin. He had first-time nerves.

He put it in his mouth, closed his eyes, and played.

He searched for its soprano sound. He always recognized the timbre of a beautiful woman's voice in the oboe. He blew and produced a miracle.

The voice had Margaux's face.

If the Pierné Orchestra wanted him, he'd be ready for his first concert soon.

He was received at the Théâtre du Châtelet with excitement, hugs, and the kinds of words you never forget. Musically, they told him yes, of course, they were missing an oboist, and they'd welcome him with open arms. Rehearsals for *Prelude to the Afternoon of the Faun* began that same afternoon. Before sitting in front of his stand, they had to catch him up on the highs and lows of the orchestra. No one knew anything about the conductor, Delphin Moureau. It was a bad sign. There hadn't been news of Imtold Lefebvre. There wasn't much hope there either. They didn't talk about it, but a year after he'd disappeared, no one could ignore his fate. On the other hand, there was a lot of discussion in the hallway about Michel Mirailles, the cellist who'd stayed in the orchestra until liberation day. When they discussed him, Damien remembered the night M. M. had thrown himself on him in the middle of the street. Mirailles had been wasted, and Damien was able to throw him off before his discomfort turned into tragedy. During the last few days the Germans were in Paris, when everyone had assumed they'd escaped, someone had spread a rumor that Michel Mirailles was the spy in the Pierné for the Germans. His companions in the string section had guessed it for some time. He'd hidden under the pseudonym Jean du Silence to act as a musical critic in *Je suis partout.* Someone had ratted him out to the Germans, and in exchange for not deporting him like all the men who loved men, they'd given him a mission: spy on the orchestra. Everything he saw and heard he must report discreetly to the office of propaganda, with the excuse that he was going there to turn in an article. At the end of August, the morning of the great parade of liberation, with the big streams of people walking from the Arc de Triomphe to place de la Concorde, Mirailles knew a squad would search for him and make him pay for his betrayal. He took off his belt and hung himself in the stairwell before they arrived at his house.

The tickets to the Pierné Orchestra concert sold out. Once music lovers discovered it was an homage to those who'd been deported, they signed up without even knowing what pieces would be played. It was a farewell to so many fears, tears, and sadness. The program was the least important of it all. When they arrived at the doors of the theater and saw the posters, they discovered they'd be listening to three works by Debussy, a compatriot.

Margaux and Michelle, who'd entered through the back door, sat in the third row next to the aisle. They saved a seat for Ferdinand, who would take off his khaki uniform for one day and sit in the main hall once the lights went out. After so many years working at the Châtelet, he'd heard a thousand and one rehearsals, but he'd never watched a performance while seated in the audience.

"Papa, most importantly, don't come out in your work clothes."

"Why not?" he teased her. "It doesn't look good on me?"

"Papa, please . . ."

"Are you embarrassed of your father?"

The response was a peach-fuzz kiss on the cheek. The murmurs in the hall quieted as the main floor was left in half light. In the reverential silence, musicians appeared, like a trained parade of black-and-white penguins, and they took their places. Last to come out was the new conductor, tall as a giant, with a white head of hair and beard, and he walked to his platform to receive the courteous applause. Once he faced the musicians to open the musical score and grab the baton, the audience realized there was an empty chair in the middle of the stage. The robust conductor stepped off his platform and left so everyone could see what happened next.

An emaciated Damien emerged from the side of the stage, his oboe in hand. He was barefoot and wore his striped uniform from Buchenwald, which had turned gray from months of wear. Slowly, the oboist walked to his seat with the dignity of a survivor.

The gasp from the audience was unanimous.

The conductor didn't have to explain anything. Everyone understood. Damien's companions from the woodwind sections were the first to stand. The musicians placed their instruments on their chairs to applaud him. Instantly, the rest of the audience stood, and everywhere the word "bravo" resounded throughout the whole hall. It was an act of patriotic vindication, an homage to anonymous heroes.

"Did you know about this?" Michelle whispered into Margaux's ear.

"No . . ." Between her enormous belly, the wooden seat, and the explosion of emotions, it was difficult for her to stand up. "He didn't tell me he'd saved the uniform."

Stoic behind the music stand, Damien bore the ovation by looking down at the floor. When he lifted his gaze and saw so many people moved for such a long time, he had no choice but to wave his hand, with a knot in his throat and his oboe in the air. The tribute went out to the memory of those who hadn't had as much luck. He immediately found Margaux in the third row. He saw how emotional she was, sitting next to her parents, the family that would be his as soon as they got married. He closed his fist, and with his eyes glued to Margi, he placed the oboe next to his heart.

The audience took their seats as soon as Damien sat. Michelle asked Ferdinand for a handkerchief, and the conductor took advantage of the magical moment of collective disturbance to raise his hand. Keeping it up was enough to silence everyone and place the orchestra on alert. Debussy began to speak immediately.

The first notes of the *Prelude* were for the faun's transverse flute.

After a few bars, the oboe entered. Damien focused with all his concentration. He followed the score and played with his heart. His fingers worked, as always, like those of a perfect stenographer. His mouthpiece did not work so perfectly. Nervously, he pressed the reed too hard, and without expecting it, he had to stop to cough. With a modest gesture, the conductor stopped the *Prelude*. In the middle of the buzz, Damien looked at the conductor fearfully. What if that survivor's cough stopped him from finishing the concert? Quickly, Ferdinand began clapping, and everyone else joined. The applause resounded once more throughout the hall. It was a knowing ovation, an understanding ovation. From the back of the theater, a man stood on his chair to shout, *"Vive la France!"* A woman from a lateral box responded, *"Vive la vie."* And while people shared in celebration of their victory, the conductor walked up to Damien. He asked him only one question. Breathing deeply and trying to find the air missing in his lungs, he nodded in response. The giant returned to his platform and raised his hand, succeeding in silencing even a fly. He turned to his musicians and said one thing:

"Sirs, da capo."

From the beginning again. Like always.

ROGER

33

White Key, Black Key

Barbara opened the window and stuck her head out to see the highway. It had been dark for hours. And it had been days since they'd stepped out onto the street.

"Tomorrow, they'll let us go out." She closed the window of the top floor and rubbed her cold hands together. "Mayor Delanoë says to be careful with the slippery ice."

"Buzz off, Mayor. We're going out now, Barbara. Paris to ourselves."

"Now?" She looked at herself and her lazy outfit. She was so comfortable in her long pajama pants and worn-out Cirque du Soleil T-shirt.

"Tomorrow, Montmartre will be infested with tourists again. They've been locked up for a week in their hotels. Once they let them out, it'll be a plague."

"The crowd will be small."

"But we'd be alone now."

"Because it's not allowed, Roger . . . We can't do it."

"But there's not much snow left, if you know what I mean." He was looking for any reason to exit through the window.

Making sure Roger couldn't see, Barbara lifted her shirt to look at her belly button. It looked like there was a cotton ball sticking out.

"No matter what, tomorrow I have to go see my grandmother."

She sneakily removed the tuft by brushing it off with a finger. "Mamie Margaux must be up the wall with all these days locked inside."

"That's for tomorrow. I'm talking about now, come on." He grabbed her by the waist, a subtle way of asking, "Why don't we bundle up and go out?"

"Will you come with me?"

"Where?"

"Tomorrow, to see my grandmother. Aren't you dying to meet her?"

"Of course I am. Actually," Roger said, cheekily, "I already know her."

Barbara looked like she needed more explanation.

Roger went on: "On a bike, in black and white, when she was a girl. The allure of the photo . . ."

"Come to the home tomorrow and ask her all about it."

"Now, put on your Nikes and let's go out for a walk."

Roger winked. In exchange, Barbara kissed him on the tip of his nose.

"Do you always get what you want?"

It sufficed for her to put on some thick socks, soft corduroy pants, and a polar lining. She didn't bother changing her shirt or her bra. "'Georgettes' were out to play," as her grandmother, who named everything, would say. They didn't have to run into anyone, she'd be wearing a jacket on top, and what the hell? For forty-one years old, she felt like her breasts were still enviably perky and firm; if she put a pencil under them, it would still fall out. Barbara gave Roger one condition.

"Don't bring the camera."

"But—"

"It'll just be me and you today. Today, you're looking at the city. Or you're looking at me, but without the viewfinder."

They playfully began their forbidden walk. They'd yet to reach Clichy Boulevard when Barbara had a vivid memory of Anne Delacourt and the piano. She was Giresse & Trésor's star author, whom Barbara had sold worldwide rights for. The day they met at an editorial dinner in a private room at Le Procope, Paris's oldest brewery, Anne Delacourt had revealed an intimate secret about her creative process.

"Writing is like a piano concert," she said. "The beautiful sound of the piano lives behind the keys. A straight back, forward gaze, and some flowing parts and some lulling. The letters and verbs emerge little by little. Peaceful sounds, fragile words. The right hand converses with the left hand. The cadences of the sentences dance slowly across the computer's keyboard. But there are other moments when the hands argue, the fingers race, they pick up speed and accelerate, and they become virtuosos, playing the notes—white key, black key—with an insatiable impulse to fill pages and pages with burning emotion. The body of the pianist links with the keys. The writer helps breathe life. They close their eyes, and the story flows without the need for a score. Suddenly, passion sprouts. Ideas, expressions, trips. High and deep, to here and there. The writer chases down paragraphs, carried along by the music of the tireless drumming of fingers. Action, dear Barbara, action. Gushing out."

That description stayed with Barbara. It's how she was feeling on this strange walk she'd never planned on taking. Action gushing out. Adventure. The solitary escape through Paris, the empty city, the door to happiness. Her feet rushed. The pure air, the cold on her face. Risk and happiness. And a man she could trust at her side. Ever since she'd said goodbye to Maurice, slamming the door shut on seven years of infidelity, she hadn't yet walked next to anyone else. Much less held someone's hand. She was disoriented. The feeling was as strange as it was new. First, she felt embarrassment, then comfort. Two arrondissements later, with her insecurities now gone, Barbara walked happily in lockstep. That stubborn home settler, Roger. That cheeky guy who'd come to Paris to take pictures, perhaps because he didn't have anything better to do. That young man, who was wounded by the death of his father, who'd softened slowly, who'd made conversation, who'd confessed to her at midnight, who'd cooked—with too much salt—during the days after a historic snowfall they'd never forget. Roger Narbona, who made her see, without saying it, that being surly was a waste of time, and that she was actually punishing herself. That robust and strong Roger, lively as his eyes, who she'd heard moan pleasurably when they made love.

But they weren't the only ones who'd escaped the curfew with just a few hours remaining. They silently smiled when crossing paths on the street with another couple who'd gone out to exclaim their joie de vivre. The mischief of good faith united them. The French: a rebellious spirit. Near the Gare Saint-Lazare, they were approached by a man who'd gone out for a run to get his blood pumping. The peace was so absolute they could hear three men breathing from far away before the breathing—like a hastening waltz—stopped as they lost sight of them. Behind l'Opéra, some teenagers were causing a ruckus. They smoked, laughed, drank, and made up for all the days they'd had to stay inside. Beyond, at rue Saint-Honoré, it seemed like they'd granted special permission to go outside to walk their dogs. Barbara and Roger spotted the light of a police car from far away, so they turned and found another path. Every shortcut felt like a game, a world to discover. Paris was still, for a couple of hours, a silent city.

The fence of the Madeleine was closed. Les Deux Magots in the dark, with its chairs tied on top of the tables. The terraces, deserted. Not a single soul at the pont des Arts. The Latin Quarter was silent, a welcome irony. In place Saint-Michel, in a square where a mass of snow had accumulated, a rat ran in front of them as if they'd been hunting it. The Louvre pyramid, all for themselves, emitted a bluish light. Surely they were hard at work inside preparing for the next morning's reopening. In a few hours, the lines, tourists, and pickpockets would return. This was always the way things were. The imperfection of big cities.

"Maybe we should start heading back. We've wandered far from home."

Barbara's suggestion produced a new idea for an adventure. Roger made her walk down a couple of stairs next to the river. "No one will see us here."

The darker, the more mysterious. The cold had penetrated the rocks. Water trickled down the walls. Thawing was a constant occurrence in the city. The dribbling sound accompanied them through their shortcut. The river snored with the buzz of the city, constant and pacifying. Suddenly, Roger stopped.

"Do you see it?" He pointed to the moon.

"It's splendid."

"There are two types of people. People who think man went to the moon and people who are convinced that Apollo 11 was staged. Which side are you on?"

"You tell me, since you're the photographer. Could they take those pictures of Armstrong and the other guy up there? How were they able to stream the images live throughout the whole world? What kind of cameras? Could they broadcast from the moon?"

"I see which side you're on."

"Which?"

He surprised her with a cheeky smile. "Your most beautiful side."

Roger gave her a long kiss on the cheek. Immediately, their lips found each other's. Hugging, they melted into each other, swept by a new passion. It was a strange feeling. Until then, they'd tasted each other only from within the walls of the apartment. In Barbara's room, or on Roger's bed.

"Hello, couple." Someone they hadn't heard approached and coughed at their side. "Everything okay?"

Barbara and Roger pulled apart. Frightened, she reacted first.

"Yes, all good, thanks. Good night."

"Good night," the man responded politely, not wanting to scare them. He was a strong man who seemed like he could have been the physiotherapist for a professional cycling team. In a familiar gesture, he took his wallet out from inside his down coat. With a flick of his wrist, he showed them a badge and then stowed it away. "Don't you know there's a curfew?"

"Get out of my face," Roger jumped in.

"Excuse me?"

"This badge is good for nothing," Roger said to Barbara, ignoring the undercover cop. "Are we really supposed to believe this dude is the fuzz? Look, I can go like this, *chip-chop* with my wallet, and this guy would think I'm part of the FBI."

"Roger, please."

"Please show me your IDs."

The man, standing with his two feet on the ground, spoke without losing his cool. Roger, however, was momentarily offended.

"*We* show *you*? You want us to show you what? *Désolé*."

Barbara felt around the pockets of her coat.

"I'm not carrying anything. We came out for a walk, and . . . I just grabbed my jacket, and that's it."

"Don't apologize, hell. I'm carrying mine, but I'm not going to show anything to this kid until he proves he's the police."

The man, in his eternal patience, took out his wallet and placed his badge in front of Roger's face. He left it there for a while so Roger could read his credentials.

"Okay. Sorry. There are so many scams these days . . ."

Barbara took a couple of steps back. The last thing she wanted was problems. The second-to-last thing she wanted was to be embarrassed. Roger took out his ID and gave it to the policeman.

"Spanish?"

"From Girona. Well . . . do you know Barcelona? Near there."

"You speak French well."

"It's not hard."

"His mother is from here," Barbara added from afar.

"Well. Not from Paris. From Besançon," he specified.

The man didn't hear him. Barbara worried Roger would start acting even more ridiculous. She hated that feeling. Another time, she might have found it fun. But he broke the rules, and, as a well-behaved woman, she felt very uncomfortable. If, on top of it all, Roger tried to be funny, that would make her mad. She'd discovered a new side of him she didn't recognize. Now that experience—which was another way of saying age—had led her to settle down, she simply wanted someone to be by her side. Not someone who'd later reveal himself to be someone he wasn't. What did she want? A man without baggage, who listened well, who didn't create big scenes, who was detailed, who knew when to act and when to be quiet. And who never made her blush in front of others. "You mean guys like that still exist?" a coworker at the press had asked her.

The policeman walked away with Roger's ID in hand, took out a phone from his pocket and made a call. He started slowly relaying the information to someone who was hard of hearing on the other end.

"Roger. Narbona. Bazin. B-A-Z-I-N. The number? 46-230-015. With a *P* for Peter at the end, yes."

While they waited for a response, Barbara approached Roger and whispered in his ear.

"They won't find anything, right?"

"Of mine?" He took too long to respond. He whispered back, as well. "Of mine, no. But with all of my father's gambling debts, you never know when you'll be surprised."

The unperturbed physiotherapist policeman returned with Roger's ID. His eyes were glued to the papers.

"You don't look the same . . ."

"I cut my hair for the picture. Better now, huh?"

"What are you doing in Paris?"

Roger was silent. He looked at Barbara. "That's a good question."

Before his silence could create more tension, she cut in. "He's my boyfriend. He came to visit. He's staying at my house for a few days."

"A few days?" He turned over the ID. "Until when?"

For Roger, it was better that Barbara answer for him. He was curious to know what she'd say. And, next to the river, in a compromising situation, caught violating curfew by the police and not knowing how the situation would end, Barbara took the opportunity of being stuck in a jam to express her true feelings.

"Maybe he'll stay with me. Here in Paris."

"Are you sure?" the officer replied.

"Hey, don't you get involved in this," Roger jumped in. "Do your job, but get out of my—"

"My love, please!"

"Okay, okay." Roger raised his hands like he had a gun pointed at him.

The officer gave him a disapproving look.

"Look," he huffed, "I should fine you two right now. You've violated the lock-in. Tomorrow morning, everyone will be able to leave the house, but not tonight, as you should know. If everyone had made the same—"

"If you have to fine us, fine us. But save the sermons for church."

"Roger, please."

The policeman ignored him. He looked at Barbara. "I don't want problems. Let's not fight, okay?"

"Okay," she said hurriedly, in a small voice.

"Go home, and I'll pretend I didn't see you."

"Thank you, officer."

The man disappeared just as he'd arrived, without saying goodbye. And with the takeaway that women in the city had a bad habit of falling in love with the wrong person. He held himself back from saying it. *Soon, they'll figure it out,* he thought.

The walk back was quick and mediated through bickering. They cut through lonely streets in search of shorter ways to Montmartre. Barbara took advantage of the time to say, "That's enough, Roger. I don't remember you being an insolent teenager."

He withstood Barbara's complaints and laughed, disarming her. She went back at him, imitating him when he hadn't believed the officer was a real policeman. "'This badge is good for nothing,'" said Barbara, parodying the voice of a full-grown man. He argued, acting like he was in the right, that if you give in to the fuzz, you're dead. The weaker you look, the harder they squeeze. And she insisted it was just the opposite. If they think you're a rooster, they'll shave off your comb. They poked and prodded, without annoying each other, like lovers in the early months of dating, until they arrived near the corner of Chappe and Tardieu.

Roger, thinking seriously about what she'd said, couldn't help himself from asking, "What you said to the policeman . . . that perhaps I'd stay here with you. Are you serious?"

"What do you think?"

"Me?"

"Are you the type that thinks man made it to the moon or not?"

"Not even in paintings, Barbara. All of that was a show."

"You see? I couldn't live with someone who wasn't as romantic, who always wants to be logical. Hope, man. Imagination. Women like men to sweep them off their feet."

"That must be a thing for women—" He stopped in his tracks. He'd learned to hold back a joke following a series of blows.

"What? Say it."

"That must be for women . . . your age." Roger started laughing.

"You're a dumbass." Barbara couldn't hold back her laughter and tried to pinch his balls with each hand while laughing and repeating he'd pay for saying that.

She inserted her key into the lock, and they entered the building. Before climbing up the stairs, and out of breath from laughing, Barbara stopped and surprised him with a question.

"Do you know the Tibetan secret to a better life?"

"Is it a saying?"

"Yes."

"Save it for yourself. I hate sayings."

"Well, now I won't tell you."

"Better. Thanks."

"You have to listen, honey. The secret to living longer and better is," she declared with the voice of an afternoon program for children, "eat half, walk double, laugh triple, and love without measure. What?"

"I can't stand sayings. Plus, being locked up here these days, we haven't been able to walk much."

"That's why we have to laugh triple."

"And fuck without measure."

"They don't say it that way in Tibet. 'Love,' I said."

"It's not the same?"

"In France, no."

"At our house, yes."

"What does 'our house' mean?" Standing in the vestibule, Barbara pointed upward with her pinky finger. "This is my apartment, boy."

"And this possessiveness? It doesn't look good on you, my love. You just told the police you want to live with me, and now—"

"You're a rascal." She got on her tiptoes to give him a kiss and climbed up the stairs.

"The day I got here . . . Do you remember? I thought you were renting your room like my brother was."

"You think I could ever forget?"

"I didn't understand the apartment was yours. I had no idea, come on."

"Such nerve. I was surprised."

"What'd you think about me? Tell me. Your first impression."

"The truth? That you were a cretin from head to toe. That's easy."

"Oh yeah?" He stopped in the first-floor hallway and unzipped her jacket. "And now what do you think?"

"On nights like these? That you're a cretin. A nice cretin."

Hulshoff started barking before they got to the second floor. The closer they got, the more he yelled, in his language.

"Is this where the Dutch man lives?"

"How strange . . . Hulshoff's never done that. The dog can't even hold in his farts."

Now he wasn't only barking. Once he heard them pass by, he started desperately scratching the door, like he did on nights with fireworks.

"Let me call Jasper to see if he's fine . . ."

"Don't bother him now, woman. It's too late. Let's watch you give the grandpa a heart attack."

"But if the dog is making this much noise—"

"Look at the time, Barbara."

"That's why. If Jasper isn't shushing him, there must be a reason."

"Because he's sleeping, you'll see."

"Jasper is old. He lives alone. He's my grandmother's friend."

"Walk up, woman. Tomorrow morning, you can come down and ask what's going on. Don't worry."

The Labrador continued to bark without end. He filed his nails against the door with a worrying obsession. Once Barbara and Roger were on the third floor, she decided to turn around.

"Look. I'll go down and ask Jasper if he's okay."

"You can't just send him a text? That'll scare him less."

Before she could respond, she was at his apartment door. She rang the doorbell. With every ring, the dog went crazier and crazier.

"It's me, Hulshoff. It's okay. It's Barbara . . . Calm down, baby."

There was no reciprocation from the other side. Little by little, it seemed like Hulshoff might be walking away, but then he'd immediately speed back up until he knocked into the door. And then he'd start scratching again.

"Those barks aren't normal. I'm sorry."

"Ring again," Roger suggested.

"Knock on the door, and I'll call the phone directly."

"When did you last see Jasper?"

"Yesterday . . . the day before yesterday. The day before yesterday, yes. I came down to see if he needed anything. It was the day of the blackout?"

Roger had enough with the doorbell. With his hand flat against the door, he began to knock. Every time, he shouted his name louder and louder. "Jasper! Jasper!" He waited a couple of seconds, then again. "Jasper!!!"

"He isn't answering the phone either. Shit."

"Jaspeeeer!"

"You know what?" said Barbara, with nervous sweat dripping down her back. "I'll call the emergency line. This is enough. Someone should come and knock down the door."

34

The Age of Boredom

Viviani. It was the name of the square. It was the name of the home that occupied an entire three-story building stretching a whole block on the other side of the Saint-Julien-le-Pauvre church. Viviani was surely named after somebody. It had to be. Roger approached the blue plaque to look for a hint and read the sign out loud:

"'Square René Viviani. 1863 to 1925. Prime Minister during the Third Republic.' Don't you see how important this dude was?"

"The people here know about the square because of the tree." Barbara signaled at it with her chin. "It's the oldest in Paris. Or that's what they say."

The black locust was still dusted with snow. At the foot of the trunk was a mountain of dirty snow, as if the brigade of good intentions had brought out the shovels. Or—Roger's second hypothesis—as if the unskilled neighbors tried to make a snowman and it melted like an ice cream cone midlick.

"It's easy for your grandmother to go to church since it's so close by. And she's got Notre-Dame so close by. She can choose. One day here and the next there."

"Mamie Margaux at Mass?"

"What?"

"If it isn't for a funeral, you'll never see her near an altar. When she goes out, if the weather is nice, she prefers coming here, to the tree."

"To pray."

"To meditate. It's not the same."

"Not even a little? What's the difference?"

Barbara improvised an answer. She said it the way such theories ought to be stated, confidently: "When you pray, you tense up, you concentrate with all your might to try to connect with someone who doesn't have signal coverage, and you ask him for things he really can't make good on. But when you meditate, you relax, you look inside, time stops, you open your mind."

"And you end up asking God to help you. It's the same thing."

"Meditation is looking for the best solutions from within. Prayer is trying to find magical formulas from outside."

"You say tomato, I say tomahto. It's the same thing."

"It's not." She pinched his butt. "Oh, my stubborn little guy."

Already at the door, Roger rang the doorbell. "How do you think she'll take the news about Jasper?"

"I don't know," Barbara huffed. It seemed like a mountainous task to have to tell her grandmother the news. "She'll be sad to hear it. Of course. But sometimes, when you've lived through so much . . . It seems like, by this age, they've learned how to compartmentalize all news, however hard it may be."

The Viviani residence smelled like disinfectant from the outset. They disinfected, maybe excessively, to cover the stench from the rooms. The white spaces, clean as a whistle, gave off a certain air of hygiene, of serenity, of a comforting peace. Altogether, a first step toward heaven. The main hall was full of the residents' family members. It was open season. After spending so many days without being able to visit, everyone had run to hug their grandpas and grandmas the morning the confinement ended. Some did it to calm their conscience, others to get a better sense of when they'd be able to call in their inheritance. With one glance, they could tell if their beloved family member would make it to

2009, or, as if it were a game, they could predict what month of the following year they foresaw ending their payments to Viviani. On the first of every month, the invoice came in, and it wasn't a cheap residence.

Margaux hadn't expected them so early. She welcomed them in while she poured the water left from breakfast onto the little plant by the window. Barbara had to wait to hug her.

"Oh, I've missed you so much, Mamie." She covered her grandmother in kisses.

"Is everything okay at the apartment, girl?"

"Well, the ceiling held up under the snowfall of the century, so . . . Speaking of home, I want to introduce you . . ."

Roger, who had lingered discreetly by the door of the room, took a step forward. With his jacket, he covered the bandage he was wearing on his left arm.

"Good morning," he said, extending his right hand.

"And this young man?"

"This is Roger. He's been living in the apartment for some time. He's renting the room."

"Oh, I thought you had mentioned another name . . . Roger? It wasn't Roger."

"What a memory you have, Mamie. Roger is Marcel's brother, who—"

"That's it. Marcel, I do know. Because I remember thinking he had the same name as that mime you really liked."

"No, I've never liked Marcel Marceau. Mimes make me sad. Well, in either case, his brother took over the apartment, and his name is Roger Narbona."

"It's a pleasure," said her grandmother.

"For me as well, ma'am. I've heard so much about you."

"And I didn't even know you existed—"

"Mamie, please," Barbara interrupted.

"What? It's true. Is it true or not, young man?"

"Of course, of course."

Mamie Margaux, who didn't want to embarrass her granddaughter, apologized. "Pay no mind to old ladies like me, boy. This place is full of people reaching the age of boredom."

"Please, no need to be so formal with me."

In no time, Roger had a mental portrait of Mamie Margaux. Her white hair was brushed back, and she had wrinkles on her forehead and a winter complexion with enough color to last all those days inside. Her teeth, which weren't real, fit well in her smile. On top of it all, her eyes captivated him. The same sharp eyes as Barbara. Less lively, maybe. They were a tired green. She offered her hand, hooked from arthritis, firmly. Her fingers were bony, her nails manicured. Even at eighty-three years old, her body had not appeared to weaken. *I hope my mother ages that well,* thought Roger, who continued hiding the lesion on his arm.

Once all three were sitting, Barbara spoke. "Something happened, Mamie."

"Oh no." She put two fingers on her temple as if to say, "What are you going to tell me now?"

Barbara explained what had happened the night before.

They'd gone out onto the street when it still wasn't allowed. Nothing big. Just a walk with Roger to stretch their legs after so many days of confinement. When they'd returned to the apartment building and climbed the stairs, Jasper's dog was barking in a bad way. Hulshoff wasn't a crazy dog or a barker, as Mamie Margaux knew well. That's why it surprised them he was barking so persistently from the other side of the second-floor apartment door. Barbara had called his name to quiet him because it was already getting into the early hours of the next day, and the yapping wasn't normal. But there'd been no way to calm him down. In fact, the animal only became more desperate. They decided to ring the doorbell in case Jasper needed anything and to ask if everything was okay. But he hadn't responded. One ring, two, three . . . Nothing. They guessed he was dreaming deeply. They called him. First on the landline, then on his cell phone, but still no one picked up. From then on, they were scared. Before calling the emergency line, they'd tried to break down the door, but there was no way. While they waited for the firemen, or the ambulance, or anyone who could help them, Roger went up to the fifth-floor apartment, opened the window to his room, and, leaning out onto the balcony, tried to tell if he could see anything through Jasper's laundry room. Not a clue. Not one. But he did see another option. He realized that by placing his feet on the water pipes and holding on to the windows, he could climb down from the fifth floor to the fourth, from the fourth to the third, and, repeating the operation at the small risk of killing himself, he could slip through Jasper's balcony. If Barbara had known that Roger was going to try to be a hero, she wouldn't have let him. But he went for it without letting her know. One foot here, one hand there, his fingers grasping a ventilation window's sill or an air-conditioning apparatus, then arriving at his target. With one last jump, he landed his two feet onto Jasper's balcony. When he fell in the laundry room, he'd hit his arm hard against the washing machine. He felt it in his forearm immediately, but there was no time to waste. First, he had to win over Hulshoff with a little bit of petting so the dog would let him enter and realize he was an ally and not a robber. Next, he went to open the door from the inside. It was then that Barbara had found Jasper on the floor with a stream of blood flowing out of his nose. He was lying near the fireplace, the embers practically out. The Dutch man was pale, wearing a shirt and a sweater, but barefoot. She felt for his pulse and found he was still breathing. While they waited for the damn ambulance to arrive, they did everything they could to wake him. But Jasper wouldn't stir. When the emergency responders arrived—a man-and-woman duo who must have been paramedics but who never identified themselves—they discovered the door open and went straight to work. They handled him quickly and professionally without asking questions. If there was nothing they could do to save him, maybe the paramedics wouldn't have acted so urgently. Within five minutes, they had Jasper tied to the bed and, between the four of them, took him down the stairs as far as they could. "Elevator?" they'd asked. "In Montmartre?" Barbara had responded. The gurney went down the stairs of the two floors and out to the street. Jasper, luckily or tragically, didn't notice a thing.

Barbara climbed into the ambulance with him and held his hand, just in case. It was a stroke. A brain hemorrhage. No one knew how long he'd been on the floor while Hulshoff had been asking for help. Still, no doctor could tell if he'd make it. The preliminary tests at the hospital indicated the stroke had severely affected his brain. Would he be able to walk again? No one knew. Would he talk again? It was too early to say.

Margaux took a deep breath. "Oh lord." It was all she said at first. After some time spent sitting motionless with a lost look, she added, "Poor Jasper."

And that was it.

Barbara and Roger respected that spiritual retirement. She seemed absent, as if she'd learned to resign to suffering another blow in life. Things don't hurt so much in old age. When someone goes through as much as she has, you ration your tears as if we have a finite amount, even though, at the end of the day, lives end, eyes dry up, and good night, the game ends. *When someone goes through what she has,* thought Barbara, *there are no gods left to convince her of anything.* Maybe that was why Mamie Margaux dismissed Our Father, the candles to the Highest, and the belief in the miracles of the Holy Spirit. She felt abandoned by Damien's death and by Édith's accident. When life takes a daughter from you, there's no God to speak with anymore.

"A good neighbor, Jasper is. A good friend."

They let Mamie Margaux's feelings flow at their own rhythm.

"He's kept you company all these years."

"I don't like it."

"What?" Barbara didn't understand her grandmother's sudden bitter tone.

"'Company.' The word. It implies . . . compassion."

"It doesn't have to."

"When someone comes to keep you company, it means you're going downhill. And I was better off than him . . . and now this is proof."

Roger snorted with laughter. He liked Barbara's grandmother's unruly air. The need to speak the truth seemed like a spark, a sign of intelligence.

"We hope he makes it through, Mamie. The doctors say—"

"Barbara," Mamie interrupted her. "Depending on things, maybe it's better if—"

She closed her eyes. One of them knew Jasper's outlook wasn't very good. The other realized it and accepted it. They paid homage to him with a foggy silence, as if poor Jasper had already kicked the bucket.

To distract her grandmother, Barbara rolled up Roger's sleeve to show his bandage.

"He hurt himself jumping from the patio. You could've killed yourself."

Mamie became interested in Roger. "What's wrong?"

"Not much. Just a wrist injury."

"Is it broken?"

"I don't think so."

"If you ask for it, maybe they'll do an X-ray for you here."

"A photographer without hands. Just picture what could have happened."

"Is that your line of work, boy?"

"More or less."

"All day, he takes pictures, but no one looks at them." Barbara poked fun at him. "That's why he says, 'More or less,' I guess."

Roger ignored Barbara and approached her grandmother.

"One day, I'd like to come talk with you. Not to keep you company, no, let's make that clear. But to talk about photography."

"Come when you want, honey. You'll find me here."

"You won't run away, Mamie?"

Her grandmother didn't hear the question. Since she'd learned the news about Jasper, one thing kept turning in her mind. And she didn't know how to phrase it. Eventually, she let it go and went ahead, guns blazing. What the hell—at her age, she didn't have to hide anything. She grabbed Barbara's hand and placed it on her leg.

"I have to tell you. It's about Jasper. Something no one knows. Only me and him."

Barbara and Roger looked at each other. He shifted in his chair as if to leave.

"No, no need to leave."

"I'd rather." He stood up. "I'll wait for you outside, Barb. I'll go look at the tree."

"What happened, Mamie? What's the mystery all about?"

"It will come as a surprise to you, but see . . . Jasper was writing a book. It wasn't just any book. It was a book about my life. About the years of the war."

"Oh man, Mamie. How beautiful."

"He insisted on it. He likes to write, he's good, and he convinced me to go on telling him about each chapter of the war. The entrance of the Germans into Paris, my parents, the city for a teenager like me, the music, the obsession with the oboe, the private lessons with Damien . . . It was supposed to be a surprise. I spoke, and he gave it shape. When it was finished, I would have given it to you. I said to him, 'This way, my granddaughter will have a record of me and can learn things she maybe never knew.' And Jasper would joke around and say maybe even the press would publish it. What's it called?"

"What?"

"The press where you work."

"Giresse and Trésor."

"That's it. Sometimes, he'd say, 'Maybe Giresse and what's-it-called will want to publish it. I'm sure they release much worse historical books. And your life is true.'"

"As true as can be."

"But now . . . Poor Jasper and I were only halfway through."

"Where does he keep all of it? On a computer?"

"No, no. I don't think it's on a computer. I don't know if he had one. At first, I would go down one evening a week, we'd have tea at his house, and I'd explain an episode. The day I saw *Peter and the Wolf*, for example, and then he'd spend seven days writing a chapter. After, once I moved into the residence, he would be the one to come here. But the routine was the same. One week, we'd speak, and the next I'd read what he wrote by hand to see what I thought."

"And?"

"It was like I was living it again. You should read it, Barbara, even if it isn't finished."

"I'd love to, of course, Mamie. That's so exciting to hear. And you two were so hush-hush about it."

"I've always thought secrets create addictions."

Her grandmother looked out the window. Roger was touching the branches of the old black locust like he wanted to guess its age.

"Jasper was a little younger than me, but we shared the luck and tragedy of both being from a country Hitler had invaded and . . . Nothing was new to him. I would say something, and he would understand all the feelings and the ambience right away."

"We're talking about him in the past. And he hasn't died. It's giving me goose bumps, look."

"Poor Jasper. A brain hemorrhage . . . It's lucky this guy of yours was able to get into his apartment."

"Roger."

"So brave, he could have cracked his noggin."

"You're telling me. Jasper wrote—Jasper writes by hand, then?"

"By hand, by hand. He's got really nice handwriting. You can read it all. He writes on these big pages. He stores them in a folder the color of goose shit. I'd call it that, and he'd laugh. Oh man . . ."

Mamie Margaux had to stop a tear, a single tear, that slid down at the pace of a snail. She didn't allow herself two tears. She'd ration the rest of her deposits. Barbara also didn't want her grandmother to soften more than necessary.

"We've been left with Hulshoff for now. We brought him upstairs with us."

"Good idea. Nicely done."

"We couldn't leave him by himself. And what you were talking about, the book . . . Now, with Jasper, where were you at? At what moment in your life?"

"The last day?" She reminisced. "The last day . . . The last evening he visited, we were supposed to talk about Édith's birth. About your mother when she was really little. Yes . . . That's why Jasper still hadn't written it. This week, we agreed that, with all this snowfall, it was time to talk about Damien's last winter."

"And why don't you tell me?"

"Your grandfather's last winter?"

"You've never told me about that." She wanted to get her grandmother going. "I have a right to know, I guess."

"Tell your friend to come inside or he'll freeze out there." She watched Roger, who walked around the tree with his hands in his pockets. "He's more than a friend, huh, girl?"

"Mamie, please."

"I saw it on your face the moment you two entered."

Barbara knew the verdict was coming.

"You know what? I like him."

35

A Happy Song Plays

"Those months went by quickly. Damien had performed the concert wearing his striped uniform from Buchenwald, and the gesture caused a certain kind of uproar. The name Damien Devère ended up coming out in the newspaper. The brief article explained an unusual event during which the oboist of the renewed Pierné Orchestra appeared to be playing while wearing the striped pajamas, just a few weeks after the liberation of the concentration camps. The same review, which we cut out and saved somewhere, complained of two things: that there wasn't a picture of the event, and that the same musician had difficulty finishing *The Prelude of the Afternoon of the Faun* on account of 'some inopportune coughing attacks' impeding him from playing his instrument.

"We didn't care. The 'inopportune coughing attacks' the newspaper critic had noticed came and went depending on the day, but we didn't pay any mind because Damien seemed not to care either. He took it all in with a silent resignation, like collateral damage as part of his passage through hell. One example of many.

"Those months, as I said, went by quickly, with everyone around me, my pregnancy, the birth of our daughter. It was a girl. Édith. She was born with ten fingers and ten toes. She was healthy, and, when she opened her eyes, it seemed like she liked us. What else could we ask for?

I chose the name, Damien was in agreement, and we wanted my father to be her baptismal godfather.

"I hardly remember anything from those first weeks and months with Édith at home. Only the nebulousness of joy remains, but I was so young, I knew so little, and everything was so new; between the breastfeeding, the crying, caring for any illnesses, entertaining her, and the washings, my life was dedicated to Édith. Lucky for me, Damien was always there; he spoiled mother and daughter, and we told everyone he was the father. And oh hell, was he. We gave her his last name, Édith Devère, so there was no doubt.

"Damien started weakening when winter came, though. He was left lifeless. The coughing got worse, at all hours. His health got even worse. He sweated at night, he had chills, and the growing pain in his lungs was oppressive. He didn't want to worry us and insisted he didn't want to be a burden, but there were whole days he didn't get out of bed. He simply couldn't. When it seemed like he was a little better, he'd begin to cough blood, and then I'd make him go to Dr. Bonnet, the old family doctor, who had a portrait of de Gaulle in his office.

"The doctor looked him up and down. He examined him. He put his ear against his back, he looked into the whites of his eyes, he said his breath smelled like old wood, and he immediately said that sea breezes would be good for him. Dr. Bonnet had screened Damien, and before Damien could button up his shirt, the doctor recommended a remedy that had to cure him: the Mediterranean.

"'For your lungs, the Riviera would be better than Paris,' he said with the credibility of a white coat and a serious voice. He suggested more than anything that we not wait until the summer. 'I can't think of anything better than sunbathing during winter in Côte d'Azur.'

"He said it with a twisted face that I didn't know how to interpret. Young as I was at the time, I didn't see the signs of the bad months to come.

"'And pills?' Damien had asked.

"'Believe me. Try the sea breeze. It's the best remedy. You'd do well in Sainte-Maxime, for example.'

"The doctor's rush made me anxious to leave.

"We went down to the coast by train. We saw France through the window at full speed. It was a day full of travel with Édith, a stroller, and suitcases that Damien struggled to drag along. When I took them from him, he said, 'Let me do it,' dry as his cough was. We settled into a hotel that was recommended to us. Maybe it was the only option. At the time, it smelled new and like wallpaper. The room had a crib for Édith, which we were one of the first to use, if not the first. It was the Centrum Hotel, a name with less fame than the nearby beaches, which immediately helps you ingratiate yourself to the seafaring population. Saint-Maxime was, at that time, a city without tourists. After the war, there were only fishermen. In the wintertime, there were barely even cats.

"We were comfortable for the first few days. It seemed like Dr. Bonnet's advice was the oil the lamp needed. Damien coughed less, he felt better, and he wanted to go out. We took small walks by the sea at sunset. We let Édith play in the sand and covered her hands and feet. We sat next to her, watching her, and aside from stopping her from putting her little fingers in her mouth, we let her be.

"'She looks like you.' I liked that Damien said it one afternoon while we listened to the sea. 'The way she lifts her head, looking curiously from side to side. It's like everything interests her.'

"Édith was quick, clever. Nosy, I guess, like all kids who discover they've ended up in a world of beautiful things. They like the waves, the birds, the trains, the dogs, toy cars, rag dolls, crusts of bread to lick, the moon, which has its own song. On the other hand, sounds and nasty men with unibrows scare them.

"Our daughter—I never said it out loud—also had something of Damien's. I knew it felt impossible, but he would put her on top of him and talk to her and stick out his tongue and make her laugh and shake her and sit on the ground to play with her and tickle her. Even if only from all the time they spent together and the loving things he said to her, Édith picked something up from him. His mannerisms.

"Damien came back to life in Sainte-Maxime. It seemed permanent. We entered December hopeful he was on a good course. He was cheered by the thought that Dr. Bonnet had suggested an effective way of holding off the sickness—damn tuberculosis—that had eaten away so many of his friends who'd managed to escape Buchenwald alive.

"A couple of days before Christmas, though, the inopportune cough came back. Damien suddenly spent entire nights without sleeping again. The nightmares of the concentration camps, which he couldn't escape even for a single night, and the pain in his lungs caused by the coughing overlapped with the sunsets and sunrises to create a new torture.

"For Christmas, on the twenty-fifth itself, something sad happened, as if holidays always marked when big things would happen. It had been a year to the day since I had told my parents I was pregnant. A year later, I lived another event in silence. The hotel prepared us a festive meal served on beautiful trays atop a linen tablecloth. Damien, who wasn't hungry, practically didn't eat. We went up to the room after because Édith was more comfortable napping in her crib, and he said he wanted to lie down because everything hurt. He said it, but he didn't do it. I saw Damien suddenly grab the oboe case. I don't know how long he'd gone without opening it. Since we'd arrived at Sainte-Maxime, he'd left it on a wardrobe shelf and hadn't looked at it anymore, as if it didn't exist. Then it did. He took out the instrument, put it together, went out in a coat to the terrace, and I thought, *now he'll play*. I watched him from inside, through the window, with the door closed and the curtain open. Outside, he was looking at nothing and holding the oboe in his hands. He didn't even bring it to his mouth. I tried to imagine what was happening and slowly opened the door without making any noise, then went out with him onto the terrace. I leaned to put myself level with his eyes. He was crying. He smothered his sobs as much as he could. He tried to control his breathing. I kissed him and I said, 'Damien, we'll make it through.'

"He didn't say yes or no. He simply didn't respond. After he wiped away his tears, he passed me his oboe.

"'Play a happy song, Margaux.'

"That sentence. I hear him say that one sentence he said to me on the balcony of our hotel room in Saint-Maxime, every day of my life. 'Play a happy song.' As if it were easy in the moment. *What should I play for him now?* I thought. *What can I play that will cheer him up, that I know by memory, that wouldn't beat him down any more than he already was?* I would put the oboe to my mouth and something would play. The duck's rhythm from the melody of *Peter and the Wolf* emerged, in the form of the happy high notes that signaled the duck managing to become revived.

"Despite my nerves, and despite feeling like I was exhausting the last of my willpower, I thought it came out good enough. He didn't clap. The person who had been my teacher and was my love didn't applaud. He did something better. Damien grabbed my hand, and, as he caressed it, he said words I didn't want to hear in that moment but that, with time, I recorded in my heart.

"'You've made my life better. With you, it's all been worth it. Thank you for letting me be the father of your daughter.'

"Is it possible to say anything more profound to someone?"

There was a silence in Mamie Margaux's room. Neither her grandmother, nor she, nor Roger were in any condition to say anything. A nurse knocked at the door and entered with two cookies and a glass of milk with a dash of coffee, then left with a friendly greeting none of the three had heard.

"Mamie," Barbara said. "The Sainte-Maxime hotel is where you took me when I was little . . ."

"Yes, the Centrum."

"The summer my mother was sick, you took me to the town and the hotel you'd been to with Grandfather?"

"I had never returned."

"But . . . it must have been torture."

"I wouldn't say that."

"Very difficult, Mamie, for the love of God."

"It wasn't easy. But I had to go back. No, no . . ." Mamie raised her finger like she was in class and knew the answer. "I did it for me. I needed to remember it. It had been years since he'd died, and the memories had begun to fade for me—his voice, the touch of his skin. *What will we do if our experiences blur,* I thought. Your mother was sick, you were a little whirlwind that had to be distracted, and your house wasn't a place for jokes. We went down from Arles to Sainte-Maxime and settled into the Centrum Hotel, which was more run down than it'd been the first time I visited, and we were fine . . . or not?"

Barbara didn't know whether to laugh or cry. The two met, simultaneously, at an emotional summit.

"Yes, yes. It was the best summer of my life. You let me do anything, I had you all to myself, and I don't remember what—I don't know. I was little, but I didn't notice if you were sad."

"We grandmothers don't allow it. And when there are problems, even less so. We always play happy music. The more the mess, the happier the face."

"But"—Roger dared to open his mouth—"I don't want to insert myself when no one is asking, but . . . the nostalgia?"

Mamie smiled. She liked questions coming from him. It was the last thing she'd expected to hear from this strapping man who'd settled into her granddaughter's life.

"Roger is right," Barbara cut in. "You took me to play in the sand and eat ice cream, through the streets of Sainte-Maxime. You had to live all of that . . . and I didn't notice anything."

"Nostalgia is like salt. In small doses. If you use too much, it'll take you to the next destination in no time."

She stirred the glass of milk and took a sip. She was left with a white mustache over her lip.

"Mamie . . ." Barbara was thinking about what she'd learned. You never know everything about your family. And if you don't know everything, you know nothing. "You went there to test yourself."

"To remember, let's put it that way. To test myself?" Mamie had to think about it. "I won't say no. To overcome it, if it's even possible to somehow move on from the life and death of a man you fell in love with. The sediments of memory . . . They're always there, I guess. You're too young to know. Memory learns to domesticate itself over the years. Memory returns until it completely leaves. Did I tell you that Anine isn't in her right mind?"

Barbara knew Anine was Mamie Margaux's friend from the room next door—the hunched woman who had picked up the habit of asking everyone what they wanted to be when they grew up. But it wasn't the time to talk about anyone who wasn't Mamie, who was rewriting Barbara's life at a steady pace. Barbara wanted to point out how much her grandmother must have suffered, having to act like she wasn't sad, but for whom, inside, everything was turning.

"Look, Mamie, let me say it. I simply can't believe you were so stone-like. You must have put a lot of energy into pretending to be happy with me all the time. Surely, come on." Barbara turned to face Roger, looking for an ally. "I'm sorry, but it's hard for me to believe it."

Before Roger could say anything, Mamie took a short sip of her milk, curled her lips, and lowered her head to make a confession.

"One day, I did break. A day you don't remember. A day I got goose bumps while we were on the beach, and you'd noticed. You even asked me, 'What's wrong, Mamie?' and I didn't say anything and simply acted like a mosquito had bitten me because I didn't want to worry you. And I began to scratch my arm with so much force it made you laugh, so then I laughed, and we ended up running through the sand from mosquitos that didn't exist."

"You're a clown."

"So what happened next with Damien?" Roger asked, not wanting to lose the thread.

"For the New Year, Damien had an idea. He didn't have the strength to endure the bells ringing at night, Édith was too little, and we agreed to stay in the room and act like it was any other day. But he had the idea to celebrate another way. We left the hotel and went to the shore to wait for midnight. It was a stormy day, and a cold wind was coming in from the sea, along with some welcome rays of sun. Damien and I took off our shoes. We also took off Édith's booties. I held the girl in my arms, and, as we neared the water, Damien took my hand. We put our feet in the cold, damp sand and proceeded up to where the undertow settled. The water barely reached our ankles. Damien began to count the waves. Every time one reached us, we jumped a little. At first, the ritual took me by surprise. The second time, he forced himself to lift his feet off the ground. The third time, he managed to do it imperceptibly. On the fourth, Édith laughed with our jumps. On the fifth, we were a happy couple. On the sixth, Damien sang them out loud. The seventh was coming with furious foam. On the eighth, I jumped to splash his pants. On the ninth, in the absence of the bells, came waves we would remember eternally. On the tenth, we said 'I love you.' On the eleventh, Damien looked at the horizon with a concentration that made it seem like it was saying something. The last wave . . . 'Welcome to 1946.' The year your grandfather died."

36

After So Many Days of a Cowardly Sun

That next morning, Paris returned to a normal city. After too many days spent shut inside by snowy barricades, the urban inhabitants slipped out from under their sheets to resume their lives. The smell of bakeries at dawn, the cobblestones wet with morning dew, the proud ringing of the neighborhood bells, the inevitable early-morning bad mood, the café au lait ordered to go, the out-of-control honking of a perpetual traffic jam, children with their big backpacks, rows of newspapers at kiosks dwindling little by little, the customary bonjour at work, and the out-of-nowhere suicide on the train track that takes down two whole lines. The yellow line won the lottery that morning—the line Barbara had to take to la Défense. After she'd spent a lot of time at the station without any explanation, the voice over the megaphone instructed passengers to evacuate the station. She filed obediently out onto the street and grabbed a taxi to Giresse & Trésor. She wanted to arrive at the office early to prepare for that evening's meeting. It wasn't every day the press's owner made an in-person appearance to negotiate the sale of international rights. And Frode Arnesen, the Norwegian editor at Cappelen, had traveled to Paris to look into buying the translation rights to Anne Delacourt's bestseller. Her dystopian novel about the surrogate mother revolution could now be found in twenty languages, but not yet in

Norwegian. Barbara, who knew Frode Arnesen from an old transfer of rights, had written him a letter inviting him to make an offer for the novel that was shaking the literary scene. Being quite interested in signing the contract, he told her he'd come down to Paris and asked her to reserve a table, because they'd be dining together.

Though it was already dark, Barbara left the house dressed in her workday outfit, which she reserved for meetings where she had to speak in front of others. A button-up shirt, blue blazer, work-appropriate heels, and the Cartier bracelet her grandmother had given her because she no longer wore it. It was an outfit that gave her confidence.

"I'll be home late today" was the last thing she told Roger before planting a kiss on him, after making sure she had her perfume bottle in her bag.

"I'll be waiting for you without pajamas," he responded, opening one eye. With one of them rushing and the other sleepy, neither realized that jokes are told half seriously.

"What're you going to do today?"

"I thought I'd go see your grandmother again, if it's okay with you. I'll bring the picture of the bike. See how she responds."

"Take care of Mamie for me, most importantly. Don't overwhelm her."

Roger stayed in bed until his heart told him it had been long enough. Once Hulshoff was able to find a crack through the door, he entered the room to keep Roger company. They'd become fast friends, but the dog was still confused. Jasper's apartment had the same setup as theirs, but the obstacles weren't the same, and it was hard for him to become confident in the new space. All curled up, neither of them was in any hurry. Before getting out of bed, Roger waited for the light to filter into Barbara's room. After so many days of a cowardly sun, there was finally a thread of spring in Paris. A good day for taking pictures.

He celebrated with a shower.

As he got dressed, he had an idea. It came to him like a bolt of lightning, and, suddenly, the thought was stronger than he was. He had to return to Jasper's house. However he could. He got the obsession in his head and couldn't get rid of it. He had to go look for the manuscript of Margaux's life. If it was there, he'd find it. It had to be there and nowhere else, because Mamie had said she hadn't had it with her at the home. And she'd confirmed there was only one paper copy that traveled back and forth. In any case, the goose-shit-colored folder couldn't have disappeared.

Roger already knew the way without a key. He opened the window into the shaft and once again looked at the pipes to see where he'd have to put his hands and feet to get into poor Jasper's laundry room. This time, he didn't have the anxiety of having to rush to save someone's life. He could calculate each step better so as to avoid making a wrong move. The key was to not look into the abyss and to leave no room for fear.

He was on the fourth floor in no time. Going from the fourth to the third, holding on with his cheek against the wall, was a little more difficult. He noticed the pipe was moving and realized that if it went up, he'd go down and, if he was lucky, break his neck. His fingers feeling like ice picks, he let himself slide until he had his foot on the railing of the third floor. He entered their laundry room to catch his breath and refine his strategy for going down the final floor. Getting into Jasper's house wasn't difficult once he calculated his moves. Two jumps was enough this time. The landing onto the second floor was smoother, because everything is easier when you have experience.

Before looking for anything, he walked through the apartment. He turned off the lights that had been left on as if it'd only been a minute ago that the medics had taken Jasper away. The place had an odor that Roger hadn't noticed on that chaotic day. The smell of a sailor's pipe, of Dutch tobacco, permeated the whole house. And the bathroom. It was the apartment of a single man—a widower with a dog as lively as he was. Nothing was completely clean, nothing was completely in order, and grays dominated all else; everything was old, the ashes were plentiful, and there was a film of dust in every corner. The TV had a belly, and it would be a miracle if the computer—if that was really the computer Jasper had used—worked. In the kitchen, the burners looked ancient, as though they'd been bought in an antiques shop in the Marché aux Puces. The fridge handle was rusted. Roger opened it to check if there was anything that could go bad if Jasper took a while to return. That is, if he ever could step back into his kitchen—because you know when you leave your house, but you're never sure of when you'll return.

He put the bruised fruit in a bag and poured the dregs of a milk carton into the sink. After, he began to look for the folder. Roger remembered well the expression Mamie had used to describe it: "the color of goose shit." A folder like that wouldn't stick out in this apartment, but it couldn't be that hard to find. Jasper didn't have any reason to hide pages filled with Margaux Dutronc's life during the war. Roger looked around the computer. Nothing. It didn't even look like he had a printer. He looked through the shelves, where a pile of books seemed to have been put away willy-nilly. It wasn't there either. At a glance, there was nothing in the room. Roger spent some time looking at a picture on top of the nightstand of a woman. Jasper's wife was beautiful, he thought. And young. The only picture the widower had framed on his intimate altar was of her at her best moment. He had likely chosen it to look at when he needed consolation. The silver frame would need bicarbonate and a scrubbing to return its shine, not unlike the poor woman, who was only an old photograph.

Intuition made Roger open the top drawer of the nightstand. There, in the bedroom, he found his treasure. The folder. Call it mustard, call it beige, but "goose shit" also captured it. It could only be that one. He sat on the bedside with the folder in his hands. He slipped off the rubber bands and took out a handful of pages. There were maybe two hundred in total. His eyes wandered to the beginning. First page, first chapter.

The convertible parked at the door of the Théâtre du Châtelet without screeching. Five German soldiers in uniform from head to toe got out of the car. They had a mission, the determination to carry it out, and the explicit orders not to be unpleasant toward the musicians. To get from the Conciergerie to the theater square, they needed only to cross the Seine River through the pont au Change. They could've arrived immediately if they had walked, but they preferred showing up in a car. It was imposing, scary, and gave the order an official air.

The guy wrote well. Roger took his phone out of his pocket and snapped a picture of the folder and the first page so he could show his find to Barbara. Without wasting another second, he continued to read. He flew through the story, but he didn't want to spend any longer there, feeling like a robber who spends his time looking at the signatures of the canvases he steals. Roger left Jasper's apartment through the front door and slammed it shut. With the folder under his arm and the fruit to throw out, he returned to the fifth floor to continue reading about the occupation of Paris through the eyes of a teenager who'd lived it from within the city. For the moment, the book was Mamie's youth. It had been worth it to risk his life. He wouldn't say anything to Barbara about how he'd gotten it.

Roger left the folder on top of the red sofa. Before heading to the retirement residence, he grabbed his camera and the cutting from the old magazine with a portrait of young Margaux atop a bike. He was dying of curiosity to see the grandmother's face when she saw her picture. Jasper's book hadn't mentioned it yet. Or if it did, Roger hadn't gotten there yet. He'd skimmed through the pages, running his finger along the words, looking for two key words: *Bike photograph.* If they were there, he'd missed them.

He took the metro toward Viviani with haste. When he arrived, Mamie wasn't in her bedroom. The workers had to call her back in from the therapeutic garden, a patio where smoking companions puffed pipes in secret, nurses acted like they didn't see, and everyone crossed their fingers that they wouldn't get caught by the health inspector.

"You weren't expecting me, Mamie . . ."

"Marcel's brother?"

"Roger, yes."

"That's it. The man who's brightened my granddaughter's face."

"That's the best compliment I've received since I arrived in Paris."

Mamie Margaux fell into the tall, winged armchair. "But the girl is older than you."

"That doesn't ruin it, ma'am." He tried to turn things around. "No one cares about that stuff anymore."

"You're right about that. Sit down." She pointed to her bed. "Don't listen to me; all of us here are made out of old mold."

Her bed was made, and he didn't want to mess it up. Instead, he sat down at the desk chair that sometimes served as a place to dine on the evenings Margaux was too lazy to leave her room. Roger struggled to find a way to begin the conversation.

"Barbara told me not to disturb you too much."

"Do you know anything about Jasper?"

"Jasper? The latest news is—" How do you phrase it when doctors aren't optimistic? "Everything is the same. He's not getting better, but he's not getting worse, they said."

"Maybe that's enough. I can't get it out of my head. It feels like a lie, well as he was doing."

"Hopefully, he'll come back to write your story."

"Who cares? I already know all of that."

"But it would be good to have it written. It's a valuable testimonial."

"For whom?"

"For Barbara, above all."

"Valuable?" She thought about it and picked out its advantages. "I don't know. It's just a life. Memories are memories. If they weigh heavily, they're more annoying than useful."

"Do you think about that a lot?"

"A little or a lot, I don't know. That's all we have left."

On the topic of memories, Roger found his moment. He took out the picture and placed it on her lap. He didn't say anything. He just watched the grandmother's reaction, how she picked up the photograph with both hands having no idea what she was about to see. She raised it inches from her nose, looked at it for five seconds, then suddenly let it go. It was as if having it between her fingers disgusted her, like it anguished her to touch it. She raised her chin up to the ceiling and closed her eyes. The photograph of a young Margaux in black and white, beautiful, on top of the bike, rested once more on her legs.

Roger didn't say anything until the grandmother, with her eyelids closed, breathed deeply and asked, "Where'd you get this?"

He had to tell the truth. "From under the bed."

"Which bed?" Mamie lowered her head and opened her eyes to interrogate him.

"From a Banania tin. It was under my bed. I put my suitcase under there, and—"

"This picture . . . The infamous bike. We went through some bad times over this damn photo. It's been years since I've seen it. Years."

"Barbara told me it was you. You have the same air."

"The girl has seen it?"

Roger didn't respond. His face answered her.

"Of course she's seen it. And what'd she say?"

"She said you shine. Or something like that."

Mamie shook her head. "She doesn't know the story."

Roger was dying to ask, "And what is the story?" But he held himself back. He was reluctant to accept firstfruits without Barbara there. Whatever it was, they had to hear it together. On the other hand, he wanted irresistibly to squeeze Mamie Margaux so she would talk about it and let fly everything she had saved up for so many years.

"Maybe Barbara will read about it in Jasper's book."

"Not all of it comes up there. There are episodes that hurt so much . . . This picture really came at a high price. Very high."

Roger paused for a long silence to give her the chance to either begin the story or save it for herself. In the end, he limited himself to basic information.

"This picture is hanging in an exhibition. In the Bibliothèque historique de la Ville de París."

"This one?" She was more surprised than scared. "My picture?"

"Yes, this one and many more. But this one, too. They created an exhibit from slides a photographer had done for a Nazi propaganda magazine."

"What's the name?"

"Signal."

"Yes, but not the magazine. The photographer."

He pronounced the name slowly. "André Zucca."

"Zucca, that's it. Of course. I couldn't remember it."

"His mother was Italian, but he was from Paris."

She repeated the last name two more times and, as though hypnotized by the repetition, was left stupefied and staring at the white ceiling.

"If you'd like, I can tell you my side of how all this happened," said Roger.

It was a matter of generating trust so Mamie, if she wanted to, would come back down to earth. He told her how he'd moved into Marcel's room to spend fifteen days in Paris, how he'd emptied his suitcase and found the box under the bedspring. In that powdered-chocolate tin, he found all kinds of photos and old clippings from a 1940s Paris magazine. But he hadn't said anything to anyone. To Barbara least of all, lest she think he was snooping through the apartment. Later, while visiting an exhibit, he'd come to realize that one of the pictures hanging in the BHVP was the same one he'd seen in the tin under the bed. He arranged things so Barbara would accompany him to the show about Parisians during the German occupation. He led her effortlessly to the hall of all the women on bikes. And when he had her in front of the photo, he moved. Barbara recognized her grandmother at seventeen. Sixteen, maybe. She said she'd never seen the picture. Roger confessed that he had. When they returned to the apartment, he took out the Banania box, and much to Barbara's surprise, she realized the photo they'd seen at the museum was the same one that had been hidden in her home for who knows how long. For sixty years, surely.

"More than sixty," Margaux emphasized. "Count them yourself. Right now we're in—"

"2008."

"We went through some hard times because of this photo. The whole family. But so did Zucca. After the war, he had to change his last name. He even left Paris for some town with a new identity. But we searched for him."

"Who? What do you mean 'we searched for him'?"

"Jasper and I. Jasper accompanied me."

"And?"

"We found him. Of course we found him."

Mamie went silent, as if she'd said too much. Then, all of a sudden, she grabbed the picture and brought it back up to her face. She looked at it with less regret than she had the first time.

"Do you really think Barbara looks like me?"

"The eyes, the nose, of course. You both have something. Elegance and beauty."

"Can I tell you something?" For the first time in the afternoon, Mamie Margaux's beautiful smile made an appearance. "I've always thought that."

Roger left the home when a nurse said they were beginning to serve dinner and that guests were no longer allowed to stay. His heart was beating fast, and he was excited to tell Barbara everything he'd discovered. And all that they'd yet to discover. He called her from Square René Viviani, next to the oldest tree in the city. After the third ring, though, he hung up. Then he sent her a message.

Your grandmother is wonderful. The photo with the bike has a lot of history. Secrets we still haven't uncovered.

Ok.

Between your grandmother, the picture, and Jasper's book, I'm dying to tell you everything. We'll talk when you get back.

Okay. Perfect. Kisses.

In the lobby of Edouard VII, Barbara put her phone on airplane mode, stowed it in her bag, and sprayed her wrists twice with her perfume. Frode Arnesen was a hair away from catching her. He appeared by the stairs, agile and nicely dressed. The editor proceeded down to the hotel hall in shining shoes and with the top button of his shirt undone.

"Ties are only for old people now."

"Mr. Arnesen." She did a half bow.

"Have you noticed no one in the literary world wears them?"

"Now that you mention it . . ." Barbara smiled without finishing her agreement.

They gave each other two kisses.

"I'm happy to see you after such a long time. You look the same, Frode."

"You, on the other hand, look better." His credibility didn't rest in his blue eyes but rather in the convincing way he said things. "Where are you taking me for dinner?"

"Close by. We just have to cross the street. I thought you'd like to go to the Drouant, where they give the Prix Goncourt."

"The Drouant? Good idea. I don't think I've ever been there. If it's very expensive, I'll pay. If not, Giresse and Trésor can pay."

"There are pictures of winning novelists on the stairwell heading up to the private salons. It's very charming. You'll like it."

"Let's do business, then," said the editor, sticking out his elbow so Barbara could grab it, and they crossed l'Opéra in dignified steps.

The restaurant seated them at a table for two next to the window Barbara had expressly asked for when she'd made the reservation. They readily accepted the courtesy glass of champagne.

"An interesting way of starting the night," he said in exquisite French.

Frode Arnesen, a dandy, had the pride of someone who doesn't think they need an instruction manual. He spoke in a low voice, smiled modestly, and had straight teeth. Even his gesticulations were elegant. He wore a dark gray suit over his starched white shirt. His neck posture seemed stiff. The cuffs of his shirt stuck out symmetrically from his blazer. At fifty, the Norwegian editor was a veteran in his field. It wasn't enough for Barbara to look at the cuticles and nails of her interlocutor to know if she'd make the sale. She wasn't used to failing. And Frode, who'd come all the way to Paris to close a deal he could have done from his office in Oslo, had a nice manicure and the hair of men who drink a lot of water. She didn't even taste the champagne throughout the dinner. They went for red wine. A Château Latour.

"Why'd you become an editor?" Barbara asked.

"That's a good question." He had to think. "Probably because of a toboggan. A new one they'd put in a kids' park near the town hall. I must have been four or five years old, and I wanted to be the bravest of my friends. It was the first time I'd tried that red toboggan, which was a big event in Sogndal. I climbed the stairs, jumped with my arms out in front, fell headfirst onto the ground, and must have knocked a neuron loose. I've always thought something inside me became irregular after that, and that's why I became an editor. It doesn't make sense any other way."

"You make me laugh, Frode."

"If it weren't for that blow, why would I have started my press?"

"Because you love the work you do. You can tell from afar."

"Very much so. My day-to-day is mesmerizing. Reading a handful of bad manuscripts, enduring the egos of good novelists, dealing with cover designers, who all have an inner tyrant. Preparing a speech for the presentation of a book that will be sold to only seven people, two of whom will fall asleep halfway through reading it and one of whom will abandon it entirely. Meeting with literary agents who are very interested in numbers and much less so in letters."

"And meeting interesting people too."

"That's true." Barbara had disarmed Frode Arnesen. "Negotiating foreign rights with you makes up for all of it."

"I see the blow to your head also sharpened your sense of irony."

"No, no, I'm telling you the truth. Dining with you, here in Paris, what more can I want?"

"That I sell you the rights to Anne Delacourt's book, maybe?"

"We'll close that over a drink at my hotel."

"I only drink to toast when I've closed a deal."

"That'll be the case. Good on both ends."

Before dessert, they established the important clauses of the contract. No more than a year could pass between the transfer of rights and the publishing of *Tomorrow* in Norwegian. Cappelen would have to reproduce the same cover design from Giresse & Trésor that the rest of the editions worldwide had used. The French publishing house guaranteed that Anne Delacourt would travel for two nights to Norway to present at an event with the publisher, attend a meeting with readers in a public library, and sit through a minimum of eight interviews. The hotel for the author would have to be four stars or higher. The flight from Paris to Oslo would have to be in first class. In exchange, Cappelen would pay fifty thousand euros for the exclusive rights to the paperback book in Norwegian. The author would get 10 percent of the royalties, and Giresse & Trésor would get 10 percent too. These were the conditions. This way or no way. Frode Arnesen tried to haggle, but he managed only to get invited to dinner.

With the petit fours on the table, the waiter asked them if they wanted coffee, tea, or anything else to drink; he said yes, an espresso. She said no.

"If I have coffee, I won't sleep."

"And?" In one word, he said it all. With the next pause, the Atlantic-blue eyes of the Norwegian revealed his intentions.

"Frode," she said, smiling. "This is a business dinner."

"And we have to celebrate that we've closed the deal."

"We've already toasted. And we're good."

"The Edouard VII has a beautiful terrace at that. I'm sure they make gin and tonics there. And you'll see the Palais Garnier like you've never seen it before."

"Are you going to be the one to explain Paris to me? You men are really—"

"Is someone waiting for you at home?"

Before responding, Barbara finished off her red wine and wiped her lips slowly.

"No. No one is waiting for me."

37

A New Feeling

The doorbell rang. Roger, who was in bed, didn't move a hair. It bothered him that they were ringing so persistently. Whoever it was wanted to wake him. Lazily, he grabbed his cell phone off the nightstand and looked at the time. Eight on the dot. He thought, *"You'll get tired of ringing, twit."* But Hulshoff barked more and more impertinently, and the tension between the doorbell and the dog continued to grow. He was surprised that Barbara hadn't gotten up either. She must have returned from her work dinner so late that she'd laid down and fallen asleep. He didn't remember her stopping by and saying, "Night, I'm here." On the ninth ring, Roger got out of bed in a bad mood. He left his room, moved Hulshoff with his leg, and answered the intercom.

"What's wrong? Is the building burning down?"

"Surprise!"

"Who is this?"

The receiver was staticky, Hulshoff wasn't helping, a truck was unloading its cargo for an early morning delivery on the corner of Chappe and Tardieu, and he could barely hear what was being said from the street.

"Roger . . . It's Marcel."

"Marcel?"

"Your brother, remember?"

"Shit, man. Come on up!"

Roger ran to his room to put on his boxers from the night before and a simple T-shirt. Barbara's door was closed, so to warn her about the unexpected guest, he entered without knocking. There was no one there. The bed was made impeccably, and Barbara wasn't hiding in her wardrobe, waiting to pop out and say, "Surprise!" Either she hadn't slept there, or she'd woken up early and gotten her day started already. There was no trace of her. Not her phone, keys, or even a whiff of her perfume.

"Barbara?" he called out in a half-hearted voice.

She wasn't in the kitchen either. Or in the bathroom. She'd disappeared.

"Hell, *tete*, what a welcome," Marcel said once he was in the apartment.

He'd entered and found Roger drowsy, confused, and wearing boxers with a stretched-out waistband. Next to the giant cactus, they looked like two dunces. The plant was just as prickly as Marcel.

They gave each other two kisses.

"I wasn't expecting you, Marcel. What are you doing here?"

"I have a room in this apartment, don't you remember?"

"But just like that, without warning." He wiped away an eye booger.

"I came from Barcelona. I took the flight before 6:00 a.m., and I thought if Barbara and Roger aren't home . . . I don't have keys. You have my keys, right?"

"Of course."

"Who's this?"

Hulshoff was sniffing Marcel's pant leg.

"It's a long story. His name is . . . It doesn't matter. He belongs to the neighbor."

The Labrador looked at the newcomer with the hope that he would throw him something to chew on. Jasper fed him better.

"She's a beauty, this dog."

"It's a male."

"And Barbara?"

"She's a female, yes."

Marcel laughed. Brothers get each other's jokes right away. "What? She didn't want to open the door for me either, huh?"

"She must be sleeping. Don't talk so loudly."

"You sleep in different rooms?"

"Sit down, *tete*, sit down." Roger was uncomfortable. "I'll take a shower, and then we'll go out for a walk."

"For breakfast, better."

Marcel fell onto the red sofa. He did it noisily, the way men do once they reach middle age.

"So are you two together or what?"

"I told you to stop yelling." He put his finger to his lips and looked toward Barbara's room so his older brother could understand that he couldn't talk openly at the moment.

"Yes or no?" Marcel persisted in a lower voice.

He doubted what to say. "I'll tell you soon."

He literally couldn't talk about it. Suddenly, Roger didn't understand what had happened the night before. Where was Barbara?

The shower woke him, but he couldn't rinse out this new feeling: jealousy.

They went down to rue Véron on foot and sat on the terrace of Chez Richard, which only had three round tables for passersby. The wicker chairs, lined up with their backs against the restaurant window, looked onto a street with little life. Roger greeted the owner, who came out to attend to them with a napkin hanging from his arm.

"I didn't know you were a morning restaurant too."

"We can't miss out on all the tourists that climb up Montmartre in the morning."

"Or the ones that climb down," Marcel quipped.

"I thought you only did lunch menus."

Richard, who stood at the ready, didn't have time for armchair psychologists. He wanted them to recite their order. Two café au laits, two croissants, and he ran off.

Marcel wandered from one subject to another, as if someone were winding him up. He wanted to know everything about Roger, about the pictures he'd been taking, and in general about Barbara, the landlady who'd been so dull with him and who, from what it seemed, had overcome her sadness with his brother. Suddenly, the lawyer wanted to talk. He told Roger stories about the case he'd won and the hailstorm that'd fallen at the airport in Barcelona just as it was time to board. Then, he realized he hadn't said the most important thing.

"Did you know Mother had a fall?"

"Mom? No . . ."

"A bad one. Like all hell in the street."

"First I'm hearing of it."

"She was walking by herself to the butcher's shop, with her cane, and she tripped on a step and—"

"You saw her?"

"Yes, the scraped knee and the wrist sprain. The wounds. The worst thing is that it's lowered her spirits."

"Stop it. Is she scared?"

"Above all else, now she's got it in her head that if another one of these falls happens, she's done for."

"She didn't tell me anything. It's weird . . ."

"But have you called her?"

"Every week."

"Roger."

"Every ten days. Or fifteen, it doesn't matter. We've been really busy here."

"I can imagine." Marcel laughed through his nose.

Roger caught the implication. "No, man, no. With the snowfall and all that, I mean. You should have seen it. It was impressive. In any case, Mom could have told me."

"You know how she is. She keeps it all to herself."

"That's very Bazin of her."

"Absolutely. But fucking call her, man. It's not hard to give her a little call once a week."

"Have you come to scold me or—"

"No. I'm just worried about your half of the inheritance."

"Me? She'll give me double what she's giving you. You're getting nothing, and I'm getting double nothing."

They laughed happily. Roger, finishing the last crumb of his croissant, got up with a jolt.

"I'm going inside to pee."

He acted as if he was going to the bathroom. He looked from one side to the other to see if Laurence was around. He wanted to see her that morning.

"In the back, up the stairs." Richard gave him the directions and turned on the light in the hallway.

Everything in the hallway was falling apart, dark. Roger had to walk carefully to avoid knocking into a bucket in the middle of the path, a trap for customers.

"Does she come in for work later?"

"Who?"

"The girl . . ."

"Laurence? Ha!"

The blunt laugh confused Roger. "Is she out today?"

"She doesn't work here anymore. She's something, that one."

"Oh no? Has something happened to her?"

Richard got closer to confide in him.

"She was a weird one, that girl. She had a lot of problems. Did you notice how she was always a sourpuss?"

"She left?"

"By force."

"You fired her?" He was surprised. "But why?"

"If I told you, you wouldn't believe me. I don't even want to say it. Forty years in the kitchen, and I've never seen anything like it. I swear, I'd never seen anything like it."

Roger waited for the restaurant owner to continue, with his hands in his pockets. Fearing Richard wouldn't tell him on his own, he prompted him to. "But what'd she do?"

It didn't matter that the establishment was empty. Richard got even closer to him.

"She spit in a customer's dish."

"Sorry?"

"I saw it in person."

Roger couldn't believe it. "But why?"

But Richard hadn't even asked Laurence for her reasoning. He hadn't wanted an explanation, and he told her to remove her apron and get out of there. Without compensation, negotiation, or unemployment . . . to the street!

Roger returned to his table, drying his hands on his pants. He couldn't find any paper towels.

"What's up with you?" Marcel asked.

"Me?" He didn't know what his brother was referring to.

"The photos. Did you come to Paris to take pictures or to fuck?"

"Are they mutually exclusive?"

Marcel the comedian became serious. "No one told you?"

"You're such a dumbass, *tete*."

After laughing, Marcel persisted, "The photographs, I was saying. How is it? Have you made it worth it?"

Roger rubbed his chin. "It's going . . . I'm making the most of my scholarship, I think. In fact—" He was dying to tell his brother, but at the same time he didn't want to tell anyone. "I'm preparing something. It's a project. I don't want to say it out loud. It's a secret."

"Now you're the big artist."

"It's not like that. I met a woman at a party in the Canal Saint-Martin. A party for the publisher Barbara works for. We went together, actually, and Barbara introduced me to her. She told me she was a gallery owner or that she had contacts, and I don't know. At the end of the party, she told me that if I ever wanted to show her my postcards, she'd happily look at them."

"Postcards."

"In a manner of speaking."

"Contemptuously, yes."

"Let's just chalk it up to a social joke. A little overboard, the woman. Maybe, yes. In this environment and in Paris . . . Everyone at that party shit gold. But I've been showing her things over email. She's seen pictures, and she's interested in doing something together. Something different, and the project, if it turns out well, would be awesome."

"And it's a secret?"

"I don't want Barbara to know. Not until she sees it."

"But I'm *tete*, I'm your brother . . ."

"I'd prefer not to talk about it. You know how I am."

"Like our mother, yes. Stubborn as mules, both of you. Not even a hint, Roger?"

"A hint wouldn't help."

"Try me."

"Fine." He thought about it. "I'll say it in one word: 'bike.'"

"'Bike'?" Marcel acted as though he was thinking about it for a while. "I've got it. The Tour de France."

"Cold. I'm not going to tell you any more."

With the circumlocutions of a lawyer, brotherly blackmail, jokey arguments, Marcel tried everything but couldn't manage to get any other information. Roger's lips were sealed.

"What about you?" Roger asked, changing the subject. "Why'd you come back to Paris like this, without saying anything?"

"I've got good news. I'm coming to pick up my things. I'm leaving. They're sending me to London."

"To London? For three months?"

"For a year. Right now. An office on Fleet Street, the kind with three hundred lawyers and a mother superior, needs someone with my profile. Four languages; no family ties; able to travel; dominates the mergers of companies, complicated trades, and international issues. So I'm going."

"Bravo. London is even better than Paris."

"The bad news is that from here on out, you have to pay for the room on rue Chappe if you want it."

"Naturally." The next words came from deep inside Roger. "Between me and you, if I stay, I hope she doesn't charge me."

"You're fucking her to save on rent?"

"No, dammit. It's not like that. You think everyone is like you?"

"What do you mean?" Marcel asked, acting offended, but also like he enjoyed whatever image his brother had of him.

"I'll explain it to you. The other day, Barbara said she'd like for me to stay with her. To live. She didn't say it like that, outright, but it was understood."

"And? What do you think?"

Roger's grimace revealed it. "Today, exactly today, is not the day to talk about it."

"But how old is Barbara? Isn't she much older than you?"

"Stop it. Not that much. She's eight years older."

"Eight years older? And you're considering it?"

"It's a possibility."

"Have you thought about the fact that when you're fifty-nine, she'll be sixty-seven?"

"Marcel, dude. First of all, you'll be in your sixties before anyone else. Second, no one can guarantee they'll be home for dinner tomorrow. Thousands of things can happen between now and then. Third of all, with this kind of old-fashioned attitude, I don't think you'll win many cases. Not here, or in London, or anywhere. And fourth—"

"Now, what's this sad face you're wearing?"

"Look, I'll tell you. I met Barbara's grandmother, and if at eighty, Barbara has the same eyes and vitality that woman has, I'd love to be with her."

"Roger, you're starting to worry me. Let's see if you go after the grandmother next."

"Oh, Marcel, you're a pig. You make the same jokes you made when you were twenty."

"Hey, it's your problem. I'm just warning you of the dangers of life, as your lawyer."

Right as they stopped jabbing at one another, Richard came to take away their plates and mugs. Marcel left a ten-euro bill on the table, and they headed back home. On the way, at around rue des Trois Frères, Roger received a text on his phone.

Where are you?

It was short. Barbara was asking where he was. She. The one who'd gone out for a work dinner and hadn't come back. Roger didn't know if he should respond, or what he should respond with. He heard Marcel chattering away like a twit, yapping and yapping, but he couldn't follow what he was saying. Not anymore. As they got closer to the corner near the house, Roger could feel that Barbara was upstairs and guessed she'd want to talk, but he didn't know where the conversation would take them. Barbara, who, from all appearances, couldn't stand men, all of a sudden . . . Maybe she'd reveal that she spent the night with the editor from Norway, or Denmark, or Sweden, or wherever he was from, whom she'd gone to dinner with. He couldn't wait to answer her message. But with what?

"Shut up for a second, please. Look, one thing, Marcel." They stopped in the middle of the street. "You can't come up. I need to talk to Barbara. Alone. Something happened last night, and if you come up now, it'll be . . . I'm asking one thing. One day, I'll tell you. But I'm asking you to take a walk. Go wherever you want. See the painters in the square. I don't know."

"What do I say to them? Make me a charcoal caricature?"

"It's not funny. I'm asking you, please. Don't come back until it's time for lunch."

Marcel looked at his watch. "Walk for two hours? At least they eat lunch early here."

"Please, *tete*."

His brother understood that, whatever it was, he'd be in the way, and so he listened to Roger.

"Don't worry about me. I'll come back after lunch. I'll call a friend from the office."

"Thanks."

Roger kissed him on the cheek and turned around. He took out his phone and responded to the message as he went up the stairs.

I'm coming.

Just as short. And noncommittal. Informative.

He went up to the fifth floor without taking any steps for granted. He could only imagine what version of Barbara he'd find. Sorry and on the defensive, chatty and sincere, or not too much of anything. Maybe she'd act like nothing had happened. And if she didn't bring up the subject, what should he do? Should he let it go, scratch the itch, or swallow the bitter pill and live to see another day? He put the key in the door with trepidation.

"Hey, it's me," he said, in a neutral-sounding voice.

He made sure not to slam the door when he closed it. Barbara was sitting on the red couch, motionless. Her back was facing him.

"Hello."

It sounded like she'd been napping. Roger didn't do any of what he thought he'd do. He saw she was weak and walked to her, kneeling on the floor. Her hand was wet. She'd been crying. Her swollen eyes and red nose gave it away. It didn't seem like she was trying to hide it, either.

"Hey, what happened?" It came out of him in a paternal tone. "Tell me as much as you want. I didn't see you this morning, and . . . I won't judge you, Barbara. I'm not one to do that."

She took her time. She collected herself to say a handful of things. She wasn't the type of woman to unleash storms. She removed her hand from under Roger's and put it on top of his. She breathed deeply, trying to find the words.

"I had to go see Mamie Margaux." A tear was sliding down her cheek. "I had to tell her the bad news."

"What happened?"

"Jasper died."

38

Always Keep a Secret

"I left dinner. It was late. I saw a handful of missed calls. I'd been closing the deal with the Norwegian editor, and it ran longer than I thought it would. After we finished our last drink, I called back this unknown number I didn't have in my contacts. It was from the hospital. They said I was the emergency contact for Jasper Repp. Bad luck, I thought. 'Ms. Barbara Hébrard, we're calling to inform you . . .' When you hear that verb, you know the gravity of what's to follow. 'Tonight, two minutes before midnight, Jasper Repp died.'"

"You should have told me."

"And what could you have done? There's nothing more we could do."

"Keep you company, at the very least."

There was silence.

"It's also true that—" She shrugged her shoulders. "I didn't want you there."

Barbara didn't feel good hiding the truth, and Roger didn't want to hear a lie. Whatever it was, Jasper was dead, and the excuse was impeccable. There were no edges.

"I thought it didn't make sense to go to the hospital. And I wouldn't have been able to sleep if I came home anyway, and I thought the most important thing to do was tell Mamie."

"Did you go to the residence?"

"I stayed with her. All night."

"Why the rush?"

"I could have waited until the morning, maybe. But she appreciated it."

"And they let you in during the early-morning hours? As strict as they are with their visitors?"

She started to worry that her alibi was falling apart.

"I told them it was an emergency. I told them what had happened, and . . . deep down, they're good people at Viviani."

"Very humane, yes." Roger's suspicions were starting to peek out.

"You don't think so?" Barbara held her breath.

"Of course I do, woman. I'm only saying . . . What confuses me—" At the very least, she couldn't think she was going to get away with pulling his leg. But then he preferred not to continue down that path. "And how did your grandmother take it?"

When Mamie Margaux heard the news, she let out a blunt "oh," shook her head sadly, and immediately said, "Maybe better that way, poor Jasper." Then she closed her eyes, conjuring his image. Remembering his voice and the smell of Dutch tobacco on his skin. Just ten days ago, her former neighbor, her fellow widower, Hulshoff's owner, the writer of her secret biography, had been a man with drive. And in no time, he'd become a heap, with hands that were shells and a weak tongue. And from that moment on, he would only be a memory. Given how it happened, Margaux preferred to not see him after the stroke and to maintain that last vigorous and elegant image—that of a gentleman.

Barbara respected the time her grandmother took to withdraw. A remorseful and serene funerary wake. Her grandmother only opened the door when she heard the breakfast cart approaching down the hallway. Every morning brought the same torturous sound.

Barbara, who'd been sitting on the bed next to Mamie, traced the veins on her grandmother's hand.

"I'd like to find Jasper's writing on your life story."

Margaux cracked a cheeky smile. "You don't know?"

"Don't know what? Tell me."

"Roger told me he already has it and that he wants to surprise you. It's important, don't tell him I snitched." It was her grandmother who was caressing Barbara's hand then. "He's a good-looking boy."

"What'd he say exactly?"

"Nothing. He found Jasper's folder in his house and planned that every night, you'd read a fragment out loud. One day you would, the next he would."

"He said that to you?"

"Jasper writes so well. Wrote . . ."

"And it's your life, Mamie. It's thrilling. And Grandfather Damien's life is like a movie."

The nurse said, "Good morning, Margaux," from behind the cart, opened the curtain with one swipe, left a boring breakfast on the side table, and closed the door with a gust of wind. She left just as she came, with an impartial effect and a trained voice.

"Not everything's there."

"I don't understand, Mamie." Barbara didn't know if she was referring to the breakfast, to the room, or what she was talking about.

"Not everything is in Jasper's story."

"We already knew it hadn't been finished. You explained to us what happened after the liberation. Grandfather's return, the concert dressed in his Buchenwald clothes . . ."

Mamie Margaux swung her head. Barbara didn't know what she was referring to.

"There's an episode missing from years after the war. Jasper and I couldn't agree on how to tell it, and we decided to leave it to the end."

"The last chapter?"

"You could say that. To close the story, yes."

"Come on, surprise after surprise."

Her grandmother kissed her granddaughter.

"Always keep a secret, Barbara. Don't let anyone know but you. Only you."

"I'll take the advice, Mamie. But can we skip to the unwritten chapter, or do you want to keep me on the edge of my seat a little longer?"

"Jasper played a fundamental role."

"Poor Jasper? That's confusing." Barbara was dying to know everything. "What would you title this chapter?"

Mamie thought about it. She picked up the slab of whole wheat toast and put it back down on the plate. The news of Jasper's death had stolen what little hunger she had left.

"The day we went to meet André Zucca."

Barbara became alert. She and her grandmother, they were joined at the hip. As much as she loved her, how could she still be learning new things about her? Barbara prepared to listen to the most unexpected of chapters.

"One day, Jasper and Hilde told me, 'Get ready. Tomorrow, we're going on a trip.' We did that from time to time. On a Saturday, three or four times a year, the married couple took me out on a trip. This must have been in the mid-'60s. I was in my forties, give or take. I wasn't the weakling I am now. It was a holiday in Paris, but stores were open throughout the rest of the country. I remember because I didn't have to ask for permission to take leave from the shoe shop I was working at. We left early in their car; they told me we'd be heading in the direction of the Loire Valley and that we'd go somewhere after we arrived. I let them lead me. The plan, based on what we discussed before we left, was to have lunch in Dreux. I don't know if you've ever been. It has a royal chapel and a historic center. It's beautiful, small, with few people, and was peaceful at the time. Jasper knew it well. He went back and forth for his cheese company, and he met people and ate at nice restaurants. They always took me to places that were worth it. On the way there, Jasper said, 'I need to tell you something.' I'll always remember it. He was driving, Hilde was at his side, and I was sitting in the middle of the back seat so I could look ahead and not get dizzy. I looked into Jasper's eyes through the rearview mirror. I knew what he was about to tell me was something important just by the way our eyes met. One of those feelings that you notice immediately, you know? And yes. Jasper goes ahead and says, 'I found him.' 'Who?' I asked. And he responded to me in kind: 'The man who took your picture. The photographer from the magazine.' I froze. And I remember saying, 'But what do you mean?' And Hilde turned and said, 'Jasper has spent a lot of time researching it. He's moved heaven and earth to find—what's his name?'"

"'André Zucca,' Jasper responded. 'Well, he's changed his name since.'

"'If it's been twenty years since the liberation, imagine how much time it's been since that day,' I said.

"Hilde opened the bag she always carried on her legs and took out a horizontal envelope. And inside the envelope was the photo. It was me as a young girl on top of a bike with a high bun. I hadn't seen it in years. I hadn't even thought about it. Not the picture, or the photographer, or all the headaches it had brought on the family. I did know that, when the war ended, my parents kept up with what happened to the people from *Signal* magazine.

"They saw that Zucca had been put on trial and mentioned it one day, but I'd lost the plot by then. I had your mother, Damien was sick, and I had a whole other set of worries. I had practically forgotten it, that whole Zucca nightmare, as strange as it sounds. But Jasper hadn't. He'd known about our story, and he became stubborn and wanted to know what happened at the trial. He'd recovered some information and had papers and things he told me about on the way to Dreux. He reminded me of details I must have known at some point but had forgotten. After Paris had been liberated at the end of August, they would have arrested Zucca in October. Him and everyone who worked for the magazine. The *dossier Signal* is what they called the case. They brought them all to trial. Him as well, and he got off unscathed. They accused him of being a collaborator. He swore in front of the jury that he 'was loyal to France despite appearances' and was acquitted. But they condemned him to the shadows. He was sentenced under national unworthiness, which was a way out that de Gaulle invented to prevent excessive Frenchmen-on-Frenchmen revenge. It was a political punishment, not a crime. He was either lucky or had a family that saved him. It's true that he wouldn't have been able to go back to photojournalism and would've been forced into an early retirement, as they say. With that information, Jasper must have somehow found a way to make it work, because Zucca wasn't that big. Following the trail farther, Jasper found out that, during the war, he'd also lived in Montmartre. That really impressed me. Knowing he passed through the same places we did . . . Hearing it made me shiver. You must think it's dumb, huh? The thing is, from what Jasper had heard, months after the sentencing, Zucca disappeared from the neighborhood and fled Paris. No one heard from him again. Not from him or his family. They all disappeared. With just that small bit of information, Jasper began to search, stubborn as only he is. The Dutch, when they get a mission in their head, you know how they are. And he decided to shout. He was looking for a needle in a haystack, and he had a good idea. Original, if anything. You'll laugh now, Barbara, but I promise you that things went the way the Repp couple told me on the way to Dreux.

"The cheese company Jasper managed sold camembert throughout the country. One day, he grabbed his network of businessmen—all kinds of salesmen, who every week visited every corner of every department to sell their cheeses. He showed them a picture of Zucca's face, a picture in which he had a nice haircut and a pipe in his mouth, and said, 'I'm looking for this man, help me find him. It's almost a matter of life or death. All I know is he worked in Paris, he left after the war, he must be around sixty years old, and he's a photographer.' And, he added, 'I'm sure he's somewhere in France. Look for him, anyone in contact with trusting store owners, cattle farms, and cheese shops in villas, towns, small cities, and cities that aren't so small. Speak to people. Ask around. Surely someone somewhere will have something to tell you. If he's French, he must eat cheese. His name is André Zucca. He might be living under a fake name, he might be wearing a wig. Don't rule out any possibilities. Anyone who brings me a good clue will be rewarded two months of paid vacation. A good prize.' And they found him. It was difficult, but they found him. Jasper told me while looking at the highway, with Hilde laughing at his side, and my head was spinning. A salesman who worked in the Eure department zone had appeared in his office and said, 'Monsieur Jasper, I'm not 100 percent sure, but I have a feeling I've found an interesting lead. Hopefully, it's him. In Dreux, in an alley, there's a photography shop that opened fifteen years ago. A man works there by himself, without an assistant. His name is André. Not Zucca, but André. He takes pictures of baptisms, communions, and weddings. A lot of wedding photography. They've confirmed he makes his living that way. He's very private, and nobody knows where he lives. The person who told me assured me he doesn't sleep in Dreux. But his shop is there. And he gave me the address.' And that's where the three of us were heading inside Jasper's car on that soon-to-be-nerve-wracking Saturday.

"It was hard to park in Dreux. After so much time spent in the car, we stretched our legs a little. Mine were weak, and I told Hilde and Jasper, 'Do you think it's worth it to find him? And what if it's not him? And if it *is* him, what do I say? And if he takes it badly . . .'

"'We'll accompany you. Nothing will happen. They told me the shop is very small, with a glass door and a single window. We'll be there soon.'

"And we found it.

"The photography shop was in a good location, on a picturesque and narrow street, a hundred feet from the royal chapel. Cars could drive by on a single lane, but I don't remember a single one passing by. In fact, we walked on the street to see if, from the outside, we could spot him. The store was squeezed between a haberdasher and the most central pharmacy, which was on the corner. It was a good way to lure customers who were on their way to buy cough syrup, who'd pass the window and discover they could also get film developed and take studio photos.

"'I'll enter and say I need passport pictures,' Jasper said determinedly.

"'And you accompany him like you're his wife,' Hilde added.

"'And you?' I asked, looking at my neighbor.

"'I'll walk outside. These things make me nervous.'

"She opened her bag, took out the envelope with the picture, and put it in my hands.

"'What are you doing?'

"'Maybe you'll need it,' she said, before heading down the street.

"Jasper and I were left on our own, past the pharmacy. We looked at each other with frightened smiles. Both our throats were dry. Slowly, at the pace of goggling tourists, we approached the store from the side of the pharmacy. Inside was a man, a retail worker in short, rolled-up sleeves who was operating a paper cutter on top of the counter. He looked up when he noticed a shadow in front of his store window.

"'It's him,' Jasper whispered.

"There was no doubt. He resembled the picture with the pipe. A clean face and sparse hair combed back. Older, neither fat nor skinny. He had a friendly face. It didn't seem like he was worried about getting caught. Inside of my coat, I was shaking head to toe. I pulled on Jasper's sleeve to stop him. But as soon as I made the gesture, he opened the door, and I don't know how we were already inside. 'Bonjour, bonjour.' Everything was friendly.

"Jasper asked if they took passport pictures, and the shop owner told him to come in, that he'd come to the right place. He took him to the back room. There was a small studio that held a stool, the camera, and a flash with a weakly lit bulb. The two of them entered, and I stayed in the shop area, not touching anything, scared to look around. The establishment smelled like chemicals, development liquid. In the background, I heard men's voices, but I couldn't make out what they were saying. He took a couple of pictures, that's true. Jasper returned to the front of the shop, putting on the coat he'd taken off. He winked at me, and I knew it was a sign of something I didn't know yet. In the back, the photographer shook a satiny paper, and Jasper's four identical faces appeared. His wrist moved skillfully. A gesture he'd made thousands of times, I guessed. In that moment, Jasper took his wallet out of his pocket, and with all the naturalness in the world, he spoke a sentence I hadn't expected.

"'What do we owe you, Monsieur Zucca?'

"The photographer stopped waving the passport picture and looked at Jasper.

"'I think you're confused,' he said, motionless.

"'You're not André Zucca?'

"'André, yes. André Piernic. Do we know each other?'

"'Not me,' said Jasper. 'You might recognize her.'

"When Zucca looked at me, I wanted to die. If I could have, I would have left the store, fled from Dreux, returned to Paris, put my head under the pillow, and cried to my heart's content. But I was too late. Jasper took the envelope out of my hands, pulled out the picture of me on top of the bike, and put it on the counter.

"'Nice picture, Zucca,' said the Dutchman.

"The man no longer denied it was him. He touched his Adam's apple, rolled down his shirtsleeves, and looked up at my face.

"'Is it you?' he asked.

"I nodded.

"'I was seventeen. It ruined our lives.'

"'I'm sorry,' he said, looking down. 'I don't remember it.'

"And then something unexpected happened. Jasper grabbed the copy of the picture of the bike from the counter, left eight francs for the passport photos, and left.

"'I'll wait for you outside,' he said.

"And there I was. By myself. Face-to-face with André Zucca or André Piernic, ready for an unplanned duel. I wasn't prepared for that conversation, but I think I put on a good act. The moment before I spoke felt like an eternity. It might have been a couple of seconds before I asked my question. The kind you ask criminals.

"'Why'd you do it?'

"He sighed. He buttoned his two sleeves.

"'I was the photographer for the press. It was work. It was only an assignment.'

"'But you worked for them.'

"'I wasn't one of them. I was never one of them. What was I supposed to do? I couldn't deny it. Once the Germans entered—'

"'You could've fled like so many people did.'

"'And condemn my family to poverty? I couldn't deny it. The alternative was worse. They had me nailed. They knew I'd been awarded as a French hero in the First World War. They liked my pictures. They sent me to the magazine. They gave me good film, color film that no one else had . . . It's really hard to escape when they grab you and you enter a spiral of fear.'

"'And you became their accomplice.'

"'That's not what it was, ma'am . . .'

"'Margaux. Margaux Dutronc. I don't have to change my name to go through life.'

"'Look, Ms. Dutronc. They tried me and absolved me. I was a professional, and the jury understood all that. I was not that kind of collaborator. I took pictures of what I saw. I documented an exact moment in history. That was my profession.'

"'You—' Would I say it or not? 'You used your camera as a weapon.'

"'Me?' He was offended. 'It's my job. I'm a hunter of images. I showed reality, and that was it.'

"'You used it as a weapon of propaganda, of course. What was *Signal* if not a disgusting propaganda magazine? And what were your pictures of? Beautiful girls on bikes in Paris, kids playing at the zoo, the full terraces of Les Deux Magots café, the fashion, the sunglasses, the heels, despite everything going on. You showed the beauty of Paris so the world would think we were happy, that nothing was happening here, that the Germans were doing us a favor.'

"'I . . .' Zucca shook his head, not understanding. 'And what do you want me to do now?'

"I didn't let him interrupt me. Suddenly everything rushed out, without me becoming daunted.

"'You hid the horror. You didn't take pictures of the ration lines. Not the deaths, not the refugees. Not the fear, not the cold. An evil thing, mister. It was there, at all hours. The cruelty. Where are the pictures of Hitler's soldiers parading at all hours like they were kings of the world? Where are the people wearing the star that marked them as Jews, just like you'd brand the pigs on a farm? Why didn't you take pictures of the Vél d'Hiv Roundup?' I slammed the table. 'Why didn't you publish them with the rest of the pictures? The enemy always came out looking good in your magazine.'

"'Those were years of political turmoil. We all did whatever we could.'

"'Yes, but some fought more than others.'

"'It's easy to talk about it now. Each family was experiencing something. Everyone endured it however they could.'

"'It's true that survival was the primary concern. But there were many who gave it all too. There are some who fought, there are some who resisted.' I caught my breath. 'You showed the happiness of people who weren't happy. That wasn't showing reality.'

"'That also existed. And I was just capturing it.'

"'Yes, of course. To tell the world that we French were so ruined, so committed, so adapted to the new life, and that was the great Nazi victory. I felt used.'

"He shook his head, denying it. It seemed like, for a moment, Zucca might surrender. He only lowered his voice.

"'That's not fair. I photographed what happened, what was on the street. I also took photos of the liberation. The Americans entering Paris, the August festival, I documented all of that. I've saved all the film in color. I have them labeled. You can see them.'

"'Many tried to change sides at the last minute, when they saw the Germans fleeing. Those were the worst.'

"'I, to put it in your terms, worked for the enemy, but also against the enemy.'

"'Don't make me laugh now with some spy movie plot. The dangerous game of the double agent.'

"'What do you want now? That I lay my regrets on the counter for you? I'm not a traitor,' he said, irritated. 'My photos—'

"I didn't let him finish.

"'If you're not a traitor, you wouldn't change your name.'

"He heard that and disappeared. He went into his studio and left me alone without saying anything else. For a moment, I didn't know if I was running a risk staying there. Through the window, I looked to see if Jasper and Hilde were watching, in case they had to save me. They were on the other side of the street, unaware of me, truthfully. At most, Zucca spent a minute in the back room. He came out calmer.

"'Can I ask you a question?' he said, in a cordial tone.

"'Try it.'

"I didn't know what he'd come up with. I even thought for a second he'd ask for some sort of apology.

"'How did you find me here?'

"'Oh, that's . . . Jasper's thing. I can't tell you.'

"Zucca resigned himself and didn't push it. When he saw my hand on the door handle, he said one last thing: 'Take your husband's pictures.'

"'Sorry?'

"'For the passport.'

"'He's not my husband. Here, no one is who they seem.'"

39

What Do You Want to Be When You Grow Up?

Roger listened to the whole story, motionless. Then, he recounted where he'd been, ending with Marcel's return. Barbara had inhabited Margaux's voice and Zucca's skin, and he'd entered the scene.

"What a life your grandmother has lived. And so many twists and turns."

"Mamie was telling me about the meeting, word for word, and I couldn't believe it." A yawn escaped from Barbara after her night of not sleeping. "Look, for my work, I read all types of plots, but her story doesn't lag too far behind any of those."

"You should publish the book. Take Jasper's writing and add this final chapter. The meeting with Zucca."

"It feels like a lie that she hadn't told me about it before. She's so secretive about some things. She told me, 'It wouldn't have been useful for you to know it before, girl.' And I said, 'Mamie, nothing is insignificant, and nothing should be forgotten.'"

"That's exactly why you should do the book."

"I'm not an editor."

"So? Go to Giresse and Trésor, tell them you have these materials, and they'll rip it out of your hands."

"It's all so clear to you, huh?"

Roger was ready to respond with a quick "They'll even translate it into Norwegian." But he knew when to drop a bad mood, and he continued like nothing happened. Things that aren't spoken don't exist.

"What's the problem?"

"I don't know, I thought about it. I'm not saying no, but . . . You can tell it's not your family history."

"That's true." Roger forced a smile. "A lifetime harvesting apples doesn't make for a storyline. Three generations of boxes, hailstorms, and harvesting apples . . . So much routine would make for a boring book. We could maybe bring something interesting out in the end with my father, but my brother won't let us stick our noses into that."

"Your brother!" She jumped up quickly. "Where'd you leave him? Where's Marcel?"

"Good question. Where is he? I have no idea. Taking a walk, I suppose. He'll send signs of life soon."

"And what's your plan?"

"Me?" It surprised him. "I don't know. And you?"

"I was asking in case you want to accompany me to the retirement home. Mamie told me she has something for me . . . It's nice out. We could walk there."

"You don't have to meet up with the Norwegian editor today?"

"The one from Cappelen?" The question caught her off guard. "We finished our business yesterday. Anne Delacourt's novel is his. Arnesen flew back to Oslo this morning."

Roger waited for Barbara, in case she wanted to add something. She, meanwhile, was counting down the seconds for things to explode. There was a restlessness in the back of her eyes.

"Better that way, huh?"

"Yes, better that way."

And they never spoke about it again.

Sometime later, they descended Montmartre to the statue of Churchill and turned at the pont Alexandre III. They walked leisurely along the river. They looked at the bouquinistes kiosks, and from time to time, they browsed the fashion magazines or postcards of Parisian skies from another generation. After, to avoid the horns of cars, they went down to the riverbank in search of eternal peace. There are places that haven't changed in sixty years. The outskirts of the Seine are one of them. The people change: the ones who walk there, who laugh there, who plant down their easel to paint a smoking moon, who lie on top of a mattress to spend the night, who pee against a wall, who seal their love with an improvised dance, who steal a watch from a clueless tourist. The stage is always the same there, tranquil. The rocks, bridges, and trees resist the years. Only the characters change. None of them remain. Nor the words uttered. Everything has evaporated. Everyone has moved forward without slowing down, true passersby of life.

"It was impressive to see how many people sunbathed here in the middle of the war at Zucca's exhibit. This is the pont du Carrousel, right?"

"This is where my mamie and grandfather swam. It's one of the most beautiful passages in the book. Jasper described it perfectly."

"I remember. You even became emotional when we read it."

"It's so horrible to think of everything that happened here. And the Nazi soldiers swam here. They took off their uniforms and weapons, and . . . It makes me shiver to think about places where time erases the important things that have happened. And the place remains intact, like a virgin each time. Who would've thought that here Mamie Margaux—" Barbara suddenly stopped, and her face shifted. "I have an idea."

Roger caught her drift. Her catlike eyes revealed it.

"Don't look at me like that, Barb. I'm not jumping in."

"You wouldn't do it for me?"

"You want to contract tetanus? You've seen how the water runs."

"You wouldn't do it for my grandparents?" She was docile. "This is where they lived their most sublime hour."

"You still surprise me sometimes. You would swim in this water?"

She knew how to delay the moment until she responded.

"Me? Not even in my dreams!"

She took off running. Roger followed her, careful to avoid her heels. He liked sprinting behind that hair that bounced on its own. You could sense a friendly beauty in Barbara's laugh.

Once he caught up to her, they walked together in silence, holding hands, and recovering their breath on the peaceful journey. To switch banks, they crossed the pont des Arts and continued on the eroded cobblestones. Notre-Dame's towers served as a sort of lighthouse in the background. Roger accompanied her to the door of Viviani.

"I'm going back home. Marcel wrote to me. He's coming by to pick up his things. I'll take the metro and go up."

"Do you have to help him?"

He took the oboe key chain out of his pocket.

"He doesn't have his key, and I'm going to say goodbye." Sarcastically, he added, "If you give me permission, of course."

"You make me so angry when you act all innocent." She pinched his hand. "Don't go away with Marcel, you hear?"

"You read my mind. How'd you guess? You have superpowers, Barbara."

"You're an ass!" She playfully slammed her fist against his chest. "At the very least, don't laugh at me."

"You remind of your mamie." He decided to put on his good-boy face. "Can I tell you something?"

Barbara opened her hands. "Go ahead."

"I like that you tend to her."

"No, don't be mistaken. I also like to think I take care of her, but she's the one who is caring for me."

When they reached the oldest tree in Paris, they gave each other a long hug, like they would never see each other again.

Mamie Margaux smelled like fresh perfume. Knowing that Barbara was about to arrive, she'd sprayed herself with the bottle she kept on the nightstand, just in case. She didn't want Barbara to smell the rancid stench of the retirement home, or think she was looking bad. She combed back her hair. She thought the pillow marks on her face were a sign of old age, and she had an obsession with always being nicely coiffed. She forced a cheery voice when her granddaughter entered the room:

"Good morning, beautiful."

"You're still alive, Mamie?"

"Still, my love." She forced a smile. "One day, you'll ask that, and I won't respond."

"I'll leave these chocolate cat tongues on the table. Hopefully, they'll last you a few days."

"Milk chocolate?"

"Milk chocolate. How are you?"

She couldn't pretend. Barbara knew her too well. When she entered, she had seen her looking sad. And she didn't waste any time in asking why.

"These are hard days. I didn't think Jasper's death . . . The days go by slowly here. You have a lot of time to think, and you think and remember. In the end, I decided to do something. I don't know. Let's see what you think."

She opened the drawer of the nightstand, returned her comb, and took out an envelope.

"A letter?"

"Yes." She gave it to Barbara.

"For me?"

"No, I finally decided to respond to Anine. You know, the woman in the room next door—"

"Who doesn't know where her head is."

"The one who always asks me the same thing five times a day."

Barbara unfolded the letter. There were four single-sided handwritten pages.

"Can I . . . ?"

"I asked you to come so you could read it."

"It's an honor, Mamie."

"I spent a lot of time on it. It's been a long time since I've written anything, and I don't know if it's worth much, anything an old hag like me can say."

"Please." Barbara sat on the tall armchair next to the window. "Don't say those kinds of things, Mamie."

"Let's see . . ." Mamie felt that old kind of nervousness, like when you're awaiting your exam grade. "Let's see what you think."

> *Dear Anine,*
>
> *You ask me what I want to be when I grow up. You ask me time and time again with this persistence of your circular ideas. And it's time for me to respond, now that I am a tired woman. Rest assured that I say it without complaining. It's simply like this. The moment has come for us—I think you share in this—when we wake up tired, and we go to bed tired, without having done anything to merit it. But when you ask that question, and I see the renewed innocence in your eyes, time and time again, I sense that you want me to respond like you were seventeen or twenty, or whatever age at which life is still an immense spring meadow opening up before your very eyes. Ready for you to jump, scream, pray to the heavens, and run across it, looking for the path among the hedges that seems the most fun to you. Youth is, Anine, the age where we have become stuck. I'm not scolding you for it. Quite the opposite. Sometimes, settling back into that playful happiness must be a small inner paradise.*

Believing that your four grandparents, all alive and well and still charmants, *are watching you while you cross the brook to eat a snack next to the fountain is a feeling of peace like no other.*

But you and I, my beloved friend, are not twenty years old anymore. We have multiplied our joys and sadness by four, and today, grandmothers like us and so many of our friends at Viviani who look out the poet's window at the oldest tree in Paris have also grown old. It's a blessed consolation to know there will always be someone more wrinkled than we, isn't it?

In the end, the big secret of aging is signing a cordial pact with solitude.

What do you want to be when you grow up, you ask me.

I acknowledge that your question has made me think. And I've never wanted to respond to you randomly with the first job that pops into my head. Given that thinking is still free, I have made the most of it. And if there's anything we do here inside our rooms, it's think. So, I've been ruminating on how best to respond to you. In such a way that this peaceful afternoon, when our sun has lost its rage, I pick up the pen to tell you, at once, what I want to be when I grow up.

I know it now.

I want to be an inventor. An inventor of time.

Maybe it would have been easier to answer that I want to be a nurse, not so much to clean the wounds of a bike fall, but so I could place a gauze on jealousy, which is humanity's silent evil.

Maybe I could have said I want to be a schoolteacher when I grow up, not so much to teach geography, but rather to learn history. What use is there to explaining the rivers that sprinkle Europe's maps if you can make an impact on the intensified hate that has jumped borders, annihilated people, and destroyed whole populations mercilessly?

If I were more ambitious, which I've never been, instead of a teacher, I could say school principal. Who knows if I could have been like Yvonne, the principal of my school, the one in front of the house, where I learned many things without realizing it and knowing I would carry them until now. The principal of l'école communale des filles *was an authority figure because she knew when to discipline and when to coddle. In the middle of the war, however, she disappeared. We later discovered she'd been deported as a member of the resistance, first to Ravensbrück, then to Auschwitz. Three years ago, I saw they renamed the street of the school with her name. Yvonne Le Tac. A whole street for her. A street forever. Can you imagine it, Anine, what that means? Posterity. She deserved it. But maybe she never lived in the hopes of becoming a memory. You have to have a certain kind of vanity for these things. One time, she wanted a life, and that was it. And now it's a home address where a man delivers pizzas. Even worse. Yvonne Le Tac is a tourist path on the way to Sacré-Coeur.*

That's why, when I grow up, I'd like to be an inventor. An inventor of time to marry things to the time when they're supposed to happen. An inventor of time to discover the formula that lets me manage the anxieties plaguing me at each age. The three silent anxieties. Fear, embarrassment, and mourning.

The three anxieties with inconvenient timing that usually arrive too early or for which we find solutions too late.

Fears, I said. They grab us when we are too tender, when we still don't understand that, after the darkness of night, a dawn will come ready to illuminate it all again.

Embarrassment perhaps makes us suffer less, but it follows us for too long. It always follows you, like a loyal dog. You know what I'm talking about, my friend? It's the feeling of not being up to speed. Sometimes, out of ignorance. Or for saying something inopportune or inappropriate. At other times, it's the gap in your teeth or your big ears or the sensation of a stench only you can smell that you think you leave behind like a skunk's trail. I said the word "sensation." And I say it to you, now that we are in each other's confidences, as someone who got pregnant at a very young age and who felt like she'd dishonored her whole family. With the years—now I can't tell you how many—you learn that embarrassment depends on each person. Only when we grow up do we realize it's not worth it. At a good time, huh, Anine?

Mourning, however, comes when it comes. There isn't an age where you learn to live with this pain, silent and cruel, that gnaws at you forever. You and I know nothing is a gift in this world. Life gives us a deal. It gives us a lot, but it compensates for it with absences. Mourning is a punishment.

Everyone knows their people, my friend.

I lost love when I was young. I lost my daughter when I was old. It was never the right time. "The side effects of war are well-known," they told me. "An accident can happen to anyone," everyone who didn't know what to say after Édith's death said. But no one should have to bury a daughter. Or a husband before her thirties.

I loved one man, and I lost him twice.

Now that, thanks to your question, I'm forcing myself to write, I realize that poor Damien is, to this day, a number in the middle of a list in an extermination camp. He is, also, one of those freed from Buchenwald in another list of names ordered alphabetically. A simple name lost on a list. But for me, he was everything, and I didn't want to let him go. I wanted to cling to him. The oboe, the case, the dedication in a book, the first kiss, the bells ringing over the waves, the farewell hug . . . a nostalgia for the ups and downs. Every memory with Édith, a daughter born of happiness, something of that nature. Her school albums, the first word she said, her tricycle, the personal conversations when she became a woman, the birth of Barbara, my granddaughter, who is still hope and salvation . . . Forgetting is impossible. The past invades. Don't get rid of all that, but my invention will help us know if there's a time where we have to let go of the dead. You have to let go of their hands. Damien's, Édith's, my parents', or any one of the people we've loved or who we've held on to. The day comes to untie the bow around our fingers and let them fly. Don't abandon them, Anine. We only free ourselves to continue. By the pure necessity of looking forward. For the survival itself of those we want to play with a little longer. Don't you see how good milk and cookies still are every afternoon?

Anine, I've made my decision. When I grow up, I want to be an inventor of this engine that tempers rampant anxieties. Until now, I've led a modest life. A whole career as a salesgirl in a shoe store on Saint-Honoré, where we supplied shoes for all types. I'm not complaining. Being a salesgirl like my mother—attending to women, having a salary, always having a smile ready for everyone, looking for the right shoe size for every Cinderella—was fun.

With more than fifty years of customer service, you can be sure I've seen it all. All kinds of feet, and shoes of all prices. Nothing, however, like those wooden-heeled shoes that click-clacked like clogs and could be heard from the other side of the street. Those became fashionable at the end of the forties. When Paris returned to being Paris.

I hope to have answered your question, Anine. Without your question, I maybe would have never had a day as nice as today. It's been a long time since I've written anything, and you can see I still have a steady hand. Who knows if I could maybe take the oboe out of its case and play it a bit.

Your friend, now and forever,

Margaux Devère

40

The Best Landscape

Barbara read the letter at the retirement home. Her grandmother, sitting next to the poet's window, didn't take her eyes off her. She didn't say anything until her granddaughter finished it.

"Can you still understand my handwriting?"

"You can understand everything." She looked to see if there was a date on the letter. "Can I keep it?"

"It's for Anine, lady."

"Mamie, Anine's not all there. I'd love to keep it."

"It's just—"

"You've said so many beautiful things about me. About my mother and grandfather. I want this letter."

"But—"

For Barbara, the matter had already been settled.

"When will we see each other again?"

"You and I?" Mamie thought about it. "Sooner than you think."

They kissed each other, and Barbara dismissed the last comment, which seemed to have been said instinctively. She folded the letter and took it home. She wanted to read it to Roger. She was excited, but she waited until it was dark. She played with the light switches until she found the exact lighting she wanted to exude peace and comfort. She wanted to recapture the ambience of the snowy nights when they were shut in and told each other stories without rush. With a newcomer, that is. Hulshoff was keeping them company still.

When she had it ready, she made Roger sit on the red sofa next to her. She took out the letter from under one of the cushions and read it to him out loud.

"'Dear Anine, you ask me what I want to be when I grow up . . .'" He listened with the attention required for Margaux's confession and Barbara's recitation. She modulated her voice, pausing, and, at times, her grandmother's voice emerged. She herself realized it but didn't stop it. It was the misty mirror of family.

"She was a brave woman," Roger said.

"It's not a letter to Anine."

"What do you mean?"

"It's not a letter to Anine. She wrote it for herself. Don't you see?"

"From Mamie Margaux to Mamie Margaux?"

"She's the sender and recipient."

They spoke of the storms her grandmother had had to weather and how she'd endured the hardships without growing sick of life. With tea on the table, Barbara became philosophical and spoke of fear as the motor of the world, of individual mysteries, and of the healing power of writing. She saw it in many of the novels she'd sold across the continents. Roger listened to her. He liked hearing her say that sometimes the lives of writers fascinated her more than their novels. She cited a couple of names. He hadn't read any of them. He hadn't even heard of them, but he acted interested, and Barbara was happy he was listening.

That night, they didn't move from the sofa to make love. The novelty excited them. The pillows moved up and down. At times, the pillows helped them prop themselves up a little better; other times, they placed them under a knee, or to stretch their neck and rediscover damp corners with their tongues. Hulshoff had never witnessed a scene like that. Jasper didn't do those kinds of things. He was motionless, one eye open, with no intention of intervening.

"I like your body," Roger said.

"I like yours too," mewed Barbara. "What if we take this to the bedroom?"

"You're more comfortable there, huh? It's because you're older, of course."

"You're so annoying when you want to be." She pulled him to the room. "Don't fear, young one. Come with me. I won't do anything you don't like."

The next day, afternoon took forever to come. Roger had been preparing for that day for weeks with the help of Madame Giroud and the secret intervention of Margaux. In the morning, with a tone of someone dreading the matter, he asked Barbara to reserve the evening. He wanted her to accompany him somewhere. She wanted to guess what it was, and she tried to wheedle it out of him any way possible. But he gave her very few clues. Next to the place de la République, cocktail evening wear, transportation by taxi—it would pick them up at six o'clock on rue Chappe—and two hours of heavy emotions. That was all he could tell her.

At six o'clock on the dot, Barbara's insistence was rewarded when they got into the taxi. She discovered they were going to an art gallery. She'd picked the right dress. A burgundy one-piece, narrow at the waist, with half sleeves and a top that could be opened or closed with three buttons. She had only one buttoned.

The gallery was two corners away from the Canal Saint-Martin. The owner, Madame Giroud, a friend of the Giresse & Trésor couple, had rented an old industrial ship of which only the structure and spirit remained. A former wire factory, it had been abandoned for some time, and when she had the fifteen-year contract lease guaranteed, she emptied it, stripped it, and gave it the appearance of Chelsea Piers in New York. Minimalist, falsely modern, so it breathed spaciousness all around. She left the iron beams in sight, installed a smooth and gray forgiving floor, and kept the little square windows at the top of the ship. She did indeed tint the glass so some light entered but so it could also stop the momentum of a stray sunray that wanted to filter through. She'd painted the walls, imperfect in their roughness and patchiness, white, because above everything, she had one obsession: that art be highlighted. She liked the idea that there, where there had once been assembly lines, no two of the same works would be displayed. Only singular pieces.

Barbara entered without knowing where she was going. Whose exhibit? Whose photography? It's all she'd asked on the way to the canal, and Roger had avoided answering her. Once they were at the door, he revealed the first of his three surprises of the evening.

"Can I put this on you?"

Barbara didn't understand where he'd suddenly gotten a silk neck scarf. Only Roger.

"A blindfold? For my eyes?"

"A rolled-up scarf, a blindfold. Call it what you like."

"You can't just cover my eyes like this? With your hand?"

"If you put it on . . . The trick is if you put it on, I'll gift you the scarf after."

"Me?"

She unrolled it. It moved like red water, subtle and elegant.

"You spent a lot of—"

"I promise that if you put it on, you'll remember this for the rest of your life."

"Tie it for me, come on."

Roger tied the knot, and using his hand, he made sure Barbara couldn't see anything.

"Let's go in?"

"Let's go in . . . But you're scaring me . . ."

"Give me your hand, and don't worry."

Her first three steps were unsure. After, she trusted there wouldn't be a trap.

"Good evening," the gallery owner greeted them.

"Good evening," Barbara answered blindly.

"Welcome to—"

"Shhh," Roger silenced her. They walked eight steps forward until they were where he wanted. "Are you ready, my love?"

"Almost," said Barbara, confidently. "I'm so nervous!"

"You can take it off when you'd like."

She slid the scarf off the top of her head without undoing the knot.

What she saw made an impression on her.

Before her stood a portrait of Mamie Margaux. Her face, in black and white, was enlarged beyond human scale. The definition was perfect. Her eyes were clear, her gaze was serene. Margaux, facing the front, smiled with the beauty of wrinkles. Her gray hair combed back, like a lady. Her fine lips, the earrings that shined, her dignified nose, her soft skin. The beauty of old age.

"But . . ." She didn't know how to take it. She didn't know where to look. "She looks beautiful."

And next to that picture, was another. And another. Twelve pictures of great dimensions framed on one wall. All of Mamie Margaux. Recent ones. All close-ups. More pensive in one, more serious or with a bored look in another. One where she was sleeping. One where it looked like the veins in her neck had taken on color. And another, the artist's favorite, where the grandmother was doubled over laughing. She looked like she was about to burst with happiness. The image communicated so many things. Barbara didn't have enough eyes to see it all. She walked with a hand over her mouth, in disbelief of what she was seeing, emotional about what was in front of her. Twelve portraits of her grandmother, nearing eighty-four years old, sitting in the retirement home. She could make out the back of the room, because she knew well those wafer-like walls at Viviani. She walked from portrait to portrait, but she wouldn't have known which to choose. Twelve works of art.

Taking a step back, Roger let her go. The second surprise had had the desired effect. Only once he made sure Barbara had looked at each of the photos did he dare ask her the question.

"Do you like it?"

"A lot. It's . . . I don't know how to say it. Spectacular. But who did all this?"

As soon as she said it, she knew the answer. He was next to her.

"I didn't want to tell you anything until—" With an open hand, he gestured to the work. "Here you have it."

"They're magnificent, Roger. Magnificent." Still disoriented, many things flowed to her head. "But how did Mamie let you . . . It's been sixty years since . . . You captured her spirit."

"How'd I do it, you ask? It wasn't easy, no. You know what? Let's have her explain it to you herself," said the photographer theatrically.

The gallery owner coordinated with Roger and pulled back the curtain hiding her office.

"Hello, love."

There, like a television-competition trophy, was Mamie Margaux in her best dress and shiny shoes, sitting in a wheelchair to conserve her energy.

"Oh!" she cried out. "Mamie, please . . ."

The third surprise.

"You didn't expect me to be here, did you?"

Her heart racing, Barbara ran to hug her grandmother. The happiness of seeing her there was the same as when she was a girl and Mamie had wiped the sand off her feet.

"But you look so, so stupendous."

"What do you have to say?"

"What I think, look—"

"Blown-up big like that, you can see all my flaws. A wrinkly raisin."

"These photos are magnificent."

"You see it. So many years holding myself back. What use is it doing that now?"

"Don't sell yourself short. Don't you see how beautiful you are?"

Margaux wrinkled her nose regretfully, as people with a sense of modesty do.

"The photos are nice, perhaps. This boy knows it. It's a shame I only a see a dried-up piece of parchment."

Barbara turned to recruit Roger. He walked toward her.

"Désolé," he said, smiling from ear to ear.

"I think you two have a lot of explaining to do. A lot. When did you do this? And you don't take pictures of people, you told me—"

"And it was true."

"And now what? What happened?"

"These last few days, I discovered something. When I spoke with your super-mamie and, after, while taking her pictures, I became aware of . . . a phenomenon."

"What?" Barbara could only take so many mysteries in a row.

"I had it here. I had it here right in front of me, and I had missed it." He pointed to the wall of twelve photos. "The best landscape is the face."

Still holding the silk scarf in her hand, Barbara caressed his face. Later, she wanted every explanation.

He had taken the photographs in two sessions. Over three mornings, when Barbara had stayed home to work, he'd gone to Viviani, and he'd won over Mamie, conversation after conversation. First, he explained his project. He told her that, after a couple of months in Paris, a gallery owner had seen his work and decided to trust him. But Madame Giroud had asked him to do a different kind of exhibition. To tell a story that stirred up emotion, a story that could be told through the media so they could dedicate a fragment of a page in the Sunday newspaper to him. This seemed to be the owner's obsession. Roger's work was to convince her grandmother to break the conviction she'd held strong for so many years. The first day, Margaux was as stubborn as granite. The second day, she'd become softer with Jasper's death, and by the third meeting with Roger—half of it was persuasion, half of it cleverness—Mamie said yes. With pursed lips and a single argument for why. She would do it for Barbara. Only for her. As a gift to her granddaughter. She said it like that.

A gift.

Who knows if it'd be the last chance for this. One never knows.

They began the sessions the next day. Roger asked her to go by the window, and he positioned the wheelchair there, where there were subtle marks on the floor. He was looking for the light to enter to the right of Mamie, like in classical portraits. Once he had her with her shoulders positioned according to his directions, he made sure there were no shadows on her left cheek. Not one. His model ready, he mounted his tripod, took out his Canon, and attached the fifty-millimeter lens. Before he began shooting, he spent some time calculating the focal distance, the velocity of light, and the depth of field. He looked for the sharpness of the face, and that was it. He'd fade the background of the room to give the images more personality. It was at that moment he decided he'd make them black-and-white.

"I'm not so sure about this, boy."

Roger began to flash. He calmly gave her directions. At first, she was uncomfortable. Slowly, as soon as she realized that she was, for once, the center of attention, she let herself go. It was best when Roger, hidden behind the camera, told her to act like he wasn't there. That's when the portraits began to come together. Of a natural woman.

Barbara's heart still beat quickly. Without taking her eyes off the wall of pictures, she'd listened to Roger's explanation, her hand on Mamie's back.

"How is it that there's no one here?" she asked, confused.

"The exhibition opens tomorrow," Madame Giroud rushed to add.

"This was a private showing," Roger stressed. "Just for you."

"From tomorrow until?"

Only Roger and Madame Giroud knew the answer. She responded. "We programmed it for a whole month."

Barbara didn't hide her satisfaction. "Does that mean you'll stay a couple more days in Paris?"

"As long as the exhibition lasts. And if you don't kick me out of the apartment."

"You're such a—"

He kissed her deeply.

"Do you want to know the name of the exhibit?" the gallery owner asked.

"Of course!"

"The Bicycle Woman."

"'The Bicycle Woman,'" Barbara said, hiding her confusion.

"There'll be a display case here with an explanatory plaque in the lobby. They'll be installed this evening."

Roger revealed what the show would be like.

"Here, when you enter, you'll see Zucca's photo of the bike. We'll tell Mamie's story in three paragraphs, and there, on the other side of the hall, will be a glass case with three objects. Only three so as not to overload it and because people walk by these kinds of things. The oboe case, which we will leave open; Damien's striped uniform, which he wore for his last concert; and the copy of *One Thousand and One Nights* that your grandfather gave her."

"Oof." Barbara breathed in deeply. "And where is all that?"

"I'm keeping it in my office," said Madame Giroud. "We won't put them out until tomorrow. It's better to wait until the last minute for these kinds of fragile things. They're all safe."

"Our book is here?" Mamie asked, overwhelmed.

"Do you want me to bring it to you?"

The gallery owner entered her office and came out quickly with *One Thousand and One Nights*.

"Here you go."

Mamie handled it respectfully and sighed.

She put the book on her lap, her palms on top, like she was swearing on the Constitution of the Fifth Republic with her two hands.

She didn't look at the dedication Damien had written her. She knew it by memory. Once she opened it, she ran her finger along the pages, brought it up to her face, and took in the scent with her eyes closed.

"This book smells like the twentieth century."

"Of course, Mamie."

"Paris outraged, Paris destroyed, Paris martyred . . . But Paris liberated," Madame Giroud jumped in, carried away by an excess of enthusiasm.

Much peace is needed to forget war.

Margaux gave the book to Roger. To break the unexpected moment of patriotism, Barbara got on her knees in front of Mamie. She wanted to know what she was thinking.

"Do you know what I would like?" It came out that way. "To dance with you."

"With me? What are you saying, girl . . . My legs—"

"Remember what we used to do when I was little? You picked me up, put me on your feet, and moved me forward and backward . . ."

"But—"

"I loved it so much. I wasn't just dancing on you. I was flying."

"You must be joking, girl."

"No. Today, we'll do it in reverse. You'll see." Barbara crouched even farther down. "Hold on."

Her mamie moved to put her right hand on her granddaughter's back. Roger gave her his left hand to help her. Bending over, Barbara unbuckled Mamie's shoes and slipped them off, careful not to hurt her. She helped her stand up, and she gave three instructions of mandatory compliance.

"Hold on to me. Hug me. Per-fect. And now, slowly, stand on my feet."

"But are you saying . . ." She hoisted her bones up as much as she could.

"Don't worry, I'm wearing shoes. And you don't weigh very much. First one foot, exactly. And now . . ."

"The other."

"You see. There are you. How is it, Mamie?"

"Fine," she said, frightened, atop her pedestal without her bearings.

Barbara began to move. She lightly lifted her feet off the ground. She gave her one hand, held her back, and she felt Mamie's rigid bones against her chest.

"Let go of your weight, Mamie. Don't worry about me. Like this."

Slowly, they slid over the tiles, from here to there in small movements.

"Don't speed up, girl."

"A turn, come on." She hummed "C'est Si Bon" and danced. "How are you now?"

"Good." She laughed happily. "Very, very good. Look, girl!"

With his eye positioned on the viewfinder, Roger began to photograph.

"It's perfect, Margaux. Like a nice waltz."

"We did it, Mamie. What do you think?"

"I'm flying too. Look, kids."

"Isn't it nice up here?"

"It's like the movies, Barbara. Let's dance, dance, dance."

About the Author

Photo © 2023 Xulio Ricardo Trigo

Xavier Bosch is a celebrated Catalan-Spanish writer born in Barcelona. The author of nine novels and two short-story collections, Bosch has been honored with the title of bestselling book of the year five separate times in his home country of Spain. He's also won two of the most prestigious prizes in Catalan literature: the Sant Jordi Award (2009) and the Ramon Llull Award (2015). His novel *Algú com tu* has been translated into seven languages.

In addition to his creative writing work, Bosch is also a respected journalist with a long and storied career. He has starred on radio and television, created several successful audiovisual formats, and worked as a newspaper editor. A sports specialist, Bosch is one of the most influential writers on the Barcelona Football Club. The author has also directed two documentaries on classical music and serves as a full member of the Acadèmia de la Llengua Catalana.

About the Translator

Samantha Mateo is a translator from Chicago. She received an MA in humanities from the University of Chicago, specializing in Catalan and translation studies, and a BA in linguistics from Columbia University. She currently works in academic publishing. She was an American Literary Translators Association (ALTA) Emerging Translator mentee in 2022 for Catalan. Her translations have appeared in the *Denver Quarterly* and *Granta*.